NEVERMORE BOOKSTORE

KERRIGAN BYRNE
& CYNTHIA ST. AUBIN

Cover Art by: Staci Hart

Published by Oliver-Heber Books

0 9 8 7 6 5 4 3 2 1

Dedication

This is for the rest of us:
Those of us born in quicksand, who had to start this journey already exhausted from surviving and/or rescuing ourselves and others.
Those of us who feel betrayed by our bodies and/or our brains.
Those of us who break damaging cycles and heal generational traumas.
Those of us who still have the audacity to dream, achieve, love, and claim our happily ever afters, even if they may look different from everyone else's.

Contents

ONE

Anticipation

{ĂN-TĬS'Ə-PĀ'SHƏN} NOUN. HOPE, EXPECTATION,INTUITION, FOREKNOWLEDGE, OR PRESCIENCE

CADENCE BLOOMQUIST STARED AT THE FAUX OLD-fashioned rotary telephone, willing it to ring.

It wasn't that she was *waiting*, per se. Waiting by the phone was absolutely *not* a thing Cady did, and especially not for a man.

Despite her best friend's completely unfounded accusations.

She was merely making herself available for Nevermore Bookstore's most lucrative customer. A customer who was polite enough to place his weekly orders every Thursday night at precisely eight p.m.

Over the last several months, Cady discovered that if she not-waited at exactly the right second, she could catch the gleaming gold dial and glossy black enamel vibrating ever so slightly before the brassy jumble of notes sang out.

And they would.

Any minute now.

Planting her hands on the silky wood of the credenza her aunt had repurposed for the bookstore's cash register, Cady shook out her legs and stretched her stiff back.

Any other evening, and she'd be upstairs life-rafting on her heating pad by now, doomscrolling or binge-watching until the day melted from her bones.

Still. The bookstore did take on a cozily creepy edge once the darkness pressed against the shop's large front window.

Cady glanced up just as a gust of early-autumn wind sent red and yellow leaves somersaulting down the empty sidewalk. Bathed in the amber glow of wrought-iron streetlamps, Water Street—the quaint seaport town's main drag—had already gone quiet, the locals safely tucked into their homes and the stream of tourists dwindling as they found their way back to their cozy bed-and-breakfasts.

From the mantel of a fireplace whose chimney had long ago been bricked up, the antique brass clock began to chime.

The mosh pit of butterflies in her stomach pulled out their tiny glow sticks and began to rave as she counted the bell-like musical pings.

Two. Three. Four...

Brrrrrringg.

She waited the customary one and a half rings before clearing her throat and lifting the handset from its golden cradle. The receiver was pleasantly heavy in her hand and cool against her cheek as she inhaled to issue her standard greeting.

"Nevermore Bookstore, this is Cady." Hearing the manically chirpy edge in her voice, she made a face at herself in the antique mirror above the table bearing teetering stacks of books still in need of shelving.

"It's Fox." Two syllables, two goddamned syllables of that smoky, sexy fireside voice, and her vital organs turned to melted butter.

Cady bit her knuckles to keep her rush of excitement from becoming the audible squeak she'd once had to blame on a smoke detector in need of a new battery. Which then led to her having to replicate the sound while she put down the phone and pretended to change it.

Not the ideal scenario for an auditory flirtation.

"Well, hello, Fox," she said in her Wish App attempt at a

seductress's drawl. Even Edgar, the bookstore's resident raven mascot, seemed to be rolling his eyes at her.

Eye, anyway. Like the other assorted critters congregating on various bookshelves, Edgar's taxidermist displayed more enthusiasm than skill when it came to lifelike reconstruction.

"How was your week?" she asked, reaching for the delicate China teacup of Earl Gray she'd put in place at exactly 7:55pm.

"Good. Yours?"

Hearing a muffled jingle on the other end of the line, Cady imagined him seated in a wide, wing-backed leather chair, the phone pressed to his smoking jacket as he rang a bell to order up a triple-distilled something or other from the loyal, silver-haired butler who'd been with his family for ages.

Conjecture of this kind had been one of her favorite parts about their conversations. With a voice that rumbly, he'd have to be tall. Or at least tall-ish. Deep-chested. Broad-shouldered, or his proportions would just be all off and he *definitely* didn't sound like a man whose proportions were all off.

Not that it would matter, with the way her lady bits stole her heartbeat when he so much as breathed on the other line.

"My week was excellent." Moving her cup and saucer onto the lacy disk of a knitted purple coaster, Cady bent at the waist to ease the ache at the base of her spine. "I just got in a brand-new shipment."

"Is that so?"

Three words already, and not even a full minute in. This had to be some kind of record. The knot of tension behind her sternum began to soften. Their calls had always begun this way—with his mostly monosyllabic answers gradually lengthening as she supplied the conversational push that turned his verbal engine over.

"Mmhmm," she said. "You'll never believe what was in it."

"I bet I would."

Four? *And* a voice-smirk?

Cady gripped the corner of the credenza to keep from swooning. "*Frankenstein*."

"Not one of the first editions of the third printing in 1831?"

"Even better," she drawled. "One of the first five hundred published with Lackington, Hughes, Harding, Mavor, and Jones in 1818."

"No."

"Yes indeedy. Speckled calf cover, brown Morocco spine label and all."

It had taken her three weeks, twenty calls, thirty-seven emails, and promises of nonexistent firstborn children and/or sexual favors to finagle it from a notoriously cantankerous rare book seller on the East Coast.

"I can't believe you actually got it."

Seven. Hot damn.

"It *almost* sounds as if you doubted me." Cady looped her index finger through a coil of the phone cord, feeling like some kind of moony retro teenager.

"I would never doubt you."

Cady took a sip of tea to loosen her stiff tongue. "I'm not sure if that's a compliment or a red flag, considering you don't actually know me very well."

"I know you have a monster kink."

Bergamot-scented mist exploded from her lips. Cady promptly managed to aspirate the rest, descending into a coughing fit that lasted a fortnight at least.

"Sorry," she rasped. "Just went in the wrong hole—er—pipe."

"Hate it when that happens."

Something about the way he said it left Cady wondering which scenario he was referring to.

She bent to retrieve a roll of paper towels from the cabinet below the credenza and dabbed atomized droplets from the counter's surface as she searched for a witty rejoinder.

"To be fair, I had only been talking to you for, like, three weeks when I made that comment about Sasquatches. *Sasquatch?* Ugh. *Is* there even a correct plural for that word?"

"I hope not," he said. "And you didn't make a comment about Sasquatch—you made a comment about me being one."

"That is *not* what I said," Cady insisted, fighting a grimace when she turned too quickly.

"Then what *did* you say?"

Caught in her own snare. Hoisted by her own petard. Grudgingly, she sank back into the memory of one of their first conversations, complete with clammy pit-sweat and burning cheeks. She'd been so desperate for any scrap of information about him then. So embarrassingly obvious in her data mining.

"I *said*, how do I know you're *not* a Sasquatch?"

"Is that what you said? Because I feel like there's something missing," he mused.

Cady blew out a gusty exhale. Damn him with his stupid raspy voice and his annoyingly perfect memory.

"How do I know you're not a Sasquatch with a really sexy voice?" she said in the unenthusiastic cadence of a times table recitation.

"So, Miss Monster Kink, will you add it to my shipment?"

Questions like this were part of what informed her mental image of Fox as a reclusive scholar with ancestral money. Well, questions like this, and gothic romance novels. Many, many gothic romance novels. Being occasionally bed-bound was for more glamorous when you could imagine yourself as the ailing but brave heroine in an imposing manor on a windswept cliff.

An ailing but brave heroine with a mysterious benefactor who never once expressed concern about the prices of the rare and sometimes almost un-gettable books he asked her to find.

The small, unassuming hardbound tome sitting by the phone would have cost her a quarter's worth of paychecks when she'd only been working for her aunt as opposed to running the bookstore. Buying it had been a significant gamble on her part. If Fox hadn't been interested, she'd have ended up further in debt, and the book locked in the glass curio cabinet containing her other unfortunate investments.

"Cady?"

The sound of her name caressed by silk and sandpaper snapped her back to the present.

"I'm sorry, what?" Reaching for one of the vintage cookbooks next to the iPad register, she began to fan herself as she frantically searched her short-term memory. If her cheeks grew any hotter, her glasses would be in imminent danger of fogging.

"Will you add *Frankenstein* to my shipment?"

"Right. Of course. Happy to." Crumpling the paper towel, she shot it at the wastebasket and missed. "Any special requests or this week's order?"

"There is, actually." Silence stretched over the line for a beat.

"I'm listening."

So, *so* hard.

"You wouldn't happen to have any more like—" Another pause. "Like the extra book in last week's order?"

Her mouth curled up at the corners.

"Extra?" she asked innocently, brushing her chin with the feathery mock-quill pen patrons used to sign for their credit card purchases.

"The mystery?" he prompted.

"*The Sign of the Four*?" Cady may have mangled seductress, but naïve ingenue she gave in spades.

Fox's epic sigh sounded like the rushing wind, followed by a mumbled "*nancygoo.*"

"I'm afraid I didn't get that."

"Nancy Drew."

"*Oohhhh.* That book." Using the full extent of the extra-long cord she'd plugged in precisely for this purpose, she walked around the credenza to stand before the set of shelves she couldn't bring herself to part with despite their slight sway-backed bowing. "You're in luck," she said, running her finger down the neat regiment of yellow spines with iconic blue lettering. "I have about forty of those. How many would you like me to send?"

"Top five?"

"Done," she said, scanning the titles and tipping them forward with her index finger.

She had gotten to *The Secret Staircase* when something touched her elbow.

Cady let out a little screech and whirled around to find a familiar face hovering just behind her shoulder.

The instant rush of relief she felt was quickly replaced by irritation as her best friend proceeded to wander around the shop, glancing behind velvet curtains, peering into the many reading nooks and shadowy corners.

"What are you doing?" she whispered, pressing the receiver to her chest.

Gemma McKendrick blinked wide jade-green eyes at her, her rosebud mouth pulled off-kilter by a smirk. "I'm checking for serial killers."

"Try the closet," Cady quipped. "He's probably trying on my hooker heels."

"Hooker heels?" Fox's voice crackled up from the region of her breasts.

Shit.

"So sorry about that. My best friend dropped by *unannounced*, but she's just leaving." At this, Cady shot Gemma an expectant look and cut her eyes toward the door. "You were saying?"

Her slide into the animated tone she reserved for Fox alone was surprisingly effortless.

Gemma dramatically batted her lashes, miming a phone snuggled against her pumpkin-colored cardigan.

Cady flipped her off and turned her back to her friend, her flush deepening to an atomic cherry.

"She has a key?" All traces of footwear fetish curiosity had vanished from Fox's voice.

"No, but she does this all the time. It's really no big—"

"Lock your doors."

A chill lifted the fine hairs on the back of Cady's neck. "What?"

"Lock your doors." Coming from a man she'd never met face to face, this ought to sound creepy instead of panty-dampening and protective in a John Wick meets Mr. Darcy kind of way.

"This is Townsend Harbor." Cady laughed, attempting to reinject some levity into the conversation. "Nothing happens here."

She would have traded her autographed copy of *Interview with the Vampire* to know what Fox was thinking in the twelve whole seconds that elapsed before his response.

"Nothing happens until it does. Lock your doors."

"I will, I promise. As soon as we're—"

"*Now.* While I'm on the phone with you."

Cady shifted her weight to the opposite hip, gazing longingly toward the chaise she would have collapsed onto already were her best friend not there to witness it. "See, I *can't* lock the door while I'm on the phone with you because the cord won't reach."

"I'll get it," Gemma sang, picking a dust bunny from her plaid skirt as she rose from the avalanche of books she'd been stacking.

"*No.*" Fox's eruption was loud enough for Gemma to hear in the otherwise quiet shop. The smile melted from her face as she raised an eyebrow at Cady. "I want you to get in the habit," he said, softer now. "Put the phone down and go lock the doors. I'll wait."

"Just a minute." Cady set the receiver on its side at the phone's base and quickly locked the front door. She'd intended to repeat the process with the building's rear entrance facing Townsend Bay, but her back and hip had other opinions.

Without missing a beat, Gemma shot to her feet, Mary Janes making the old floorboards creak as she swiftly sprinted up the steps leading to the back. Cady's chest tightened.

Most days, her determination not to feel sorry for herself was enough to wall off the ever-present envy she felt watching her best friend bounce around like a brunette Tinkerbell in a body that didn't randomly declare mutiny.

Gemma reappeared in the doorway, tossing her dark braid over her shoulder and giving a thumbs-up.

Cady mouthed *thank you* and returned to the phone and her self-appointed security guard.

"Doors locked, windows shut, hatches battened, and lights lowered to discourage the late-coming retail scourge," she said. "*Now* can we talk about books?"

Fox cleared his throat. "Rain check?"

Cady's already heavy heart sank into her guts. He'd spoken to her from this chilly distance only one other time—when he abruptly ended their discussion about *The Count of Monte Cristo* after Cady had flippantly suggested Edmond Dantès should have gotten a good therapist and invested his fortune in aeronautics instead of wasting it on weasel-faced Fernand.

"Of course," she said. "Listen, if it's something I said—"

"It's not," he said, cutting her off. "Just need to go."

"O-okay," she stammered. "Until next week?"

"Next week."

The dial tone stung her ear.

Cady returned the phone to the hook, blinking away silly, childish tears. It shouldn't hurt her feelings.

Shouldn't, but did.

Gemma clomped down the steps and leaned against the corner of the credenza, a guilty grimace tugging at the corners of her mouth. "I'm sorry," she said. "I didn't mean to interrupt."

"Yes, you did. But it's okay." Cady should have known that her attempts to evade her friend's not-so-subtle attempts to discover more about the man she'd been spending her Thursday evenings with would only serve to amplify her curiosity.

It was only a matter of time.

Running through the modified closing ritual reserved for her "bad body" days, Cady tugged the dangling brass chain to click off the knockoff Tiffany lamp at the register and picked up her teacup. The purple knit coaster below it jogged a memory.

"Before I forget, do you have any yarn in hideous colors or terrible textures that you'd be willing to donate to a good cause?"

Gemma folded her arms across her chest. "Are you suggesting that Bazaar Girls lacks a carefully curated inventory?"

Hearing the name of her best friend's knitting and craft shop conjured soothing images of the orderly rows of colorful knots and skeins interspersed with other odds, ends, and notions.

Emphasis on *odds*.

"Wouldn't dream of it," Cady said. "I was telling my mom about the Stitch n' Bitch club, and now she wants to start one with her friends."

"Is that even allowed?" Gemma asked.

"I'm sure they don't give them metal needles or anything, but yeah, they do crafts."

"In that case, absolutely. I'll put something together tomorrow if you'll remind me."

"Of course." Cady had already made a mental note to do just that. For all her many excellent qualities, short-term recall had never been Gemma's strong suit. "I just need to grab a few more books for an order and we can get out of here." Ambling over to the bookcase, Cady smiled to herself as she plucked the Nancy Drews she'd selected for Fox.

When she'd included them in last week's box on a whim, it had been a toss-up between these or the Sweet Valley High books. She'd plowed through two or more a night sometimes during her high school hiatuses—Aunt Fern's prescription for the insomnia that had plagued Cady in the early days of her condition.

Judging by the rate at which he placed his orders, Fox achieved similar results during the restless hours of the night.

The image of him beneath the brocade covers of a four-poster bed, nursing a burgeoning grudge against the scheming Jessica Wakefield provided a balm to Cady's still-smarting soul.

"You know that thing is a lawsuit waiting to happen," Gemma said over her shoulder.

Cradling the stack in the crook of her arm, Cady pressed a palm to the side of the bookshelf that had developed a pronounced starboard lean. "Aunt Fern said Mt. Rainer will crumble before this thing does," she said, thumping the solid oak.

Gemma searched Cady's face, not-so-subtly looking for evidence of the grief her best friend obviously thought she was hiding. "We can talk about it, you know."

"I know," Cady said.

"I mean, the funeral was only three weeks ago."

Three weeks ago...today.

So *that* was the reason for her friend's impromptu welfare check.

"I remember," Cady said.

"She practically raised you."

"Are you actively trying to talk me into a depressive episode, or are you doing shadow work again?"

Gemma's eyes skated toward her shoes.

Guilty on both counts, Cady guessed.

"Anyway, she didn't raise me," Cady pointed out. "Aunt Fern took me in when I was sixteen. I'm not a real Townsendite, remember?" That she could joke about it now was a testament to time's pain-dulling quality.

As an already self-conscious teenaged transplant, Cady had been handed the dubious task of penetrating social circles that had been in place since...since forever, really. Had it not been for Gemma, she likely would have graduated without anyone recognizing her face in the yearbook.

"And yet you pulled Townsend Harbor's most eligible bachelor," Gemma said, her dark eyebrow raised.

Cady huffed a whisp of hair away from her face in mock exasperation. She was immeasurably grateful for the subject change. "There will be no pulling of any kind where Sheriff Townsend is concerned."

Together, they migrated toward the back of the shop, turning off additional lamps and pulling down the shades. Gemma held the swinging door that opened on a hallway leading to the narrow alley between buildings. Townsend Harbor's postcard-quaint historic downtown area was full of these strange intersections, impractical collisions where buildings had sprung up to service the Victorian seaport before city planning was a thing.

"So things aren't going well for the two of you, I take it?" Gemma asked.

"They're not going at all." Stopping at the landing at the bottom of the stairs that served as part storage, part work area, Cady tucked her armful of books into the box labeled FOX with large, marker-scrawled letters.

"I got a new shipment in today," Cady said, attempting to re-change the subject.

"You did?" As predicted, her unfailingly curious friend floated over to the bench with her recent deliveries.

Too late, Cady saw which box her friend was reaching for.

"Not that one—"

Gemma shrieked and leapt back a full foot, her eyes wide as duck eggs and her cheeks pale as milk.

"Jesus." Her best friend glared at her, a hand to her heaving chest. "What is wrong with you?"

From this angle, Cady had to admit the package's contents looked pretty unsettling.

Poking up from the snowy mound of packing peanuts, a small pink paw stretched heavenward as if to catch a game-winning fly ball.

Seized by a fierce pulse of joy, she began digging through the contents. Her newest acquisition entered the world nose first, followed by a conical, black-lipped maw bearing yellowed teeth jutting out at odd angles, and, finally, two glossy onyx button eyes below small pink ear folds. The gray body was the size of a cat's, but longer and...lumpier.

"This is Roderick," Cady said. "He's an opossum."

Gemma shuddered. "Where do you even find these things?"

"Etsy, mostly." Cady carefully wiggled the stiff body back into the peanuts. "He was on—" A gasp stole her breath as her lower back tensed up. "He was on sale," she continued after the unwelcome twinge had passed.

Concern creased her best friend's face. "Astrid remodeling today?" The name she and Gemma had landed on after deciding that pronouncing ankylosing spondylitis stole too many seconds from their day, Astrid was Cady's unwelcome tenant. The ever-present but always-unwelcome squatter who had moved in when Cady was seventeen and had been renovating her spine ever since. Some days, Astrid was content to chill and admire her handiwork. Others, she'd call up a few friends and annex Cady's hips or neck.

Today had been the latter.

"A filthy cockbiscuit, more like."

"One cockbiscuit eviction notice, coming right up." Unsnapping her satchel, Gemma reached in and produced a box whose logo Cady immediately recognized.

"You went to Baked?"

"I thought you might be able to use some cannabinoid consolation."

A relatively new and controversial addition to Townsend Harbor's commercial makeup, the cannabis-based vegan bakery had proved an instant hit with tourists and a source of constant and very vocal consternation for its residents.

Cady's would-be suitor among them.

But at only four dates in, it wasn't like she *owed* him every detail about how she spent her free time.

Right?

"Couch and Kush cookies?" she asked, finding a weak smile.

"Now you're talking." Gemma began climbing the stairs, glancing over the banister when she noticed Cady wasn't following.

"I can't just leave him down here," Cady said, motioning toward the box she didn't dare lift in her present state.

"You're right," Gemma agreed. "We should put him in the alley so he can be with his own kind."

Cady widened her eyes in a pleading look.

Her best friend exhaled a long-suffering sigh as she stomped back down and leveled a mock-serious look at Cady. "I'll bring that thing upstairs under one condition."

"What's that?" Cady asked.

"You're going to spill about you and the sheriff. None of this vague 'it's not going at all' stuff. I want details. Times. Dates. Bases reached. Got it?"

"Deal." She almost felt a little guilty for agreeing. Gemma was about to be incredibly disappointed.

With her arms stuck straight out in front of her and her face accordioned in disgust, Gemma picked up the box by its flaps and followed Cady up one flight to the front door of the two-floor living space she and her aunt had shared.

Until recently.

Cady opened the door and allowed Gemma to enter first so she could rid herself of her unwelcome cargo.

"Just set him on the kitchen table."

"The hell I will." Gemma set the load down on top of several file boxes stacked on a bench near Aunt Fern's office. "I plan on eating in there at some point in our future."

Guilt gnawed a pit in Cady's growling stomach.

How long had it been since she'd invited her friend over? They'd grabbed the occasional drink at Sirens after work, slurped coffee together from the one semi-decent coffee cubby in town before starting their days, but they hadn't had a proper hangout since before Aunt Fern's diagnosis.

Stage four metastatic lung cancer, officially.

The decline had been so fast that Cady was still reeling from the hellish merry-go-round of medical terms, medications, well-meaning mourners. The evidence of her emotional vertigo littered nearly every surface of the lovely, lofty second-floor space that Aunt Fern had converted into her home.

Wilted condolence bouquets she hadn't gotten around to tossing out sat on the dusty sills of high-arched windows. Piles of unopened mail littered the antique sideboard. Stacks of probate paperwork and file boxes huddled near the thick, intricately carved baseboards on a parquet floor badly in need of waxing.

"I'm sorry it's such a mess," she said, toeing out of her sneakers and kicking them near the front door before proceeding to the kitchen.

"You *have* been to my home, right?" Gemma set the Baked goodies on the counter and slung her coat and satchel on the back of a kitchen chair. Using it to balance, she wiggled out of her chunky patent-leather Mary Janes before padding to the dishwasher. "These clean?" she asked, holding up two wine glasses.

"Yep," Cady said. "That's pretty much the dish cabinet now."

Her best friend placed them on the oversized kitchen island and grabbed a bottle of red from the small wine fridge tucked under the subway-tiled counter. "Mind if I do the honors?"

"By all means."

Gemma made quick work of opening the wine and pouring them each a glass.

Cady gratefully accepted hers, waiting for the next part of their ritual to commence.

"If the ocean was beer and I was a duck..." Gemma began.

"I'd swim to the bottom and drink myself up," Cady finished.

They clinked glasses and sipped in solidarity.

"Now then," Gemma said, all business. "Wine is all you're getting until you spill the tea, so you might as well get on with it."

The French Cabernet was burgundy silk in Cady's throat. Spicy and full of dark fruit. She willed it to loosen her tongue.

"About Ethan?"

Gemma waggled her brows suggestively. "*Ethan*, is it?"

"I mean, that's his name. What did you think I call him?"

"*Daddy*, in a perfect world." Her wine-kissed lips curved in a suggestive smile. "Or *you iron-cocked Adonis*, or— Balls!"

"No way am I calling him *Balls*," Cady teased. "I don't care what you say about the bulge in those perfectly pleated khakis."

The gentleman dresses to the left. This information, her unhelpful brain had filed under Things I'm Trying Not to Know.

Gemma turned her leg to examine the runner in her opaque black tights. "You have any clear nail polish?"

Cady didn't. But she knew who almost certainly did.

"I'll check." She drew in a deep breath, pointed her socked feet toward the living room, and continued down the hallway to the master bedroom. Sweat bloomed on her palms as she stared at the floral ceramic doorknob.

"I can do this," she whispered to herself, flexing her fingers in preparation. "I can do this."

Turning inward to find some secret reserve of strength, she was surprised to find Fox's voice waiting for her.

I never doubt you.

That made one of them.

She got as far as closing her fingers over the smooth, cool shape before jerking her hand away as if it had burned her.

Nope.

Not yet. Not today.

The distance back to the kitchen seemed to have doubled.

"I'm sorry. I didn't—" The words died on her lips as she spotted her best friend frantically pawing through one of the file boxes on the kitchen table. Cady folded her arms and leaned against the doorway. "Want to tell me what you're doing?"

Gemma jumped, her lightly freckled cheeks flooding scarlet as her eyes darted around the kitchen.

"See, what had happened was, there's been a lot of talk about the Townsend Building since Aunt Fern's probate information has been published."

An unlikely member of Townsend Harbor's city council in her tender early twenties, Gemma had maneuvered herself into the mainline of constant, covert conversations that ran the town like the river beneath a mill.

Cady's recent misfortunes had apparently upgraded it to hydroelectric.

"I can't imagine *who* might be doing the talking," Cady said, her face beginning to slide down her skull.

The Pacific Northwest's near-constant drizzle hadn't yet flattened the dirt on Aunt Fern's grave, and already Cady had been fielding thinly veiled questions about what she intended to do with the building. Whether she would sell it back to the Townsend family, or perhaps sublease it to one of the many businesses clamoring to slide into the bookstore's coveted Water Street spot.

The idea of Cady keeping it and running the bookstore on her own never seemed to be included in their potential plans.

Gemma straightened out the tassels of the kitchen rug with her stockinged toe. "Mayor *Spewart* did mention something about the property taxes being in arrears, and I thought if I could find proof to the contrary, he might shut his stupid face."

Ever since his appointment, Deputy Mayor Stewart (*Deputy*, because he'd been designated as interim by the city council and not by democratic process) had become Gemma's official nemesis. A mansplainer of epic proportions, he'd made it his business to oppose her every idea and suggestion on principle.

As if he had any.

Cady deflated on an exhale. "In this case, Mayor Spew's stupid face is right," she admitted.

Her best friend chewed her lower lip. "If you need help—"

"It's not that," Cady said a little too quickly. "I've just been hyper-focusing on getting the business's paperwork caught up. I promise, getting those taken care of will be the next thing on my list."

Thanks to Fox's purchase of a ridiculously expensive book at a healthy fifteen percent markup.

Satisfied, or pretending to be for Cady's benefit, Gemma returned to her wine glass and grabbed the bakery box. "Shall we?"

"We shall."

They shuffled into the living room and plopped down on the well-worn leather couch. The sticky-sweet scent of vanilla with a distinctive herbal undertone wafted up from the box as Gemma opened it and offered Cady a cookie.

"I thought I didn't get one until *after* I tell you about Ethan."

"I changed my mind," Gemma said. "We both know your filter dissolves after even half of one of these."

With the day she'd had, Cady wasn't about to argue with that logic. She lifted one of the sugar cookies and bit through the thick blanket of pink icing.

Her friend swiveled on her cushion to tuck her feet beneath her skirt. "Let's have it."

Cady stretched her legs out and leaned back against the mound of throw pillows. The blessed relief of not having to support her own body weight was nothing short of a miracle.

"There's really not much to have," she said, fighting a topic-appropriate yawn.

"What did I say about the vagaries?" Gemma asked.

"That's not a vagary." Cady took a sip of wine to wash down the mouthful of doughy cookie. "That's an empirical fact."

A crumb fell from Gemma's open mouth. "You're saying he hasn't touched you, like, *at all*?"

"He did brush my boob once, but I think that was really an accident." Cady felt a flicker of fondness at the memory. The sheriff had mounted a rickety stepstool to reach the cobweb and dust-caked one-legged partridge on top of the long-neglected top shelf of Nevermore's nonfiction section. He'd misjudged his reach by a couple cup sizes on the way down and spent the rest of the evening spurting apologies at odd intervals that Cady suspected coincided with his involuntarily reliving the moment.

Every time he did, his ears glowed like they'd been dipped in lava.

All because Townsend Harbor's ginger Dudley Do-Right had been his helpful, gentlemanly self.

Glancing down at her graphic t-shirt, Cady willed her nipples to harden. Demanded that the telltale warmth gather behind the zipper of her wide-leg trouser jeans.

It was no use.

One man alone had mastered her body's cheat codes, and she'd never even seen his face.

She'd imagined it, though.

Frequently. Feverishly. And usually with a battery-powered device within arm's reach.

"Helloooo." Gemma snapped her fingers near Cady's face. "I asked you a question."

Cady dug her socked feet beneath her best friend's hip on the couch cushion. "Ask it again."

"You're telling me that I'm over here giving you all the space, being all sensitive to your grief by *not* asserting my right for the dirty details, and the whole time, there *were* no dirty details?"

Cady wiggled down on the cushion to adjust her lumbar support. "We're taking it slow."

"You're taking it slow," Gemma repeated.

"That's right."

"For this, I carried that rat up the stairs?" Gemma's eyes took on a wild look as she stabbed a finger toward the entryway where Roderick's paw was still visible above the cardboard flaps.

"He's an opossum," Cady pointed out.

"Have you given no thought at all to how this affects *me*?" Gemma demanded.

"*You?*" Cady snorted. "How could my lack of action with Ethan possibly affect you?"

"Here I am, a pillar of our community—" Gemma began.

"Who has twelve unpaid parking tickets."

"I'm on the city council," she continued.

"And were nominated as a prank."

"I'm the founder of this town's fastest-growing recreational organization—"

"Of women who you bribe with free booze."

"—the best friend of the woman dating Townsend Harbor's most eligible bachelor—"

"Who his mother set me up with," Cady reminded her.

"—and you expect me to bring my constituency something as lame as 'they're taking it slow?'"

Cady shrugged. "Seeing as it's the truth, yes."

Gemma dramatically flopped back against her side of the couch. "This is a disaster."

"You want me to flash him next time he comes to pick me up for dinner? Maybe straddle his lap at the Drunken Clam?"

Gemma brightened. "You'd do that?"

"Hell no," Cady said, batting her friend with a pillow. "I may fake smiles for retail purposes, but I'll be damned if I'm going to fake a lady boner."

"You didn't seem to be faking much while you were on the phone with Book Batman."

Cady flushed with pleasure at the memory. "That was a genre-specific lady boner. We were talking about Mary Shelley's speculative fiction masterpiece, and I don't even want to know the motherfucker who doesn't get moist for Mary Shelley."

Gemma shifted to stretch her legs so they sat feet to hips. "What do you know about this guy, anyway?"

Cady had known this question was coming, had seen it in the dogged, determined focus her easily distracted friend had demonstrated downstairs while Fox was still on the line.

"I know he was raised on a ranch in Wyoming. I know that he has a younger sister who's an architect in Cleveland. He doesn't read literary fiction but likes it when I summarize the plots for him. He hates the desert but loves high Sierra sunsets. He can't stand anything that's orange- or grape-flavored. He loves Thursdays and hates Sundays. His favorite sound is rain on a tin roof. He hates the beach because he can't stand the feeling of sand on his skin. I know he can quote the romantic poets and dissect story arcs. I know that he's traveled all over the world, and he's brilliant, and funny, and—"

"Is *that* all?" Gemma drawled.

It wasn't, but it was all Cady could say without earning herself a new avalanche of questions from Gemma.

I know that his calls are the reason I didn't go insane when Aunt Fern got sick. I know that just the sound of his voice makes my skin tingle and heart fly.

"His favorite color is blue," Cady added, for all the other things she couldn't tell her friend.

"It's a good thing men don't lie ever." Gemma set her wine glass on the coffee table and reached for the remote. "And what does he know about you?"

The implication behind the question was clear and, if Cady was being honest with herself, not entirely ungrounded. Her conversations with Fox had started innocently enough but were definitely beginning to dip into the realm of flirtation as of late.

And flirtation with a man who had become her emotional anchor and the chief source of revenue for a business she was terrified of losing was, she admitted, not the *best* idea.

"The kind of things you find out during a friendly conversation," Cady said. Like the fact that she was into monster porn, apparently.

"See, the funny thing is, because I *am* your friend, I know what your friendly conversation voice sounds like, and that wasn't it."

Cady let her head drop back against the pillow, too tired to try to convince anyone of anything.

"Look, I totally get the *man of mystery* fantasy," Gemma said, making air quotes with her fingers.

"It's not a fantasy, Gem."

Okay, so she might have the *occasional* daydream about being tied spread-eagle to the rolling ladder in Fox's library—which she was a hundred percent sure he had—but what provincial governess *wouldn't* be curious when the troubled and darkly seductive laird of a crumbling manse invited her to peruse his private collection?

"I'm just saying, I think you should be careful."

"You're one to talk," Cady said around a yawn. "Remember that time you gave a ride to that hitchhiker just because he was wearing a yellow beanie?"

"Umm, yellow is my lucky color."

Gemma and her signs.

"Right," Cady said. "As in, you're lucky you didn't end up the pretty face on an episode of *Dateline*."

"I was perfectly safe," her friend assured her. "Someone setting out to do harm to another human would never accessorize with something so easily identifiable on a police sketch."

"Have you shared this theory with the FBI's Behavioral Analysis division?" Cady asked, picking a crumb from the shelf of her breasts. "I'm sure they'd be riveted."

A rolling cloud of mellow began to fill her limbs with warm honey, and her joints mercifully surrendered their grudges against general existence.

"Feeling better?" Gemma asked.

"Much," Cady said.

"Stand-up or tits and dragons?" Gemma aimed the remote at the flat screen mounted above the fireplace mantel.

"You pick." Letting her body become one with the couch, Cady felt a rush of gratitude. For the reprieve from Astrid. For cannabis cookies and her best friend's comforting presence.

But especially for the man whose smoky voice chased her into dreams.

TWO

Hermit

[HÛR'MĬT] NOUN. A PERSON WHO HAS WITHDRAWN TO A SOLITARY PLACE

TRAPPED.

No, *hostage.*

Fox's heavy limbs strained against the bonds cutting into his skin with such animalistic frenzy that his veins bulged as large as ropes.

The only part of him left unrestrained?

His rage.

A bell jangled in the distance, doing the same to his nerves.

A phone? His heart threw itself against its cage in the direction of the sound.

She'd never called *him* before.

The bells again. Not a phone. What the motherfuck was that sound?

Santa?

"They call you Fox, but you are not so hard to hunt." A smooth, accented voice slid into his ear like a venomous serpent, slithering down his spine until his veins turned into writhing, foreign invaders. It was all he could do not to peel off his own flesh.

The frenzy became something else. Something even darker. Driven by the presence of a sensation so foreign and yet...recently familiar. All he knew was he needed to escape it. His senses sharpened, and yet he could see and hear nothing but the sounds of his struggles echoing off the walls.

Walls too close. Too low. Pressing down. Down. And on all sides. Trapping his arms. Squeezing the air from his lungs. Stealing the space his ribs needed to expand. Kicking his heart and sweat glands into overdrive.

The sensation had a name.

Terror.

An odd hiss struck his sensitive ears as he peeled his eyes open, only to be assaulted with brilliant white light. Struggles turned to flails as his bonds, astonishingly, loosened enough for him to bend his elbows, then his wrists. Kick out with his legs.

The hiss grew louder, more insistent. Rhythmic, even, as he fought his way out of some clinging substance shaped like a coffin. Forcing blinks against the light, he leapt to his feet and gyrated like his sister Rochelle that one time he'd tossed a jumping spider in her hair. He ripped off the shirt that sweat had molded to his skin. Kicked heavy bindings away from his legs.

The sole of his foot landed on something burning hot, and he leapt in the opposite direction, careening into a gritty wall and slipping on something satiny.

Catching himself on one knee, he exploded forward like a sprinter, escaping the walls.

Fucking figures. A disassociated auditory snarl in his own voice echoed in the contorted, half-conscious shit-soup between his ears. *I knew I was headed toward the Light sooner rather than later.*

A brutal chill ripped into him like a blade, cutting through to his marrow. This time, the cold burned his bare feet. Stumbling, he scrambled to regain his balance, claiming enough of his wits to sink into a fighting stance and identify the direction of his adversary.

One of them was about to die.

The air turned to ice crystals in his lungs as brilliant sunlight reflected off the first late-autumn snow and punched from above *and* from the reflection below into stubborn pupils refusing to contract.

He stood in front of the only shape that wasn't either tree or stone and bared his teeth. "Let's do this, motherfucker."

It wouldn't be his first bare-handed kill, but it *would* be the first with his dick swinging in the breeze.

Unutterably gentle doe-brown eyes dispelled the vestiges of his recurring nightmare, yanking him from the gnarled, clawing fingers of sleep and back into full consciousness.

Literal deer eyes.

Fox and the doe stood like that for a moment as sweat froze to his exposed flesh. They stared at each other as their hasty, heaving breaths made matching clouds in the crisp morning air.

She was a young adult. Less than a handful of years. On the small side, like they all were in this area of Washington state's Olympic Mountains range, easy for navigating the dense forests and uneven terrain.

The bell sounded again. This time from behind him.

His creature alarm.

Whirling, he caught sight of a teenaged fawn as it frolicked toward one of the bells hanging from the rope he'd surrounded his den with. Completely unbothered by the six-foot-three nude man separating her from her mother, she booped the bell with her nose and jump-twisted away with playful excitement at the sound.

A breath he hadn't known he was holding exploded from his aching chest.

The dream wasn't real.

He wasn't *there*.

He was *here*.

Here: the Pacific Northwest lovingly referred to as the PNW. The other side of the country from where he was born, high in the Olympic Mountains, above where most women his age had once been children who believed sparkly vampires and indigenous werewolves resided nearby.

Better them than the monsters living in his nightmares.

They were real...and they did unthinkable things.

An entirely different noise chuffed from behind him, and he glanced over his shoulder to see the mother pawing at the ground, looking from him to her offspring with naked fear.

Only when he unclenched his teeth to speak did he realize he'd been grinding his molars to dust.

"Don't worry, Mama." His unused voice sounded like sandstone and razorblades. Turning back toward the den, he cleared his throat. "I didn't know it was you."

They'd crossed paths before. He recognized the white blaze beneath her throat. Early spring, her fawn had been the height of a golden retriever and just as bouncy. Probably the first birth for the young doe.

Even if he took his bow out later, he'd starve before bothering with those two.

He didn't kill children. Or their mothers.

His difficult swallow landed in the abysmal void in his chest as he strode back toward the coal bed of last night's fire. He stepped on one of the stones he'd laid around the fire just beyond the ingress in the smooth rock.

He slept here when the weather turned, though he preferred to stare up at the moon. This was the next best thing, however, as he could at least *see* the sky, the dense woods, and was still protected from the worst of the weather by the cliff face.

Mostly. So long as the wind didn't shift in a very specific way.

He identified his camo winter sleeping bag as his perceived captor, the fabric the source of the strange hiss he'd perceived in semiconsciousness.

Fuck. What if he was getting worse? If the sleeping bag became more confining? If the nightmares drove him out of it...

Then what?

Though Fox had selected the PNW for the fact that it was forty-five to eighty-five degrees basically always, a changing climate was beginning to cause the summer to kiss a hundred. On the other side of that, winter would bring significant exposure hazards.

He'd been able to survive thus far. But if it got much colder... it would be shelter or die.

And at this point, Fox wasn't certain he'd bother with the shelter.

If he wandered east of Seattle, he'd be in fire season country until he cleared the Rocky Mountains. Same if he went south, with the added complications of higher population densities and less hunting and fresh water, all the way down to Mexico.

Fox followed the limp path of clothes he'd torn off his body, snatching them up along the way.

The nightmare lingered in here, too, smelling of dank, damp stone and stale fear.

His skin reeked of it.

His body thrummed with it.

Digging his palms against his eyes, he dragged his hands down his face and a beard Thor might have been proud of.

He was almost warm and dry when the tremors set in. Almost ready for a late breakfast when the nausea and vertigo nearly drove him to his knees. His bones were held together by crepe paper and glass, rather than connective tissue and hard-earned muscle.

He needed to run. He needed to hunt and climb and push until he'd exhausted the adrenaline coursing through him.

Or...

His eyes swung to his satellite phone. His *one* link to the world.

Programmed with the *one* number he ever called.

The *one* voice he wanted to hear from the *one* person he could fucking stand.

No. *No*. Things had become much worse than that. He longed for the sweet husk of her animated voice. So much so that he denied himself all contact except for Thursdays.

Thursdays belonged to Cadence Bloomquist.

"Cady."

He didn't realize he'd said the name aloud until it landed south of his belly button, and he had to turn from the fire to avoid a wiener roast.

Checking the tick marks on the stone wall, he cursed and stomped about the den like a bear awoken early from hibernation as he gathered his gear.

Fucking Monday.

Three more nights of this, he reminded himself. *Three nights before I can sleep with her voice caressing my dreams.*

He often didn't have the nightmare on Thursdays.

Which was why he *shouldn't* call her more often.

Attachments were dangerous. Furthermore, no one should be burdened with his specific flavor of fuckery.

Heaving a breath, Fox braced for the cold day's work ahead. The routine never altered. He'd check his traps and treat and store the food and pelts. He'd track the three small herds of deer in the area and pick an old-timer to sacrifice to his winter stores of jerky. He'd do target practice. He'd do pull-ups on the oak by the lake. He'd exhaust himself so his body forced him back to sleep.

And he wouldn't call Cadence Bloomquist for three more nights.

Until then… He looked out toward the lake dusted with a scrim of frost. Time to take God's own cold shower.

THREE

Guardian

(GÄR'DĒ-ƏN) NOUN. A PERSON WHO GUARDS, PROTECTS, OR PRESERVES.

It'd been dark for a while when Fox closed the book, but he'd been so engrossed, he barely noticed the time pass.

Jaw cracking on a yawn, he considered turning in.

The second the thought landed, his body seized. The ghosts of his morning nightmare had been exorcised with punishing physical labor.

Until now.

Swallowing around a constricting throat, Fox closed his eyes and reached down into his ever-dwindling reserves for fortitude. For disassociation. For...for something he'd stopped believing in.

Peace.

If only he didn't know where it could be found.

Above a bookstore in the—and he never used this word —*cutest* goddamned town in the entire planet.

And he'd seen most of this world.

Three more nights.

The soft peal of an outgoing call ringing through physically startled him.

When had he reached for the phone?

When had he dialed her number?

Hang up, he commanded himself. *Hang up, you selfish fu—*

A click. A feminine sneeze. A crash.

"Oh, shitsnacks."

Fox sat up, every muscle tensed as her faraway curse was muffled by the sounds of her fumbling with the phone.

"Cady?" He cleared the rust from his voice again. "Cady? You okay?"

"Sorry! One sec!" Another sneeze. A plaintive meow. A sound like falling marbles. And...either he'd called a WWII-era radio, or the receiver was being dragged against sandpaper? "Um...oof... ouch. Sat down too fast." At least, that's what he *thought* she said.

"Cady?" He willed his heart to slow. Pain injected a concerning note into her voice. But he detected no fear...probably. It was hard to tell.

"Ugh. Balls." It seemed like the receiver might be making its way in the right direction, as he heard that loud and clear. "Why do you have to be such a weapons-grade dick? I mean, whoops. I mean—" The phone finally made it to her mouth. "Um, thank you for calling the Nev—"

"Who's being a weapons-grade dick?" he barked in a voice he'd not used since... Well, it didn't matter how long. You *did not* use that tone with a woman.

Ever.

Before he could apologize, she answered, unconcerned, "Fox? *Ohmigod*, did I forget it was Thursday?"

Brow furrowed, he tossed the book into the dirt, his entire energy homed in on her voice. Was she drunk? Had she hit her head? Had a "weapons-grade dick" done something to hurt her?

Was she currently in the room with a dead man?

"Cady...it's Monday. What's wrong? Are you alone? Say, 'Order for the Christmas season,' if you're not safe."

"Oh... I'm all the way safe." She giggled.

"Did you suffer trauma to your head?" He only asked because she wasn't acting like herself. "Are you experiencing—"

"I mean, I wouldn't claim *trauma*, per se, but I did almost clothesline myself getting out of the Lyft earlier." The giggle turned into a rich laugh, and suddenly he could breathe a little.

But something was off. *Seriously off.* Cady Bloomquist was a shy, sensitive soul with an acute awareness of her place in the world and how she moved within it. While she was a ray of sunshine, he'd only heard her giggle when he made her nervous.

Not that he blamed her. He made everyone nervous.

It was kinda his thing.

"I'm so glad it's you." The words gusted on the breath of someone who'd just sprinted up several flights of stairs. "I was about to make the most awkward apology ever... Well, maybe not *ever*, but ever over the phone at a bookstore in the middle of the night on a Monday."

Was it the middle of the night?

She was glad he called?

"Who was being a dick?" He managed to keep the primitive bullshit out of his voice this time.

Barely.

"My spine."

He blinked. "What happened to it?"

She paused a beat too long. "Mmmmust have wrenched it or something. It's NBD—speaking of Mondays, did you lose your calendar?"

Adorable that she thought she was misdirecting. Almost as adorable as her habit of using text acronyms in her everyday speech when she had such a literary mind.

"Cady..." His voice was as soft as it could ever get. "Drowning a rough Monday in alcohol?"

"*Au contraire, mon frère,*" she said in the *worst possible* French accent. "Celebrating a *splendiferous* Monday with a root beer soda made with—get this—the devil's lettuce. We put it over ice cream, and it tasted like cream soda, and now I'm *the most highest* because I didn't know that there were ten regular servings of THC in one bottle. And I had thirds!"

He didn't realize how tight his skin had stretched across his tense expression until the explanation of her unusual mood threatened to relax his lips into a smile. "Someone with you?"

"I don't see how that's any of your business," she remonstrated with half-mock petulance. "I'm a strong, independent woman. I can hold my substances. I don't need a *man* to babysit me."

He'd stepped into some shit in his life, and he could smell it on his shoe now. "No—uh—I didn't mean to pry. It's none of my business, I just..." If his team could see him like this—they'd take his man card, rip it up, and throw it in the fire, then piss on the ashes, wait for them to dry, and dump them from a plane into the most remote center of the ocean.

And that was if they were feeling pity.

"I'm teasing." She laughed again, and the sound lifted every hair on his body. "I mean, I'm alone. No one needs to witness this chaos."

He didn't want to identify the bleak note beneath her pitch when she said *alone*...

Nor could he analyze the relief he felt that another man wasn't in her shop in the middle of the night.

"Shit, I called too late, didn't I?" It was too cloudy outside to tell the time. When she said *middle of the night*, he'd assumed hyperbole. "I was going to leave a message with my order if you'd closed," he explained, hoping relief wasn't the only fond feeling she had toward him for an unexpected call.

"If? I closed five hours ago."

Regret shanked him in the sternum. "Fuck. Sorry. You just getting home from...a party?" Had she started forwarding her landline to a cell? She wasn't aware he already knew the number to her mobile, but he never used it.

"Yeah, it was Myrtle's *fifth* fifty-fifth birthday, and Vee threw her a not-sixty party."

"Sounds"—*fucking weird*—"fun."

"*So* fun," she strenuously agreed. "I had three root beer floats. Did I tell you how much cannabis that was?"

"You sure did." Jesus Christ, she was adorable on a regular day. Inebriated? He'd met certain sociopaths who would be charmed by her.

"Say what you want about that generation, they know how to handle their weed."

A gruff sound escaped him, somewhere between a cough and a grunt. Could have possibly been interpreted as a laugh? It'd been so long, he didn't remember. "What are you doing at the store instead of partying or sleeping?"

Her gusty sigh ended on a breathy little groan. "Oh...you know, gathering data for taxes, profit and loss statements that are due to my accountant tomorrow that I forgot about until my Google Calendar sent me notifications at midnight. You know... the sexy stuff..."

Fox bit down on both of his lips. When her voice went liquid like that, his veins turned from ice to honey.

She'd never done that before.

"Oh yeah?" He hoped his own groan sounded a little teasing as well. "Tell me what your dividends are wearing."

Nope. No. Negative. Abort. He had no business talking to her like this.

"To be honest? Not much."

For the billionth time, he thanked the Nine Princes of Hell she couldn't see him. Or read his filthy mind. Or knew anything about who he was or what he'd done.

"Wanna hear how low and nasty these numbers are?" She saw his tease and raised him one of her own.

"Only if you go real slow." He'd listen to her read the phone book in that voice. *Keep talking. It's the only thing connecting me to my sanity. The only thing connecting my mind to my body.*

She cleared her throat as if to prepare, but what came out was shy. "Hey, so...why *are* you calling on a Monday?"

After he was done being disappointed, he'd be grateful she was the one to break the spell and pull them away from a ledge he'd vowed to avoid. "Out of books early," he answered honestly, eyes going to the embarrassingly colorful cover almost glowing next to the faded exterior of his unzipped sleeping bag. "Couldn't put down that last Lady Lavender mystery."

It used to hurt to say it. Like someone poured napalm down his throat. Lady *motherfucking* Lavender. Victorian spinster archaeologist and amateur sleuth.

Probably crack was less addictive.

But something like six weeks ago he'd asked Cady what book *she* thought he would like the most. Fox'd nearly given birth to an entire cow when she suggested the title, obviously marketed to women.

While the plots could be a bit melodramatic, it read like *Downton Abbey* meets *Game of Thrones*, and he'd ordered the entire twenty-one-book series.

"OMG. The next one was *just* released early—I'll overnight it to you, no charge."

A harsh laugh burst from him in another surprising gust. She was too sweet for her own fucking good. It was going to get her in trouble. "The overnight fee will be four hundred percent of the book's actual cost."

"I know, but you *have* to read it yesterday! This isn't a spoiler, but it has this twist that will make your soul jizzzzzzz."

Two chuckles in a row she'd caused. This woman was some kind of witch.

"I won't be checking my mail for another few days, so no overnight necessary." If this was how she conducted business, no wonder her store suffered financially.

"Okay, well, when you read it, you have to call me and tell me what you think. I have questions. I have big thoughts for you. *Yuge* thoughts. The most *tremendous* thoughts ever thoughted. No one has ever thought about a book like I think about this one..." she said, adopting a flat-toned spoof they often used as an inside joke before dissolving into giggles.

He had something *yuge* for her, too, something twitching against his thigh and threatening to become a fucking problem.

Slamming the iron bars closed on that thought, he realized she'd not stopped talking.

"...know when you reach episode four. Because don't watch before you finish the book. There are spoilers," she was saying. "But call me after, because you are going to shit your *mind*! I bet it would be fun to watch high. The colors would be like..." She made a noise between an explosion and a sea wave.

"Episode?" He struggled to grasp her meaning through a haze of sudden lust-fog.

Being a dude sucked sometimes.

"You know, *Lady Lavender* on PBS. It's an abomination, but they won six Emmys this year. Don't tell me you're not watching. The whole fuckin' *world* is watching..."

"The whole fucking world minus me."

"Ugh, I can't let this stand. Go and watch episode one right now! I'll wait up. You can call me back. I can't believe this. It's as if you missed *Star Wars* or something. Do you even exist if you haven't seen it?"

"Ummmm..." He glanced around the smooth rock face cluttered by his sleeping roll, bag, lantern, bow, rifle, and pack. The entirety of his possessions weighed just over seventy-five pounds. "I can't manage an episode tonight, I'm afraid."

"It's okay. You can catch up while I send the book off, but again, don't touch season three, episode four or there will be consequences."

Why that silly threat turned his body into a fucktangle of desire was beyond his mortal understanding. But here they were —her having an innocuous conversation, and his hand moving restlessly from his chest toward his cock.

It wouldn't be the first time.

"Sorry. Can't," he rasped, hoping she couldn't hear the strangled note of need.

A mock noise of disbelief. "Wait just a minute, *Mister* Fox... *Do not* tell me you're one of those people who are all, 'I don't watch TV.'"

"'Fraid so." Why watch *GoT* when his own memory was dripping with just as much blood, geopolitics, and betrayal?

"Ugh. Gross!" She laughed. "Can we even be friends?"

"Hey. Aren't streaming platforms sending bookstores like yours out of business?" he quipped with his own chuckle. Three in a night. A recent record.

"Touché!" Her voice glowed with warmth and laughter, and suddenly the night didn't press in so close. "Monday you is mean."

"I'm mean every day."

"I'm sending you something extra," she announced, as if the decision had just struck her.

"You don't have to—"

"No, it'll be so fun. It'll keep you occupied. Hold on a sec, I have to switch to the store landline—my cell is about to die."

Several clicks later, she reappeared, sounding a little further away. He liked her fascination with all things analog, including the antique turn-of-the-twentieth-century rotary phone with one of those mile-long twirly cords.

"Want to know what I sent?"

"Man like me doesn't get many surprises. Let me want it for a while." Christ, even *his* voice wasn't *that* deep. If she didn't hear the impossible, unarticulated *sex* in it, she needed to get her hearing checked.

"Can I ask you something?" The tone of her voice pierced his warm haze with doubt.

Running a hand over his still-drying hair, he tugged with frustration at his uncharacteristic lack of control lately. "Nothing good ever follows that question, but...yeah."

"Are we... And tell me if I'm totally up in the night...or if I'm reading things weirdly...or if... Well, I'll just ask it. Are we, like, flirting? Er. Were we *just* flirting? I felt like we were flirting, but I'm not always super great at telling. I swear, in order to get me to realize someone is interested in me, I'm pretty sure they'd have to bash me over the head and carry me back to their Neanderthal cave." Her nervous laughter repeated when he didn't instantly reply.

He surveyed his surroundings. He'd bash his own brains out before rendering a woman unconscious, but a Neanderthal cave?

That, he had covered. Kinda.

There was no way around it. "Yeah. One could say we were flirting just now," he answered carefully.

"Okay, phew, I just didn't want to be inappropriate with a... a...? Customer? Frrrriend?" Her audible swallow charmed him more than that little fawn and her obsession with his bell.

"Be as inappropriate as you want." He needed to hang up. *Hang up now! Think of a reason to let her go, you sack of shit!*

He opened his mouth to inquire as to why she was doing her financials so obviously impaired when she cleared her throat. "Can I ask you something else?"

"Of course."

"Why don't you ever, like—I don't know—send me pictures of your dick?"

Fox had been choked by many things, but swallowing his own tongue was entirely new. "Do you...want pictures of my dick?" Because they didn't exist—he had no camera, and also, why the *fuck* would anyone send one without a very obvious request?

She paused. "No?"

"Was that a question?"

He could feel her squirming in her chair, so strong and obvious was her silent distress. "You're different from most guys our age, that's all. We've been talking for months, and...you're always... Well, you're just...you know, you're so... Well, you're great."

"*Great*?" The word tasted like "I love you like a brother." Which should have been fine...but also made him want to lick a skunk's ass to get rid of the flavor.

"Ffffffantastic?"

Ouch. He'd prefer *weapons-grade dick*. "Do you know how many question marks would be in this conversation if someone transcribed it?" he joked, trying to give her a way out of a very perilous situation with levity.

"I can't land on a word!" she complained, as if she couldn't decide which chocolate to pick from a fancy box. "Something exciting and attractive and considerate and intense and mysterious. I daresay enigmatic."

It'd been an entire eternity since Fox blushed, but a warmth creeping up his neck and into his ears told him he was the most pathetic human alive. "You're landing on a whole mess of words there, Cady."

Audible swallow. "Too many?"

"Not if you mean it." He literally bit down on his lip so hard he tasted blood. *Stop. Fucking.* Talking. *Man.*

He should just walk into the sea. End it.

There was torture he could take. And then there was *this*. This inconceivably exquisite torment.

Somehow his hand had worked its way to the waistband of his pants.

Fox sat listening to her fight for breath as he grappled with his own lungs. All her feminine thoughts audibly vibrated through him with detectible delicacy, like cogs in the most intricate watch.

He should say something.

"I'd never send you a picture of my dick."

He should have said anything but that.

"Well, *now* I'm wondering if there's something wrong with it."

"Trust me, woman, it gets the job done." Was that a sexual challenge? From him?

How did they get here?

"I-I'm not— I didn't mean— I'm not *requesting*—" Laughter warmed her embarrassment as she took a moment to find the words. "Well, the whole point of the question was, like... We've been chatting for several months. Friendly. Er...flirting, one could say. And you've never tried to take it further or push boundaries."

Well. Yeah. "Is that bad?"

"Not so much," she said after a pause. "It's refreshing, actually. But I guess I just wondered if... Well, I thought we might... I mean, since you have your deliveries picked up by hand, you might be local-ish..."

A wave of dread threatened his teeth-clenching arousal. Here it was. The capital-T *Thing*. The conversation that would shatter the purity of what they had.

He couldn't ask her to dinner. A movie was so far out of the question that the very thought of it made his ass itch.

He certainly couldn't take her home.

He couldn't love her. Touch her. Talk to her.

He could *not* want her.

He'd never wanted anything so bad in his life.

"Cady... I can't—"

"Shh!"

"I'm sorry?" Did she just *shush* his gentle rejection? Had anyone dared shush him in his entire godforsaken life? His rancher mother, from whom he'd derived a tough hide, the work ethic of an ox, and a backhand Conor McGregor would envy, was the lone person in his memory.

And when she shushed, you shushed the fuck up.

Or you would answer to his father. A quiet, simple, patient man with a green thumb and fists the size of jackhammers.

A paternal trait he'd inherited. The fists, not the green thumb.

He was better at killing things than making them grow.

"I thought I heard something downstairs..." Cady took a moment to listen, and he took a moment to not lose his entire mind. "It's fine—it's probably just Gemma."

"Probably?"

"Yeah, no one else comes here this time of night. She's probably making sure I got home and into bed okay."

Probably was his least favorite word. "Why would she do that?"

"Um..." She hesitated.

As much as Fox's well-honed instincts told him he could trust Cady, she was a woman who kept a secret from him. One he wasn't entitled to know...

One he ached to discover.

"You know how fierce female best friends can be. We take care of each other."

He couldn't think of anything sweeter. "I guess we're both about to yell at you for not locking your doors this late."

"What's *weird* is that I swear I did," she said in absent wonder. "Like, I remember because I am watching Mr. Henery's cat, Kevin Costner, and he's a wily little escape artist."

"Kevin Costner? Or Mr. Hen—" Whipping his blanket off, Fox bolted upright, struck by a dark bolt of dread. "Last time we spoke, you said Gemma doesn't have a key."

"Oh yeah." Hesitancy crept into her tone. "Um... Hey, Gem?" she called out. "Gemma, is that you? I'm on the landing."

"Jesus fucking Christ, woman, don't give away your position!" he barked.

Calm down. It's probably just the fucking cat.

"Oh, *please*, this is Townsend Harbor—we have fewer break-ins than Fort Knox," she replied. "The last violent thing to happen here was before I lost my—"

The abrupt cessation of her words jarred him into action. "Cady?" he said as he surged to his feet. "Cady, what's happening? Talk to me."

"They—they broke something," she whispered.

Fuck.

"It's not the cat?"

"I just remembered I shut him in Fern's old parlor." She sounded so small. And so *fucking* far away.

Nine miles, to be exact.

His blood froze, heart plummeting from a cliff into a void.

The flat of his hand struck the stone. He wanted to punch, to roar, and destroy.

But he needed to save his knuckles for a deserving face.

"Get behind a locked door, Cady," he said in a tone measured with precise elements of authority, gentleness, calm, and urgency. "Get behind a locked door and call 911."

"Okay." Uneven footsteps echoed across the line, and she made several concerning sounds that reminded him of her wrenched back... She was moving waaaaaay too slow. How bad was it?

The thought of someone accosting her while she was injured sent his vision swirling into crimson chaos.

"Fast as you can," he urged her, fighting a strange squeeze in his chest. He needed intel and had exactly no time to gather it. Blueprints of her store. Her place in it. Tactical positions close by. "Do you see them? How many?"

"Don't know." Frightened tears choked off her whisper. "More than one."

Jesus Christ, he'd never been so alarmed and frustrated at one time. "Locked door. Where is it?"

"Over there."

He closed his eyes, fighting a surge of visceral panic at the idea of anyone being trapped. It was for her safety. She was hurt and inebriated. Extra vulnerable. Panicked and confused.

And this world was full of men who struck at the first sign of weakness.

"Lock yourself in," he managed around a closing throat.

"But...but the phone cord won't reach that long."

"Now, Cady! I'm going to call 911."

"No. *No!* Don't leave me alone!" If he could have reached through the connection between them and clapped his hand over her mouth, he would have.

"I have to get help there," he explained. "Is there a weapon close by?"

"What about— No, that won't work. This stapler is kind of

heav— Nope. Oh, wait! I've got it. *War and Peace*! Hardcover with super-pointy edges."

"No, dammit, you need—"

"I can almost reach it."

"Cady—"

"Got it."

Her triumph was interrupted by a cry that ripped his heart from his chest and tossed it, still beating, into the snow.

"No! Oh no! *Nononono*. Don't. *Please*."

He roared her name, but his voice was lost to a sound like an avalanche.

Then a dead line.

Stringing together every curse word in every language he'd learned, he dialed her number.

Nothing.

Again.

Same.

And just like that, a calm stole over him, as still and frigid as the crystals sparkling in the frozen air. He pulled it around him like a mantle of ice and dialed 911. Somehow he was able to connect with a dispatcher with a smoker's voice named Judy. As the woman sent law enforcement to Nevermore, Fox kicked snow and dirt over his fire, donned his boots, checked and secured his gear, and abandoned anything nonessential that would slow him down.

As he began to march, dark emotions swirled beneath his disassociation. *What if she—?*

Nope. Shut it down.

His heartbeat became the syllables of her name. *Cady. Cady. Cady.*

If one hair on her head...

Keep it together, Fox. Lock it away. Casualties are inevitable. The person next to you might matter most, and if they went down, vengeance was swift and merciless.

Only then he could think about grief.

Nine miles would take him at least three hours over this terrain. He could sustain that, no problem. He wanted to run. To sprint. To plunge headlong into the increasing wind and hurl himself through the inky black until he landed at her feet.

He had to be smarter than that. He couldn't arrive too exhausted.

In case there was blood to be spilled.

FOUR

Contrition

(KƏN'TRIΣƏN). NOUN. SINCERE PENITENCE OR REMORSE.

"WHAT DO YOU THINK HE'S DOING?" GEMMA'S COFFEE-scented whisper tickled Cady's ear.

They stood behind the credenza/register, sipping their lattes and watching Sheriff Ethan Townsend…sheriffing. Lean in khakis and a sky-blue dress shirt, he stood immobile and erect, the muscular wedge of his torso diminishing into the black utility belt circling his waist.

For the last seven minutes, he'd done nothing but stand there, motionless, silently staring at the sprawling chaos of books and papers before him, one knuckle notched beneath his chin cleft.

"Beats me," Cady said. "Catatonic episode of some kind?"

"You think he'd notice if I tried to hit that freckle on the back if his neck?" Gemma asked, picking up the feather quill pen and aiming at the neatly shaved, Marine-precise hairline at Ethan's nape.

"Which one?" Cady shrugged out of habit and sucked in a breath as lava flashed down her arm. The cumbersome canvas sling she'd been strapped into after being diagnosed with a dislocated shoulder at the Townsend Harbor Allcare Clinic had so far failed to remind her not to move it.

And yet, clipping her aunt's ancient bookshelf hard enough

to cause a *posterior subluxation* while reaching for a book to use as a weapon was by far the least humiliating consequence of the previous evening.

Nope.

That unique and dubious honor belonged to her having to assist the man she'd been dating reconstruct the scene of a maybe-crime while trying to remember if she had accused Fox of having a Quasimodo cock.

...I'm wondering if there's something wrong with it, she heard herself say in a voice dripping with sass.

Shame scalded her anew.

How the hell had they gotten from a flirty back-and-forth about the store's tax paperwork to conjecturing about Fox's man-root?

Why, oh why, had she allowed Myrtle to talk her into a third round of beer pong? Cady didn't even like beer. Or pong. Or anything that could be played with a ball, for that matter.

She forced herself to continue the process of dredging her sludgy memory despite the other various horrors it continued to produce.

It will be so fun.

Make your soul jizz.

Send me pictures of your dick.

How hard?

Gemma's pointy elbow dug into Cady's ribs on the side of her body the bookshelf hadn't attempted to pulp in its epic face plant.

She glanced up to see Ethan's clean-shaven jaw angled over his shoulder, a sandy brow lifted in question.

"I'm sorry, what?"

Ethan's lips tugged downward at the corner. "I said, how hard did you hit the bookshelf?"

"Um...pretty hard?" Her insides lurched, and Cady wasn't sure if it was gas or her soul attempting to escape her body. "I was trying to get to a copy of *War and Peace* to use as a weapon and I must have misjudged."

Send me pictures of your dick?

Oh dear God. No no no no no. Had she really requested dick pics from the customer single-handedly keeping her in business at this point?

Worse, what if Fox had actually sent them, but she hadn't responded?

What if—trapped in the pulverized remains of her cell phone —right now, this very minute—nay, *second*—there were pictures of Fox's rigid, perfectly veined—

"Which side?"

Cady blinked to clear the screen of her mind from another man's imaginary penis before returning her attention to Ethan. "What was that?"

The translucent tips of Ethan's lashes lowered as he squinted at her. "Which side did you run into?"

"The side that's closest to the register?" she said, sounding exactly like the kid in class who'd been fiddling on a device instead of paying attention.

"Right." Ethan turned to face them, his posture so stiff he looked like he was rotating on his own personal axis to the earth. "So why'd it fall in this direction?" he asked, gesturing toward the pile.

Whether it was the weed hangover from Myrtle's "Skunk-beer," or a goodly section of her temporal lobe still making frantic queries of her codeine-addled memory, Cady couldn't quite follow his logic.

Noting the ponderous crease in Cady's crumpled forehead, Ethan pivoted and held out a hand to Gemma. "Come here."

"Me?" Gemma's dark brows vaulted up by an inch.

"You." The palm he held out to her was wide and callused by years of engaging with his hobby of choice.

Woodworking. Making hand-crafted benches, to be precise.

She and Gemma had nearly torn something the other night

howling about potential taglines should he ever decide to open a storefront.

Smooth enough to satisfy, hard enough to last.

You'll never want to sit on anything else once you touch our wood.

Get knotty on our porch swings.

Gemma discreetly kicked Cady's ankle coming out from behind the register. Payback, she guessed, for her being drafted into service on her best friend's behalf. Hesitantly, Gemma picked her way around the sprawl of books and placed her hand in Ethan's.

His fingers closed over hers in a flash, and, in a move that made Cady dizzy, he looped Gemma's arm over her head to twirl her to face the rectangular patch of wall where the bookshelf used to be.

"You were here," he said, glancing back at Cady.

Her teeth clicked as she snapped her gaping jaw shut. "Mmhmm."

His hands were anchored at Gemma's waist and swiftly rotated her hips toward the stairs. "Like so?"

Cady's tongue had turned to taffy.

"Or like this?" he said, and Gemma's pleated skirt flared as he spun her a quarter turn toward his chest.

She shot Cady a look over the shoulder of her eggplant-purple cardigan.

Cady widened her eyes in a silent *I know, right?* She'd never seen Ethan so...in charge. So...in control. So...*I can move your body however I want you, and you'll like it.*

And it wasn't *not* working.

"Like that," she agreed, not wanting poor Gemma to get vertigo before he could finish his reconstruction.

Ethan's voice dropped to a conversational register as his hand hovered near her shoulder. "May I?"

"Please do." Gemma sighed dreamily.

He carefully lifted her braid and moved it to her opposite

shoulder, guiding her torso forward with a hand planted between her shoulder blades.

"The impact happens here." His piercing blue eyes locked on Cady's. "Then what?"

He *would* ask that of a woman with weed-addled memory.

"I kind of bounced off." *And let fly a flash flood of fucks.*

Ethan hooked his hands under Gemma's armpits and lifted her until the patent-leather toes of her Mary Janes barely kissed the wood floor. "Here?"

"I mean, I wasn't exactly recording geo-coordinates by that point, but roughly, yes."

Ethan set Gemma down. "Then?"

"Then I heard a cracking sound and realized it was tipping toward me." Closing her eyes, Cady allowed herself to drift back into the moment. The sense of a shift in the darkness. The hair standing up on her arms a split second before the impact. "I tried to jump out of the way, but it caught my shoulder and knocked the phone out of my hand."

"You were on a call with a customer at the time of the incident," he observed in a flat, *just the facts, ma'am* monotone.

"Yes."

"And he was the party who placed a call to 911."

"Yes," Cady confirmed.

"Do you recall about what time that was?"

Sometime after I insulted his manhood but before I proved Gemma annoyingly right about the bookshelf didn't feel like an exceptionally helpful answer.

Cady conjured what she hoped was a thoughtful expression. "Hmm..."

"I heard he sounded like a cross between Benedict Cumberbatch and Jason Momoa." This helpful tidbit was offered up by none other than Myrtle, who looked surprisingly none the worse for wear—relatively speaking—despite having thrown a rager that had half her guests yarking on her ceramic-animal-littered lawn.

"One of those voices that comes with a hand around your throat. But a hand that knows just how hard to—"

"That'll do, Myrtle," Ethan interrupted.

"Not a local, either," she added, leaning in the doorway. She, like many of the town's core residents, had been milling around the shop's exterior, hoping to catch a snatch of gossip through the old and not very thick plate glass window. *Unlike* many of the town's other residents, Myrtle had had the stones to slip in via the front door. "Judy said that—"

"Judy said that she's going to keep her mouth shut if she wants to retain her job as a county dispatcher." The suddenly thunderous swell of the sheriff's voice dropped all three women into stunned silence. "That's confidential information, and I'll thank you to keep it that way."

Myrtle's crepey neck contracted on a swallow. "And I'll thank you not to raise your voice to me," she said, drawing herself up to every inch of five-feet-two. "I was fighting fires in Canada before you'd figured out how to properly point your pecker at a toilet bowl, and I'll say what I want, to who I want, when I want. Got it, kiddo?"

In addition to a frequent lack of discretion, Myrtle's take zero shit policy was the stuff of legend in Townsend Harbor. Because, Cady supposed, the woman had plenty of her own. As the proprietress of Fertile Myrtle's Manure, she moved it by the ton and wasn't about to add a single turd to the pile.

Not even for a town hero like Ethan Townsend.

"Beg your pardon, Mrs. LeGrande," a reddened Ethan said with a deferential duck of his head. "But if you'd be so kind as to let me finish my investigation, we can get things back to normal as soon as possible."

Which was, as everyone knew, Ethan Townsend's prime life directive.

Myrtle gave them a curt nod before turning on the sole of her leopard-print rain boot and scuffing out.

Ethan folded his arms across his chest, the thick-soled boots he favored when he was working planted at a *just try to move me* distance. "This customer you were talking to, he always call so late?"

"Usually it's at eight p.m.," Gemma offered before Cady had a chance to answer.

Suspicion darkened Ethan's eyes to the color of lake water. "*Usually*?"

Cady eased her weight onto the leather stool to prevent herself from lobbing it over the counter at her best friend.

"As Myrtle so helpfully pointed out, he's from out of town," she said. "He calls to place an order every week."

"A *huge* order," Gemma said, glancing up at Ethan. "Don't you just *love* a man who reads?"

Judging by the scowl hardening Ethan's already stony features, Cady guessed he did not.

"I'm going to need his name," Ethan said, reaching for the phone clipped to the utility case on his hip. "And address."

"Didn't Judy get that?" Cady's arm had begun to itch and sweat within its canvas prison. She hadn't showered since before Myrtle's party, and she longed to dissolve the swampy film on her skin in the paradise of a long, hot bath.

"Called from some kind of sat phone," Ethan said. "He didn't give his name. Only reported there'd been a break-in at this location."

"*And* threatened to rip out the spine of every officer in Townsend Harbor if they didn't get there within the two minutes," Gemma added.

Cady's heart fluttered like a spastic bird. Surely Fox wouldn't be promising musculoskeletal rearrangement if he was upset at her for insulting his dick, would he?

"Sorry," Gemma said sheepishly, ducking her dark head. "I ran into Judy at the Coffee Spot this morning."

That was when it clicked. Her gossipmongering traitor of a best friend was trying to make Ethan jealous.

His eyes narrowed to slits as a walnut-sized knot appeared at the hinge of his jaw.

"I'll have that name now."

Cady cleared her throat. "Fox."

"First or last?" Ethan asked.

"Ummm...yes?"

Ethan's thumbs ceased their typing. He looked at her from beneath a furrowed brow. "Come again?"

"She's not sure which," Gemma helpfully supplied.

Cady dearly wished they were behind the register still so she could pinch the back of her best friend's arm. "He mentioned that he would prefer not to disclose it for security reasons."

"What sort of security reasons prevent a man from providing a bookseller with his full legal name?" Ethan asked.

"My money is on the witness protection program," Gemma said. "Otherwise, why wouldn't he be able to provide an address?"

"How is it you're shipping books to this man on a weekly basis if you don't have his address?" Ethan pinned her with a skeptical look.

A bead of sweat trickled down Cady's ribs.

"I box them up and leave them in the delivery area by the alley. My regular UPS guy picks them up, and from there, I'm not really sure how they get to him. I just assumed they have some kind of arrangement."

"Arrangement." Ethan spat the word like it had just peed in his mouth.

She nodded, beginning to feel the first prickles of irritation. "Frankly, when someone places an order that big, I don't concern myself with how they're getting their books or why they don't want me to know their private information. I just respect their privacy and thank my lucky stars for the revenue."

And she had.

Fervently.

For the third time since he'd arrived, Ethan reviewed the

details she'd provided, point by point, before jamming his phone back into its holster and shaking his head in disgust.

"This scene makes absolutely no sense." And Ethan Townsend was a man who liked things to make sense.

He stalked the length of the storefront, moving with athletic efficiency. "You locked your doors, but someone gets in without there being any sign of forced entry?"

Mostly true.

She *thought* both doors were locked. But she'd also been tripping balls. One of the facts she had decided not to share with Sheriff Townsend.

"You're on the phone, you hear a noise, you attempt to get to the stairs but run into the bookshelf on the south side, but it somehow falls in the opposite direction."

Admittedly, that part had her stumped as well.

Ethan stormed over to the credenza and yanked out the vintage attaché case her aunt had used as a makeshift cashbox.

"You insist that not a dollar was taken. No merchandise was stolen. And not a thing is missing from the premises. So, our working theory is, an incredibly sophisticated thief is able to access your secured store for the sole purpose of—what? Un-shelving books and breaking a lamp?"

His gaze burned a hole in the atmosphere between them.

"Is he asking us?" Gemma asked out of the side of her mouth.

"I don't think we're supposed to talk," Cady whispered back.

She had never seen him so perturbed. Not even when they'd exited a movie theater to find a drunk tourist relieving himself on the tires of Ethan's immaculately maintained county-issued SUV. He had merely told the guy to zip it or lose it before opening her door and driving them through the Suds Studs after-hours auto-wash.

Frankly, he seemed more bothered by the somewhat suggestive wash options in the automatic drive-through.

He'd gone with the Quickie, naturally.

As swiftly as it had gone, Ethan's mannered calm returned,

transforming his features into a stoic mask. "You mind giving us a minute, Miss McKendrick?"

Gemma glanced between them, self-satisfaction smeared all over her elven features. "Not at all," she chirped. "I'd be happy to. Delighted, even. I'll just be in the back."

Eavesdropping on every word they spoke.

When her clunky footsteps receded, Ethan turned to Cady.

"If you weren't the target, I'd say this had to be something personal." He met her eyes as his ears began to flush a candy-apple red. "Can't think of a single reason anyone would want to hurt you."

Damn if his kind words didn't make her feel like the shittiest shithole who ever shat...

"I can write you a list, if you want," she said, deflecting the compliment. "Take Roy Dobson."

"Wish someone would," was Ethan's deadpan reply.

They both glanced across the street, where a man with silver hair and an epic scowl shooed people away from the section of the sidewalk in front of a drab and unadorned storefront. The windows had been (poorly) tinted, silver bubbles pockmarking the dingy glass with (also poorly) painted letters.

You Want It, Take It.

Below it, in a smaller and more insistent font:

No refunds

No exchanges

No exceptions!!!

The last was underlined twice and punctuated with not one, but *three* exclamation marks. One of those emphasis dots had become a drip that meandered a good ten inches down the filthy window.

Ethan's grunt of disgust likely had more to do with the store's untidy exterior than its occupant, who Cady herself doubted was responsible for her current predicament.

His feud with her Aunt Fern had been legendary, but typically contained to perma stink-eye and sternly worded letters to the city council.

"Until we figure out who got in here and how, I'd feel a lot better if—" Ethan halted abruptly, his prominent Adam's apple bobbing above the neatly creased collar of his shirt. "What I mean to say is—" he began again, then froze.

Feeling a surge of warmth for the decent, earnest man before her, Cady rested her hand on his wrist. "Go ahead," she encouraged, not at all convinced she wanted to hear what he was about to say.

"I have room—I mean, *we* have room. At the house."

The house.

A vast understatement of the sprawling Victorian manse looking down its nose at the town from its perch high on the hill. Yet another reminder of the Townsend family's indelible ties to the town's history.

"You could stay with us," Ethan continued. "Just until we get this resolved. You'd have your own suite. Plenty of privacy. Even has a kitchen. In fact—"

"That is so, *so* incredibly generous of you, Ethan." Welling panic made Cady squeeze his firm forearm a hair harder than she'd intended. "And if I didn't have so much work to do around here—"

"You'd have help with that too. Half the town is already out there," Ethan said, jerking his head toward the window. "Soon as I'm gone, they have the okay to put this place to rights."

Cady glanced at the gathering of loitering onlookers, glad she'd heeded Gemma's suggestion to grab a couple boxes of doughnuts as a bribe.

"I mean, I really, *really* appreciate that, but Gemma and I already have some people coming."

His face fell, and with it, her heart.

At times, she wished she could dig the empathy out of her brain with a grapefruit spoon. Being able to identify the precise moment Ethan Townsend registered her rejection of his offer of kindness as a rejection of himself blew soggy chunks.

"Maybe you could call me later, though?" she said, knowing he was bright enough to recognize it as a consolation prize.

Ethan nodded, his lips pressed into a tight line.

"Just not too late," she added. "I'm going to try to turn in early tonight."

And work up my nerve to call Fox and apologize.

"Copy that. I'll let you get to it, then." Ethan kicked the rock Myrtle had slid into the front door to keep it cracked on his way out.

Gemma's footsteps announced her arrival, but Cady kept her eyes on the mix of locals on the sidewalk across the street.

"Not that I ever seek to align myself with uptight lawmen, but I really don't like the idea of you being here alone," Gemma said as she returned.

"I'll be fine," Cady promised. "The door to the upstairs has a deadbolt and a security chain."

"That you also never lock," Gemma pointed out.

"Tonight, I will," Cady said.

"I know you will," her friend said. "Because I'm going to lock it."

Cady picked up the attaché case cashbox and slid it back beneath the counter. "That's going to be hard to do from your house."

"Which is why I'll be staying with you," Gemma said.

"As much as I appreciate the offer, I'm looking forward to a long bath and a short evening."

Gemma set the boxes of doughnuts on the entry table next to the front door in preparation for soliciting help from the rabble outside. "Seven years of friendship and you still think you can lie to me."

"About what?" Cady laughed despite the deep, angry ache waking within her shoulder.

"The reason you don't want me staying over." Popping open

the lid of the bakery box, Gemma helped herself to a glazed doughnut. "You're going to call Fox."

Sometimes, it really sucked to have someone who knew her so well present for these pivotal moments of potentially regrettable decisions.

"He probably thinks I'm dead."

"For all we know, you're lucky that you're not."

"Gem, I was literally right here and practically blind after I knocked the glasses off my own face. If someone had wanted to hurt me, it wouldn't have been hard."

What she'd meant to be a reassurance for her friend suddenly made Cady's stomach feel hot and queasy.

Were it not for Fox, she'd have been an even easier target.

Gemma wiped flakes of glaze from her fingers and squeezed the wrist of Cady's uninjured arm. "Are you sure you know what you're doing?"

"No," Cady admitted.

But after tonight, she would.

By the time the early dark found its way into her windows, Nevermore had been mostly "put to order," as Ethan had described it. Broken shelf hauled away by a Goliath-sized passerby who'd watched two grown men wrestle with it for the better part of half an hour. Books neatly packaged into boxes to wait until she found a suitable successor. Volunteers rewarded by effusive thanks and pastry bribes. The locks on both the front *and* back doors replaced by Ethan himself, and every last living soul evicted from the premises.

Bathed and in her comfiest yoga pants and oversized book-nerd-themed t-shirt, Cady could at last retire to her cozy room on the third floor of the building, and wait.

Which, she was one hundred percent terrible at.

Buzzing with nervous energy from the day, she crossed to the window of her loft and wrangled her blinds open one-handed. A half-moon hung in the clear night sky, grinning a Cheshire Cat smile at her from the star-studded bolt of deep blue velvet.

Her gaze drifted down to the empty street, and her mind played tricks with the moonlight.

Were it not for two columns of bluish smoke rising from the mouth of the alley next to You Want It, Take It, she might not have seen them at all.

Two shadowy figures just outside the pool of jaundiced yellow security lights mounted on the side of the old brick building.

Cady removed her glasses, breathed on them, and polished the lenses with the tail of her well-worn t-shirt. Squinting through the darkness, she could just make out the distinctive vertical swoop of a hairstyle favored by a certain nineties late-night TV host.

Mayor Stewart?

Since when did he join Roy for an evening cigar?

She jumped when her phone rang, smudging the glass with her nose.

Glancing down at the glowing screen, she saw three letters that sent a frisson of excitement shimmering through her.

Fox.

"Hey there," she said, trying not to sound out of breath by the simple act of being startled.

"Jesus *fucking* Christ."

The expletive was bellowed from the receiver at a decibel level that would rival a rutting elk. All the anxiety that a day of worry and physical labor and a hot bath had evicted returned to her in a single, searing rush.

"*You.*" The syllable was raspy and vehement enough to make her spleen shrivel into a raisin. "Do you have any idea...any idea at *all*"—the word was strangled out by a sound she'd describe as something between a growl and a grunt— "how relieved I am that you're okay? Christ, woman. I've been fucking sick with worry, you know that?"

Her own relief was so powerful that it dragged a surge of

nausea in its wake. "Actually...no. I thought you were upset with me."

"Upset?" he scoffed. "What the hell would I be upset with *you* for?"

If his fear that someone may have un-alived her had erased her errant comment about his meat puppet from his short-term memory, Cady certainly had no intention of reminding him.

"Because I didn't call you back sooner?" she suggested.

"On second thought, yeah. I'm willing to be pissed with you about that," Fox said. "You could have ended my agony hours ago."

Her toes curled into the shaggy bedside rug as he dipped into the lower register that turned her blood to warm honey in her veins.

Now or never.

"What do you think about ending it in person?"

A pause.

A very, very *long pause.*

"How's that?" he asked.

Cady let her eyelids fall closed and filled the four corners of her lungs with a long, slow breath. She had to do this. Had to know what they were.

Or what they weren't.

She scrunched her face into a grimace that made her infinitely grateful he couldn't see her and commenced with shooting her shot. "Do you think it's time we meet in person?"

FIVE

Voyeur

(VOI-YÛR') A PERSON WHO DERIVES SEXUAL ENJOYMENT FROM BEING AN OBSERVER.

Do you think it's time we meet in person?

Fox swallowed around a sandpaper throat as every word for *NO* in any language he ever knew became the only vocabulary available to him, forcing him into silence.

Because regardless of what his brain *knew* to be the truth, other parts of him were screaming *yes*.

It'd always been an intriguing impossibility, the reality of finding out what she looked like. A daydream he often entertained in the vast silence. A fantasy that brought him pleasure and release on occasion through empty physical solo operations.

The attachment—no, *attraction* to her had been perilous *before* he saw her for the first time.

It was lethal now.

As in *actively* killing him.

He'd known she was okay, because he'd beaten feet down here and arrived in time to find Gemma driving Cady home from the emergency room in a sling and helping her pop several painkillers.

Still, he had to pretend there was distance, so she'd never know he'd been close enough to reach out and touch her.

Which was one hundred percent more painful for him, he was sure.

To be fair...he could save himself the suffering by *not* committing several crimes as he gazed up from beneath the shadow of a tree as the silver half-moon battled with the ambient golden glow of her bedroom. But who would have guessed she'd be prancing around in there with her floor-to-ceiling window wide fucking open right after a *break-in in which she'd been injured*?

Taking a centering breath, he forced himself to not say anything that would give him away...such as *Close your fucking windows, woman; every perv and perpetrator could just—*

Shut it down, man. Tighten your shit all. The. Way. Down.

As he'd been securing the perimeter in the dark and simultaneously carrying on a (not so) casual conversation, Cady had wrestled the drapes and blinds open with one-handed enthusiasm, revealing herself clad in the furthest thing from seductive garb as one could get.

And yet...

Edison bulbs turned her riot of long hair into a golden corona fit for an angel.

Halo and all.

As she peered out into the night clad in yoga pants, a baggy tee with stacks of vintage books framing the words *I HAVE NO SHELF CONTROL!* interrupted by the shoulder strap of a sling, and hair mostly escaping her braid rather than being contained by it...

Fox had to remind himself that goddesses weren't real.

Her head tipped in such a way that reminded him of a Florentine statue he'd fallen for at the Ponte Santa Trinita. An artist's dichotomy of succulent details. Small mouth, plump lips. Wide, but heavy-lidded eyes. Pleasant, round cheeks, angular chin.

And a body to which he might dedicate the immortal poetry of Sir Mix-a-Lot.

Thank God she had clothes on (thought no one ever). The fact that she was head-to-toe covered still didn't save him from being nine kinds of pervy fuck-knuckle for staring at an unsuspecting woman through his PVS-7 Focus Range Night Vision tactical binoculars.

But how else was he to gather intel on her interior layout and monitor every person who dared to approach the shop day or night?

Okay. Admittedly not helping with the creepiness factor. But even with the new locks, no one could deny that the sliding glass door to the waterfront walkway was the furthest thing from secure, storm windows or no storm windows. Fox had been lingering at the shop earlier, and now couldn't get that smug lawman's irritatingly astute observations out of his head.

Without a motive or a suspect, there was no way to accurately gauge what sort of danger she was in. And whenever he decided he should turn around and march back into the mountains, the notes of helpless terror in her voice that night would surge into his memory, planting his boots.

Harbor County, over which Ethan Townsend presided, had a handful of deputies to span about two thousand square miles. In the hours Fox had been conducting surveillance, he'd counted only two sheriff's department cars driving by, and one from Townsend Harbor Police. Those safety checks would wane as more time elapsed after the incident.

Who would protect her then?

Well, Fox had nothing better to do, and could think of no purpose on this earth more important than Cady's security.

And he would be a goddamn gentleman. Shouldn't be so hard. He couldn't remember a single time he'd kinked out on voyeurism. Hell, he didn't even like strip clubs. Not that he disliked the idea of scantily clad women dancing beneath flattering lights and all, but he wasn't a look-not-touch kinda guy. And, because his brain was his brain, he invariably noticed things about women other men didn't.

Or maybe what they didn't care to see.

Possible emotional damage. Boredom. Desperation. Fear. Vice. Sexual trauma. He believed with his entire self that women should be able to do whatever they wanted for money and be proud of it. But he just couldn't get hard if a woman showed interest because it was her job.

This—admittedly—morally gray situation in which he found himself was something different. He wasn't watching Cady for his guilty pleasure.

That was just a bonus.

What about that ginger-twatted sheriff? his inner Jiminy Cricket chirped. Sure, the guy was a boring Dudley Do-Right type, but muscled enough for some small-town vandals to be intimidated. Trained to protect and serve. Carried his gun like he was comfortable using it. (Though Fox would investigate range qualification scores, just to be sure.) The shiny-badged, clean-cut Townsendite struck him as more of a politician than an enforcer. Not to mention the all-American flagpole wedged so far up his ass he had to swallow around it.

Plus, the sheriff obviously wanted to fuck Cady, which meant Fox had forced himself *not* to spring into backflips when she didn't take him up on the offer to come home with him.

Her best friend, Gemma, had smarts and cunning, if not so much physical strength, and was a fierce and protective ally who kept a close eye on Cady. That he appreciated, but even so, she was tucked into her own bed down the street.

"Fox?" Cady's voice sounded closer, somehow, as if proximity made the connection between them stronger.

"Hmm?" Oh fuck. He'd maybe not-so-accidentally let his mind wander (run away screaming) from the suggestion that they should meet.

"I thought I'd lost you."

That was where she got it wrong. *He* thought he'd lost *her*. And to live in a world where she didn't exist seemed like as good a reason as any to take his own header into Hell.

Aaaaaand...there was the crux of why he wasn't fit for human consumption.

He was broken.

"I'm here," he murmured. "I'm right here." An ache opened up in his chest, and he both anticipated and feared she'd look out into the night and spot him.

She wouldn't.

"Did...did you hear my question?" A note of hesitancy crept into her voice.

"Your question?" He lamely bought himself some time to cast about for a "hell no" answer that would cause the least damage to her feelings.

"Do you think we should...meet? Maybe just for coffee or a walk by the water in the middle of the day, so it's not even an awkward thing. It just... I don't know. Does it feel like... Do you want... Does it seem like a good idea to you?"

Nevermore Bookstore was a beloved landmark and the proprietress a cherished townsperson. She had a good, full life here.

And he was a frag bomb waiting to shred her idyllic existence, leaving nothing behind but shrapnel wounds and chronic pain.

"I wish I could tell you why it's a bad idea," he lamented. Why it was a guaranteed train wreck.

Caused by a jetliner.

Followed by the Black Hawk it collided with midair.

And then all of that would crash into an overpass.

At rush hour.

That would begin to cover the regret she would eventually feel if she were to become entangled with him in any real-life situation.

"There's a chance we've already met and didn't even realize. Is Fox your first or las—"

"We haven't." That came out pithier than he'd intended. "Met, that is. We haven't."

"How do you *know*? I have a great memory for faces. What do you look like?"

"I look like..." He touched the hair he'd tousled and faded with powdered silt. His purposely grimy face. Wiped his fingers on clothes he purchased from the local Goodwill...and then beaten up. "Well, I look like hell. What do you look like?"

Backing away from the window slightly, she turned to her right and very obviously observed herself in a mirror out of view. Frowning, she sucked in her cheeks like a Kardashian and pinched at a roll of skin at her stomach. "Right now? I look like the Pillsbury Doughboy and Miss Piggy's love child." She laughed her own joke, and, time was, he might have too. Would have told her she was being silly, while appreciating that she could laugh at herself.

It wasn't often a beautiful woman didn't know exactly what that currency was and how to wield it. And well they should. He'd not been above leveraging his tough jaw, thick, dark hair, and size to charm a woman into asking him to do the things he wanted to do in the first place.

But he didn't like that the question drove Cady back from the window. That she carefully tumbled into bed, pulled the covers to her chin, and tucked her knees together.

"I could tell you what you look like without ever seeing you," he murmured, not waiting for a reply as she settled in. "Your eyes are wide and wild and wise, as open as they can possibly be, so they don't miss anything. They're the hue of a nebula, maybe. Like those pictures you see taken by the Webb. Such vivid, unusual colors that we haven't even invented names for them yet. Your skin is smooth, as if spun by merchants along the Silk Road a thousand years ago when colors were pure. The color of moonlight."

"Okay, Lord Byron, what color is moonlight?" she asked, audibly fighting for breath.

"It doesn't matter. Moonlight is the most perfect color on any shade of skin."

She covered a dreamy sigh with a huff of disdain. "Pretty words there, book man, but you don't know if I'm a supermodel or a troglodyte."

"I know what I like. And I know I'd like you." *And the award for understatement of the year goes tooooooooooo...*

"You have to stop!" she pleaded in a mock-plaintive whine. "Compliments from deep-voiced men give me the nervous urps." She squirmed as if her skin had become suddenly uncomfortable. "Men always pretend a woman's looks don't matter, but that only works when they're already physically attracted. So tell me, Mr. Fox, what are your preferences? What color do you think my hair is?

He had to be careful here. To not make her feel nervous or threatened. "B-brunette?"

She opened her mouth as if to disavow him. Then closed it, her lips twisting wryly. "Like brunettes, do ya?"

"I don't care if a woman's hair is forest green, if she feels herself in it."

"Okay then, what about personal style?"

"Um...Michelle Obama power suits."

"I wish!" She gave a soft scoff. "I'm a jeans and graphic tee kinda gal. I don't even think I own a suit. I barely own matching socks. So...strike two."

"Nothing wrong with jeans and t-shirts." It was sort of his style too. In the summer, anyhow.

She paused, and her lower lip disappeared between two teeth.

She very obviously didn't mean for it to look porny, but here they were. "What about...what about size? You have any poetry there, Longfellow?"

"No. No, I can only say with absolute dead fucking honesty that there could never be enough of you in this world. No matter what size."

She sniffed, and he watched her run her fingertips across her face as if to wipe away an errant tear. Lifting his binoculars, he zoomed in on her face and watched a tiny pool of moisture gather her lashes into spikes.

"Men don't usually want to hitch their proverbial carts to a woman they can't carry across the threshold."

Sure, too many men allowed society to tell them whom they wanted to fuck, but Fox had always been stronger-willed than that. His sexuality was tied to more primitive notions of beauty. His pecker was old-fashioned, he supposed, because the larger the curves (especially those related to biological fertility imperatives), the more physically interested he became.

"I could do it," he boasted with a certainty he shouldn't have. "No problem."

"Psssh. You don't know how much I weigh."

"Doesn't matter. I could do it."

Her answering scoff contained multitudes of disbelief. "You can't even reliably claim that! What if you're wrong?"

"I'm not wrong." He'd already done the math.

"I-I'm a big girl." It was the first time she'd said so to him.

"I'm a big man."

Giving in to a halfhearted sound of frustration, she shifted on the bed, writhing awkwardly as she fluffed (punched) her pillow one-handed and grunted into a more comfortable position. "I wish you were here so I could win this argument..." She paused, blinking back over to the window. "I mean, even if I lost the argument, I'd still be happy you were here. I'd feel safer, I think, which is weird, because I'm not entirely convinced you're not some kind of phantom...or serial killer. You act a bit *sus* sometimes."

"Honey, I ache to be there." The confession was ripped from his throat in a voice made of equal parts velvet and steel. After clearing his throat, he added. "Also, I'm not a serial killer."

"Oh, well in that case, you could come over..."

Every muscle in his body clenched as his eyes latched on to her face. She sounded as though she were teasing.

But she looked dead serious. Hopeful, even.

Fuck. Fuck fuck fuck fuck.

Was she inviting him to be a shoulder to cry upon?

Or a booty to call upon?

Did it matter in terms of desire? Not one fucking little bit.

The reasons he shouldn't/couldn't were losing a bit of their contrast. Fading into something less substantial.

But they'd never disappear. "Funny that you seem more worried about what you look like and don't seem that worried about my appearance. For all you know, I could have leprosy. Or a mullet."

She coughed out a laugh, then a moan. "Do you have either of those things?"

"No, but that's not the—"

"Well, barring any breach of CDC protocol, I vow that you can just walk right up to me and say hi, and you could look like the love child of Rowan Atkinson and Steve Buscemi and I'd still kiss you like a returning WWII hero."

Christ, you couldn't just go around saying stuff like that to a guy in his current—engorged—physical condition.

"First of all, both those men are stallions, and you'll never convince me otherwise," he joked in an attempt to break the tension as thick as a Howitzer and just as terrifying. "And second...I can't."

"You. Can't," she repeated, chewing on her lip. "Are you sure you're not married?"

"You know a married man with the time to read as much as I do?"

"Good point." She sighed, rubbing at her forehead. "Then why—"

"I can't because I'm not— I have one intensely important job, and if I fail— Well, I can't fail. It's the truth. I promise."

"Oh." Her brows drew together, and she shook her head as if berating herself. "Some other time, maybe."

"Cady, I—"

Down the frigid, deserted Water Street, a pack of women spilled out of Olive or Twist, the town's only late-night, underground speakeasy. They tottered in strappy heels he wouldn't trust his own ankles in, whooping in exaltation at a friend's newfound, and probably well-deserved, freedom from an unhappy marriage.

"Hey, I've got to go, Cady. You get some rest, okay?"

"O-okay." She sat up, her face pinched with concern. "Talk to you next we—"

"Wouldn't miss it." He disconnected the call just as the noises of a half-dozen women came closer.

Another second on the line with Cady and she'd have known he was close by.

With a breath of relief, he looked up toward his campsite, pleased to see that he'd hidden it well from this vantage.

When he pitched his tent here, so to speak, he'd been pleased to find such a tactical vantage in the middle of town. Water Street, where Nevermore Bookstore was located, ran along the Pacific shoreline and sometimes even out over the tides with several piers, boardwalks, and shop/apartment balconies.

The rest of the town crawled up a hillside where pretty, old Victorian homes bared their beams like painted ladies pulling up can-can skirts. A five-story stone staircase built into the slope of the hill connected Water Street to the residences, other shops, and churches on the hilltop, an area locally known as "Uptown," as opposed to Water Street's "Downtown."

Townsend Harbor left the wilderness on each side of the staircase as untouched as possible. A thick swath of forest in the middle of the city. Fox had found a perfect, body-sized plateau on which to take up residence. It took an act of God to get a permit to cut down a tree in this place, so the pleasantly overgrown wildland in the middle of town had been there long enough to produce thick layers of moss on the trunks of the trees.

The area had been dubbed a sanctuary for the deer herds that moved into Townsend Harbor proper, and decided they were now city folk. They could be seen grazing on park lawns and getting fat on the gardens of wealthy retirees. Not to mention juncos and titmouse, bunnies, squirrels, coyotes, and foxes, the occasional stray cat...

And, for the indefinite future, one feral human.

Because, just like coyotes and foxes, once he sank teeth into his prey, he didn't stop shaking until it was broken and dead.

With the divorce party bearing down on his position, Fox didn't pause to appreciate the bronze fountain in the middle of what was considered the "town square" from which the staircase led. A replica of Galatea bared perfect bronze breasts to anyone who might wander past. He recognized the sculpture from what he'd seen of the original back in the day.

Not because he wasn't interested, but because the women had begun to teeter toward the steps as well, and from what he could make of their conversation, they'd collectively hand the next man they came across his ass in their own personal version of *The Hurt Locker.*

After leaping up the stairs two at a time, he ducked beneath the iron railing and climbed the face of the hill on all fours, careful not to disturb the darkness with his shadow.

Cresting the plateau upon which he'd spread his bedroll, he sank down on his haunches and scanned the night. He could almost see all of the hamlet from his vantage. The tall steam stacks of the paper factory belching puffs of vapor into the atmosphere. The bright lights of the small hospital on the south hill of town. The various masts from the harbor, many of them singing a haunting song as the evening breeze picked up.

Scents of late-night pizza and the brine of the cold sea mingled with a cloud of incredibly expensive perfume carried to him from the Pilates- and spin-class-honed battalion of ladies taking the stairs like it was the beaches at Normandy.

"...does that guy think he is refusing a drink from *us*—from you, Stefanie?" The faint gas-lamp-style lights perched on each stair landing glowed off the speaker's brassy hair and smeared makeup. "I don't know what you saw in him. I'd take a bottle brush to my own vulva before letting a man whose tattoos indicate he's obviously been to prison *think* he had a chance with me."

Ears perked, Fox crouched and listened closer to the Real Housewives of Townsend Harbor.

"Those were too pretty for prison tattoos," sighed another. "So much color."

"So much muscle," purred an accented voice from somewhere south of the border.

"So much fucking attitude," growled the first. "New guy doesn't realize how shitty a place like Townsend Harbor can be if you don't make friends."

"Judy told me the town is getting a new master mechanic to replace the last one. He's from one of the desert states, I think."

"I'm about sick of all these Californians relocating and claiming to be climate refugees," the first one spat. "They're driving up the house prices and bringing their Botox, fillers, and lash extensions like it isn't hard enough to get laid around here."

Someone's heel broke, and the most sequined among them lost her balance, clinging to the iron railing for dear life. The part of Fox raised by his mother urged him to leap to her rescue. Instantly, the women rallied around her, pulling her to her feet and saving her from a tumble, so he settled.

Besides, in *this* crowd, his help would be as welcome as a turd in a hot tub.

The night stilled when the party eventually reached the top of the stairs and disappeared into their respective homes.

Fox sat on his bedroll and immediately stood as something beneath dug into his ass muscle. A tree root, maybe? Scouring beneath his bedroll, he found something smallish and cylindrical. As he held it up to the light, his brow furrowed with a sense of trouble.

The butt of a cigar. Half smoked. Half chewed. Had it been a cigarette, he might have assumed some local kids came to ditch class and used this a haven for their youthful discretions.

But he'd never met anyone under twenty smoke a cigar halfway and not end up praying to the porcelain god in heaving gags.

Glancing back over to Nevermore, he felt a sense of unease lance through him.

What if someone else perched here with the same intent? To watch Cady.

It wasn't easy to see her entire loft from this vantage, but with binoculars, her place was basically exposed.

Speaking of... He lifted the lenses to his eyes and checked the bed.

She'd fallen asleep with a book on her chest.

Fox's own constricted as his heart doubled in size.

Seaside tourist towns always had their share of indigent and un-homed—which he technically was. If he kept to himself and kept his head down, he could protect Cady without threatening her sense of serenity further. For a man as large as he was, he'd always been adept at remaining unseen.

With humans, the trick was to make yourself so pathetic, people couldn't help but look away.

He wouldn't stay long. Once he'd dealt with any threat to Cady, he'd take himself back off to his mountain and stay there.

But he had to be the one to deal with it.

Because the sheriff would put the perp in jail...but Fox?

Fox would put him in the *ground.*

SIX

Rejection

[RIˈDƷEKΣƏN] NOUN. TO REFUSE TO ACCEPT (SOMEONE) AS A LOVER, SPOUSE, OR FRIEND; REBUFF.

"I'M GOING TO KISS ETHAN TONIGHT."

Cady punctuated her declaration to the universe with a lusty bite of burrito. The taco truck she and Gemma favored in the aftermath of a devastating emotional blow sat adjacent to one of Townsend Harbor's many ocean-view-friendly public gathering spots. Following her last call with Fox, Cady told herself she was well within her rights to skip her usual Chicago Special—spinach, tomato, egg, and cheese—and go straight for the California Calamity: French fries, steak, pico, guacamole, and shame.

"Who are you and what have you done with my platonic life partner?" Gemma narrowed her eyes as she peeled back the foil wrapper from her own, much more modestly sized breakfast. Her assault was far more delicate, owing in no small part to the lipstick she was attempting to keep on her face instead of the tortilla.

"I mean it," Cady said. "If that man hasn't made voluntary manual contact with my physical person by midnight tonight, he can find someone else to not-seduce."

Gemma blotted her mouth with the napkin she'd secured beneath her handbag against the gusty morning currents of air. "Is our good sheriff aware of this romantic ultimatum?"

"Not yet," Cady said, setting down her burrito so she could

pick up her napkin. Three more days with this wretched sling. "But he will be."

A briny wind off the water carried the high shrill of seagulls as they sailed on the gusts overhead, likely eyeing the breakfast Cady was mangling with her nondominant hand. She and Gemma huddled closer around the standing table they'd chosen for its proximity to the outdoor heater. Like the cold, the torso-forward stance required to avoid anointing her coat with burrito shrapnel woke the ache in her lower back. Once woken, Astrid would helpfully make sure the rest of her body kept her company.

"I'm curious as to why this novel solution wasn't on the docket last time we talked." Gemma saw her struggling with the tub of green sauce and popped off the lid before opening her own.

"A lot can change in a few days." Had Cady not just reached the bacon that the truck's proprietress had added to her order with eyebrows raised, this declaration might have sounded bitter.

"Such as?" Gemma asked.

After an exhale that very likely brought up lung tissue, Cady made herself say the words. "Fox is officially out of the running."

Gemma's burrito paused mid-journey to her mouth. "I'm going to need some context here."

"I...may have suggested an in-person meeting on our call the other night."

"Bookmarking that statement for further discussion, but continue," Gemma said.

"Things got all weird after that, but basically he said an in-person meeting wasn't an option and then got off the phone as fast as fucking possible."

"What *exactly* did he say?"

Cady was back in her bed again with Fox's voice in her ear, her heart soaring like a paper kite one minute, a sad pile of broken sticks and tangled string the next.

"He said, 'I can't. I have one job to do. I can't fail.'"

"What the hell does that even mean?" Her best friend began wrapping up the remains of her burrito, neatly tucking the corners in the expert fold that had made her so popular at The SandWitch, Townsend Harbor's now-defunct humanely sourced Wiccan deli.

"Right? It's clearly an excuse. It's not that he can't. It's that he *won't.*"

"Any theories as to why?"

In the lonely hours after he had abruptly ended their most flirtatious conversation yet, Cady had generated about a thousand of them, but narrowed them down to one. "He thinks I'm ugly."

Gemma pinched the freckled bridge of her upturned nose. "You are a fully ridiculous human. You understand that, right?"

Better than she knew. "What else am I supposed to think when he spouts all these poetic words about my eyes being wild and wise nebulae, and my skin the color of silk roads or moonlight or whatever? It's obviously bullshit."

"Whoa, whoa, whoa," Gemma said, holding up a hand. "He said *what*?"

Flaying would have been preferable than to recall such beautiful words in a moment when Cady realized they may have been no more than carefully calibrated verbal catnip for lonely girls.

"It's not important. The point is, I made the mistake of asking him what he thought I looked like. He clearly peeped me on social media, couldn't think of anything nice to say in real time, and hit up a Cyrano de Bergerac compliment generator. I suggested we meet up, his dick retracted like a turtle, and therefore, I'm kissing Ethan Townsend tonight."

Stubbornly refusing the offer of help, Cady used the fingers poking out of her sling to hold her burrito in place while she twisted the ends of the metallic wrapper like a Christmas cracker with her opposite hand.

Zero points for neatness, but it would serve.

They gathered their breakfast litter and dumped it in the trash before turning face-first into the bracing wind.

Gemma's cold grip closed around Cady's wrist, forcing her to slow her pace.

"Look over there," she whispered.

Cady followed her eyeline just in time to see a figure roughly the size and build of a professional wrestler disappear into the mouth of the alley next to Roy Dobson's wildly unenthusiastic secondhand store.

"Wasn't he hanging around here the day after the break-in?" Round red spots of color painted Gemma's milky cheeks.

Cady blinked at her. "If by 'hanging around,' you mean 'carried the broken bookshelf from the curb to the Junk Hunk's truck *by himself*,' then yes, he was hanging around."

Having been conscripted by bribes of glazed pastry, their task force had been an amalgamation of locals looking to score shareable details, the pack of ever-changing van-dwelling bohemian poet/artist/musician kids, and several members of Townsend Harbor's resident un-homed.

The man in question could have belonged to one of the last two categories, but would have stood out in either, due to his sheer size.

"'Kay." Gemma gave her a wary look. "But why is he skulking around Misanthrope Alley?"

"First, he's too big to skulk," Cady said. "Second, he needs to get out of there. You remember what Roy did to the last guy that got caught sleeping there?"

"I think the entire town remembers that." Gemma shuddered. "I still can't look at a muffler the same way."

"I'm just gonna go give him a heads-up." Cady started down the sidewalk but was quickly tugged back by the tether of Gemma's hand on her wrist.

"Just because he helped you move some broken furniture doesn't mean you owe him."

"I'm not warning him because I think I owe him. I'm warning him because it's just basic human decency to prevent a man from being assaulted with auto parts."

"Something tells me he's not in any danger from old Roy. Did you see the size of his hands? He could squeeze the eyes from your head like a classroom hamster." Gemma widened her eyes demonstratively.

"I wasn't looking at his hands. I was looking at his face."

"Because it looked hungry?"

"Good point," Cady said. "Do you think he would want my burrito leftovers?"

Gemma brushed dark strands out of the corner of her mouth. "I think he might want some of your soul by way of your ass."

"You're welcome to call the authorities if he tries."

"Hell with that." Gemma reached into her macrame shoulder bag and pulled out a retractable knitting needle. "If Hot Hagrid so much as lays one sausage finger on you, this puppy is going straight into his temporal lobe." She twirled the pointy metal object in her fingers like a baton and closed it in her fist.

They walked across the street together, but Cady stopped her friend short of entering the alley. "You wait here, Dirty Harriet. I'm trying to give the guy some food, not a lobotomy."

The air between buildings was a few degrees cooler, heavy with the scent of old wood and damp earth. Cady stood at the mouth, scanning for a size eleventy-seven boot sticking out of the potential shelter spots.

Nothing protruding from the pile of old pallets leaned against the mossy brick wall outside the back entrance to Roy's store. Nor from behind the black trash bins nearly twice the size Townsend Harbor typically allowed. The cans, like the pallets, were a special dispensation given him by the city council, who were sick of his endless complaints about the sanitation department, the foot traffic through *his* alley to access the stairs up the hillside, and the existence of other humans in general.

"Hello?" she called.

A faint dripping sound was her only answer.

"I really appreciate your help the other day. Also have some leftover burrito if you're hungry," Cady called in case he was still in earshot. "Just FYI, it has extra cheese and bacon on it, so if you're lactose intolerant and/or vegan, maybe give it to someone else. But if not, it will restore your faith in humanity. If you had any to begin with."

"I didn't."

Cady whirled around to find the man *behind* her. Which should technically be impossible, unless he was capable of camouflaging himself as a brick wall.

He certainly looked as solid.

Even without Fox here to provide tactical advice, Cady knew the idea of letting a giant man get between her and the closest exit was most likely a bad one.

And yet the chest-tightening panic she would usually feel in this kind of situation failed to materialize. Somehow, she had the feeling that he was the one in danger of bolting.

"Would you like this?" She held the burrito out with the wrapper side toward him.

Gemma had been right. His hands were *huge*. The palm he held out to her was the size of a salad plate. His knuckles were reddened, the large square fingernails ringed with dirt.

The tip of his index finger felt like sandpaper when it brushed hers.

From this close position, she could see the chiseled wedges of his cheekbones above the woolly tangle of his beard. His skin was a sun-weathered tan. His eyes downcast, framed with long lashes bleached golden at the tips. His lips red and chapped from the cold.

"You know," she said, "I have other things around the store you could help me with if you ever wanted to make a little extra money. Unless money is a system you're choosing not to participate in, which, in that case, respect. I personally think that capitalism should die, but while I still have to pay off my credit cards, it's books or stripping."

His thick, dark eyebrows notched upward.

"That was a joke," she explained. "Not that I'm saying there's anything wrong with sex work," she quickly added. "Just that I'm not cut out for it. With my stiff hips and back, they might as well strap a Fleshlight to a hobby horse. Aaand now I am standing in an alleyway, complaining to a complete stranger about why I wouldn't make a good prostitute."

At the end of the alley, Gemma frantically signaled to her with wild hands and even wilder eyes.

"I better get going before my friend has a stroke," Cady said. "Just know you can come by anytime. I usually keep tea and snacks on hand, and there are lots of places to sit and get warm."

"Thanks," he rasped.

"I'm Cady, by the way." She held out her hand again, but the man only stared at it, his non-burrito-bearing hand flexing at his side.

"I'm sorry," she said. "I didn't even think. Maybe you don't like being touched. It could hurt for all kinds of reasons, and not all of them are easy to see."

She let her hand drop to her side and smiled at him. "See you around, then."

Glancing back to give him one last grin, she stepped in a puddle and felt an outsized surge of irritation, adding to her mental list of complaints that the cuff of her trouser jeans would be flapping damply around her ankle until it dried.

Gemma launched into her lecture the second Cady rounded the corner. "Do you have any idea how unsafe that was?"

"Sharing my half-eaten burrito with a stranger?" Cady asked. "I guess I can see where that would be kind of insulting. I did put my mouth on it."

"Oh, yeah." Her friend's lips twisted in a wry smirk. "Men just *hate* it when we put our mouth on things."

"But not, like, things that are going in *their* mouth," Cady said.

A dreamy smile spread across Gemma's face as they fell into step. "That reminds me. If things don't work out with you and Ethan, I think I might have someone else you should consider."

"But we know all the same people," Cady said.

"Exactly," Gemma said, shooting Cady a mischievous smile.

"Speaking of mouths, how are you planning on getting yours on Ethan Townsend?" Hearing the leaves crackle behind them, Gemma glanced over her shoulder. "He's following us."

"I know," Cady said. "I told him he could."

Gemma's shoe caught a raised edge of concrete, and she stumbled before quickly righting herself. "You did *what*?"

"I told him that if he wanted to make a little extra money, I had some things he could help me with around the shop."

"Are you absolutely positive that bookshelf didn't hit your head? Because—"

"Do you or don't you want to know about my plans for the evening?" Cady said, heading off another round of interrogation.

"I do," Gemma said, finally taking a hint.

"We're doing dinner and a movie."

"Again?"

"Yes, but he said it was my turn to pick the movie," she explained.

"And?"

"Your brilliant best friend chose that new buddy cop flick."

"And you're hoping your selection of a film within the genre of his chosen vocation will bring about the desired surge of ardor?" Gemma guessed.

"No," Cady said. "Since he's going to *have* to lean over at some point to tell me what they're doing wrong procedure-wise, all I have to do is turn my face and pow." She smirked at Gemma. "Game on."

They slowed at the crosswalk just as the rent-a-cop Ethan had hired to patrol the block rolled by. He gave them a stiff nod, his eyes obscured by tinted Aviators.

"If he doesn't kiss me back," Cady continued, "then I'll know that he's not really interested. If he does—"

"You'll know whether you are," Gemma said.

"Exactly," Cady said. "Foolproof plan."

"And what about Fox?"

"What *about* Fox?" Cady repeated sourly. "I'm moving on to

adult males of the species who I can hold hands with, and watch terrible TV with, buy those stupid 'As Seen on TV' gadgets for—"

"You're not going to stop buying them for me, though, right? Because that hands-free can opener?" Gemma chef-kissed her fingers.

"*Right?*"

"Genius," Gemma said. "Go on."

"That's it, really. Until the other night, I hadn't realized just how much I want that. The good stuff. The silly stuff. The everyday stuff." An ache that had nothing to do with various medical diagnoses or improbable injuries lodged itself behind her sternum.

"May I raise one small ethical question?"

"If you must," Cady said, slowing in front of Nevermore to unlock the shiny new deadbolt Ethan had installed by hand.

"Returning to the controversial topic of putting your mouth on things, are you sure it's fair to kiss Ethan when you still have feelings for another man?"

"Who says I have feelings for Fox?"

"Your face, mostly."

They waved to Myrtle, who was walking one of her and her partner's gigantic wolfhounds and cheerfully flipping off Roy Dobson through the window of You Want It, Take It.

"Feelings can change," Cady said. "Or they can be locked away in a vault never to be looked at, thought about, or generally acknowledged again."

"Because that sounds healthy." Gemma held the door open, then followed her in.

Cady inhaled deeply, holding the comforting smell of old paper, ink, and leather in her lungs.

This had always been one of her very favorite things. How the sensory delight of this place could find her anew after she'd been gone for long enough.

"Jesus." Rather than taking her coat off, Gemma hugged it

tighter around her. "When did you stop heating this place at night, Ebenezer?"

Setting her bag down on the adjustable stool behind the front desk, Cady cranked the dial on the circa 1970s thermostat. The old brass radiator located somewhere that the building's original architect had considered "central" began to hiss then knock. "Does that make you Bob Cratchit?"

"Fingerless gloves and all," Gemma said. "Which reminds me." She rooted around in her bag and came back with an eggplant-purple ball that she tossed at Cady.

"Gem," Cady said, unfolding the downy-soft bundle and slipping them onto her hands. "You didn't have to do that."

"Tell that to Hilda." Cousin to Astrid, Hilda was the nickname they'd chosen for the hyperfocus aspect of Gemma's ADHD. "Which is why I also have pairs for your mom, Lyra, Kevin Costner..."

"Good luck getting those on him and retaining the use of your hands," Cady said, beginning her round of turning on the shop's many lamps. "How is Lyra, by the way?"

"Disgustingly happy," Gemma reported. "She just won a major case against Merck, and her trust-funded dick-wrinkle of a boyfriend is now her trust-funded dick-wrinkle of a fiancé."

"Still doesn't believe you about the dick-wrinkle part?"

"Of course not." She pouted. "It's a total crock that I'm the one who has to go around with a name like Gemini when I'm still not convinced we're actually twins."

"Except for the whole identical faces thing," Cady pointed out.

"Probably not even that anymore. I can barely manage a skincare routine, and she's out there exploring the brave frontier of subdermal neurotoxins." Gemma frowned at herself in the mirror as she pulled at the lightly puffed lower lid of her eyes. When she spotted something in the reflection of the front window, the frown deepened. "Rip Van Stinkle's here," she said.

Cady glanced out the window to see her furniture-hauling

friend from the alley seated on the oversized cement planter on the sidewalk. His broad back was to them, collar of his jacket brushing the disheveled tufts of hair at his nape.

"One, his beard isn't nearly long enough to earn that moniker, and two, he smells like pine needles and rain."

Having cared for her aunt during the final phases of a terminal illness, Cady could no longer be shocked by anything the human body was capable of producing. She had walked into that alley prepared for anything.

Except that.

"I don't like this," Gemma said.

"Then maybe you'll like this." Cady took her best friend's hand and ran it carefully beneath the lip of the counter until they reached a small, round protrusion.

"What is that?"

"A panic button. I press this, and Sheriff Townsend receives a text giving him the green light to ride to my rescue."

"Uh-huh," Gemma said slowly. "And how is it that you're still not sure whether the man is interested in you?"

"Or maybe he's interested in keeping the number of calls to emergency services low so as not to mar Townsend Harbor's near-perfect record," Cady proposed.

"That's a distinctly unromantic assessment of his gesture."

"It's a distinctly odd gesture to make if romance is the goal," Cady countered.

Gemma let loose an exasperated sigh. "If you're going to have Silent Bob in here, you at least need to take the cashbox and put it somewhere that you can lock."

"If that would make you feel better." Cady floated out from behind the register, surprised at the subtle stab of disappointment she felt when she noticed Burrito Man wasn't there.

"What the—" Gemma stood at the register with a quizzical expression on her face and a pair of lacy red panties dangling from her outstretched finger. "Times hard enough that you're giving these away as bookmarks?"

Blood boiled into Cady's cheeks.

"I've heard some people keep paperwork beneath their cash register, but—"

"Hilarious," she said. "Give those to me." She made a grab for them with her good hand, but her friend snatched them away.

"Not until you tell me what a box of crotch floss is doing at the register in the first place," Gemma said with an impish grin.

Cady's face broke out in a furious flush. "Because wearing them made my body feel like more than just a problem," she said, grabbing the underwear and shoving it back in the box. "But the only time I didn't feel ridiculous with them on was when I was talking to Fox. Some days it was too much for me to get up and down the stairs to the apartment before he called, so I changed in the customer restroom."

Gemma blinked at her as if she'd just revealed that she swallowed live scorpions recreationally. "How come the most upset I've seen you in the last three weeks is when I find underwear stashed beneath your cash register?"

"I'm not upset." Cady fired up her iPad, swiping a finger to scroll through email notifications for new orders that had come in overnight. "Just busy."

Gemma folded her arms across her chest. "Busy being passive-aggressive?"

"Busy being humiliated," Cady choked out.

"Humiliated?" Her best friend's tone had softened along with her expression. "Cady, no. I'm just trying to—"

"I know what you're trying to do," Cady snapped. "You're trying to get me to realize that instead of grieving for my aunt, I poured myself into a phone flirtation with a man I've never met and probably never will. You want me to be worried about the break-in, and the property taxes, and the fact that the whole town now thinks I'm a deadbeat who doesn't deserve a man like Ethan Townsend."

Gemma's eyes widened. "That's not it at all. I just wanted to—"

"What good does it do?"

Cady knew better than to have a conversation like this on what was shaping up to be a bad body day of epic proportions, but now she'd started, there was no way out but through.

"What good does it do to think about how I only got six years with an aunt I didn't even know I had until I was fifteen? Or how ever since the break-in, Nevermore feels a little less mine, and it's never felt much like mine to begin with? Or how I still haven't been able to find any paperwork proving that Aunt Fern left the building to me, but I still have to come up with the money to pay property taxes she was too sick to deal with? Or how instead of dealing with any of that, I choose to create a whole-ass fantasy about a man who doesn't feel about me the way I feel about him? How worried do I have to be before you stop worrying *for* me?"

Cady's shoulder began to throb within its sweaty, itchy canvas prison, and her lower back offered up a dull, radiating duet.

Gemma didn't answer. Her gaze was trained on the oversized desktop calendar, forever fixed on July. The 22nd had been haloed by Aunt Fern's signature purple pen, *Dr. Appt.* scratched there in script far more casual than its outcome would prove.

With robotic movements, Gemma gathered her bag and coat. "I need to get the store opened," she said. "I'll call you later."

Guilt set in while the shop bell's brassy note announcing her exit still hung in the air.

She and Gemma had experienced a few minor verbal tussles over the years, but had never ended a conversation or a call without having made up. Without having made their way back to each other.

Cady's face crumpled as the tears spilled over her eyelids and streaked down her cheeks. A strangled sound tore loose from her constricted throat, and she sank down behind the register where her unraveling couldn't be witnessed from the shop's front window. The body-racking silent sobs united the patchwork of pain into one.

Her shoulder. Her back. Her hip. Her heart.

Gemma was only trying to help.

Everyone was always only trying to help.

With her grief. With her condition. With her life.

Most days, she could smile, and nod and accept whatever lukewarm consolation or unsolicited advice was being offered. About her posture, her diet, her energy, her plans.

You know, my friend's cousin had AS, and she gave up gluten...

My cousin is a reiki healer, and she said that energy work could really...

You poor thing. I just don't know how you do it.

Behind every breezy "I just take it a day at a time" lived a thousand bitter retorts.

Wait, is not *doing it an option? Why wasn't I told?* Or *I don't die. That's how I do it.*

But the real answer, no one but Fox had ever understood:

I escape.

She'd learned to love long shadows. Hints she'd soon be able to crawl beneath the covers and disappear into the space between black letters on a white page. Become something else. Some*one* else.

Someone not in pain.

The self-pitying thought was obliterated by the familiar squeal of hinges as the front door opened, followed by the bright *ping* of the hanging bell.

Someone *would* pick this time to need something from her.

"Just a minute," she called in a hopelessly congested voice she hoped to pass off as seasonal allergies. "I'll be right with you."

No answer.

The hairs lifted on the back of her neck.

Had it been Gemma returning to make up, she would have made some smart-ass quip to the tune of *yeah, you will*. Even the most entitled of the tourists would usually offer at least a grunt of acknowledgement.

Not Gemma.

Not a customer.

The first tendrils of icy fear reached between her ribs, plunging her back into the night of the break-in. Then, Fox's eminently sane voice in her ear had been her anchor.

WWFD.

What would Fox do?

No sooner had she asked the question than he answered it inside her own head.

You already gave away your position. Protect yourself. Find a weapon.

Grateful for the sizzling adrenaline that temporarily turned down the volume on her body's various complaints, she shifted on the soles of her sneakers to face the cabinets beneath the register.

Cady wasn't sure whether she successfully opened the latch without an audible click, or if she just couldn't hear it over the primal rushing in her ears. Either way, she felt a fierce pulse of satisfaction when her fingers closed over something smooth, cool, and *heavy*.

Her quick mental scan revealed no possible matches until she pulled it out into the lamplight.

A leather sap.

How the hell had a weapon wound up on the shelf where she kept biscuits for dog visitors and the disastrous paper book totes with the "CAWm Again" logo that no one had gotten but her?

Ethan.

That was how.

He must have tucked it in here when he'd come by to change the locks.

She spelt a spark of warmth for his protective gesture and willed it to catch fire when they met later that evening.

If they met later that evening.

Even with a cudgel, she was nothing like certain that her left arm's aim would be accurate enough to connect weapon to skull, even if her maybe-assailant was kind enough to put his within reach.

Slowly and with great effort, she pushed herself up until her eyes cleared the counter—and felt a deluge of relief.

"Oh, hi. It's you."

The same hulking stranger who had accepted her half-eaten gratitude burrito now stood in the entryway to her shop, dwarfing the eclectic displays and vintage furniture.

"Did you get enough to eat?" she asked, covertly dipping down to quickly toss the sap in the panty box. "I know those burritos are big, but you look like you probably take down a solid dozen of them and still have room for horchata. Speaking of which, I have bottled water, coffee, root beer—if you promise not to tell my GP. He's always telling me how reducing my sugar intake will reduce my inflammation, but he fails to understand that reducing my sugar intake also reduces my will to live."

The crinkles on either side of his eyes deepened. And was that the flicker of movement at one corner of his beard-bracketed lips?

"Water."

"Coming right up." Cady marched up the steps leading to the tiny kitchen and opened the three-quarter-sized fridge she'd had to source at a consignment store. The half-empty bottle of prosecco in the rack on the door kicked her hard in the feels—left over from her and Gemma's celebration of their last Idle Tuesday. A holiday they'd concocted one very high night when they both decided that they felt sorry for basic bitch September having to precede October, November, and December. She grabbed the water and closed the fridge door on the thought.

When she returned, she was somewhat perplexed to see her guest standing just outside the front door, his eyes closed and his face aimed skyward. Taking a few steps backward, she ducked behind a curtain and waited until she heard the door squeak open before breezing out like she'd only just arrived.

"Here you are," she said, holding the water out so he could approach at his comfort level. "One doctor-approved, completely boring, but life-sustaining beverage."

"Thanks." He twisted open the bottle and drank the entire

thing in just a few powerful gulps. A film of condensation still clung to the outside when he glanced around in search of a trash can.

"I'll just...recycle this," she said, setting it next to the phone on the register. "Well, you're welcome to look around. There's a really comfortable leather armchair that's just your size over by the home improvement and gardening section. Also, almost no one ever looks in that section, so it's pretty quiet if you want to rest."

Just looking at him made Cady want to rest. The perpetual grimace pulling his chin downward. The concerned crease chiseled into his brow. Those dark, watchful eyes that looked like they'd witnessed every atrocity the world could unleash.

Twice.

He cleared his throat, shifting on battered boots. "Came to help."

"Oh! Well, in that case. Right this way." She made it to the steps again before she realized he wasn't following her. His hooded lids obscured the exact point of his focus, but she could see his breath had quickened. His deep chest moved in and out like a bellows. Sweat had bloomed on his forehead below the dusty shoreline of his dark hair.

"There's a door right next to where we're headed," Cady said gently. "You can step outside any time you need."

Seeing the naked gratitude written on that weather-beaten face threatened to snatch the soul straight out of her tiresome, irritating meat suit of a body.

She started again, somehow comforted by the wall of person hanging a respectful distance behind her. He followed her through to the storage room, where the sight of an empty box with Fox's name on it in bold black marker stirred up her sadness like pond silt.

"So, all those stacks of books in the front of the store need to come back here. And the ones back here," Cady said, gesturing to a disintegrating cardboard box with the toe of a sneaker, "need to be transferred to those." She pointed to the not-yet-assembled stack of cardboard file box bottoms and lids against the wall. "It's not really difficult work, unless you're down an arm or your back is being a weapons-grade dick."

The trench-deep furrow appeared between his eyebrows. Cady guessed the term *weapons-grade dick* might have caught him but wasn't sure the official medical diagnosis would land any better.

"I'm fine, really. I mean, I'm not, but I am. You know?"

For the very first time since they'd "met," her stranger looked her directly in the eyes. The suffering she read in them made Cady feel like someone had just dropped a brick on her heart.

"I know."

She wanted to throw her arms around him and reassure him that it would get better. That whatever it was that led to his current difficulties, she could help him. Listen to him. Do whatever it took to see that bleak emptiness filled with even one positive thought.

And damned if that wasn't exactly the same kind of thing she had snapped at her best friend in all the world for earlier that morning.

Cady cleared her throat. "Well, I better go sell books and stuff. Help yourself to whatever's in the fridge and let me know if you need anything."

Back in the shop, Cady set about willfully banishing the ghost of her fight with Gemma, the break-in, the general pong of sadness that had hung over every nook and cranny since Aunt Fern got sick. She dusted. Organized the register cabinets. Windexed the front window. Hell, she even lit one of the palo santo sticks one of the clean-up volunteers had left.

By the time Burrito Guy reappeared an hour later, the air felt a little easier to breathe. The gray day, a shade lighter.

"Done already?" Cady followed him back to the storage area, where not only had he moved and re-boxed all the books, he'd also separated them out by genre. It was everything she could do not to stare at him in open-mouthed wonder and offer him the second bedroom in her apartment. "I'm sorry, but if I'm going to heap effusive praise on you, I'm gonna need a name."

She instantly regretted what was meant to be a lighthearted second attempt at an introduction when he flinched.

"Pick one."

"Bob?" she suggested, remembering the most complimentary of Gemma's earlier nicknames.

"Fine."

"Pleased to meet you, Bob." For reasons she couldn't quite understand, Cady held out her hand to him despite his earlier resistance.

His dark eyes moved from the tips of her fingers down to her wrist. Up her arm. Back down.

Engulfed—the only word Cady could source to describe the sensation of having her small, soft hand disappear into his large, warm, leathery one.

His fingers—not at all sausage-like, thank you very much, Gemma—flexed against her knuckles, gently holding the most delicate bones of her body within a sandpapery grip that felt like it could crush rocks into sprinkles.

But it was Cady's heart he somehow squeezed with his half-hesitant, half-triumphant flicker of a smile.

"Now that we've officially met, you think you'd be up to some more sorting?"

He was.

The next six hours were this exact cycle on repeat.

Cady giving Bob a task. Bob completing in record time what would have taken her a week of working around the hours of her body's impossible-to-predict cooperation.

They finished out their day by addressing the impossible item that had been on Cady's task list for the last several months: taking down and dusting all of her taxidermied critters. Towering oak of a man he was, Bob didn't even need the ladder to reach all of them.

"Initially, it was just Edgar," she explained, accepting the raven by the small wooden stump his delicate black feet were mounted on. "But he just seemed lonely, so I started buying him friends."

Picking up the barely damp cloth, she carefully stroked it over the bird's small, sleek head. "Since Edgar is so, um, *special*, I tried to pick ones that also had...character," she said, landing on a word that felt accurate without being insulting.

Bob's nod communicated none of the patronizing pity she'd come to resent when explaining her collection.

Which was the distinct advantage of those strong, silent types.

"There," she said, placing Edgar on the card table she'd set up as a work surface. "I need to run upstairs and feed Kevin Costner, then we can get to work on the squirrel family?"

Bob grunted his acknowledgement.

When Cady returned, she saw that Edgar had migrated to the register. Propped open before him against the phone's base was a tiny but surprisingly well-made booklet complete with a cardboard cover bearing a title in looping, fancy script. Edgar's single eye leered at the tiny book through a silver monocle that, upon closer inspection, was a paperclip Bob had bent into a tiny circular frame. When Cady saw *what* Edgar was peering at so intently, she whooped out a laugh that gripped her abdominals and didn't let go.

Cady was still howling like a banshee, tears streaming down her dust-streaked face, when Ethan showed up smelling of aftershave and looking like he'd tried. She had no idea how long he'd been there when she noticed him standing there, staring at her like he was trying to figure out if he needed to call someone.

"It says..." she began, gasping for breath. "It says...*Carrion Cooking.*" She howled anew, slapping a hand on the silky wood.

Bob appeared to be as baffled at her sudden hysterics as Ethan as he shifted on his battered boots and glanced toward the front door.

The sight of his discomfort, combined with the mantel clock chiming the six o'clock hour, finally finished her fit.

"Oh balls," she said, picking a cobweb out of her hair. "I'm so sorry. Give me fifteen minutes. I'll be so fast." Remembering that she had no idea where Gemma had stashed the cashbox, she grabbed several twenties out of her purse and stuffed them in Bob's giant paw. "Thanks again," she said to him. "I'll be right back," she said to Ethan. "Have a good night," she said to Bob.

Upstairs, she set new land-speed records in sticky-bits washing, bare-essentials makeup application, and would-be-seductress outfit selection. Examining herself in the full-length mirror next to the door, she wasn't entirely displeased with the effect.

Upon her return, she found Bob gone and Ethan standing opposite her ragtag congregation, his jaw set and his small, shapely mouth in a tight line.

"Don't they look *so* much better?" Cady asked. "We finally dusted them all." She ran a demonstrative finger over Edgar's glossy black head. It could have been her imagination, but the small black oubliette at the center of his one googly eye seemed to glow with a jaunty little spark of pride.

"I don't like to meddle in a person's business"—a quality that pretty much made Ethan a unicorn in this rumor-mill-fueled town—"but the guy who was helping you..."

Cady felt a nibble of irritation at Ethan's use of the word "guy" as opposed to "man." From what she knew of Sheriff Ethan Townsend, the list of requirements to earn the latter designation would be extensive and inflexible.

"Bob?"

"Bob," Ethan said. "His coming here going to be a regular thing, or...?"

"I'm not sure," Cady said, studying his profile. "Why?"

Ethan was many things, but stupid wasn't one of them. He knew his rugged work boots were sliding onto dangerous territory. "He have a last name, or..."

"I'm sure he does." Cady smiled warmly. "You going to tell me why you're asking, or..." She trailed off, mimicking his not-so-subtle game of interrogative Mad Libs.

Ethan scrubbed the back of his reddening neck with the palm

of his hand. "I was just thinking, until we get some answers about the break-in, might be good for you not to be alone in the shop."

"I agree." Cady brightened, grabbing her sweater off the back of the chair behind the register. "Which is why I invited him to come back tomorrow."

The satisfaction melted from Ethan's all-American features. "That's not quite what I—"

"I know what you were getting at, Ethan," she said. Bending down, she opened the cupboard and carefully extracted the sap from her box of panties before placing it on the counter.

Ethan looked from the sap, to her, back to the sap. "Were you waiting for me to say something, or..."

"Something like 'why did you leave a deadly weapon in my place of business without asking me?'"

"But—"

"Or maybe, 'do I really look like the type of woman who's capable of rendering another human unconscious if shit goes sideways?'"

"Cady—"

"It's not that I don't appreciate how protective you are," she said, trying to soften her tone. "It's just that I don't think we're quite at the point in our relationship where gifts of potential violence are a thing."

Ethan's sandy brows gathered at the center of his forehead. "That's what I'm trying to tell you. I *didn't* leave a sap in your cupboard."

Cady's face flooded with heat as she grabbed the braining stick and tossed it back under the counter. "So, dinner?" she asked, willing a sinkhole to open up and swallow her whole. "I'm starved."

Ethan, God bless him, let it go at that.

Her brain proved not to be quite so benevolent.

One endless meal and a twice-as-lengthy movie later, Cady's plan for seduction had gone right off the rails. The precise moment of opportunity she had described to Gemma occurred not even five minutes in, when the embittered senior officer with an axe to grind was assigned the feisty rookie who broke all the rules.

Just as predicted, Ethan leaned in to inform her how a law enforcement administration with any degree of oversight would never pair two officers with problematic conduct records.

Ethan's clean-shaven, soap-scented face was mere inches from hers. Hell, his eyes had even flicked to *her* lips for a split second, but Cady choked.

Afterward, they drove back in awkward silence that thickened the air in his county-issued SUV to concrete. She felt a gust of relief when he finally eased the vehicle to a stop in front of her shop, killed the engine, and walked around to open her door.

Now she would get out, and he would escort her across one and a half cement blocks to stand a full three feet away from Nevermore's front door. There, he would say something to the effect of "I had a really great time," and, keeping his pelvis a good four King James Bibles' worth away from hers, hug her shoulders and pat her exactly twice before hightailing it back to his vehicle and driving away.

Whether it was a function of the moon or her impatience to be upstairs in something with an elastic waistband, Cady couldn't face it.

Not now.

Not ever again.

They'd gotten as far as the door when, instead of waiting for his gentle lean in, Cady captured his square jaw between her hands and stretched up on tiptoes to place her actual mouth parts on his face.

Their alignment wasn't quite plumb at first, but he quickly corrected it.

And that was when shit got *real.*

Cady had prepared herself for the stiff, tight-lipped, tongueless smooch she would have to carefully coax Ethan out of.

What she *hadn't* prepared for was his walking her backward against a brick wall with a masculine growl that temporarily short-circuited her fine motor functions. Just as she hadn't prepared for his burying a hand in her hair. Or finding the curve of her hip and squeezing it through the fabric of her knit dress as, right there on the sidewalk, he did things with his tongue that she wasn't entirely certain would be permitted by Townsend Harbor's public decency laws.

Her eyes fell closed, and the hands were no longer his. The heated voice in her ear was deeper, smokier.

Fox's.

"Can I come up?" Ethan asked.

Cady wrenched free, panting and dazed, her palms planted against his chest.

"I'm so sorry, Ethan," she said. "I'm sorry. I can't."

"My bad." He stalked back toward his car, got in, then got out again before walking around to the hatchback and popping it open. He reappeared with something shaggy and green that she recognized as a potted plant when she no longer had to squint to see beneath the streetlights.

"Almost forgot," he said, thrusting it at her. "This is for you. From Mom."

Cady stared at the glossy green leaves climbing the center spike of substrate. "Oh," she said. "Thanks. Could you just— I just need to..." After digging in her coat pocket for her keys with her good hand, she unlocked the front door.

Like the gentleman he was even then, Ethan carried the plant in and set it down on the counter before marching back to his car. He waited until she had re-locked the front door before driving away at the prescribed speed limit.

His taillights became a red blur through Cady's tear-filled eyes. She stared at the plant and snatched up its beribboned card.

So sorry to hear about what happened. Thought this might brighten your mood. -CT.

In other words, *Sorry about your break-in. Here's something you need to take care of or feel guilty about neglecting if it dies.*

Under normal circumstances, she and Gemma would have been deep into psychoanalysis of Caryn Townsend's motives by this point.

Under normal circumstances, Aunt Fern would still be alive. Cady wouldn't have a sometimes-debilitating chronic pain condition. She wouldn't be involved in a one-sided flirtation with a customer who was probably only toying with her because he could.

Because she was just that hungry.

For something good.

Something real.

Something she was terrified she'd never feel again.

Cady's body began to quake until she could no longer stand still. She grabbed the plant and stalked through the shop and upstairs, overcome by the overwhelming need to break something.

SEVEN

Imposter

(ĬM-PŎS'TƏR) NOUN. ONE WHO ENGAGES IN DECEPTION UNDER AN ASSUMED NAME OR IDENTITY.

NORMALLY, FOX WASN'T A FORTUNATE MAN.

But to find an industrial-sized demolition/remodel waste container in the alley between Nevermore and Spill the Tea & Spice Emporium the same moment he might barf? Could almost be considered lucky.

Not only for splatter control, should he need it, but also to put something very substantial between the sight of Cady and the self-righteous sheriff in a lip lock.

Cady kissed *him.*

As in actively grabbed and kissed the square son of a bitch. She didn't wait for the Look. Or the Lean. Just went for it—crushed her lips against another man's lips with an artless enthusiasm that broke his fucking heart.

Now he had a new plot line to add to his nightmares. Behind door number one was what'd driven him to the woods in the first place.

Behind door number two was whatever the hell Cady and the sheriff got up to.

Choose your own headfuck.

Fighting a gag, Fox knew two things for sure: Lunch would be just as spicy coming up as it was going down.

And he'd rather have his eyes pecked out by a diseased raven than watch something like that again.

Cady's lips crushed to another man's hard, undeserving mouth.

Swallowing profusely against the tingle in his jaw, Fox finally allowed himself to unfurl the fingers he'd been clutching around the ghost of her touch all day.

Didn't matter—his fingers still buzzed with an arc of energy, electrifying the thrill until he swore he could feel every whorl of his fingerprints locking away the sensation of her skin.

Today had been an intense reminder of just how much fire he was playing with here. Enough to burn them both.

Him...quite literally.

Cady Bloomquist might be a bit absent-minded, but she wasn't an idiot. Just the opposite. And if she spent a good deal of time in his presence, the chances of forgetting himself and making a mistake that gave him away increased exponentially.

Not that he wasn't fucking good at this kind of thing. He'd become so adept in the past that he could do a job one night, and encounter a rare witness the next day with a friendly handshake and no trace of recognition.

But Cady...she didn't just look at people.

She *saw* them.

She called to his humanity. Rekindled it with her struggles. Beckoned it out with her tears.

She hadn't approached him on the street with the same caution and preconceived notions others had about his supposed life circumstances. Her eyes didn't skip over him to shield her heart from the ache of pity or the fear of contamination.

Which made things more complicated. Fox relied on people's need to avoid responsibility for the suffering of others by looking away.

He'd need a different tactic with her.

Fuck that. No. He couldn't be making plans. No tactic necessary. He should back off. Keep a bird's-eye view rather than lurking around her shop making everyone feel uneasy.

Besides, that sheriff was asking for a punch in the mouth, and with every encounter, Fox was more and more inclined to comply.

It wasn't even so much that she'd kissed the sheriff.

He'd even brightened when he thought she might come away unaffected. Then he noticed the shift in her features. The arrangement softening from determination to anticipation to...

Yearning?

Rapture?

The sight drove him away.

It was that or act on one of the myriad inappropriate instincts coursing through him.

He swallowed the acid trying to crawl up his throat and let his shoulder blades meet the brick wall of her shop to prop him up. Lifting his head to the sky, he did his best to slow his breathing.

His bones felt cold. Heavy. His lungs tight and aching.

She'd spoken of Fox to Gemma today. A lot.

I'm right here.

Crazy as it made him, he had to admit to himself that she was kissing the right man. Someone who wanted her. Someone who could stay close. Protect her.

This was good.

In fact, this could speed things up.

Sheriff Square Pants wasn't exactly his favorite human alive, but they were *not* technically at cross-purposes. In fact, the man could be helpful, though he wouldn't know it.

The problem with that shiny badge was he had to toe a certain line. Count all his empty brass once he discharged his weapon. Explain all forms of violence.

And he should. His job was to protect and serve.

Fox, however, was held to no such creed. Didn't rely on the chains of morality. If he had a god, it was an ancient, wild one, and he'd moved to a place where the laws of the forest made more sense than those governing the people in their cities.

The lawman was useful, though. In a boots-on-the-ground kind of way.

They were satellites pulled into her orbit, neither of whom would want to be released from her gravitational pull.

Christ. What a fucking day.

A deep, deep fatigue rolled over him, born of muscles that had refused to unclench the entire time he'd been inside her store. He was lucky hers was the corner shop on Water and Raven Streets.

The open doors helped, the floor-to-ceiling windows allowing the fall sea air to keep moving around him, giving the illusion of a somewhat open space. It had not been unbearable, but nor was it easy.

He'd been mentally screaming at himself to leave her alone. At one point, he'd possessed a will of iron and a resolve someone had once called supernatural.

Apparently, though, Cady's tears were his kryptonite.

He was such a shitheel. He'd known that forever, but it was like he'd been a cockroach, and was now a goopy crunch at the bottom of God's combat boot.

It was a cruel thing to keep calling her, to establish or maintain any sort of emotional or mental intimacy without the chance of ever actually *introducing* himself to her.

She needed someone stable. Steady.

Normal.

Today had been an anomaly. He'd seen someone in pain. In need. And he couldn't allow it to stand.

But...

He couldn't be the man who carried heavy things for Cady. He couldn't be someone she relied on. His past was too dark, and his future too uncertain.

Fucking all the way off was best for them both in the end.

He was a weight no one should have to carry. This heavy brick of dysfunction. Cumbersome on a good day, a menace on a bad one.

Just as he reached the depressing realization that his life had become the lyrics and/or title of a Creed song, something hit the ground next to his feet at terminal velocity.

If he'd not stepped forward to check, he might have missed the impact of what crumpled against his crown, exploding into a shower of shit.

Or, more exactly, dirt.

Soil.

What the fuck?

Instant rage surged through him, akin to the kind when someone's head was bonked on a kitchen cabinet and they instantly considered the homicide of whomever left it open.

"*Ohmigod,* no!" That familiar voice coursed down his spine, cooling his ire with a visceral shiver. "Oh shit. Bob? Bob is that you? Are you okay?"

Fox scrubbed at his mat of hair, dislodging some dark soil flecked with little white fertilizer balls before craning his neck to look up.

Cady was a disembodied, head-shaped shadow against the evening sky, leaning over the waist-high wall, sweet lips twisted with mortification.

Though his scalp smarted and stung, he noticed the pot she'd dropped on his head had been in one of those expendable plastic jobbers that crumpled if you squeezed them too hard.

No harm done.

"I didn't think anyone was in the alley! I swear I was intending that for the dumpster—I just have perpetually shitty aim. How bad are you hurt? Do you need me to call an ambulance?"

He shook his head, half in denial and half to check for concussion. No swelling. No dizziness. Vision was okay. So far, so good. "I—"

"Stay right there! I'm coming down!"

Spitting some grit from his mouth, he held up a staying hand. "No—"

She'd already disappeared.

He had *just* decided to restrict contact or interaction with the woman! He *needed* to stay away from her. For both their sakes. So, of course, she dropped a fern on his head.

Of course she did.

He swore to God, if she brought the motherfucking sheriff down with her to assess his injuries? He'd slit his own throat and throw himself in the dumpster.

Trash glinted in the moonlight against the honest-to-God cobbles, and he stooped to retrieve some and huck it into the dumpster. Plastic sheeting. Window molding. A mess of wires that may have been salvageable as a security camera or something if the dirt hadn't exploded all over.

Might have been handy during the break-in.

Cady's hurried descent down the balcony steps reminded him of what a tactical and security nightmare this building was. Both were connected by a spiral staircase that reached from the waterfront boardwalk to the third floor, only interrupted by decorative gates with—he guessed it—no locks.

Fuck, this world was too dangerous for her to live in.

When she reached the first-floor landing, she started chanting his name in a panic. Well, not his name, but the one they'd assigned him.

"Oh my God, Bob! Oh my God, Bob! Oh my God! Bob! Are you okay? Are you bleeding? I should call you an ambulance." Her phone was in her hand before he could finish a blink. "How is your vision? Are you dizzy?"

She rushed him like a fraternity, arms reaching, desperately doing her best to examine him while he refused to allow it.

To keep himself from enfolding his body around her, Fox shrank away instead, using the last of his willpower to create space between their bodies.

"I'm okay." He adopted his patois from this morning—diction more precise than his own, three octaves of separation from the regular pitch, and signifying English from another part of the country in minute ways, so as not be thought of as an "accent."

The devil resided in the details.

Especially his.

"You might not be okay!" She clutched at his elbow, and he had to stop or give up his balance. "Head wounds can be way unpredictable, and worse than you initially think." She dropped her arms, correctly reading his lack of enthusiasm for physical touch. "Listen. Let me take you to the urgent care, at least. They'll do a quick scan and make sure there's no damage to your brain." She must have read the denial in his posture, because she hurriedly added, "I have workman's comp insurance. If you need it. Please. This is my fault. Let me help you."

Go to the urgent care and say what? That he lost a fight with a ficus?

No thanks.

"No injuries," he said. "It glanced off."

She shook her head. "But you don't know that. Sometimes injuries are hidden until they make themselves known."

She had no idea.

"No hospital." He remembered this time to keep his voice gentle, but still her mouth snapped shut. Eyes the size of tea saucers filled with moist concern.

Blinking grit from his eyelids, he squinted at the pile of leaves, stems, and a disarray of dirt. "What'd it do?"

She cringed, looking up with only her eyes and blinking rapidly against a gather of damp emotion. "Actually...a patch in my roof is leaking again. I'm closing it off for, um, for repairs. Just getting rid of extra stuff."

Fox also glanced up, as if he could diagnose what the roof needed from this vantage.

"It buckled last year beneath storm debris," she explained, turning to the stair railing and mounting the first step. "Aunt Fern was supposed to hire a contractor, but she got sick...and it didn't seem to matter to either of us after that."

"Yeah?" he asked as she climbed slowly and carefully, keeping her Keds on the wide parts of the spiral steps.

"I should be getting a payout from the insurance from the break-in for damages—I figured I could use that to pay for work on the roof and do a lot of the indoor stuff DIY to save funds."

He couldn't think of a single thing to say but "huh" as she passed the second-floor landing and kept on climbing.

That ass. Not just plump and wide in sexy jeans, but round, too. It shifted so dramatically as she walked, making an eternal figure eight.

Eternity. That was how long he'd want her.

"Aunt Fern was a bit of a hoarder," she admitted sheepishly, glancing down almost in time to catch his eyes where they ought not be. "I keep finding things up here on the roof that should have been thrown away years ago. Old, rusty installations. Broken furniture. Plastic totes of stuff she never planned to use again but couldn't part with... It's just so overwhelming sometimes."

From the roof, they caught the last of the light as it disappeared over the mountains.

Casting his eyes around the flat roof-turned-veranda, he frowned at the mess illuminated by a string of decorative outdoor lights. "Who helps?"

"No one." She shrugged. "I just get to it when I have the...the time."

"Your back," he reminded her, frown deepening to a scowl.

She waved her hand as if to bat his ire away. "Oh yeah, my back's an asshole, but, as you have been made painfully aware, I can roll a thing or two off the roof without too much problem." Her lips twisted in a wry grimace as her eyes made their way to his soil-caked hair. As if of its own accord, her fingers reached toward him. "Are you sure I can't just look at your head? It's the least I can do."

He jerked away, realizing for the first time that he'd followed her up three flights of stairs without even meaning to.

Like some pathetic stray puppy.

Fox was forced to pause his self-criticism to be astounded. Somehow, she'd Jedi-mind-tricked him out of his bullshit willpower using some sort of Pacific Northwest Bookwitch magic and then dangled that ass in front of him like a carrot in front of a mule up two flights of stairs.

He needed to get out of here.

The pole in the middle of the spiral staircase seemed sturdy enough to slide down, and the only thing that could stop him...

Was a hole the size of a small car in her motherfucking ceiling.

Knowing her like he did, Fox had expected a bit of chaos in her life. But this?

As if just noticing he'd stopped dead in his tracks, she turned to follow the direction of his stare.

"Yeah." Her nose crinkled as she gave a soft, nervous laugh. "We had an old friend sort of patch it using nails, polyethylene plastic sheeting layers, and this nifty little post that props it up like a tent so the water doesn't just gather and make it heavy. I suppose I need to get it fixed at some point."

Some point being yesterday. The tarp and waterproof fasteners were made for slanted roofs and temporary fixes, not the flat roof of an old Victorian building. Even for a temporary fix, she needed rolled PVC membrane roofing materials at the very least.

"Easy patch." It was absolute last thing he'd meant to say, but here they were.

"You think?" She looked at him askance. "It's not getting any smaller, that's for sure."

"Take me three days, tops." He should eat a bullet. It would make less room for his foot in there.

Brightening, she clapped her hands together and linked her fingers as if in prayer. "Tell me you mean it," she pleaded. "I've been looking for a contractor. But people around here are busy and expensive. Are you saying you'd be interested in—"

Absolutely not.

"Sure."

Fuck.

Around her, his brain didn't make connections to his mouth

or his dick, allowing them to work on their own. But they were sure as shit talking to each other. *And apparently* making all the decisions these days.

"Last you through the winter, anyways." Now that he'd gone and done it, he instantly warmed to the idea. How better to keep a bird's-eye view on her than perching on her roof for a couple of days?

Easy there, cowboy, he cautioned himself. *Don't go lowering your guard now.*

Not when it was the most dangerous. When he was weak from a head wound. Yeah. Maybe that pot hit him harder than he'd realized. Brain damage could be the only explanation.

"Excellent!" She clapped her hands again, this time in celebration. "Let's talk about hourly compensation for— *Ohmygodyourebleeding.*"

Before he could register the abrupt shift, she was in front of him, reaching up toward a trickle above his eye he hadn't yet noticed.

He regretted the emotion he read in her eyes at the rejection of her touch, but a woman like her didn't need to handle his kind of filth.

Face hardening with determination, she seized his soil-dusted elbow. "I know you don't like to be inside, but I need to take a look at the wound, so you are coming with me," she insisted, able to drag him a few paces toward the door until he recovered enough of his wits to plant his feet.

"I'm fine," he protested.

Cady's expression gentled as she turned back to him, not releasing her grip on his coat. "The first and third floors of Nevermore are paneled in windows to maximize the view of the sky and sea. I know you don't like to be inside, but could I tempt you long enough to clean the cut? It could get infected or worse if you don't get the soil out of it." She released him, looking down at the grime left on her palm. Mostly her doing, with a little help from himself and the wet earth he slept on. "Maybe take a hot shower?"

When he realized she was tugging him toward the roof door, panic clamped around his ribs like a vise. “I shouldn’t.”

“Don’t worry,” she soothed in a tone that made him hesitate. “Nevermore restrooms are on the second-floor balcony inside, but my personal bathroom is on the third floor in my loft, which has no walls and floor-to-ceiling windows. Plus, the balcony stretches across the entire back of the building with a door off the bathroom. It faces the water, so the view from the boardwalk is blocked by the lower-floor balconies. You can be buck-ass naked in front of the window and no one could see in—unless they’re using binoculars from a boat, I suppose.”

Or the plateau above the fountain.

Fox fought not to stumble. She’d intuited that he was a claustrophobic nutcase, because he wasn’t the sort of man who could hide his trauma anymore.

“Please? What if I made food and we talked shop on the picnic table off the second-floor balcony? It’s sheltered by the deck over it, so we’ll stay dry.” Her gentle eyes showed no pity. No fear. No judgment for his weakness, just patience and...hope?

To some men, a rooftop picnic wouldn’t sound like heaven, just a regular Tuesday.

But to him?

“I guess I could use a shower,” he heard himself say. His longest sentence in her presence thus far, he was pretty sure.

“There we go!” She turned and enthusiastically pulled him toward the door in the middle of the roof. Cautiously, she led him down a switchback staircase to her loft.

To the place over which he stood sentinel, watching her sleep.

Jesus Christ. His sister had watched enough Lifetime movies in high school for him to recognize himself as the villain.

He eyed the stairway dubiously. “Your”—gulp—“sheriff sweetheart won’t like it.”

She made a rude noise. “He’s *not* my sweetheart. He’s more like...” She paused to think of a word. “Well, anyways, no one tells me who to invite into a building I own.” She turned from him and kept moving. "Or at least hope I own..." he thought he heard her mutter.

He cocked his head to the side like a dog learning something new.

Something interesting.

The staircase threatened to constrict him between its walls before dumping them into the airy loft. Two of the four walls were constructed of stormproof glass, above which glow-blocking blinds lurked, eager to be used.

He was so glad she didn't tend to lower them. The view from both inside and out was unparalleled.

Oddly enough, the sinkhole-sized gap in the ceiling wasn't too apparent from the main room, which was completely open but for a handful of columns holding up the ceiling.

Well, in theory.

The edge of the fissure peeked from over the solid wall, in front of which the kitchen appliances and cabinets lined up like a vintage vignette.

"The bathroom is tucked behind here." She led him to an impressive alcove in the corner that cut several feet from along the sea-facing windows. After kicking off her boots in the general area of a shoe basket, she retrieved an elastic from her wrist and gathered her hair into a high ponytail.

He did his best not to notice her breasts beneath the words *My Favorite Season is the Fall of the Patriarchy.*

Despite the windows, he still catalogued the exits. Basically, the roof, the stairs, and a front door.

This fucking place would never pass code if it were built sometime in the last century. And yet these Victorian brick buildings lasted so much longer.

His heart only pounded a million miles a second because he was indoors. Sweat slicked his spine with hair-lifting awareness because of how he'd been ruined.

It had nothing to do with her.

He wiped at his temple, where a second trickle of blood slowly joined the first, before it could drip into his eyebrow.

Reaching into the enclosed room, she clicked on a light, and he froze.

"Pretty cool, huh?" She surveyed her own bathroom as if seeing it through his eyes. "My aunt had expensive tastes and tended to date rich men." A grim note lurked beneath her obvious fondness for the woman. "They often gifted her the upgrades she requested, rather than diamonds or expensive perfume."

"Smart woman," he remarked, drinking in the space.

No toilet in view—he surmised it probably hunkered beneath the half wall away from the windows.

Cornered by the two glass walls, a gigantic copper tub stretched beneath a rain shower that might actually be tall enough for him. The shower curtain hung from an oval suspended by antique-looking copper pipe.

Floor-to-ceiling drapes closed over the wall for privacy, so it wouldn't be very easy to see in from the walkway three floors up with your vision impeded by the large balconies.

It was kind of perfect.

"Sorry, it's been a minute since I cleaned it." The chagrin in her voice struck him as funny, and he wondered what she'd think when she realized he usually went in the woods and bathed in a lake.

"Doesn't matter."

The room smelled like her—something earthy with undertones of fruit, but free of musk or florals. There was nothing even the most talented perfumer could do to recreate the scent. Any attempt would be trite and underwhelming. Some things were so pure, they couldn't be captured. Like books and rain.

He breathed so deeply that his lungs complained before he was forced to exhale in a gust.

"You doing okay?" She craned her neck to look up at him as

he loomed in the doorway, almost tall enough to put his chin on the top of her head.

No, he was not doing okay.

Only the whisper of a butterfly's wing existed between him and the woman he'd promised never to touch. He suffered distressing thoughts and attachments to said woman. Not to mention, he was in a city.

In a building.

Also, there was the head wound and shit. Probably should wash that before his demons caught up and drove him outside.

"I'm good."

Instead of retreating, she strode into the bathroom and peeked inside the freestanding sink, opened a linen closet on the left to show him where the towels were, and walked to the tub to pull back the curtain and peek in.

"I'll get out of your hair," she said. "I'm just making sure Kevin Costner isn't hiding in here again."

Fox stared at her for five full, uncomprehending seconds before she blinked and shook her head.

"Sorry, Kevin Costner is old Mr. Henery's cat from the Cyclery down the street. I offered to watch him while he went in for a minor procedure. But for such a big fellow, he's certainly good at hiding and escaping..." She must have caught his skepticism, because she clarified, "Kevin Costner, not Mr. Henery."

"It's fine." He didn't *not* watch her bend over and check the cupboards. And averted his eyes just in time for her to straighten and whirl to face him.

She backed up toward the door, staring at him oddly, as if seeing him for the first time. Maybe his pitiful, dingy state was more appallingly apparent beneath a chandelier.

"Okay, well, the shower is all yours. If you need trimmers or a razor, you'll find them in the wicker drawers next to the bathtub. Sorry in advance that all my stuff smells so girly. Hope you don't mind mango shampoo..."

He knew what she was thinking—he could see it on her face.

In this room built for people the size of a century ago, he probably looked like Sasquatch or something.

Whereas she resembled one of Renoir's famous bathers—eyes wide and luminous as the moon. Something so secretive and sensual about her smile that the sight of it would make the devil whimper.

Clutching the door latch, she chewed on the inside of her cheek, assessing him one last time. "I mean, I should probably ask because... Well, people will ask me if I checked... But you're not a serial killer, right?"

He shrugged. "More of an oatmeal guy."

It was more words than he'd strung together in her presence. An echo of a man who used to be well-liked for his sense of humor.

She blinked three times, her face crumpled with confusion before the joke hit her and crinkled her eyes.

Fox recognized the nervous undertone to her laugh. She was having second thoughts.

"I can go," he offered gently, shoving his fists in his pockets to keep them from view.

Her features softened and then became resolute. "No. You know what? *No*, you're a new employee, and my aunt treated all her employees like family."

Guess now wasn't the time to tell her that most violent crimes were perpetrated by the members of the victim's family.

Words crowded his mouth. He wanted to extol her virtues, to express his gratitude, to praise her *and* punish her for having such an open heart and a fucking death wish.

Instead, he faced the window, staring hard at the violence of the waves as the wind calmed his own stormy spirit.

She was gone when he turned back, and he hoped he'd not seemed too skull-fucked if he missed something she said.

As he turned toward the bath, his reflection caught his eye.

Jesus, it was worse than he thought. The silt he'd rubbed in his hair had clumped in the moisture of the day. He'd let his hair grow too long and could no longer hide its tendency to curl. His beard almost hung to his sternum, and at thirty-three, he wasn't supposed to be sporting this much gray.

Soil still clung to his clothes along with those little white balls of fertilizer.

Peeling off his layers, he uncovered a body marked, pocked, scarred, inked, and hard.

Of course she was afraid of him...she had every reason to be.

Fox tried to silence the roar of his empty stomach with a hand over the noise as he stepped from the shower.

He had some cash for fast food, but he'd take a doggie bag of whatever she was making.

After taking the time to wipe any evidence of him from the tub, he stepped around the shower alcove to retrieve his clothes.

Not finding them after two cursory inspections, he checked the linen cupboard, the sink, and the chest of drawers from which he'd taken some old-fashioned male grooming scissors—the origin of which he didn't want to know—a razor, and a washcloth for his shower.

Fox froze when he pulled out the third drawer down.

End-to-end pills. And not "medicine cabinet" pills for coughs, colds, allergies, aches, fevers, food poisoning, and minor first aid. But prescription drugs all written to Cadence Bloomquist.

More than a woman in her twenties should have to take.

Shut the drawer, he ordered himself, but he'd already retrieved one of the pill bottles from its orderly spot.

Tramadol. Not an opioid, but a great deal stronger than ibuprofen. The next one lifted his eyebrows. Dilaudid. Basically morphine. Recently filled.

Holy shit, did sweet, naïve Cady have a pill problem?

Or had her back injury been that bad?

Actively hating himself, Fox searched through other bottles.

Cosentyx, an IL-17 inhibitor, steroids, both creams and pills, muscle relaxers, immunosuppressants, all with several refills.

Not an addict...

So much made sense. Her pinched face today, the tears and the hard words for her friend. The impatience with the sheriff.

Not asking him up after that hot kiss.

He shut his eyes and let out an eternal breath through his nose. She was ill. Chronically ill. And lived alone, and tried to fix roofs by herself, and shelved books, and invited random, large men into her shower, taking his word that he wasn't going to murder her and do weird stuff like wear her skin before anybody missed her.

Fuck me, I can't go yet. He scrubbed callused hands over his face. There were too many unanswered questions. Too many people in Cady's sphere could be problematic.

People were most often hurt by those they loved.

What he needed was a reason to believe she was safe. He needed information.

But first, he needed his clothes.

After slicking damp hair back with his hand, he tucked the towel around his waist and ventured to the door she'd thoughtfully left ajar.

"No, *I'm* sorry," she said around a strangled little sob. "I was so out of line. I felt like everyone was surrounding me telling me I couldn't function the way I wanted to, and today was so uncomfortable and hard, I felt like they were right. I didn't mean to take it out on you. I just love you so much." Her voice wobbled dangerously.

Fox swallowed as his heart dropped into his stomach.

He might have to just die in here, because he'd be goddamned if he was going out there while she was sniffling on the phone with the saintly sheriff.

"No, I love you!" Sobbed another disembodied voice, this one grating through a smartphone speaker.

A woman. Fuck yeah.

"I was too bossy. This mouth, it gets me in trouble. I just worry, okay? What if someone hurts you?"

"I'm more worried about losing the store, Gemma." The naked anxiety in her voice threatened to pull his heart from its cage and drop it, still beating, on the floor.

"You're not going to lose the store," Gemma soothed.

"I can't be a Walmart greeter!" Cady wailed.

"Oh, honey. No danger of that. They'll never allow Walmart to touch Townsend Harbor. That would kill the small-town vibe."

"Well, I can't work at Fronks. They'll just put me in the light-duty section with that guy Willard the diabetic racist."

"Listen to me, Cadence Bloomquist. That isn't going to happen. We'll figure it out, even if I have to do some weird, illegal shit at the county building."

"I'd never ask—"

"I know. I do what I want." Gemma gave a saucy laugh. "And I want to help you."

"I love you, babe." Cady sniffed. "OMG, not to change the subject, but look at Kevin Costner."

"He's such a handsome boi! When did you finally get him to sit on your lap?"

"Just now. He's never done this before..." Cady's voice dropped to a whisper.

Okay, the conversation had turned a corner—it seemed safer to venture out into the open.

"Cady?" Fox murmured in acceptable "you're on the phone" tones.

He found her on the comfy-looking overstuffed couch facing the window and the wild sea beyond. Perched on her chest was one of the biggest Maine Coons he'd seen in his entire life. With a long coat of black, orange, and brown, he was a majestic creature, even if his ears did look somewhat like a gremlin's.

"He's never let me pet him before, let alone snuggle," Cady

stage-whispered as Gemma made gooey eyes at the creature vibrating like a well-oiled Harley.

After clearing his throat, Fox asked in a louder voice, "Hey, uh…have you seen my clothes?"

"What?" came the squeal from the phone.

Both the cat and Cady swiveled their heads, the rest of them frozen in surprise.

"Um, Gem, I have to go."

"Cady? Who is there?" came the demand at such a decibel level that he worried for the structural integrity of the glass. "Is that Sher—"

"Talk tomorrow!" Cady ended the video call then shoved the phone under a couch pillow as if it'd done something to be ashamed of.

Acting as if he'd discovered nothing about her illness or financial desperation, he adopted his generally blank expression and jerked his chin toward the cat. "Kevin Costner?"

She didn't seem to be able to blink. Or swallow.

Her jaw loosened so much that she was apparently no longer able to form words. Cobalt eyes touched him everywhere—his shoulders, chest, each ridge of his abdomen—before dropping to the towel. Before she had too long to contemplate what was going on *beneath the towel*, her eyes snapped back up to his face. The sight didn't seem to do much for her auditory capabilities.

"Should I…"

Finally she turned away, burying her face in the cat's mane. "I was so excited about snuggling with Kevin Costner, I couldn't bring myself to move him and cook, so I ordered Thai. I got you two dishes in case you had one of the top five allergies."

Well, fuck, now he felt bad she'd spent money. "You didn't have to do that." Also, hadn't she just been to dinner with the sheriff?

"Psssh. I promised you food, and I am the mediest-of-ocre chefs. I had a salad course earlier, and people seem to think that's a whole meal…so I hope you don't mind something heavier." She pursed her lips at Kevin Costner and stroked along the cat's spine, threading her fingers through fluffy hair with apparent delight.

If Fox watched her much longer, his hard-on might split the towel. "My clothes?"

She startled, causing the cat to launch off her lap and zoom under the bed.

A bed Fox refused to look at. What with its fluffy, silky, dark purple coverlet and an intense array of pillows.

Who decided to make lofts, anyway? No one wanted your guests to come over for dinner and automatically be in your bedroom. No man could be in the space with Cady *and* a bed and not be dying to use the mattress for its second-most-intended purpose.

Wincing, she stood. "Oh, sorry. I was so stricken over having dropped so much dirt on your jacket and jeans, I popped all your stuff in the wash. I'll switch them to the dryer, so they'll be done while we eat." She shuffled over to a closet off the kitchen and opened it to reveal a washer and dryer.

She reached in, squeaked, and pulled out, grabbing her back.

Fox was at her side in a minute. "Let me." He snatched the handful of stuff in the washer and bent to load it in the dryer before pushing the buttons to dry as quickly as possible.

"Show-off," she muttered, and turned too slowly for him to miss the fact that she'd been watching the towel against his backside when he bent.

You can't know that shit, he yelled at himself. *Don't even consider...*

Making herself busy in the kitchen, she unpacked containers of noodles, curries, and kabobbed meat. "Dish up whatever you want."

Thai in a towel?

After clearing her throat twice, she said, "I have a robe you could wear if you're cold. It's a kimono, and it has a few orchids and a peacock on it, but it's warm and huge."

He didn't even have to think of a reply. "I'm good with the towel."

A pause. "I guess I should have asked before touching your things." She wouldn't stop glancing up at his hair.

He'd cut it above his ears, shaved the sides, and slicked it back like he had a million years ago. He hadn't taken off the beard, but he'd trimmed it to a respectable shape and shaved his neck. He almost looked human.

It was a lie he hated the sight of, but he had to admit, he looked decidedly less serial killery. So he had that going for him.

She gestured to the four-person table she'd somehow bullied over to the windows.

He took a seat across from her, and both of them looked out the window toward the lights across Puget Sound.

"I saw your meds." It was a confession he hadn't meant to make, but here they were.

He had so many questions that he didn't know what to ask first. *How much pain are you in right now? How much pain do you live in every day? What can I do to fix it? To alleviate it, to cover you in bubble wrap so that you don't have to suffer?*

"Snooping, were we?" she asked around a soup spoon of curry.

He glanced up to see a sparkle of mischief in her eyes as she chewed.

"Looking for my drawers in your drawers," he said, shifting in his towel and reaching down to make certain it stayed secure. How did women even do skirts?

Cady's friends were right—she wasn't careful enough. Shouldn't allow strangers into a place where all her medications were not secure. People had been killed for fewer narcotics than she possessed.

She frowned at him, narrowing her eyes and setting her chin at an obstinate angle. He almost hoped it was suspicion in her expression, but it looked more like irritation.

It'd been decades since he'd lowered his eyes in shame. "I shouldn't have snooped," he told his pad thai, stabbing it.

She stunned him by snorting. "I'm not mad. There are certain times it's totally permissible to snoop."

He blinked.

She shifted in her chair and crafted a huge bite.

Intrigued, he leaned in, pretending not to notice how she watched his shoulders hunch when he put his elbow on the table to steeple his fingers. "You snoop?"

"Not that much..." Her grin melted. "Just like my boyfriends, my girlfriends, my parents, my ex, my ex's new girlfriend, and one time his boyfriend. My ex's ex, my doctor, my therapist, my physical therapist, my aunt, distant relatives, employees and employers, and, lastly, any stranger that allows me alone in their bathrooms, kitchens, or libraries. Although I'm weird about bedrooms, because who knows what you're going to find? And if it's sanitary..." She made a face and shuddered.

Blink.

She shrugged. "What? I'm a curious woman."

He blinked again.

"You're hard to read, Bob. I need you to tell me what you're thinking," she said, fondling the chain around her neck.

I want you.

"I—thought...you'd be bothered."

"I'm bothered that every strong, capable man in my sphere seems to be convinced that my kindness is stupidity," she said, her even tone not exactly matching the gravitas of the message. "I mean, I listen to the serial killer podcasts and murder porn like every other basic white lady, so I know what men are capable of. But I *also* know that I'm not going to become cynical and callous on the off chance someone will murder me. I mean, let's get real here—statistically *you're* less likely to kill me than anyone else who has been in this store today. Including a cop *and* my best friend. So yeah, there's all sorts of things you could do to me, but I imagine you would probably want to commit murder before a shower and not after." Her eyes narrowed in mock suspicion. "Unless you are a true psychopath."

Somewhere in the middle of her tirade, his lips had tilted upward, and he held on to a shaky, unused smile. She'd homed in on that, and since then, her eyes had remained glued to his mouth.

Grabbing his napkin, Fox wiped his beard and his lips. Twice. Then he searched his teeth for hitchhikers with his tongue, as if they would explain her intent gaze.

To avoid doing anything embarrassing, he applied himself to his dinner. A dinner he'd have to compensate her for.

"I have ankylosing spondylitis," she announced as if she were telling her family she'd decided to be a vegan—confident but defensive. "It's autoimmune spinal arthritis, painful, chronic, not curable. That's the TL;DR version."

He'd have to read up on it. "What does it do?"

"Oh, basically it causes inflammation of my spine and sometimes bonus joints and is generally a fuckwad of awful sauce wrapped in a shit-stained tortilla."

He chuffed. "Glad we didn't have Mexican food tonight."

Her laugh. The most welcome sound in the world.

Talk less, he admonished himself. He was getting too comfortable... Which was saying something at an antique table with only a towel between him and revealing his nut sack to Kevin Costner, who was staring daggers at him from around the corner of the kitchen island.

They ate in silence for several minutes as she seemed to take social cues from him. After a few bites, the atmosphere relaxed into something like companionship.

When she shivered, he stood up and shut the door, but not before gulping in deep, cleansing breaths.

The air was getting closer. The night was colder, but the fireplace seemed to be blasting out heat like a fucking supernova.

"I...I don't know why, but I thought you were older," she

shyly informed his turned back. "How long have you been...in town?"

He couldn't bring himself to look at her, lest he give something away. He had to work harder on his voice. On the shift in pacing and diction. "Longer than your sheriff likes."

He'd settled into the mountains three years ago and had expected the wilds to take him down long ago.

Bears were kind of small here.

An embarrassed little groan escaped her. "I'm sorry about Ethan. He's protective, and...there have been some issues with a little more violence than usual this tourist season. The town is a bit divided on some things, and—"

He held up his hand when he turned to face her. "Protecting you is his job."

This time she looked down at her food, and the slightest hint of peach crawled up her cheeks. "There's protective, and there's condescending. I'm a woman with a condition, not a child."

He nodded, sufficiently chastised. "Fair point."

"Where did you learn to patch a roof?"

"The army," he answered honestly.

"Oh?" Both eyebrows shot up.

On deployment, he'd had to put up and take down a base in a hurry. It often needed a lot of patching if there was bad weather or...explosions, heavy artillery fire, drunk marines—

"Did you spend a long time in the army?" she asked, her eyes alight with interest.

"Too long..." he said without thinking, the incredible food turning to ashes in his mouth.

"I see." It was the first time he'd read a note of pity on her face.

He didn't like it.

He ate the rest of his food as if it were the military mess hall, doing his best to remind her that he was an uncouth creature. He might be cleaned up ever so slightly, but was no different than before.

No less dangerous. No less horrible.

For her part, she chatted about the roof, invited him to an upcoming book club, whereupon he'd be joined by other local un-homed who liked to show up for coffee, tea, and snacks and to listen to the hilarity. Her conversation escaped in a stream of nervous consciousness, but he didn't mind. It saved him from having to say anything. To explain himself. All he had to do was focus on her voice, the only thing distracting him from how badly he needed to run a few miles to get this extra adrenaline out of his system.

He'd been inside too long.

"I need to go." He stood abruptly, and the chair scraped loud enough to freak the cat into some kind of Scooby-Doo scuffle on the wood floors.

She stood as well, hurrying to swallow her bite. "Oh, okay. Let me get your stuff out of the..."

"I'll do it."

Turning his back to her, he tugged his things out of the dryer, barely giving their continued dampness another thought. He'd freeze to death if he had to.

Almost too frenzied to remember that she was most certainly watching him, he yanked on his boxer briefs and thermals. Jeans came next, then undershirt, long-sleeve tee, jacket, flannel, and sweater.

"Thanks for dinner." Grabbing his socks last, he strode to the door and picked up his boots. "I'll be here tomorrow to start on the roof."

"I'll walk you out," she offered, wiping her mouth and making her way to the door.

"No, I can—"

"I've already locked everything up and gated the back steps to the balcony. I need to let you out the front so I can lock it again and pull down the new storefront security grate." She scrunched her face into an expression of distaste.

"Sure." He gestured for her to go ahead of him, hating himself for wishing she could walk faster. A cold sweat had begun to spread across his skin, and the tremors would hit any moment if he didn't get the fuck out.

As they reached the second-floor landing, his clothes were already starting to chill in the late-fall darkness. She didn't heat the store in the evenings, probably to save money.

After turning on one overhead chandelier, she moved to the door, reaching to open it before freezing in place.

"OMG," she whispered, stepping back until her shoulder blades met his chest.

He steadied her with gentle hands on her upper arms, and his heart kicked even higher at the note of pure horror in her voice.

He searched for danger, but couldn't find a thing in the shadows.

"The ghosts put Edgar the raven back over the door." She pointed, eyes owlish and mouth agape.

Fuck.

Fox knew he'd placed all the taxidermized weirdos in one place, facing the corner of the far wall, where their soulless, creepy-ass faces belonged.

Starting with that goddamn googly-eyed raven.

But there it was, staring down at them with its one wonky eye.

"I don't believe in ghosts," he muttered.

But he knew that someone had to have come into the shop and moved that raven...

All while they were upstairs together.

EIGHT

Confliction

(KŎN'FLĬKT'ION) NOUN. AN EMOTIONAL DISTURBANCE RESULTING FROM THE OPPOSITION OR SIMULTANEOUS FUNCTIONING OF MUTUALLY EXCLUSIVE IMPULSES, DESIRES, OR TENDENCIES.

Bare-Naked Book Club Presents: Blind Date with a Book Boyfriend.

Looking to fill an empty evening? Why not take a duke between the covers?

Cady snorted into her glass of wine, nearly turning it into a Neti pot. "Nope. No. Absolutely not. If we put that in the *Town Crier*, I don't even want to know what kind of people are going to stop by our booth."

She had only been half listening while the Bare-Naked Book Club's usual suspects attempted to cobble together a description of their booth offering for Townsend Harbor's annual fall festival.

Myrtle looked up from the pad she'd been taking notes on. "Why not take a duke between the *sheets*?" she suggested.

This time, she nearly got Gemma. "It's the duke part that's the problem, Myrtle," she explained, dabbing a dribble of Cabernet from the corner of her mouth.

"If these novels had any sense of historical accuracy, they would know that a marquess would be far more desirable in terms of a match. Honestly, I don't know how anyone reads genre fiction." Caryn Townsend tossed the brown-paper-wrapped book on the table, lifting her pale blue eyes to meet Myrtle's warm brown ones.

Pushing fifty-five, Caryn had the kind of dewy skin that suggested regular facials or perhaps a deal with some minor underworld deity. High cheekbones, minimal crow's-feet, and a jaw line probably created by the kind of plastic surgeon you had to be referred to by a secret handshake. Even on a night like tonight, where a howling wind turned a steady drizzle into a diagonal assault, she'd shown up with her silvery-blonde bob stubbornly sleek.

She was the kind of woman who would never *not* be beautiful. Or wealthy. Or well respected.

Worse, she was Ethan Townsend's mother.

"If you're going to be so picky, then why don't you be the scribe?" Myrtle held out the glossy black raven's feather quill that she insisted on using for the book club's meeting minutes. Which she also insisted on recording. To what end and for what purpose, none of them had ever figured out.

Seated directly across from Myrtle in the circle of chairs, Caryn glared at the quill as if it were crawling with some mysterious avian disease. "That's quite all right, Myrtle. I'd hate to distort the *official* record."

Caryn somehow managed to make this sound both patronizing and complimentary at the same time. Like the minutes and the elaborate leather-bound tome where they were recorded, Myrtle had come up with the idea of the BNBC needing a scribe.

"Of course, we wouldn't be experiencing this problem had we gone with *my* suggestion," Caryn added.

Cady and Gemma locked gazes from across the circle, and Gemma crossed one eye on the non-Caryn-facing side. Cady had first seen this particular trick during the tenth-grade summer school algebra II class where they'd initially forged their friendship —Cady to make up for the semester she'd lost to Astrid's onset; Gemma to retake what dyscalculia, a symptom of her yet-undiagnosed ADHD, had cost her.

Though they had initially bonded over a mutual hatred of correlation coefficients, they'd soon begun mapping other uncanny convergences. The same lucky number (thirteen). The same food aversions (tomatoes). Even matching seventh-grade boyfriends named Ben.

And most recently, a mutual dislike of Caryn, who had been instrumental in getting Melvin Stewart appointed as deputy mayor when her late husband vacated the position.

"I mean, *of course* a booth about beach reads would have been amazing," Cady said. "It's just that the group couldn't seem to come to a consensus about which books we should recommend."

And by *couldn't come to a consensus*, Cady meant *nearly resulted in a lawsuit*.

In Myrtle's defense, she hadn't meant to throw *Ice Planet Barbarians* at Townsend Harbor's former first lady. The septuagenarian's half-inch-thick bifocals just tended to make depth perception a challenge.

"I read *The Poisonwood Bible* while we were summering in St. Paul de Vence, and the Mediterranean was a deeper blue for it. I believe Townsendites and even the...tourists," she said, encasing the word in ice, "would be better for it." Myrtle took a lavender shortbread from her plate and dipped it into her teacup. "And I still say *'Harbarians'* need blue alien dick."

Either an elephant had sneezed, or Bob's sinuses had just tried to violently exit his head. Seated at the table Cady always set up for anyone who wanted to come in out of the cold on book club nights, her new handyman coughed into his fist as a kid with ear gauges and blond dreads thumped him between the shoulder blades.

"You'll get used to it, brother," the kid said, reaching for a scone with a hand sporting a brand-new pair of Gemma's fingerless gloves.

"Must our conversations always devolve to this topic?" Caryn asked crisply. Her masterfully rejuvenated lips pursed as she sipped the Sauvignon Blanc she'd poured from a bottle she brought then stashed beneath her chair.

"Bare-Naked Book Club *is* a romance-centric reading group," Gemma pointed out. Egging Myrtle on was one of her favorite pastimes, and considering the obvious discomfort it was causing Caryn, Cady wasn't about to stop her.

"I, for one, think Myrtle makes an excellent point." Vivian, proprietress of Townsend Harbor's first vagina-centric boutique, had entered the chat. A retired sexual anthropologist in her Mirren-esque mid-seventies, Vee had a way of legitimizing even the wildest of Myrtle's observations.

It was the accent, she and Gemma had decided.

"I thought the author's decision to fit the male *Sa-Khui* with ridged phalluses bearing clitoral stimulation glands at their base is an important statement about the prioritization of the female orgasm. Which, you don't have to be an anthropologist to know, is frequently not reflective of lived experience."

Gemma reached out and bumped knuckles with Vee, flicking her fingers in a dramatic mic drop.

"Isn't that the truth." Myrtle took another cookie from the tray. "Beautiful man, but my Frank couldn't find a clit with a GPS pin and a headlamp. And that was *before* the cataracts."

Cady glanced back at Bob to find the back of his neck had turned an alarming shade of crimson.

"If you'd had my Nigel, God bless him, you'd have *wished* he couldn't." Vee ran an arthritis-afflicted hand through her shock of ash-gray hair. "He'd rub so hard I wasn't sure whether to he was trying to turn me on or burn it off."

"Question?" Gemma said, raising her hand.

"Of course, darling."

"If Nigel was so terrible at it, why did you keep having sex with him?"

A misty look came into Vee's gray eyes. "Because I loved him. And it's what you did then, wasn't it? It wasn't until I discovered Judith Krantz that my *real* education began." Her cheeks lifted in a mischievous smile. "Of course, Nigel was a bit scandalized at first. But he was a quick study. I think he might have enjoyed E.L. James had the aneurysm not got him."

"May he rest," Myrtle said. An unintentional moment of silence followed. "What about you, Caryn?" she asked, attempting to draw their mostly silent member back into the conversation. "Was E.T. the Third a secret sexual dynamo, or were you counting cracks in the ceiling like the rest of us?"

Cady felt herself cringe hard enough to fold her own liver. Though Myrtle had become one of her favorite humans in the world, she had the subtlety of a dump truck.

Setting her wine glass down with a decisive clink, Caryn pulled herself to her full designer-heel- and pantsuit-wearing height. "There *are* no cracks in Townsend Hall's ceilings." Lifting her expertly enhanced chin, she turned on her red-soled shoe and marched toward the bathroom. "If you'll excuse me."

"Definitely a dud," the fertilizer maven diagnosed.

"Maybe we could take it just a little bit easy?" Cady scooted forward in her seat, careful to keep her arm close to her torso. When she was finally free from her sling, she intended to burn it and dance naked over the ashes.

Having finished all the cookies on the plate, Myrtle turned her attention to the truffles. "Excuse me all to hell for speaking ill of the dead. But she didn't seem to like him very much while he was alive."

Cady had formed a similar impression. The pictures of Townsend Harbor's royal couple featured in almost every issue of the *Townsend Leader* showed an attractive but stiff pairing. The handsome silver fox of a patriarch's hands always floated near his wife's elbow or shoulder. Never her hip, her waist, or the small of her back.

The realization punched Cady straight in the solar plexus and brought on an unexpected wave of sadness.

No wonder Ethan struggled with expressions of affection.

He'd grown up an only child in a household where he hadn't seen much in the way of PDA.

Cady's heart broke for him a little then. The serious man from a serious household with a serious family name to uphold. A man who had very likely been a serious boy who was seriously lonely.

A man whose love language had likely become acts of service by default. Like installing new locks. And panic buttons. And security cameras, like he was set to put in after the book club finished this evening.

"There are all kinds of reasons a person may not feel comfortable displaying affection—we're talking about their sexual preferences," Cady said. "That's why we put rule number three in place, remember? We don't yuck someone else's yum. Like alien dick. Or voyeurism. Or bondage. Or voyeurism."

"Precisely that," Vee said, angling her slim shoulders to Myrtle. "I know she gets right up your nose and seems to enjoy doing so, but there's enough misogyny out there without our helping those bastards tear us down. Our antagonizing one another—"

"Only benefits the patriarchy," Myrtle finished in the grudging tone of a chastised schoolgirl.

"It's like we said when we created this club in the first place..." Vee said.

"Maiden, mother, virgin, whore. They don't write our stories anymore..." Cady began.

"Vampires, lairds, pirates, earls—we're taking smut back for the girls," Vee, Gemma, and Myrtle recited in unison.

Though Vee's remarks were aimed at Myrtle, Cady felt chastened as well. She hadn't exactly harbored the most charitable feelings toward Ethan's mother for a variety of reasons not altogether Caryn's own fault. Radiating money and petite, pretty privilege, Caryn Townsend always made Cady feel...ungainly. Uncouth. Uncultured.

All of the *un,* basically.

"I think I'm going to go check on her," Cady said, carefully rising from her chair.

She found Caryn not in the bathroom but outside it, squinting as she ran a manicured fingertip along a jagged hairline crack in the old plaster.

"Bob will be starting on that once he's finished with the roof," Cady said.

"Oh dear." Caryn's eyes widened in polite concern. "I'm not sure if you realize, as you've only taken over operations so recently, but as it's a building on the national registry of historic landmarks, all repairs to the Townsend Building must be completed by a licensed contractor preapproved by the city council and Historical Preservation Society."

Cady felt her intended apology turned to ash on her tongue. "I did, actually. I reached out to a contractor on the mainland, but he's booked solid until February. I didn't want the crack to get any worse."

"Dick Sullivan?"

Cady nodded.

Caryn's eyes lit with pleasure. "He's an old family friend." Because of course he was. "If you like, I could ask him about moving you up the schedule."

"I couldn't ask you to do that."

"You're not asking," Caryn said, reaching out to squeeze Cady's elbow. "I'm offering. We're neighbors, after all. The sooner this beautiful building is restored to its former glory, the better for the entire town."

Cady's stomach knotted around the single oatmeal chocolate chip cookie she'd eaten this evening. "That's very kind of you," she said through a tight jaw.

"Not at all," Caryn said. "I told Ethan that after what had happened the other day, you could probably use a little cheering up."

"That reminds me," Cady said. "I've been meaning to thank you for the lovely plant. It brought me...so much comfort."

"Of course, dear. There's nothing like a little greenery to brighten up the place." Caryn touched a dusty leaf from the fake fig plant parked in the corner. "Isn't it amazing how lifelike they can make these look these days?"

"Amazing," Cady agreed.

"Well, I shouldn't be keeping you. Ethan mentioned he'd be stopping by after the book club is over. He'd never forgive me if I contributed to your tardiness." Caryn's beauty-pageant-worthy white smile was dazzling even in this context.

Cady ducked into the bathroom and took several deep breaths. When she no longer felt the urge to smash the old-fashioned shaving mirror, she removed her glasses and cleaned them before putting them back on. Rather than rejoining the group, she made a beeline for the card table near the front window.

Bob sat up straighter at her approach, confirming her suspicion that he'd been listening to every word of their discussion. And was most likely scarred for life now as a result.

"Everyone doing okay?" she asked.

The weathered-looking men seated there murmured their assent, none of them bothering to glance up from the assortment of magazines she typically left out for them.

"Anything I can bring anyone?"

"Got any more of those dairy-free vegan carob brownies?" Dreads glanced up from a 1970s issue of Italian *Vogue*.

"I think so," she said. "Anyone need a coffee refill while I'm back there?"

Four hands, each bearing a different color of fingerless gloves, rose.

"I'll help." Bob scraped back in the folding chair she hadn't been certain would hold his considerable mass.

"You don't have to do that," Cady assured him. "I can get it."

"Could use a breath of fresh air," he said.

Their eyes met, and she understood.

As he worked wonders on her roof upstairs, the time he could spend indoors had slowly increased. She'd moved the card table closer to the window for his benefit, but more than once had noticed him glancing longingly at the door.

"All right, then." She headed back past the bathroom and didn't miss Gemma's raised brows as she looked up from the paperback she was busily covering with a deconstructed brown paper bag.

Now with sixty-five percent less beard and fifty percent more flannel, and occasionally a hundred percent less shirt, Bob was giving hardcore lumbersnack.

And Cady wasn't immune.

Only yesterday, she'd come upstairs to find him at the top of a ladder, low-slung jeans revealing the infamous V muscles, and caught herself lingering a few breaths longer than strictly necessary before making her presence known.

She did the same now as he stood in the open doorway, gulping in breaths of air heavy with rain and wood smoke.

The tension in his jaw seemed to have eased incrementally when he joined her in the kitchen and closed the door.

As he stood at the counter filling the coffee carafe, she couldn't help but mentally map the location of the various tattoos she'd noticed during yesterday's ladder incident.

Tattoos, and *scars*. The worst of them was the angry purplish gash that snaked from the bottom of his shoulder blade and around the left side of his rib cage.

However he'd gotten it, it hadn't healed pretty.

Opening the fridge, she pulled out a bakery box and lifted the lid in search of the requested confection. "You doing okay out there?"

"Yep," he grunted.

"But I mean, like, really okay," she said, lifting a dense, sticky square of "brownie" onto the plate.

"Yeah," his broad back answered.

"Like, *really* really?"

He glanced at her over his shoulder. "Really. You?"

"Mmhmm."

"Really?" he repeated, eyes slightly narrowed.

"Totally." She nodded enthusiastically, deciding to add some fresh strawberries to the plate for some color.

Bob set the coffee carafe down on the counter and turned to face her, angling his long legs out in front of him and leaning back against the counter to bring them closer to eye level.

Closer being a relative term.

He cocked his head, studying her with an intensity that made patches of heat break out all over her skin. "Really?"

What sort of wizardry he had attached to the last round, she couldn't be sure. Only that she felt her tongue loosening, her mouth opening, and, following a shrill laugh, a torrent of words erupting.

"Yeah, no. Totally not okay. That woman out there? The expensive-looking one with the annoyingly perfect hair? That's the sheriff's mother, and I'm pretty sure she thinks I shouldn't be trusted with this building. And if that weren't bad enough, she's also the one who gave me the plant that I gave you head trauma with. And Ethan is supposed to stop by later, and now I have no idea what to say to him, because he's installing security cameras that I really need, but now I'm afraid that it's some strange nice-guy gesture of affection? So, I'm not sure if I should ask him not to do that because it might be considered leading him on? Even though I know better, I can't stop thinking about this other man whose voice basically haunts me twenty-four seven despite the fact that he's a completely dysfunctional human being with more red flags than the Daytona 500 and who doesn't want to meet me in person."

His no-longer-chapped lips curled at the corners. "That all?"

"Also, I'm afraid that our booth at the fall festival is going to be a fucking disaster because Jesus Christ, Myrtle."

Bob crossed his massive arms across his equally massive chest. A puff of air scented of soap, clean skin, fabric softener, and the pheromone equivalent of pure heroin floated over to her nostrils.

Her nipples hardened against her bra.

Was she ovulating?

"Let him put them in."

Cady's eyes widened as she felt the unmistakable rush of heat between her thighs.

She *had* to be ovulating.

Bob pushed himself away from the counter and positioned his big body between her and the several sets of curious eyes pretending not to be peering through the doorway. "Whether or not you and the sheriff have a future together, he'd want yours to be safe."

As soon as he said it, Cady knew he was right. And somehow, that made her feel even worse.

"As to this other man. Maybe you ought to call him. Tell him how you feel. If he has any kind of honor at all, he'll either tell you how he does, or let you go."

"Tell him how I feel," Cady repeated, chewing on a thumbnail. "I can do that."

She hoped.

"That ought to do her." Ethan stood back, admiring his handiwork.

Any woman in her right mind would have been admiring *him*. In jeans and a white undershirt, he looked as wholesome and delicious as hot apple pie.

Emphasis on hot.

Cady always cranked the radiator up on BNBC nights to accommodate the soft-tissue- and subcutaneous-fat-lacking elderly members of their number, as well as those who got to spend a precious hour or two out of the cold. When it had come time to un-crank, the knob elected not to cooperate, and now hissed to life every few minutes.

All the while, Cady imagined the numbers on her gas bill steadily climbing like an old-fashioned ticker tape.

"Thanks so much for doing that," she said, fanning herself with the stack of mail she hadn't yet convinced herself to open. "I really appreciate your help."

"Happy to," he said, folding up the foot ladder he'd brought from his personal collection of Useful Objects Adults Owned.

These few phrases represented the sum total of their communication for the evening, and Cady couldn't help but hope it stayed that way. The sooner Ethan packed up and left, the sooner she could take her night meds and go stick her head in a freezer.

"About the other night..."

Everlasting shit balls, please, dear God, no. Not now.

"It's totally okay," she insisted. "We just got caught up in the moment. I mean, who hasn't?" A bead of sweat crawled from under her breast down her stomach. "You don't need to apologize."

Ethan set his tool chest down on the table and took a step toward her. "I wasn't going to."

"Oh." Cady's mail fan accelerated from *Is that so?* to *I beg your pardon?*

"I liked it." Beneath the sable tips of his long lashes, Ethan's eyes flickered over her lips before rising. "I like *you*, Cady."

Coward that she was, Cady had been hoping they could circumvent this conversation altogether. That after her performance the other night, Ethan would quietly turn his attentions to any of the more proportionally appropriate, climate-tolerant bachelorettes who practically hunted him like a prize elk.

"I like you too, Ethan. So ridiculously much."

"But..."

"What's that?" She covertly mopped her chin and upper lip as he turned to glance out the front window.

"There's always a 'but' when someone says it like that."

Always. The word deepened the sinkhole in the center of her chest.

"But..." She sighed. "I'm just in a really weird place right now. Ever since Aunt Fern died, I just feel kind of...lost? I have no idea what I'm doing, or what I want. And it's just not fair to you." Despite the fact that her skin had become its own heat source, Cady laid a hand on his forearm. "You're such a good man, Ethan. And any woman would be so lucky to have you."

He nodded slowly. "I understand."

She wanted to ask him which part. Maybe all of it. Maybe none.

"I better go." After shrugging into his flannel, he picked up his tools and looped an arm through the ladder. "Have a good night, Cady."

The reflexive "you too" died on her lips. She had pretty much guaranteed that he wouldn't.

Her night, on the other hand, hinged on one simple possibility.

Whether the phone would ring.

NINE

Deviant

('DI:VIƏNT) ADJ. A PERSON WHOSE BEHAVIOUR, ESP SEXUAL, DEVIATES FROM WHAT IS CONSIDERED TO BE ACCEPTABLE

LOOK AWAY.

Fox repeated the order to himself for the eleventy-ninth time as he dragged his binoculars away from Cady and back to the first floor. Willing his racing heart to slow, he surveyed the visible perimeter, finding nothing at either entrance or window, and checked Nevermore's balconies, on which he'd installed motion detector lights.

Quiet. Dark. Good.

He snapped his sights back to her window before giving the action any conscious thought.

Holy. Fucking. Shit.

Cady getting ready for bed had to be sexier than actual porn. Even the good stuff.

Look away. It doesn't matter what she said about voyeurism being hot. Look away.

Despite the ice-needle rain barely held at bay by the quick shelter he'd built from driftwood and a camo tarp, he was suddenly sweltering enough for his blood to catch fire.

She'd danced out of the bathroom with her earbuds in, wearing nothing but a barely there tank and some boy-briefs, attempting to wrestle a brush through her chaotic hair with one hand.

The feverish rushing in his veins had heated him at first. But now it headed to his dick, and before long, he'd lose feeling in his bloodless fingers and toes.

You can protect her without peeping on her, dipshit. His conscience biffed him upside the head.

She could also not prance around in front of the third-floor window with her heavy, unbound tits threatening to bounce out of her tiny tank.

It was damn obvious she was cold. And that her nipples were small compared to her breasts. They were probably pink.

Slamming the door on that thought, he scowled. She should put on a sweater.

Or a long, fluffy robe.

A nun's robes.

Nope. Sexy, dammit.

A HAZMAT suit might do it. Like those yellow ones they wore back in pandemic early days. That might be enough coverage to put his pecker back to sleep.

Except just then, she turned away from the window.

Every one of his muscles jerked as he ripped the binoculars away, emitting a pathetic sound somewhere between a groan and a whimper.

Didn't matter if he stabbed himself right in the cornea—the sight of her pale, plump ass playing peekaboo with the edge of her cheeky shorts would be the one image he clung to until the bullet out there with his name on it found its forever home.

Hell, the sight was tattooed on the back of his eyelids now.

Attempting a peek, he immediately slammed them shut again, as he'd caught her bending over a drawer.

Without the binoculars, he hadn't seen anything. Not really. Not the outlines of her sex against the thin cotton. Not the generous backside exposed to the entire fucking world.

But he could, though. His fingers itched to bring the binoculars back to the bridge of his nose.

He didn't.

He wanted to.

She liked it. If what she claimed at Book Club was to be believed.

Still, he didn't. If this sort of self-control didn't win him back a few points from the devil, he'd fight the fucker for his throne.

Swallowing from his water bottle did little to cure a mouth gone terminally dry. Jesus Christ, he needed to put a stop to this. Someone could be coming up the stone steps from Downtown to Uptown anytime and get an eyeful of his Cady.

Wait. Of Cady. *Not his.* She was her own woman.

Never his.

Don't be overprotective. His inner voice dripped with disgust. *The median age in this town is fifty. Who's trying to climb these stairs at midnight on a fall Thursday?*

Putting the phone up to his ear, he listened to the peal on his end, then watched her react in real time.

She shuffled toward the charging station with her electronics and checked the number on the phone.

He ached to see her face.

Not that the view wasn't incredible from this end.

Still, how often had he dreamed about this very thing? Months. Since the first time he'd heard her voice on the other end of the line. A singular sound that brought his body...his *soul* back from the very nearly literal dead.

Fox's heart plummeted when she returned the phone to the charging station.

Closing his eyes, he shrank into the dank ground threatening to soak even his water-resistant bedroll.

She wasn't going to take his—

"I was worried you wouldn't call."

Peeling his lids open, he drank in the sight of her adjusting her earbuds with a smile so wide he couldn't just hear it in her voice.

He could see it. He could watch it illuminate the vicious cold and threaten to summon warmth.

He could feel it.

The timbre of a woman so genuine, of vibrations of pure pleasure emitted by her lovely throat. He tried to consider how far those sounds traveled into the cosmos only to bounce from a satellite to land just when his heart threatened to forget what warmth felt like.

"Fox? You there?"

Shit. "Yeah. Sorry. Lag in the connection."

It was nice not to have to carefully modulate each word, to relax his voice enough to allow his throat a much-needed break.

"It's okay." Across the way, she grunted, panted, and strained. If Fox couldn't see that she was struggling into a pair of pajama bottoms with disembodied coffee mugs on them, he'd have assumed he'd interrupted great sex.

Still, using some sort of one-handed woman magic and way too much wriggling and bouncing for his physical comfort, she succeeded before collapsing on the edge of her bed with a burst of relief.

"You...okay over there?" he asked, pretending ignorance.

"Oh. Ha. Sorry. I was just wresting with my... Erm." She looked down at her lap, hand going to her belly where it stretched the waistband of her pants. "With my conscience. Guess what? I won." Snickering at her own misdirection, she began an awkward, adorable three-legged crab walk back to her pillow before collapsing like a starfish-sans-left-arm in the middle of the bed.

From his vantage point, he had to look up her body to see her face, starting at the soles of her feet where the bottom of her socks demanded, BRING. WINE.

Wow, her evening fashion sure was passionate about beverages.

"How is your shoulder?" he asked, frowning when she winced and adjusted the strap.

"Hurts," she grumbled. "But what's new? How's the..." Her

foot bounced like a metronome for a moment as she searched for a word. "How's the job?"

Fucking killing him right now.

"Good. Taking longer than expected."

"You don't sound upset about that."

"I'm not."

An odd silence, pregnant with all the things said and unsaid between them, seemed to even blanket the storm with its oppression.

He should say something.

"Fox?"

"Yeah?"

"What do you do?" Her foot was bouncing again. Back and forth. Back and forth.

A pendulum.

And he was the pit.

"I work in...deliverables."

"What kind of deliverables?"

"The kind people get paid to protect. Usually human."

"Is that what you are? Usually human?"

He snorted. "Less than that. More like barely human."

He was an animal. A beast. For watching her like this. For lying to her. For the things he wanted to do to her.

And what he wished she'd do to him.

"You're quiet tonight," she said. "You remind me of Bob right now."

Fucking shit snacks. "Bob?" He very, *very* distinctly did not say that like Bob would have.

"Yeah, he's this... Well, he's a..."

Forcing himself to breathe, he wondered if anyone ever actually died from anticipation.

And he'd spent thirteen straight hours on a sniper hill, for the sake of all fucks.

"He's the...handyman I hired to fix my roof." Her voice stiffened, along with the rest of her. She was feeling defensive.

About Bob.

Interesting.

"I'm trying to decide if you're complimenting me or insulting me," he teased. "How do you feel about this Bob, who, I'm hoping from the name, is some beer-bellied contractor who plays Santa for his grandkids?"

Her laugh didn't break the tension, but it certainly made it more flexible. "Bob? Oh, he's... Well. He's like... I mean—most of the time he's just..." She cleared her throat. "I'm not exactly sure how to describe Bob. He can do just about anything, I think. But people don't see that about him. He's terse but really patient. Kind but damaged. Probably the best employee I've ever had."

Fox had to swallow twice before replying. "And...how are we alike?"

Another laugh shimmered in the moist air between them. "Well, mostly it's that I've had just about enough of awkward silences from you both," she chastised him with a wry grin. "But you're better now."

He basked in the sparkle of warmth between them. "I started that book you—"

"So about these deliverables," she interrupted in the way of polite people who are embarrassed to interrupt. "Do you protect them for, like...private entities such as drug cartels? Or like the government? Oh my God, or are you Taylor Swift's bodyguard?"

"Think about as far from the glamor of Taylor Swift as you can get." He eyed a leak forming in his shelter.

"So...government, then."

"Yup."

"Just because I've heard people are listening over the phone, let's be clear...*our* government, right?"

That elicited a chuckle from him. "Yes. Rest assured, I'm not a spy or a terrorist."

"I don't know. I'm pretty sure that's what a spy or a terrorist would say."

"What would it take to convince you?"

"A last name would be a great start." Levity still hung between them, but the laughter had disappeared.

With a big sigh, he said, "I could tell you, but..."

"Rude."

"Ask me anything else, Cady. I'll answer."

She paused, then sat up a bit, propping herself on a pillow. She didn't look victorious, but, rather, troubled. As if she'd not expected him to relent. "I don't know... Um, if you had been voted most likely to do anything in high school, what would it be?"

A hand went to smack her forehead as if by memory of repetition.

"I was, actually," he answered honestly.

"Shut up." Her jaw dropped open.

"Most likely to succeed."

"Of course." She snorted. "Of course you were popular. Bet you were homecoming king too, huh?"

Prom king. Didn't matter. "I was...different then."

She cocked her head. "Different how?"

The woman was trying to get to know him, and to allow it would be... Well, it'd be cruel in the end. "In all the ways that matter," he finished lamely. "What about you? Voted most likely to...?"

Her laugh was an astonished bark. "Are you kidding? People know better than to vote for me! But I'd say it would have been most likely to choke on Lucky Charms in bed...which I did. Twenty minutes ago."

"You're in bed?" Damn, he hadn't meant it to sound like he'd been waiting for her to admit it.

"I am."

"Did I call too late?" Usually they spoke all hours, but she was still on pills for her injury and had had somewhat of a shit week. "Should I go?"

"No. Don't go. I haven't slept lately, and I'm glad I have you to chat with instead of listening to all the voices in my head until

I'm driven toward multiple snacks. The later the time gets, the more the future gets very dark...very specific." She laughed, but this time it was her nervous laugh. An audible LOL to lighten the mood and fill space.

"Are you okay, Cady?" he asked.

"Probably? I'm having a break, but whether it's a *through* or a *down* is yet to be decided. But I ended things...well, with this guy I went on a couple of dates with. His mother is sort of a big name in local happenings. Founding town family and all that clichéd shit. She could make my life difficult."

"Yeah? Why do you think she'll be upset?"

"I don't know." She let out a frustrated sigh and flopped a bit. "The same reason she goes south of the border and sucks the blood of little children. She gets off on terrifying local villagers."

Damn her for making him laugh.

"Why break it off?" he asked before he could think better of it. "Is he the kind of guy that would put truck nuts on his Toyota Corolla?"

Or...did it have something to do with the fact that, even at this moment, she might be feeling the need to change her panties?

The thought of the panty stash in her desk made him bite into his knuckles.

"No. He's a great guy. The best, really. It's just... I saw a glimpse of our future, and trust me, it ended in a bitter divorce."

Good. Then he wouldn't have to divorce old Ethan's head from his body.

"His mom's a real chupacabra, then?"

"The worst. I keep trying to run her out of our Bare-Naked Book Club, but she keeps insisting on *showing up* and then spending the entire time shitting all over the books. I keep pushing the genre into deeper and deeper kinks in hopes she'll just give up altogether." She ticked them off on her fingers. "I've tried the bondage, the reverse harem, the bullies, the spanking, every paranormal creature you can think of and then some. Tonight we discussed the pros and cons of barbed blue alien dick...and do you think this woman left? No! She hated it. I could tell. But I think she's a secret *freak*."

"Blue alien dick...is that what women are into these days? With the barbs and whatnot? If so, I'm in trouble. I mean...it can get a bit purple when it's been too long or something, but no barbs."

She gave a shy giggle, lifting her finger to twirl in her hair. "Do you have a kink, Mr. Fox?"

Yeah. You.

"I-I don't know...maybe. You ever read *Fifty Shades* or anything like that?"

"Couldn't own a bookstore and not read it."

"What did you think?" Jesus, he was on thin ice here...

"I mean, it was sexy, but not a fantasy of mine."

"You don't like to be tied up?" This felt like something he already knew without asking.

"I think I'm just too boring for that kind of thing."

"I hear you. I'm about all different flavors of sex, but that's not one of them for me, either." If he couldn't stand four walls, handcuffs would make him lose the few marbles he had left.

Her giggle lifted in pitch with her shyness. "Am I mistaken when I say sex only has one flavor? I guess more if you have the flavored condoms."

"You don't know how wrong you are," he said. His body, having relaxed to half-mast, was now hard as a diamond again. "There are all sorts of flavors," he mused, wrapping his fingers into a fist so they didn't go where they ought not to. "Soft and sweet. Salty and sweaty. Hard and..." *Fucking Christ, you masochistic shitsack, shut your mouth.*

"Jiggly?" she finished.

He almost managed a laugh.

She sobered. "You've...been with a lot of women, I suppose."

"Not really." He lifted the binoculars to his eyes. "I married young."

"Oh?" He watched a shifting-eye argument she had with

herself while she chewed off half the inside of her cheek. "What happened?" She clapped her hand over her mouth as if she'd not meant to ask.

"I promised her the world. What she got was me." A familiar pang alarmed him. Not because of its presence. But because of how muted it'd become.

Jenny had moved on before he came to the PNW. He was just a bad memory to her now. Some short-lived mistake in her past. They were too young to have married, both eager to see the world and be adults.

She wasn't prepared for the soldier who returned home. No one could be.

"It's in the past. All for the good."

"So...we're both...free?"

"I'm single. But not necessarily free..." He was a prisoner of his own mind and would never be free to give her the life she deserved.

He'd tried for Jenny. He'd done everything he could. The boner-killing, mind-numbing meds. The endless therapy. The—

"Still more than me, probably."

"What?" As per usual, she pulled him back from a dark place.

"Women you've had sex with," she said in a stage whisper.

"I mean...how many women have *you* had sex with? I'll tell you if my number is higher." Fox allowed the heat of the conversation to rekindle the cold places he'd exposed.

"That's not what I meant, and you know it!" She threw a pillow at the wall, and it absolutely would have been him if he'd been standing there to catch it.

He ached to be.

"You want my sex partner count?" he teased.

She pressed her lips together. "Um...is it more than you can count on both hands?" she asked.

"It is."

"Then no. Is it fifty? Wait, don't tell me. It's not over a

hundred, is it? I don't want to know. It probably is—you sound insanely hot."

Shifting uncomfortably, he scratched at his mostly wet hair. "I'm—"

"It's not that I care," she rushed out. "I'm just...jealous, I guess."

"Jealous?"

"Of women who got to"—she slapped a hand over her mouth—"meet you," she finished, the words garbled through her fingers.

He didn't know what to say to that, and the silence stretched out for a beat too long, like a decision had already been made, but neither of them wanted to admit it.

"Is the reason really your job?" she asked. "Why we can't meet, I mean?"

"Yes."

"When will you be done?"

Never. "I can't say."

She did a little silent tantrum on her bed that would have been so cute if he'd not been the cause of it. "You keep calling. We keep...connecting. Flirting. And after last time I just thought—I don't know. If you really *can't* meet, I understand, but I just need to know. Am I barking up the wrong tree here? Do you...even *want* to meet me?"

"It's because I want to so much that makes it so dangerous," he blurted.

"But *why* would it be dangerous?" she asked. "Who are you, Jason Bourne? I mean, come on." She flailed her one good arm.

Not even close.

"Cady, if I ever meet you, I will have a hard time stopping myself from fucking you on the first hard surface I can find."

Choking on a gasp, she sat all the way up and clutched her heart as if it might give out. "You would?"

He didn't relent. If she could drive away Caryn with alien dick, then he could show her a bit of shock and awe.

Give her a glimpse of his dark desires where she was concerned.

"Woman, I'd do things you haven't thought of yet."

As he spoke, she lifted her fingertips to her mouth, lightly tracing the full seam before charting a course down the gentle column of her neck. She let an idle touch drift over the swell of her breast before meeting the line of her tank.

Fox fell silent, his entire body thrumming with unspent need.

"I'd like that," she said in that small voice she had when the truth made her shy and bold at the same time.

Her finger dipped beneath the thin fabric, edging toward her nipple.

Fox could almost feel the especially creamy delicacy of the thinner skin of her breasts, the tighter gather of her areola, the puckered nipple waiting to be stroked.

"Do it," he ordered her in a harsh rasp.

She froze. "What?"

"You want to touch yourself, don't you?"

"Um..." She glanced at the hand paralyzed in exploration.

"The truth," he demanded darkly. "You can't hide from me, Cady. I see you."

"I wish you could." Her breathy confession nearly did him in. "I wish you would order me around so I knew what you liked. I wish I could see you, too..."

"I'll tell you what I like." He should be gentler. Coaxing and tender. She'd had a tough day...they both had. But his frustration made his voice as hard as his dick.

A tension in her features pulled him in—a pinch of need mixed with uncertainty that broke his heart and inflamed his body at the same time.

"I'll tell you what I'd like, woman. If you do what I say."

Her body went limp as she indulged in a silent freakout. "Okay...probably."

"I'd like to make you come."

That did it.

Cady bit her lip and squeezed her eyes so tightly shut, the creases turned white. Were they going to do this? He fucking hoped so. It was the only way he could ever allow himself to make love to her.

By making her love herself.

"Okay..." she breathed. "Tell me what to do. What you like."

He was glad she couldn't see how many teeth his smile exposed. He must look like a wolf about to dine.

"I like soft women." He did nothing to keep the gravel from his voice now. "Are you soft, Cady?"

"Too soft." Her moan was half lament.

"No such thing," he growled. "Talk like that will get you punished."

Fox wasn't close enough to see the flash of interest in her eyes, but he did hear her sudden intake of breath. "I'll be good."

"Not when I'm done with you."

He knew she'd not meant to whimper by how fast she choked it off.

"What would your tits feel like in my hands, Cady? Cup them. Stroke them. Do they want attention tonight?"

Her chin lifted, and a hint of bewilderment and wonder broke through her gathering mask of arousal. It almost seemed like he'd pleased her in a way that had nothing to do with sex.

With a deep breath, she slid her fingers around the orb of her breast and lifted, caressing it with her thumbs, testing the tight peak with an audible gasp.

"Tell me, Cady."

"It's, um... They're...heavy. And...not firm."

A smile stole across his lips again, this one filled with infinite tenderness beneath the pulsing need. "Soft. Just like I need them... Go lower."

She cleared her throat and tugged her hair in mortification, but finally said, "Okay," and angled south, toying with the waistband of her sleep pants.

"Your ribs," he said. "Your stomach. Caress a path down to

your hips, but take your time. Make sure every part of your skin knows where you're headed and will be alive when you finally get where I'm taking you."

To her credit, she followed his commands, fingers drifting down a long torso with dramatic curves. "You can't see my ribs," she warned him. "I don't have abs."

"Remember what I said about soft," he murmured. She was everything he wanted. Someone not hardened by the hatred in this world. Not toned by toughness. Nor shaped by an industry that hated the curves women were supposed to have. Not just tits and ass, but shoulders, arms, tummy, and legs.

A woman was everything. Everything. Everything. The smallest could be the strongest. The largest could be the most sensitive. The gentlest heart could have the toughest walls built high around it.

Cady was beautiful because of her softness, in all the ways.

"I like to find something to hold on to when I reach for a woman," he said honestly. "Now open your legs."

She squeaked a little, but her knees drew up and fell apart.

Holy *fucking* Christ, he'd never hated the sight of a coffee cup more in his entire life than the one on the seam of her sleep pants over the promised land. He'd suggest she get naked if he wouldn't feel like a shitheel for making her struggle with an injury.

Besides. The way his heart was beating in his chest, it would explode if he could see everything. And, damned as he may be, as permissive as her language was...there were lines he shouldn't cross.

"Touch your pussy for me," he growled.

"Oh. Um. Okay." Her voice hitched as her elbow straightened and long, manicured fingers disappeared beneath the drawstring and found her core. Her gasp was an echo of discovery.

"Tell me what you feel."

Her breath hitched and she squeezed her eyes shut. "I'm wet," she admitted tightly.

In the sling, her hand squeezed into a fist, as if it wanted to help hide her face and couldn't.

"I want you drenched, Cady. Listen to me." His voice became as hard as his cock. "Don't touch your clit. Go lower for me. Go deeper. Find where my cock would spread you open and dip your fingers inside."

"I-I'm... I-I've never like...without a toy or something." Her voice was tight. Tormented.

Tantalized.

"Get your fingers slick, honey. Just do what I say."

A soft sound, this time with more interest than agony. She'd brought her knees up further, rolled her hips forward. The way she would for a deep, deep dicking.

If he passed out, no one would blame him.

"What do you feel, Cady? Smooth silk?"

"No," she said with a soft sense of wonder. "It's...ridged. Pliant."

God love a woman who was a reader during naughty talk. Was there anything sexier?

"My fucking favorite," he growled. "Now take your slick fingers and softly stroke your clit for me."

"Dear God." The mortification had trickled back into her voice.

"No, Cady. No God in this place. Just me. And you. And the slippery folds of sex beneath your fingers."

She'd forgotten to say anything back, to give him affirmations or even acknowledgements. Lost in a sea of emotion that changed with each rolling wave, he watched her hand beneath the layers set a rhythm that planted her head far back in her pillow.

"That's it. Yes, baby. Stroke it for me." She did, her rhythm increasing along with her hitches of breath. "Would you like my mouth on it?"

"Yes," she panted.

"How?"

Her speed increased once more, and her hips lifted and squirmed.

Moisture flooded in at the suggestion, and though Fox had known hunger in his lifetime, nothing had even come close to this throbbing, pulsating, possessive, yawning emptiness.

A lifetime of this could never see him sated.

"Kiss it," she said.

"Soft brushes? Or..."

"Hard." She groaned. "Like you can't help yourself."

"I'm going to fucking devour you, Cadence Bloomquist."

"Yes."

"I'm going to wrench your legs open and crush my mouth over your clit, and you will get a savage tongue-lashing. I will be ruthless. Relentless. You will beg for mercy, and none will be given."

"Fox," she sobbed. "You can't say that. You— I can't—"

"If I was between your legs, woman, you'd never see them closed again. I'd dine like a man granted his last meal, drink your desire, and start an entire new course until you could physically take no more."

"Oh." It wasn't a word but a plea. "Fox. I..."

"You're close, aren't you?"

"*Yes.*"

"Come for me, Cady." He'd meant to order her, but it escaped as a supplication. "Let me hear you. Let me fantasize it's me bringing that throbbing little clit into my mouth and finishing you off."

Another sob washed him in chills as she snapped her legs closed and arched from the bed, driving her shoulders into the pillow and lifting her hips. She thrust against her hand in gentle rolls belied by the strength of her cries.

He counted the waves as they coursed through her. So strong at first, and then gentler, until she collapsed against the bed in a heap of limp limbs and labored breaths.

"Fuck me," he said, feeling something slick seep into the thin fabric of his boxers. "Cady I...I have to go." He was about to make a fool of himself in a minute, because the release gathering in his spine promised to be something a man in a rainstorm didn't deserve.

"Wait." She sat up, facing the window at such an angle that he feared she could actually see him for a moment. She couldn't...but the effect was eerie. "Not yet. I haven't... What about you?"

Tenderness swamped him in silence for a full breath. "What about me? Your pleasure is my pleasure. I'm not going to—"

"Fox." The strength in her voice stunned him into silence. "Fox. I'll let you go on one condition."

"What's that?" She'd better tell him before he died from lack of blood to the brain.

"You tell me truthfully that you want to hang up. Tell me... that you don't want my mouth around your cock."

TEN

Seduction

(SĬ-DŬK'SHƏN) THE ACT OF SEDUCING. ALSO. THE ACT OF BEING SEDUCED.

Cady lay on the bed, weak-limbed and pleasure-slack, dumbfounded by the words that had just exited her mouth, waiting for words to exit Fox's.

The speedball of endorphins, adrenaline, and oxytocin had already begun to be reabsorbed by her busy mind.

Ecstasy's short half-life.

Soon, there'd be a click. That almost imperceptible shift in sound that preceded the line going dead.

Only, it didn't come.

His silence broke with a strangled groan. An impossible tangle of pain, anger, pleasure, and surrender.

"Woman, I want your mouth on my cock more than I want air."

Cady buried her face in the pillow to stifle a squeak born of equal parts triumph and terror. Past the cock/mouth thing, she hadn't really assembled a plan. Should she guide him as he had her? Tell him what to put where and when?

Right. Because it wasn't like he already knew how to jerk off or anything.

"You still with me, baby?"

"I'm here. I just... I've never done this before, and I know this is super lame, but I don't even know what to say to...to make you—"

The sound of his hushing was like the summer wind through curtains.

"Baby, after listening to you come, you could talk about re-grouting your shower and I'd still be hard as a diamond."

"See? You said that like you didn't even have to think about it. You're so much better at this than I am. I don't even know how to pretend touch you in my head."

"Yes, you do." His voice held the thick husk of early morning. Of a body that would be warm beneath the covers and hard against her back. "You've thought about it before."

"Yes," she admitted.

"Tell me."

"I understand what you're trying to do here, and with any normal human it would probably work," she said. "But, like, *talking* my fantasy?"

"So it's your voice, then."

"Excuse me?"

"You don't like hearing yourself express what you really want. Or you're afraid you're doing it wrong."

"You don't know me," she teased.

"I know what you sound like when you come."

Cady pulled the sheet over her face like a shroud. "Loud?"

"Not loud," he said "Ecstatic. Like a Valkyrie who's just arrived in Valhalla to remember that she *is* Odin. That her voice caused the rocks to rise and the oceans to come together."

The warmth at her center spread like warm honey. "Mostly I thought I sounded like a car alarm."

"Did someone tell you that?" His voice darkened with the promise of retribution.

Someone had, in fact, but she wasn't about to tell him that. She already knew he was a man with a certain set of skills, and she wouldn't be surprised if disappearing bodies was one of them.

"Something tells me that won't aid our current conversation," she said.

"I have an idea," Fox said. "You know that toy you mentioned earlier?"

"Yes," Cady said.

"Get it."

Swallowing the lump in her throat, Cady crawled to the side of the bed and opened her nightstand drawer, where her Vibromax 5000 Jackrabbit with extendable ears and detachable suction cup base waited to be summoned into service. "Gotten."

"Good. Now close your eyes."

"Closed."

"Now, tell me like you would if it were a scene in a book. First-person present."

Already the images were forming in her mind. Fast and furious, the world assembled itself around her. The steep cliff over a storm-tossed sea. A tiny cottage with ivy growing up one side. A witchy forest, dark and deep, across a meadow strewn with wildflowers.

"What kind of flowers?"

Cady had barely registered that she was already describing what she saw until he asked.

"Lupins," she said. "I'm out gathering them when the storm clouds break, and I get caught in the downpour. I hadn't realized I'd wandered so far into the forest. I'm trying to shelter under a tree when I see you."

"What am I doing?" His voice was coiled tight as a bowstring.

"Riding toward me on a big black mount. I'm afraid at first, but then I see your eyes."

"What do they look like?"

"Kind," she said. Not unlike another pair of eyes she had grown especially fond of over the past week. "You ask me if I need help."

"And?"

"And I tell you that I live in the little cottage on the bluff. You offer to give me a ride and pull me on to the saddle in front of you. I can feel your powerful thighs against the backs of mine."

"You're not riding sidesaddle?"

"I wasn't raised as a lady," she explained. "Stop interrupting so I can get to the good part."

"Apologies, my non-lady."

"The rain is lashing our face as your horse speeds through the forest and across the meadow. Our hips begin to move together as we settle into the horse's gait. I can feel you starting to get hard against the small of my back."

"What does it feel like?" Fox's voice was breathy.

Cady rolled her hips against the mattress, mimicking her mind's movement inside her own body. "Powerful. I love knowing that I make you hard."

"You do, Cady," he ground out.

She whimpered as heat rippled through her core.

"What are you going to do about it?" he rasped.

"I reach behind me to the lacing of your breeches and move the wet leather to wrap my hand around your—" Cady swallowed hard "...cock."

Fox emitted a low *unh* that landed directly in Cady's already tensing abdominal muscles.

"You're so hard," she breathed. "So smooth. So hot." Cady's hand began to drift upward, lightly squeezing the hardened pearl of a nipple. "You're whispering the filthiest things into my ear as I work you up and down, up and down in time with the hoofbeats on the rain-soaked earth."

"What kind of things?"

Cady's fingers drifted downward over the round softness of her belly toward her inner thigh and the still-electrified flesh there.

"You tell me you want to be inside me. That you can tell how wet I'm going to be for you. That when we get back to the cottage, you're going to fuck me within an inch of my life."

She was rewarded with a groan.

"We don't say a word when we get there. You dismount and

lift me off, carry me across the threshold, and kick the door closed. We tear away each other's wet clothes before the fire, and I drop to my knees beside the hearth."

"Are you touching yourself, Cady?"

"Yes," she admitted. She wasn't certain when it had begun, only that somewhere in the world she'd built for them in her head, her words and her body had become one.

"You're so much more beautiful than I had even imagined," Cady said. "Like a god cast in glowing copper. I can't live another second without tasting you."

Fox's guttural grunt detonated a wave of gooseflesh that tightened her nipples.

"I trace every inch of your cock with my tongue." She could feel the flames dancing on their skin, hear the crackling against his ragged exhales. "I wrap my lips around you and take you in my mouth. I just hold you there at first. I can taste your heartbeat when you nudge the back of my throat. You start to move your hips. Curling your spine to fuck my mouth.

"Just when you're about to lose yourself, you tell me to kneel. You guide me down on all fours, and I can feel you there behind me." Her hand resumed its former rhythm, sliding through silken folds his words had inflamed. "You bury yourself inside me so deep, I can feel you in my soul."

"*Cady.*" Until now, no one had ever made a plea of her name. Certainly never one filled with such fire and demand. "Fuck yourself for me."

Eyes fastened shut, she reached for his proxy and coated it with her moisture before easing it inside. Behind the screens of her eyelids, that delicious fullness could be him. Stretching her, plumbing the parts of her nearest the source of her pain. Planting pleasure in its place.

The strangeness of using her left hand made the sensations harder to anticipate, teasing her to an awkward, exquisite agony.

"Make yourself come, baby," Fox ordered her. "I'm almost—"

Cady cried out as the world of her mind and her body fused at the orgasm that ripped through both at once. "*Fox.*"

"Oh fuck, Cady. *Fuck.*" His answer was heedless. Barely human. A roar that reset the world.

Only the sounds of their breathing filled the open channel between them.

"Cady?"

"I'm here," she said, lifting her face from the downy pillow.

"I wish," he rasped.

With those words, the idea clicked into place. She wasn't there, but she could be. In her mind, and in his.

"Tell me what you see," she said.

Another extended stretch of silence unfurled between them.

"I see the stars."

Cady rolled herself onto her side to face the windows. "I see them too."

A long beat passed.

"Fox?"

"Mmm?"

"I'm laying my head on your chest now. I can feel your heartbeat against my—" The rest of her sentence was hijacked by yawn.

"Your cheek," he finished. "Sleep, Cady."

With her imaginary head against the imaginary wall of his torso, she did.

ELEVEN

Uncertain

(ŬN-SÛR'TN). NOT CONFIDENT OR ASSURED; HESITANT.

Cady ought to be miserable.

The perfect storm of conditions had conspired to make the opening night of Townsend Harbor's annual fall festival a living hell.

The day drew near its end with the kind of damp chill that would quickly seep into her bones. The wind off the water was just strong enough to continually wreak havoc with the t-shirts, bookmarks, and bumper stickers she'd had made just for this occasion. And her booth had been relegated to the ass end of the block along with the other festival undesirables.

Technically speaking, the perineum end, seeing as her and Gemma's displays were sandwiched between Vee's Lady Garden booth on the right and Fertile Myrtle's Manure tent—complete with the soft-serve swirl tip of a poop emoji topper—on the left.

Directly across the street, Roy and his junk heap of distinctively un-festive offerings sat beneath the last working streetlight before scenic Water Street gave way to the boatyard, marina, breweries, industrial lots, and one of two strip malls the city council allowed.

On any other day, it would have made maintaining a sunny disposition a real challenge. Today, with the memory of Fox's rumbling moans in her ear and several phone-sex-induced orgasms under her belt, Cady couldn't manage to wipe the smile from her face.

"So are you going to tell me what the dopey smile is about?" Gemma plopped her bag down on the folding table where Cady was serenely creating stacks of their paper-bag-covered blind date books. Already, the air already held an intoxicating bouquet of festive scents. Kettle corn. Spiced nuts. Crisp apple cider.

Cady shrugged. "Just having a good body day," she said.

"Nice try, Bloomquist." Gemma's dark brow arched inquisitively. "I know a good body day smile, and that is *not* a good body day smile."

"Then what kind of smile is it?" Cady challenged.

"You really want me to say in mixed company?" Gemma jerked her chin toward Bob, who was securing the pole of the shade tent he'd single-handedly set up after dragging the folding table out of storage. A significant improvement over last year's installation, which saw Cady, Gemma, and Aunt Fern wrestling with the ancient canvas structure her aunt had insisted would be "a cinch" to set up.

Cady pushed the thought away before it could deepen into the ache she had been chasing away at all costs

"Bob? Would you mind grabbing a couple more of those easels for me?" Cady asked. "I think there's still a few left on—"

"The register," he finished for her. "On it."

They watched him stalk away with the single-minded purpose of the T-1000 water-cyborg thing from *Terminator 2*.

"He's certainly cleaned up nice." Gemma bit her thumbnail, her eyes fixed on Bob's jeans-clad ass.

Cady turned her attention to the garland of flowers made from old book pages Gemma had assembled after seeing one on TikTok. "Uh-huh."

"Is he still cleaning up in your shower?" her best friend asked not quite casually.

"Sometimes."

"And eating dinner with you?"

"Sometimes."

"Are these the only 'sometimes' activities I ought to be aware of?"

Cady held the garland to the end of the table for Gemma to secure with a clip. "Surely you're not suggesting that Bob is the cause of what you so judgmentally refer to as 'a dopey smile.'"

"*I'm* not suggesting it." Gemma smoothed the table skirt, picking off an errant dust bunny from the dark cloth. "But it is being suggested within certain circles."

"And which circles would those be?" Squinting at the arrangement, Cady swapped out a beautiful old leather-bound copy of *Moby-Dick* for a 1970s cookbook that cotton-candy-sticky fingers would be less likely to ruin.

"The Ethics Society, the Tourism Board, the Civic Engagement Collective. And the city council." Gemma handed her a second clip. "Just FYI, the city council also feels that it's too soon for you to be dating after breaking things off with Ethan."

The buoyant balloon of Cady's happiness began to deflate.

"My tax dollars at work." As soon as the words were out of her mouth, she wished she could call them back. "And before you say anything, I wrote the check, it's sitting on my desk, and I'll be sending it Monday."

"Well, that will be one less item for Mayor Stew to yammer on about."

Cady squatted to pull a canvas tote full of their blind date books out from under the table skirt. "First you complain about my not giving you enough gossip, and now you complain about my giving you too much?"

"It's not a complaint. Just an observation," Gemma said, stepping back to assess their display.

"Like you were observing Bob's ass just now?" Cady teased.

"Can I help it if I'm an aesthete?" Gemma asked. "How long are you planning on keeping our bearded, brawny shop bro, anyhow?"

"As long as he needs the money, or I need the help." Cady shrugged. "Is this you, or your constituency asking?"

"You know I'm not supposed to tell you official council business," Gemma said, accepting an armful of books.

"Since when has that mattered?"

Arms folded across a sweater with hand-crocheted leaves, Gemma had a shrewd gleam in her eyes. "I'll tell you if you tell me what the dopey grin was about."

"Fine. But we say it at the same time." This ritual had been established early on in their friendship when Cady discovered Gemma's unfortunate tendency to forget whatever juicy tidbit she'd been about to relay by the time Cady had ponied up hers. "On the count of three," Cady said. "One...two..."

"Ethan thinks Bob is wanted—"

"I had accidental phone sex with Fox—"

"*What?*" they said in unison.

"You had phone se—"

"Shhhht!" Cady hushed, grabbing her best friend's forearm. "Do you want the whole town to hear?"

"Hear what?" The silky, sophisticated voice of Caryn Townsend floated over them like a veil.

Cady steeled herself, taking a deep breath and plastering on a smile before turning to face the inevitable.

The Inevitable wore a cashmere turtleneck sweater dress of deepest ochre that hugged her still-trim figure and spiky oxblood boots that Cady wouldn't last five minutes in.

"Hear just how...excited we are about the costume contest," Gemma said quickly.

Caryn's eyes flicked over Cady's quite obvious lack of a thematically appropriate outfit.

"I was actually just about to go change," Cady explained.

"I just wanted to apologize for the last-minute shuffle," Caryn said, completely ignoring the perfect exit Cady had created for herself. "I know we promised you one of the spots in the town square, but Meadowlark Farms brought a booth two feet larger than we'd thought, and you know how much of a crowd favorite they are."

And, by extension, how much of a favorite Cady was *not*.

But far be it from her to deny anyone the glory that was freshly fried cheese curds. Her salivary glands contracted painfully at the thought.

"I hope you understand it's nothing personal." Caryn pouted and squeezed Cady's wrist with a kid-gloved hand.

"Of course," Cady said through a brittle smile.

They both knew it was patently bullshit. If she and Ethan were still an item, her book booth would be stationed directly next to Caryn's, smut or no smut.

"Oh, there's Mayor Stewart." Caryn waved down the street. "Don't these look...festive," she said, giving Cady and Gemma a simpering smile before pivoting on the slim point of her bootheel and sauntering off.

"Do you smell brimstone, or is it just me?" Gemma picked up one of the book stacks and began arranging them on the secondary layer of easels.

"Just you," Cady mumbled.

"Quick, tell me everything about the phone sex before Bob gets back."

A question that might have delighted her even five minutes ago now made her feel small and trashy in the wake of Hurricane Caryn.

Joy was hard to hold in a body like hers. It had a way of hemorrhaging when provided any outlet.

"I don't really feel like it, Gem," Cady said, deflated.

"Oh, come on." Gemma bounced impatiently. "At least tell me what Fox's orgasm noise sounds like."

"Gemma!" Cady scolded, rearranging the bookmark tree for the ten thousandth time.

Gemma folded her arms, the bright orange beret perched atop her dark head cocked at a jaunty angle. "He's not one of those quiet ones, is he? The kind where you're not sure if they actually came or they're just thinking real hard?"

Trouble was, in answering her friend's question, Cady found herself reliving the moment of Fox's unraveling all over again. His hoarse, shuddering breaths. His grunts and growls and beautifully filthy words. At least she could blame her glowing cheeks on the cold instead of a retroactive sex flush.

"Not that it's any of your business," Cady said, "but no, he's not."

"So, what then?" Gemma asked. "Rutting elk? Silverback in heat? You've got to give me *something*."

"Well, now you have me worried I did it wrong, because he didn't make any of those noises."

"Define 'wrong,'" Gemma said.

"Like his was all hot, and he used words, and I could barely describe him feeling me up on horseback."

"Horseback," Gemma repeated. "Nice touch. What kind of words?"

"I was reading a lot of *Outlander* at the time," Cady said. "And words I am definitely not repeating out loud." Every time she thought about some of the things Fox had said, she found herself with a case of the atomic sweats.

"Please," Gemma whined, "I told you about the time I had that one-night stand with the traveling pan flute player who had balls the size of avocados."

"And I'm still trying to forget."

"Speaking of men who would look like they could be hiding some serious avocados..." Gemma's teeth sank into her bottom lip as she stared over Cady's shoulder.

Bob marched down the block toward them, the scowl affixed to his iron jaw enough to send pedestrians scattering to the opposite side of the street.

Cady been so mired in her own verbal shortcomings, she'd nearly forgotten what Gemma said about Ethan thinking Bob might be on the lam.

And now there was no time to ask.

"The second he hits up a Porta-Potty, we're discussing your half of this," she told her best friend.

"Can he even fit in a Porta-Potty?"

Valid question.

Bob set the requested easels on the table before her. "These work?"

"Perfectly," Cady said. "Thanks for doing that."

"Anyone want anything from the food trucks?" Gemma asked, plucking her wallet out of her bag. "There's a funnel cake with my name on it."

Cady looked to Bob as she dug through her cashbox. "What do you want? I'm buying."

Bob swiveled his shaggy head to look down the block. "I'm good."

"Are you absolutely positive?" Cady asked. "They have sustainably sourced tilapia tacos, organic free-range smoked turkey legs, kimchi corn dogs—"

"In that case, I'm extra good."

These moments felt like a victory. To coax humor from a man who had so little reason to own it. She knew nothing about him, and yet she knew him. The same way she knew that water was wet, and the sun was warm, and that carrot cake counted as a salad.

More than once, she caught herself looking forward to the moment when his large frame filled the glass pane of her shop doorway. She'd come to draw comfort from his big, quiet, soothing presence. They never had to talk much, but when they did, the bassy rumble of his voice never failed to lower her blood pressure by a couple points.

"Surprise me," she told Gemma. Then, peeling off a couple extra bills, "Surprise him too."

"On it," Gemma said, mimicking Bob's earlier acknowledgment.

"Do you think we should put Lenore over here, where she can

attract foot traffic?" Cady asked, holding the toothless beaver toward the south corner of their booth. "Or here, where she can greet newcomers?" she suggested, swiveling the squat brown body to the east.

She glanced at Bob, the hairs on the back of her neck rising at the change in his body language. His shoulders were squared, his jaw set. If he had hackles, they'd be raised. Looking past the brick of his fist, she found the reason.

Ethan Townsend, making a beeline right toward them.

Cady's stomach did a triple Salchow, and the abrupt reversal of gravity was enough to send a late-lunch-flavored burp up her esophagus. She stood a shade too quickly and had to steady herself against the table when the edges of her vision dimmed.

"You okay?" Bob's ability to sense the slightest shift in her balance, her energy levels, her mood had proven to be more than a little uncanny.

Cady nodded, gulping water to lubricate her suddenly parched throat.

"Evening." Despite being attired in what Cady had come to think of as his "off-duty ensemble" of stubbornly unfashionable straight-leg jeans and a flannel shirt (neatly tucked in behind a belt, of course), Ethan moved like a man on official business. Boots stationed hip width apart, arms locked in place at his sides where he wouldn't be tempted to do something so frivolous as browse.

"Howdy." *Howdy?* Christ. Could her discomfort be more obvious? "You look ni-*erp*-ce," she said, the *nice* snapped into two syllables separated by another burp.

Apparently, it could.

Double shit.

"In the market for something to read?" she asked. "I have action, adventure, fa-*erp*-antasy—"

"I don't think we've been officially introduced," Ethan said, interrupting her dyspeptic sales pitch. "Sheriff Townsend."

Bob stared down at the hand Ethan had jabbed toward him like a bayonet.

Cady swallowed sand. She was reasonably certain the man at her side could tear Ethan's arm off and beat him with the ball-socket end if the urge took him—and she really hoped it didn't—but leaving him hanging was only slightly less painful to witness.

"This is Bo-*erp*-b." She nudged Bob's elbow, and his hand closed over Ethan's and squeezed for exactly two pumps.

Up. Down. Drop.

The exchange that followed was equally warm and effusive, accompanied by much jaw flexing and eye narrowing.

"Got a last name, Bob?"

"Smith."

"Whereabouts are you from?"

"All over."

"What brings you to Townsend Harbor?"

"A train."

Ethan's cleft chin notched upward. Bob's eyes narrowed into slits.

They were deciding how far they wanted to take this. Weighing the content of their mutual grudge against the venue.

Cady had picked up on her unofficial employee's dislike for the sheriff the night she nearly brained him with a potted plant, but was only now considering that it might have something to do with a past he'd rather not have exposed to Ethan's eagle-sharp eyes.

"You enjoying the festival so far?" the lawman asked.

Bob shrugged. "It's all right."

"Always get lots of folks coming through," Ethan said, taking a step closer and scrubbing a hand over his jaw. "A little taxing for a small-town police force like this, but for a couple days, we can manage. Once everyone moves off, we have a lot more time on our hands."

For Ethan, it was as good as slapping Bob's cheek with a glove.

"Cool," Bob said. "Maybe you'll figure out who broke into her store?"

Just when Cady thought they might devolve to Neanderthal grunts and simian chest beating, salvation arrived in the form of Vee and a large scroll tucked beneath her arm.

"Might I conscript one of you strapping lads into service?" she asked, unfurling a cartoonish but exceedingly accurate anatomical drawing. "I need to hang my vagina."

Ethan stared at the three feet of labia with his mouth slightly ajar, his face turning an adrenal-fatigued shade of puce.

"See, I like to set mine on the radiator and let it dry naturally." Ever the wing-woman, Myrtle had moseyed over to amplify the interruption.

"I got it," Bob said, casting a withering look in Ethan's direction before following Vee toward her very pink tent.

"You are never going to believe what I just heard." Gemma breezed up with her tray of food truck goodies, completely oblivious to the conversational standoff that had become a stalemate. "Someone bought TrashPanda Hollow."

Just outside Townsend Harbor proper, the sprawling five-acre parcel had once been a lavender farm and pygmy goat rescue before the elderly couple running it pulled up stakes and moved to Montana to be closer to their son and grandkids. The now-dilapidated barn they'd left behind had proven an irresistible lure for local raccoons, who had successfully defended their fair kingdom against three separate potential buyers over as many years.

"You're kidding," Cady said, happy to steer the conversation onto (somewhat) safer ground.

"Dead-ass serious." Gemma began unpacking the various items, sliding a cardboard trough of kimchi fries toward Cady. "Straight from Judy's lips. Her friend's cousin's daughter knows the realtor who brokered the deal with an out-of-town agent."

Cady glanced at Ethan, whose left eye had begun to twitch.

"That deal hasn't been finalized yet," he ground out.

Of the few personal details he had shared during their brief courtship, Ethan's desire to buy back what had once been part of the Townsends' substantial holdings to build his own microbrewery had been mentioned not once, but three separate times. Which was basically the Ethan equivalent of an obsession.

"Judy says it should be inked any day now," Gemma continued, her cheeks flushed with excitement. "But that's not the crazy part. The woman who bought it is some sort of burlesque dancer. Judy's friends' cousin's realtor said she just got back from a three-year stint in Paris at the Moulin Rouge. Wouldn't it be amazing if she started some sort of revue or club out there? This town is so dull I could just—"

Cady covertly kicked her friend's ankle below the tablecloth.

Red had risen above Ethan's collar like the mercury in a thermometer. "Better be getting back. Enjoy your evening."

He didn't even look at her as he walked away.

"Who took a cattle prod to his O-ring?" Gemma huffed.

"Mayor Pipe Bangs'd be my guess," Myrtle said.

Gemma and Cady paused mid-bite of their respective carbs to gape at her.

"Saw them getting into it earlier over by the crepe truck. Never seen Ethan grab anyone by the shirt collar before, but I gotta tell you, if I were twenty years younger—"

"You'd still be twenty years too old for him," Vee pointed out, returning with Bob at her heels. "Are you absolutely certain you won't accept this a token of my sincere gratitude?" she asked, holding a small, eyedropper-topped bottle out to Bob.

"What is it?" Gemma asked.

"All-natural PH-balanced lubricant," Vee explained. "Even if you're just having a wank—"

"I'm good," Bob said, Adam's apple bobbing conspicuously. "Thanks, though."

"If you're sure," Vee said. "Looks as if I'd better get back to my quarters," she said, glancing out at the street.

The first visitors were beginning to filter their way to the Bumfuck Egypt section of the festivities.

"Step right up!" Vee invited with a carnival barker's vociferous zeal. "Come one, come all."

"She means it," Myrtle added, capturing the sleeve of a passing tourist. "Her capsaicin warming lubes will ring your devil's doorbell in ten seconds flat."

"There are children present!" Roy shouted, apoplectic with rage.

"And how do you think they got here, duck?" Vee challenged. "Someone had to come in a vagina before they could come out of one. Unless it's in vitro. In that case, the latter still applies."

Roy's sallow face crumpled in a pinched frown as he retreated back to his lair.

"Speaking of female ends, does this need to go somewhere?" Gemma asked, holding up an extension cord.

"Shit snacks!" Cady looked up at the adorable string lights shaped like miniature books she'd found on Amazon. In all the excitement, she'd completely forgotten to plug them in.

Crouching, she felt around below the tablecloth to find the outlets she had seen while they were setting up. A shriek escaped her as her fingers brushed over something furry...and warm.

Time blurred as Bob launched into action, lunging into a swift and graceful ninja crouch and putting himself between Cady and the danger.

The danger blinked out at them from the darkness below the table, his glowing golden eyes sleepy.

"Kevin Costner?" Cady gasped. "How did you get out here?"

"He must've been in one of the boxes," Gemma said. "I thought those t-shirts felt extra heavy."

"Come here, you," Cady said, carefully hefting his considerable bulk. "We need to get you back to the shop."

"I can do it," Gemma offered. "Your shoulder—"

"It's not too bad since I lost the sling, actually," Cady said, too embarrassed to admit that, after their recent bonding session, she didn't want her four-legged friend changing his mind about their compatibility. "It won't take me a minute. I should probably grab a lint roller anyway if he was in the t-shirts."

"Want me to come with?" Bob had phrased it like a question, but his dark eyes blazed with a protective insistence she had never seen there before.

Ethan thinks Bob is wanted...

What else might those eyes be hiding?

"I'm okay," Cady insisted. "I promise I'll just be a minute."

What Cady hadn't counted on was Kevin Costner becoming an attraction in his own right.

Surrounded by a tightening crush of bodies, Cady's heart began to hammer in her chest. Phone camera flashes flared off her glasses. Hands probed his fur from all sides, adding weight to the already significant burden in her arms. Overwhelmed by the attention, Kevin had begun digging his claws into her shoulder and hip.

Cady attempted to elbow her way out of the circle, only to have someone else fill the pocket she'd created.

Her verbal attempts to drive them back were even less successful, either ignored by the admirers or eaten up by the noise of the festival.

"Excuse me, could you back up?"

"Oh my God, would you *look* at him!"

"Please don't, he's a service cat."

"That is an absolute unit! Ashlyn, get a picture for the Longboi group!"

"I just need to get to my store—"

"Is he a real Maine Coon?"

For the first time, Cady began to feel real terror.

What if she dropped him? What if he bolted? She may never see him again in the crowd. The thought of the docile old love lump lost and hungry, hunkered in an alley and wondering where his home was, brought terrified tears to Cady's eyes.

"Back *the fuck* up."

The voice boomed like thunder, scattering the clutch of enthusiasts like startled pigeons.

Bob stood behind her, baring his teeth at one of the kids who didn't move off fast enough. They were given a wide berth the rest of the way to Nevermore.

"Keys?" Bob asked.

"In my back pocket." After holding on to the cat for dear life, Cady wasn't certain she could have unfolded her arms to reach for them if she wanted to.

Bob retrieved them and unlocked the door, herding her inside and shutting it behind them.

With more gentleness than she would have believed a man of his size to have, Bob worked his big hands beneath her arms to lift Kevin and set him down. He then turned his laser-focused attention on Cady.

"You okay?" he asked, scanning her for obvious injuries.

She shook her head, surprised when hot tears spilled down her cheeks. "I was so scared he was going to get away."

"But he didn't," Bob said. "You held on to him. Looks like he held on to you, too." With the rough pad on his index finger, he pushed the neckline of Cady's sweater away from her collarbone. "We should get this cleaned up. You have a first-aid kit?"

Cady nodded. "In a box under the register."

"Sit here," he said, guiding her down on the chaise.

"This is why I only adopt things that can't get hurt," she said, staring at the threadbare Oriental rug. "Can't count on myself to be able to take care of them."

"Funny," Bob said, digging around in the cabinet. "You've been taking care of me. And I'm a lot bigger than a damn cat. This one?"

By the time her anxiety-addled brain processed the words, Bob was already opening the box he'd placed on the counter.

And staring down at the colorful assortment of panties inside.

The humiliation she expected to feel failed to materialize. As did the embarrassment she had preassigned to him.

His eyelids lowered, hooding his eyes as his breathing deepened. He looked at her, trailing heat in his gaze.

Was he imagining her wearing them?

Or was Cady only hoping he did?

And why did the thought of his looking at her like that while she stood in front of him in nothing else make her heart beat harder in her chest?

"Tupperware," she croaked out. "The first-aid kit is in a *Tupperware* box."

Bob snapped the lid shut and came back with the supplies. Slipping her sweater from her shoulder, he quickly got to work.

"This the kind of thing they had you doing in the army?" she asked.

"Sometimes."

Goosebumps lifted the fine hair of her arms as his knuckles brushed her collarbone. Which she told herself was a totally normal reaction when a big, handsome man with big, gentle hands was dressing a cat-inflicted wound.

"There," he said, pressing the bandage down on the no-longer-stinging spot.

From this vantage, she noticed the threads of gold and bronze toward the center of his irises. The thinnest of scars toward the corner of his top lip.

He'd been hurt too.

And whatever his past, Cady would make sure he had a future.

TWELVE

Vibrator

(VĪ'BRĀ'TƏR) NOUN. ANY OF VARIOUS MACHINES OR DEVICES CAUSING A VIBRATORY MOTION OR ACTION, ESP. ONE USED IN MASSAGE OR TO PRODUCE SEXUAL STIMULATION.

Fox surveyed the second-day festival crowd, looking for one large pain in his ass.

The fucking sheriff.

Morning dawned overcast but mild, and until yesterday's interaction with the cornfed shirt tucker, he'd almost been enjoying himself.

Working outside. Watching Cady interact with other book enthusiasts. Food trucks. Watching Cady bend over and retrieve things. The ocean view and brine-scented breeze. Watching Cady eat a deep-fried Twinkie. Everyone's friendly dogs. Watching Cady defend herself to her health-conscious friends for eating a deep-fried twinkie.

Retrieving random books that caught his eye from the storage cart, Fox began a stack to replace what had been sold.

He wasn't going to let Ethan ruin this. It was a nice fucking morning—the first one in possibly forever he'd spent not lamenting the idea that he had to wake up. If he could just go a handful of hours without Cady's clingy cop ex lurking around, he could have something that looked like a great day.

Taking in several breaths, he was astonished to find himself so—relaxed?—in a crowd full of people.

Also, food trucks appreciation bared repeating.

The untouched forests would always remain among his soul-feeding scents, but it was hard not to appreciate sizzling onions from Pablo's Paella. To identify the spices of the shawarma, or the fruit in fresh-made-to-order crepes. Add that to the taco truck slinging smothered burritos the size of a well-fed toddler, and his mouth hadn't stopped watering for a good hour.

Maybe he was just hangry this morning. He had to admit, it'd been nice to buy his meals and enjoy food he hadn't caught, killed, and cleaned himself.

"Anything else you need?" he asked the gravel beneath Cady's feet.

One of these days he'd be able to meet her eyes and not remember what she looked like when she came.

Today was just not that day.

"I'm just so glad our sales haven't sucked despite the placement in BF Egypt." She clapped and held her hands together, surveying the display table of new, used, and rare books with obvious pleasure. "And they say people aren't reading anymore."

He was glad for her, too. Happy to see some of the stress drain from her shoulders enough to peel them away from her ears. Happy to help her carry books to her table and unload the inventory. Hell, even the customers didn't piss him off as much as he'd expected. For a well-attended outdoor event approaching Halloween, it was surprisingly calm. People were happy and friendly.

It'd be creepy if it wasn't so damned charming.

Readers. If he were to have a category of people he could stand... Well, Cady would be the lone card-carrying member. But for her sake, other bibliophiles were tolerable.

"Want food?" Looking at Cady, he thrust his chin toward the trucks on the other side of a Main Street of bounty-laden white festival tents as long as Eight Mile Road.

"You can have some of this vegan crepe if you want," Gemma offered. "They gave me Texas-sized portions."

"Vegan crepes?" Vee piped in from the other table. "What could they possibly put in that to render it palatable?"

"Chicken, I think." Gemma deconstructed it with her fork, shredding the obvious meat. "That has to be chicken."

"Who puts chicken in crepes?" Cady asked.

"I know, right?" Gemma took another bite. "But, like...so good though."

Bustling around like a bee that couldn't decide on where to land, Cady answered Fox's question without looking down as he crouched to check boxes beneath the table. "*Normally*, I'd say yes to a snack, but I'm too obsessed with reorganizing the table. I'm going to move the tchotchkes over here. Artisan bookmarks next to the mugs with Poe quotes. Then the raven paraphernalia can be in the center, beneath the book display. I should have ordered more shirt sizes. We're out of mediums. Always. Always get double mediums. Most people don't have all *of this* to test the seams of a shirt." She ran her hands down her torso, then pulled the hem away from clinging to her curves to show off the saying beneath the ubiquitous shadow of a corvid perched on a skull. *Support your local murder...*

At least, that was what Fox was pretty sure it said. He wouldn't allow himself to look in the direction of her breasts long enough to read it clearly.

"Well, actually, it's only a *murder* if it's *crows*." They all turned to a sharp-dressed guy in his mid-twenties wearing way too much aftershave on his sparse beard and elbow patches on his Irish wool sweater.

Fox remained crouched by the edge of the table, out of the way. He got the sense the ladies appreciated when he was sitting or making himself smaller some other way so he didn't scare away customers.

This customer—way more interested in Cady than her wares—took a long drag on a vape as big as a cell phone and twice as thick as the trendy glasses on his nose. Which, Fox noticed with an eyeroll, were empty of lenses.

"A grouping of ravens is called a conspiracy," they were informed with the superiority of someone who'd never been kicked in the veneers with a steel-toed boot.

Fox's toes curled with longing.

Were hipsters still a thing? This chucklehead looked like one, but worse. Like some sort of douchecanoe 2.0. Christ, Fox was only thirty-three and couldn't remember what these fucking kids were calling themselves these days.

While he might have stood and death-stared the guy into wandering away, Cady's capitalistic instinct kicked in.

"Not to worry! I'm an equal-opportunity t-shirt dealer and book broker." She shot an almost-genuine smile at the mansplainer as she grabbed a shirt from the table and unfolded it to show several ravens circling the words IT'S A CONSPIRACY! "I discriminate against no black birds, regardless of whether Poe waxed poetic about them."

"I like it. Triple ring-spun organic cotton?" The dude leaned closer, pinching the fabric of the tee and rubbed it between his fingers as if testing the thread count.

"Ummmm..." Cady fumbled for the tag, not finding it in the collar. "It's made out of t-shirt. I think the site said they were pre-shrunk, if that helps."

"That's okay." He waved off the shirt with a shake of his head, his interest caught by a beam of sunlight in Cady's long ponytail. "You own the local bookshop?"

"Nevermore Bookstore." She pointed down the street three blocks, where her shingle stuck out in wrought-iron curls.

"So lucky." He laced his hand through artfully tousled hair, slick with product. "A business owner, huh? Don't look like you're out of your twenties."

Another cloud of vapor escaped his lips, releasing a distinctly skunky odor.

Cady tucked an escaped wisp of fair hair behind the shell of her ear. She did that when she was nervous or uncomfortable.

"Just about to jump out of that decade, actually. I inherited the shop. Family business."

"That's so dope."

Yeah, dope enough to mourn her aunt every day, you pretentious pile of hot garbage.

"What do you like to read?" Cady's smile turned brittle, and she put the table between them, straightening a perfectly straight stack of books.

His cursory, uninterested glance at the books told Fox all he needed to know. Harry Potter and the Half-Baked Prince over here hadn't cracked the spine of a book since he dropped out of community college, probably. His kind got his information from Reddit threads and videos less than three minutes long.

"What do you suggest?" The dude leaned over the table, if only to get his head closer to Cady's.

She smelled like strawberries and rosemary today, and this kid didn't deserve to breathe the same air.

Kid? The guy was less than ten years younger than Fox, if that.

"What kind of subjects are *you* into?" she pressed, a bit of impatience with the non-customer beginning to show.

Running his manicured fingers over the books, the hipster gave the spines an actual read. "Got anything on growing your own adaptogenic funguses?"

It's fungi, you ridiculous cocknugget.

Cady didn't skip a beat. "I have a fantastic book on how to grow your own medicinal herb garden, complete with all sorts of healthy mushro—"

"Nah, I was thinking about something a little more... psychedelic." His wink made Fox's own eye twitch.

This pencil-necked punk bitch couldn't handle a woman like Cady. She was almost as tall as him and probably twenty pounds heavier. Autoimmune disorder or no, she'd fucking choke this guy out with her thicc thighs.

What a great way to go.

No reality existed where this asswaffle would have a chance to get so lucky.

"I'll bet you I have a book on it at the store," she offered. "You can stop in tomorrow, or order it from nevermorebookstore.com. That's probably faster."

"If I drop in tomorrow, will you be there?" The guy shifted an almost unused, unoiled, expensive leather messenger bag from one shoulder to the other.

"I will indeed." Her tight smile had no teeth. She did it for the sale.

Myrtle, who'd been lingering beside Vee's Lady Garden booth, leaned down toward where Fox crouched, the top of her poofy white hair showing a little bit of scalp as it blew in the wind. "Get a load of this poser," she said in a stage-whisper. "Trying it on with our Cady."

Our Cady.

Even though he was still perched in a squat, Fox stared *over* at the clear-eyed old lady all of five feet tall. A woman who'd never once looked at him like anything other than a human being...

Not surprising, considering the business she was in. She dealt with pieces of shit for a living.

"She's not buying what he's selling," he rumbled beneath his breath.

"And he spent too much on that man purse just to look that stupid." She nudged him with her elbow. "Bet you could get rid of him faster."

Without thinking, Fox grabbed a book from the top of the post-Ethan Townsend pile he'd stacked and shoved it in the guy's hands. "Here. This book's screaming your name."

The guy looked at the title and blanched. "*Dead Man Walking* by Helen Prejean."

"Ohhhh, that's a good one," Gemma chimed in from her table to Cady's left, not glancing up from the professional-looking baby sweater appearing in her ever-busy hands. Her dark, side-swept bangs had slid down to cover her green eyes, but Fox got the distinct impression she wasn't too impressed by Professor Elbow Patches either.

"I don't know." The guy set the book down on a t-shirt pile, pretending like Fox didn't exist. "One condition—tip me with your number?"

"Isn't the customer supposed to be the one tipping?" Vee asked from next door, not even pretending that she wasn't listening in.

"Oh, sorry...I don't think that's a good idea," Cady hedged, her skin turning pink.

"I mean, you can't make up your mind about someone so quickly..." the guy pressed. "Maybe you can help me pick a stack of books to buy for our first date. You have a coffee shop in your place, like B&N?"

Really? This guy was suggesting a date at *her* place of business and dangling a big sale as the incentive? Just when Fox thought this interaction couldn't get more pathetic.

"I don't have any coffee," Cady said, pretending like he'd not mentioned the date and very obviously leaving out the fact that she often had coffee brewing just for free. "But there are plenty coffee shops in town, and another one going in by the Coastal Highway. If you're looking for a bookshop that might carry what you need, there's one called Reading the Rainbow in Uptown."

"How about I go get us a coffee?" The clueless man gave Cady a once-over that drove Fox to his feet. "I bet I could guess your favorite."

"Take the hint." Fox handed the next book to the guy's chest. Hard.

An Appointment with Death by Agatha Christie.

"What the hell, man?" Pink-rimmed eyes lifted with the slow, unfocused gaze of someone under the calming influence of cannabis. Once they'd traveled all the way up and into Fox's eyes, the guy shrank into himself. "I mean... Whoa, dude." Fumbling in his bag, he retrieved a shiny new smartphone and pointed the camera at Fox. "Don't try anything—I'll stream live, and I'll cancel your tragic lumberjack life before tomorrow's breakfast."

Aw, wasn't that cute? He was mad and terrified at the same time.

Fox had once been about the most violent man he'd known. His superiors called his body count "impressive."

But he couldn't get hard enough to even fantasize about doing damage to this queef of a human being. It'd be like a lion chasing a bunny. What was the point? Not enough substance to even gnaw on the bones.

Instead, he bent down over the table to bring them to eye level. "The real tragedy was when Sasquatch got fucked by your dad, and together they birthed the Abominable Fuckboi into the world. Now either buy a book, or clear off immediately."

To no one's surprise, the guy didn't buy a book, instead melting into the crowd with a bravely grumbled, but unintelligible curse.

"Another pothead bites the dust," Gemma said. "To think, you could have spent an evening with someone who would begin every sentence with 'well, actually…' Wouldn't that have been a fascinating, panty-melting time together?"

Cady pretended to vomit in her mouth and swallow it before turning to Fox. "You were amazing." She soft-punched him in the shoulder. "You just pulled those books with perfect titles out of nowhere."

"Not nowhere—you should see this stack he made after the sheriff left yesterday." Myrtle stepped aside so Cady could scan the titles. "*Death of a Salesman*, *Blood Meridian*—props for Cormac McCarthy—*In Cold Blood* by Truman Capote, *As I Lay Dying*—Faulkner." She glanced up. "*American Psycho*?"

"I liked the picture," Fox mumbled, turning away from the several sets of eyes performing all sorts of uncomfortable assessments.

Where was a proctologist to make things less awkward?

"That was almost as painful to watch as your interaction with the sheriff." Vee patted Cady's arm. "Don't worry. That awkwardness will pass...we *all* hope. Especially if you both move on quickly."

Cady made a bitter sound, probably supposed to be a laugh. "I've recently decided that I'm probably going to die alone. I'll fall for some unavailable man, he'll disappear, I'll get a cat like Kevin Costner that thinks it's people... I'll complain about 'kids these days' and wait for the alt-right to ban the last book so I can retire and only wear cardigans I knit myself—" She turned to Gemma. "Oops, sorry, no offense."

Gemma looked up from her knitting, never dropping a stitch. "None taken. I'm planning on being the Rose to your Sophia."

"Awww. I love that. Lyra can be Dorothy," Cady decided.

"Obviously. Now all we need is a Blanche."

"Who's Lyra?" Fox asked.

"Gemma's twin."

"You're a twin?"

"That's the rumor," she said wryly.

"They look exactly alike, and couldn't be more different," Cady said.

"We're a twin cliché," Gemma muttered. "Complete with the getting sick at the same time... She had this affair with a congressman once, and I didn't sleep for a month for weird sex dreams about doing it on the pulpit for the Speaker of the House. And the Oval Office, which makes zero sense, and one time Pete Buttigieg was there, which I don't know why he would be, but I guess I have been reading a lot of M/M romance lately. It all started with this one." She handed him *Song of Achilles* by Madeline Miller.

"Sold!" Vee plucked it right out of his hand. "Wait. Which congressman? He better have been a Democrat. Here, Gemma, trade you for this." She placed something small, silver, and oblong into Fox's hand to pass to Gemma on the other side of him. When he realized what it was, he tossed it like a hot potato.

Gemma dropped her knitting in her lap to catch it. "What

is..." Her eyes went owlish as she clapped her other hand over the. "Vivian! You're not supposed to sell the pleasure stuff outside. It's against the law."

The Brit gave a shrug. "Oh, please, you Yanks are all so prudish. It isn't like I handed you a twelve-inch strap-on in front of a preschool class. That's just travel-sized and quiet, so you can use it anywhere."

Fox felt *himself* vibrating. *Don't look at Cady. Don't look at Cady.*

He looked at Cady.

She was looking at him.

"That's kind of you, Vee," Gemma said. "But I'm okay without...without a bullet. Also, I can't trade for Cady's merchandise, and you gave me that one very strong opinion on why you left the U.K. that included a very lengthy explanation about why a knitted sweater shall never again touch thine flesh, or the wrath of—"

"Don't be embarrassed, honey," Vee breezily continued. "Masturbation is completely casual, like when you sneeze or rub a sore muscle. Just a release. Best done daily."

This time, everyone's eyes widened. *Daily?*

Fox remembered what it was like to be a lad under twenty and shrugged. Daily. Made sense.

Standing, Gemma handed the bullet-sized vibrator back to its owner. "I don't want to buy my...any of *that* in front of all my nearest and dearest, thank you... There's a difference between casual and—weird."

"Not the way I do it." Myrtle plucked the little machine from Vee's hands and added it to her book find. "I'll pay cash."

"Again...different stores," Gemma reminded.

"Are you sure that's the one you want?" Cady teased Myrtle. "You need to get the exact right one to make you happy."

"Psssh. I don't expect to be happy, young'un—I'm from a different generation."

Fox's laugh happened without his noticing.

"See?" Myrtle clapped him on the back. "He knows what I'm

talking about. He's an ancient soul."

This time, he was able to meet Cady's eyes.

Goddamn, she was pretty. Creamy skin kissed pink by the sun. Glossed lips shimmering. He bet they tasted like fruit. Or peppermint.

Say something. Say something. Say anything.

"Getting late. I'll bring you lunch." Lame. Lamest thing to say.

She snuck a longing glance at the food trucks before saying, "That's okay. I haven't decided what I'm going to order."

Fox shook his head. She did this every day—read every menu in her drawer, considered twenty million options and combinations, and then ordered the same thing. "Meat skewers with peanut sauce—dark meat chicken or lamb, both grass fed—garlic green beans, and a bubble tea. Mango matcha with an extra scoop of...whatever the fuck the bubbles are."

"Did he just say fuckbubble?" Vivian whispered to Myrtle.

"Shut up, he's doing a thing," Myrtle replied.

"Tapioca balls," Gemma supplied.

He didn't care what they were—all he knew was that Cady bought one a day and sucked those motherfuckers through a huge straw with the vigor of a well-paid porn star. "Back in a bit."

"That's a good employee you got there." Myrtle's not-whisper followed him toward the crowd.

"I know..."

Fox walked slower so he could enjoy the feel of Cady's eyes on his back.

"That's why I pay him the... Well, I can only afford medium dollars."

"Well, give him a raise. Good work is hard to find."

"Only for the fertilizer," Cady teased.

Myrtle's noise was rude enough to draw the attention of several people. "These kids don't know the value of literal shit these days," she grumbled, giving Fox the hairy eyeball. "And sometimes they can't see what's right in front of them."

THIRTEEN
Rival

(RĪ'VƏL) NOUN. ONE WHO ATTEMPTS TO EQUAL OR SURPASS ANOTHER, OR WHO PURSUES THE SAME OBJECT AS ANOTHER; A COMPETITOR.

"WHERE'S CADY?" FOX ASKED, RETURNING WITH A couple grease-stained bags.

Gemma smiled over at him from where she was selling some mittens to a woman with a purse dog. "She was wondering if you could hold down the fort awhile." She had the woman sign her iPad and sent her off. "Cady forgot her lunchtime meds, again. And they say *I* am the one with ADHD," she added, sitting and stabbing her project with renewed vigor.

After stashing Cady's food beneath the table, Fox did two cash sales before Myrtle shuffled over. "Watch Vee for me, will ya?" she asked. "Her pervs are older than Cady's, but pretty as she is, she has to fight all these widowers off with a cattle prod."

"Seems like she can take care of herself," he said, futzing with the cashbox.

"So can Cady, but here you are."

Their eyes met and held, and for once in his life, he backed down. "Touché. I'll do my best for your woman, ma'am. You all right?"

She put a shaking hand up to her temple. "Headache."

He instantly melted at the pinched look in her eyes. "If you want to stay with Vee and sit in the shade, I can get you meds."

"No thanks, I've had it since adolescence. It flares in the company of assholes, and we're surrounded by them." She cackled at her own joke before laying a hand on his arm. "Really, Bob, I wouldn't mind a break from people and to pee somewhere that isn't made of plastic and smells like work." She eyed the line of blue Porta-Potties with distaste.

"Ten-four." He saluted her as she waddled off.

He made another sale, and learned it took a *very* secure man to be taught how to use a glitching credit card reader from a half-blind British septuagenarian. And he'd had an affair with a male Iranian cabinet member that lasted three months before he finally got his hands on the intel they'd sent him for.

If he wasn't all the way straight before, he certainly was after that ordeal.

After he'd spent about fifteen minutes alone, Myrtle's shifting gait and peppermint-scented breath announced her return from behind him. "Psst. Heads up. It's the fuzz!" she whisper/screamed into his ear.

"The what now?"

She shook his shoulder. "The five-oh. The fuzz. The po-po."

"Okay! Thank you, Myrtle, for your subtle and *not at all* culturally insensitive alert." Gemma jumped to her feet and herded Myrtle back to the vagina tent using her knitting needles as a prod.

Ethan Townsend shouldered through the crowd, stopping intermittently to accept a fist bump or a handshake. He was gracious, if curt, as his eyes had lasered away anything but Fox. Head down, his nostrils flared like an approaching golden bull about to charge.

This man wants to hurt me.

It was a knowledge Fox hadn't recognized in a while, and it kicked his blood into overdrive.

Shut the smile down, he admonished himself. *You don't fight civilians.* It wouldn't be fair to have to hand the town hero his ass with everyone looking on.

Also, it was a special felony to hit a cop.

Instead, he treated the man as he would anything he could squish beneath his boot.

He ignored him.

Heroes tended to *hate* that.

The man's shadow fell over him, and he let the sheriff stand there expectantly for what was probably the longest forty-five seconds of his life.

A life the span of which diminished the longer the fucker blocked Fox's sunlight with that blond, blue-eyed, all-American, Cobra Kai menace.

It'd be adorable if this guy hadn't put that grim mouth on Cady.

"Aren't you supposed to be manning the booth?" Ethan finally asked, voice gravelly with irritation.

"Aren't you supposed to be serving and protecting someone who needs it?"

"What do you think I'm doing?" Ethan spat on the ground, shifting his weight to his right foot. A southpaw. Fox wouldn't forget that.

The sheriff was here protecting Cady.

From him.

"You don't have to worry about me." Fox did his best to put the guy's mind at ease. "I won't be here long."

"The sooner you clear off, the better it'll be for all involved." Ethan's Nordic face was hard and his eyes dead serious.

Fox snorted. "You get your one-liners from old westerns, cowboy?" He affected the sheriff's stiff demeanor and clipped tone almost to perfection. "You're not from around these parts, and we don't take to outsiders." He tossed his arm out in challenge. "The fuck out of here with that. You may be a big fish in a safe little tourist town, but even you have to know that this is bordering on harassment."

"I'm not here as the sheriff," Ethan said, glancing down the street toward Nevermore. "I'm here to tell you that if something happens to that woman—and I'm talking anything; if her blood pressure raises three fucking notches because of you—you'll wish I'd treat you like a lawman should."

Beneath his bristle, Fox had to admit the guy was genuine.

And wasn't afraid of him.

Big mistake.

"She dumped you, man. No reason to threaten police brutality."

The sheriff's trigger finger twitched. "This has nothing to do with that. It's that she can't afford to give whatever you think you're going to get from her. Got that? She's halfway to disabled, in serious financial and possibly legal trouble. She has a lot of friends in this town, but she's without any family or inheritances."

Legal trouble? "I'm not going to take her money. I have my own."

"Clearly," Ethan said, dragging a scathing glare down Fox's well-worn jeans and shirt.

Fox had zero need for a department store in the woods. He washed his clothes when they were dirty and cycled them for new ones when they were threadbare using the same PO box he gathered his book orders from.

"I'm not going to take any kind of advantage of Cady. I'm just doing some paid labor before I move on, is all. I've worked in construction my whole life."

Ethan's closed fist landed gently on the table, and he leaned on it, eyes glinting with a victorious knowledge. "Now why would you tell a lie that *major*?"

Fox narrowed his eyes, turning from warm muscle to cold iron in the space of a blink.

"That's right." Ethan's lip lifted in a sneer. "I know your identi—"

A deafening crash sent seabirds lifting off every flat roof in Townsend Harbor Downtown, screeching their displeasure. Customers, musicians, artisans, farmers, and all other festival-goers turned toward Nevermore with a swell of audible exclamations.

Fox's feet were already flying. Most people were smart enough to dive out of his way. Those who weren't could rely on the sheriff to catch them, as his boots pounded the pavement only seconds behind.

"Cady?" Fox burst through the door hard enough to send it rebounding off the wall, causing several books to fall from their displays.

"Up here!" Her voice was strong. Good.

Taking two stairs at a time, he nearly bowled her over on the third-floor landing and had to wrap both of his arms around her and scoop her up for a few steps until he could apply the brakes.

They stood panting together until the sound of Ethan surging up behind him drove them apart.

Her entire shape would be forever imprinted on his body.

As would the fact that he'd plunged into her building and up her stairs without one iota of hesitation.

"You hurt?" he asked, even though it was obvious she wasn't.

"What happened?" Ethan demanded from behind Fox. "Is everyone all right?"

She nodded, her eyes not completely focused. "I was downstairs in the back room looking for— I don't remember what I was looking for now. But I thought there was an earthquake, the building was shaking so hard."

No earthquake, but she still trembled with pale-faced aftershocks.

Had they been alone, it would have been impossible for Fox not to sweep her back into his arms.

"The...the roof." She pointed past the kitchen and archway through to where her bed faced the wall of windows.

"Holy shit! Cady!" Gemma raced past them both and scooped her friend into a gigantic hug. "Oh my God, your roof is on your bed! Were you up here?"

"Downstairs," Cady explained, extracting her limbs from her clinging best friend.

"What happened?" Gemma gaped at the mess through the dust swirling in the air. "We have to leave—these buildings are often infested with asbestos."

"Not mine. Aunt Fern had it removed. It was super expensive."

"What happened was this dipshit's shoddy work could have gotten you killed," Ethan said, jabbing a finger in Fox's direction.

"Guess again." Fox stepped forward. "I only temporarily patched a roof that'd become a problem because whoever did the remodel cheaped out on the materials." He distinctly remembered learning that the Townsend family had greenlighted the project and approved (see: insisted on) the contractor.

Cady turned to Ethan. "Is that true?"

"It's bullshit," the sheriff said. "He's the best in the state. Specializes in buildings this old."

It was Fox's turn to narrow his eyes. "Wouldn't be the first time a public official received kickbacks."

Ethan's fists curled at his sides, "I don't need kickbacks—you know that, Cady. I have a fortune of my own."

"Yeah, because men who name their children after themselves are famous for only taking what they need," Fox jeered.

The doubt in Cady's eyes when she glanced back at him skewered him through. She was too nice to say anything out loud. Too eternally sweet.

But she *was* wondering if this was his fault.

Stalking to the pile of rubble burying the bed, Fox extracted a heavy hammer by its head so as not to disturb fingerprints on the handle. "This isn't mine."

"You could have planted that," Ethan accused.

"Where would I pull these tools from, my ass? I don't *own* anything, you dickstain." Fox tossed the hammer at the sheriff's feet. "Fingerprint that."

Murder glinted in the man's eyes, and Fox kept an eye on his gun hand. You never knew with these brick shithouse Viking motherfuckers.

"You don't have to fingerprint it—that's *my* hammer." Cady picked it up. "I think I left it upstairs last time I was trying to pry temporary roof cement from where I spilled it on the wood railing."

Fox hadn't known she'd been up there working when he wasn't around. What if it had collapsed when she was up there? She could have been seriously injured.

Or worse.

Ethan took a second to visibly swallow, temper turning his face beet red. "Don't throw things in my direction," he told Fox. "I'll warn you once."

Fox lifted an eyebrow. "And then what do you imagine you'll do to me?"

"Guys." Cady shook herself and left Gemma's side to intervene. "Can we pause the dick-measuring contest and take a second to *freak out* about how I'm going to fix this?" She swept an arm to the Mack-truck-sized hole in the ceiling. "This is—There's no way I can pay for this."

"You have insurance," Gemma reminded her. "And the town will help. It'll be okay."

"I think someone did this," Fox said, stabbing a hand toward the mess. "It won't be okay until we find who."

"*If* there is a culprit other than the weather or you, *I'll* find them." Ethan put his hand on Cady's elbow, causing Fox's vision to bleed crimson. "Hey, why don't you pack some stuff. We'll get you settled somewhere for a few days, and make some calls to work this out, okay?"

Something about the way Cady looked at the sheriff put Fox's hackles all the way up. She doubted *Ethan*, too.

The sheriff victoriously placed himself between Fox and Cady. "I don't think your help will be needed around here anymore. You can get the fuck out."

Cady shook her head, pulling her elbow away. "Hey, there's

no cause to talk to Bob like that. You've been an ass to him all day."

"Bob?" Ethan's icy glare glinted with triumph. "You don't know what this guy is capable of, Cady."

"Neither do you. I'm not capable. I need him." She glanced over, clearing her throat. "I mean, I need his help. I can't lift things and I can't afford a W2 employee."

His face softened. "I know, Cady, but that's illegal, technically. Your business could get into a lot of trouble."

"Are you threatening her?" Fox stepped closer.

"Step off, you shitheel," The sheriff's temper wasn't lost, but his grip was slipping. "She's not someone a man like you should be toying with."

A man like *him*? What about Mr. One Percent parading as a Man of the People? "Fuck you, and the fortune your mom rode in on!"

Ethan advanced, an obvious directive in mind.

Fox's demise.

Cady's loud clap didn't break the tension but interrupted a murder. "Oh look!" She put her hand on the doorjamb. "This door is open. It is amazing for going through. To leave and such. You both should make use of it."

Shame immediately cooled Fox's ire.

This was why he lived away from people. He was too reactive. Too used to war and instability and the rules in that court.

This? Society was a battleground with rules he'd forgotten.

"Yeah, it's time I get the fuck out of here," he said. "Before it gets dangerous."

"Come on," Cady said. "Ethan's not the kind of officer that would—"

"I meant for him." Fox didn't bother to hide his sneer.

"I'll meet you outside, motherfucker," Ethan snarled, and the darkness in his eyes surprised Fox. And intrigued him. Was the mild-mannered, mama's-boy sheriff someone dangerous?

"Come on, guys." Gemma put a staying hand on Ethan's arm.

"You don't want an altercation to spill out onto the streets. Lots of camera phones out there..."

Irony. It was delicious when it worked on your side.

Fox nodded. "Don't worry. I'll go."

"No." Cady's sure voice surprised them all and glued Fox's boots to the ground. "Wait." Turning to Ethan, she said, "Are you going to treat this like a crime scene?"

The sheriff shut his eyes as if praying to every deity past and present to grant him the patience not to punch a private citizen. "Cady, there is no indication of foul play here. You have roof damage you need to fix immediately—by someone licensed and bonded—or something drastic will need to be done about this building."

Fox, already on alert, let Sheriff Townsend's words hit like a threat.

"I guess we're done here, then." Cady gave the sheriff a polite but distinctly cold and distant smile. "Thanks for your help, sheriff—I'll spend all the time I don't have searching for the one document I can't find so I can stop your mother from being an eternal hurdle to my proprietorship of this building... The insurance company insists."

"I'll talk to her," Ethan grumbled, turning on the heel of his shiny shoe. "This can't be allowed to continue."

Fox couldn't agree more, though it remained unclear, as he watched Ethan Townsend's broad shoulders disappear down the stairs, just whose side the sheriff was on.

FOURTEEN

Thunderstruck

(THŬN'DƏR-STRŬK') ADJ. AFFECTED WITH SUDDEN ASTONISHMENT OR AMAZEMENT.

It was a dark and stormy night...

She'd always wanted to say that but, like, for real.

Townsend Harbor's resident weather vixen had predicted a record-breaking squall, complete with likely flooding from the overenthusiastic king tide.

Bob spent the entire afternoon storm-proofing Nevermore while Cady ventured into the Black Friday-esque hellscape that was the local co-op. Shoppers driving their carts like *Fast & Furious* extras, Tokyo-drifting into the wine aisle to grab the last bottom-shelf econo-size box-wine blends—nearly hamstringing one another in their haste to get at the last of the fresh produce.

Cady's back still ached after her frantic scurry home. She held a four-pack of single-ply toilet paper tucked under her coat, lest the rabble who had nearly denuded the shelves be tempted to take it off her by force.

She'd learned what became precious when a community was threatened by disaster.

She had never really understood the concept of marriage until Bob met her at the door with a hot toddy in one hand and a heating pad in the other. At that precise moment, she would have gratefully borne him an entire rugby team of barbarian babies, giant, chubby fists and all.

Outside, the wind's howl had been muffled to a dull roar by the storm shutters Bob had secured to keep the coastal gusts at bay. The effect was strangely cozy amid the candy-colored, glowing lamps and silent menagerie of the bookstore.

Cady lay wrong-end-up on the chaise longue, her socked feet dangling from the inclined headrest and her head propped on a throw cushion to relieve the tension in her lower back.

"We're friends now, aren't we, Bob?"

"S'pose so." The rocks glass clutched in his meaty paw looked like something out of a toy kitchen.

"Friend to friend, can I ask you something?"

Bob swallowed with an audible gulp. "Sure." His already raspy voice was smoky from his scotch.

She let her face roll toward him. "Why do men suck?"

He stared down into the amber pool of his drink as if expecting the Lady of the Lake to emerge from it, Excalibur in hand.

"Present company excluded, of course," she added.

Bob swirled the cut crystal glass in his hand. "I wouldn't be excluded, if you knew me better."

She rolled onto her side to set down her mug. Lemony steam fogged her glasses when she took a sip. "And what have you done that's so terrible?"

"I don't have the energy, and you don't have the time."

"Oh yes I do," she countered. "What else are we supposed to do for the next three hours?"

Her lighthearted question landed heavy in the space between them, thickening the air.

It wasn't like she'd never thought about it. In fact, the morning after the roof incident, she'd woken still in the grips of an exceedingly vivid dream where Bob and Ethan were doing a lot more than just measuring their respective appendages.

She blamed the reverse harem bestseller that the BNBC had chosen for their next read.

Sleep-splooshing aside, she had definitely registered the change in the temperature of their conversations. In the length of their looks. The tingle when skin accidentally brushed skin in the close quarters of the fall festival booth. The pop of pleasure it had brought her when she'd realized Bob was jealous of Fuckboi McSkinnyJeans.

"How about we stick to your original question?" Bob's eyes lasered a hole through the floor. "This about the sheriff?"

Cady wished. Unlike so many men of his age and station, Ethan had mastered the fine art of fucking off. He'd left her entirely alone and resumed his polite ignorance of her general presence following the almost-fistfight with Bob.

"You remember the phone guy?" she asked.

Bob nodded. "What about him?"

Cady pivoted on her heating pad to bring her feet to the floor. How to tell him about this without telling him about this... "We have this kind of standing call? Anyway, things got a little—intense the last time we spoke."

"Mmhmm."

"I thought that we, um...finished on a positive note," she said, searching for a truth that didn't sound obscene, "but I haven't heard from him since."

The chair's wooden legs groaned in protest as Bob sat back. "When did this intense conversation happen?"

"Two weeks ago, tonight."

"He ever missed a call before?"

Cady shook her head. "I literally set my mantel clock by him."

Bob scraped his palm over his beard, and the tendons did a magical dance beneath the hair-roughened skin of his forearm. "Then he must have a good reason."

Hope flickered in her heart like a foolish little flame. Why was it that she could attempt to convince herself of this between eleven p.m. and three a.m. to little effect, but when a very large man who nailed things to other things with his hands said it, some of her was willing to believe? "You think?"

"I've never met the guy—"

"Neither have I, technically," she pointed out.

"But it seems like something about him has you upset a lot of the time."

Wrapping her hands around the mug, Cady sank back against the pillows. There was something about Fox, all right. Something that invaded her every third thought. Something that lingered on her skin even though she'd never felt his touch. Something that had grown roots into her soul. "I guess you could say that."

Bob finished his drink and set the glass aside. "May not be what you want to hear, but maybe he needs the distance." The floorboards creaked beneath his battered boots as he scooted forward in his seat. "Could be he has some shit to sort out."

He sounded so incredibly tired and sad when he said this that Cady felt a pinprick of guilt. All this time he'd spent fixing her roof, patching her walls, repairing her psyche, and even being her booth bouncer, for crispy Christ's sake. But other than money, showers, and the occasional meal, she'd never given any thought to what *he* might need help with. What other plans he might be putting off for her sake.

"Bob?"

"Hmm?"

"Is there something you need to sort out?"

A crease appeared in his formidable brow. "Why do you ask?

She took another sip of her now-tepid toddy, a slice of lemon bobbing against her lips. She had debated with herself hotly whether to bring up what Gemma had revealed on the opening night of the fall festival. Having matriculated from the school of Mind Your Own Fucking Business, Cady strenuously avoided providing unsolicited advice or information.

But having earned a masters in toxic positivity, she also knew that those who needed the most help were often the least likely to ask for it.

"I know this is none of my business, but, seeing as we're friends now and all, I just wanted to make sure you were aware that, if you *did* need to sort some things out, you're fully covered under the Acts of Fuckery policy."

"Don't follow," he said.

"Say, like, it's three o'clock in the morning and you've been out at a bar when some neckbeard decides to get handsy with a waitress, so you relocate his gonads to his rib cage, only to discover that one of his trucker-hat-wearing friends is actually an off-duty cop in a town where the breeding pool is more like a breeding puddle and you end up in jail?"

Bob snorted. "That's a very specific example."

"I'm just saying, under the Acts of Fuckery policy, you could call me for bail money."

"Good to know." His jaw had taken on the stone set that often preceded his descent into less verbal realms.

"Or, like, if you end up roughing it outside a tiny town fueled by gossip and a paper mill that smells like cabbage farts once or twice a month, and the local sheriff who's actually a good person at heart but definitely has deep-seated daddy issues around authority decides to make it his personal mission to run you out on a rail because he doesn't understand that people do desperate things when faced with survival—your policy entitles you to a warm place to stay, at least part-time work at a bookstore as long as the maybe-owner still maybe-owns it, and all the toddler-sized burritos you can eat."

"Cady—"

"You're a good man, Bob."

He grunted as if he'd just taken a gut punch. His eyes slammed shut, and his mouth drew tight in a grimace. "No, Cady, I'm not."

She scooted to the edge of the chaise to force him to look her in the eye. "Yes," she insisted, "you are. You can try to convince yourself of that all you want. But you're not going to convince me. Where you came from, what you did—it doesn't matter to me."

"It would," he ground out, pushing himself to his feet. "If you knew."

Cady rose and padded over to him, all too aware of their height differential.

"Next you'll be telling me I'm too naïve. Too trusting. Well, I'm not naïve, Bob. I know there's a reason you've never told me your real name. I know that you wouldn't choose to live the way you do if there wasn't something that made you choose it. I know that I like having you around and that I feel safer with you here. I know that I don't want you to go."

His wide shoulders rounded forward on a short, sharp exhale that usually accompanied a sucker punch.

Cady had seen him after taking a potted plant to the head from three stories up. She had seen him after smashing his thumb with a rubber mallet, nearly taking off the tip of his finger with a box cutter.

But until now, she'd never seen him in pain.

Where had he been, this gentle giant? What had he seen? What doors had her words opened in the maze of his mind?

"I have to, Cady." The bronzed tips of his lashes lifted from his weathered cheeks, and he gazed at her with a look of such tormented longing, it threatened to cleave her chest in two. "You've been kinder to me than I had a right to ask."

"But you're not asking," she insisted. "I'm offering. You belong here." Closing both of her hands around the brick of his fist, she squeezed it, subconsciously injecting it with the warmth for him in her heart. "With us."

Bob's nostrils flared as his chin lowered to his chest. "I don't, and you know it. Your sheriff may have gone quiet, but he hasn't given up. I'm only going to make more trouble for you by being here. It was selfish of me to stay as long as I have."

Only when the rough pad of his thumb brushed her cheek did Cady realize a tear had escaped her brimming eyes. A man in her life, a good, kind man who helped her, who made her feel safe, was leaving.

"Would it help if I trotted out my daddy issues?" she asked through a watery sniffle. "Tell you about the string of terrible boyfriends my mother had growing up? You should definitely stay at least until I've had a chance to do my shadow work. You know, how to make myself feel safe instead? That's what Gemma says I need to do, anyway. Which I totally plan on as soon as I figure out whether or not I am going to lose my bookstore. Oh!" she said, having a sudden flash of inspiration. "Are you absolutely positive that angle isn't enough? Because I could definitely leverage that if it would make any difference."

His sad smile held equal parts tenderness and resignation. "My being here isn't gonna help you keep your shop. In fact, I'm pretty sure my working on your roof is the reason someone targeted you a second time."

She folded her arms across her chest and cocked her head at an angle that made looking up at him less of a strain on her neck. "But if you really feel someone is targeting me, wouldn't that be even *more* reason to stay?"

A shadow fell across his features. "There are ways of making sure nothing bad happens to you without my being here physically."

"If you're talking about another rent-a-cop, I have to tell you, I'm not in favor."

"I'm not," he said.

Cady plucked the glasses from her face and wiped the smeared rims on her shirttail. "Okay, fine. I'll allow you to go, but on one condition. You can't go tonight." She motioned toward the darkened window. "You saw how disgusting it was out there."

The shutters rattled against the windowpane at that precise moment, helpfully illustrating her point.

"Seen worse."

She hugged her emotional support blanket tighter around her. "They don't give out trophies for the most shitty weather survived by a rugged but stupidly stubborn outdoorsman in a single season, you know."

"I know."

Translation: he'd already made up his mind.

Something began to ache deep within her. "Am I allowed to ask why?"

Bob searched her face as if committing it to memory, gaze slowly moving from her hair to her forehead, from her eyes to her cheeks, her chin, and at last her mouth.

An electric tether arced in the air between them.

She couldn't move. Couldn't breathe. The world beyond his face blurred as he lifted his large, warm hands to lightly cup her chin. His fingertips fanning on the sensitive skin just below her ear, his thumbs brushing her damp cheekbones. "Because I want these tears be your last for me, Cady Bloomquist."

She closed her eyes as he leaned in. Peat fires from the scotch on his breath mingled with the comforting scent of old books and rain rising from his clothes. Firm, feverish lips brushed over her forehead, and his beard tickled her jaw line as he moved to her ear.

"Thank you, Cady."

She stood there with her eyes closed until the shop's bell tolled his departure, determined to keep her fingers away from phones both analog and digital.

She lasted all of about five minutes after he was gone.

A good four of them were spent standing at her register, staring at the phone, willing it to vibrate. Willing the ringing in her head to spread to her ears.

When her mental prowess proved to be insufficient, she turned to her cell phone. Holding it in her hand while she held Fox in her mind produced an instant flashback to their last conversation. How she'd fallen asleep with the line still connected, and woken with the phone on the pillow beside her, a smile on her face.

She wasn't smiling now.

Cady pressed the callback button, only to be informed by a mechanized voice that her call couldn't be completed as dialed.

She tried it again.

And again.

And again.

Each time, her anger rose like the tide, carrying her further out to sea.

A flash of lightning plated the sea and sky silver seconds before a deafening clap of thunder rattled the windows. The rain sounded like a spray of tiny bullets strafing the glass from ever-changing angles governed by the gale-force winds.

The ghost of Cady's face floated in the second-floor living room window, the wind-whipped waves in an endless stretch of swarming black beyond her reflection.

It has to let up. It has to let up. It has to let up.

She had repeated these words until they'd become a mantra in the hours since Bob's abrupt departure.

She hated storms. Had as long as she could remember.

In the small, manufactured Kansas home she had shared with her mother for the first fifteen and a half years of her life, every stiff wind made her feel like they might wake up to find Munchkins peering in the windows. The floor was forever threatening to disappear from beneath her feet.

When she first came to Townsend Harbor to live with Aunt Fern, she'd felt like a hotel guest. Always taking care to put her clothes neatly back into her suitcase. Leaving her loft as empty of her presence as possible so as not to be a nuisance. Slowly, patiently, Aunt Fern had made this place feel like *theirs*. When she got sick, she kept promising to show Cady where all her paperwork was, "when it was time."

Time came before she could.

Aunt Fern had to go and catch a regular old cold that turned into pneumonia that shut down her entire body within two days.

The one place that had ever felt like a real home to Cady, and the bookstore that had become her whole world, could be slipping away at this very second. The thought shot a renewed wave of anxiety through Cady as she paced the length of the living room.

If only she could find *something*.

Only one place she hadn't yet looked.

And she really didn't want to look there.

A hundred times, Gemma had offered to do this with her. A hundred times, Cady had turned her down.

But if the storm caused the kind of damage to the building she was afraid it might, the possibility of waging a legal battle to hold on to Nevermore would be more unlikely than ever.

Just go in there now and get it over with.

If nothing else, it would be a different kind of fear.

Cady took one step. Then another. Then another. Across the living room. Down the hall. Her damp palm hovered over the doorknob, closed over it, and turned.

The door creaked open with a dramatic horror-movie whine.

Just as she'd left it.

Aunt Fern's mug still sat on the side table next to her reading chair. The small white flag of the tea bag fluttered in the draft from the overhead fan they kept on to combat the chemo-induced hot flashes. Her house slippers sat exactly where she'd stepped out of them on the way to her closet. She had insisted on changing for the paramedics, despite Cady's insistence that they didn't care what she was wearing.

"One of them could be a handsome divorcee," Aunt Fern had insisted. "You don't know."

Which had struck Cady as exceptionally odd. Her aunt had often spoken of having a wealthy suitor who provided the capital for her many home improvement projects, but Cady had never actually met him.

Astrid's onset only a year and a half into their cohabitation had meant that Aunt Fern spent more time with doctors than with gentleman callers.

Yet another source of guilt.

Another flash of lightning made lanterns of the windows. Cady jumped, almost dropping her cell phone.

Just stay, she told herself. *Just breathe.* The same words she had spoken to Bob what felt like a million years ago.

How she wished he was here now. A big, comforting presence hovering in the doorway, anchoring her to a world beyond her panic.

Thunder boomed so loud she let out a little shriek and leapt back, knocking her aunt's ceramic music box off the shelf in the process. Cady watched it fall in slow motion, hit the parquet floor, and explode in a shower of ceramic shards.

As she stared down at the rubble, her chest hitched once, twice, and a sob tore free.

Another mess.

Another way that her body, her budget, her brain had fallen short.

Sinking to her stiff knees, she swept the shards into a pile with gentle fingers.

Her breaths were getting away from her, her heart fluttering like a nervous bird.

She needed someone. Anyone. A human voice on the other end of the line to let her know that it only *felt* like the end of the world.

Too late to call Gemma.

With shaking hands, she reached for her phone and dialed, already preparing herself for the automatic shunt to voicemail.

"Cady."

"Fox?" she asked, almost nauseated with relief. "I...wanted to give you another week. He said I should, but I can't—"

"Cady, slow down."

"I'm... The storm. I just—" Her words were coming out in

fractured pieces in time with their hectic exhales. "You didn't call. Why didn't you call?"

"...wanted to... I—" The line hissed and crackled with static, and for a terrible moment, she thought the call had dropped.

Scrambling to her feet, she hobbled out of her aunt's room and into the living room in hopes of improving the signal. The lamps flickered, dipping into an amber glow before brightening again.

Shit. The power.

Every time Townsend Harbor was hit by a Big Blow, she could almost count on at least one blackout. Bob had prepared a box of emergency supplies, which, of course, Cady had left downstairs in her angry rush up to the second floor to distract herself.

"Cady? Are you there?" Fox's voice grated through the speaker.

"I have to...get—" She gasped as darkness enveloped her. She froze on the stairs, but her eyes refused to adjust. The murky light that usually spilled in from the alleyway was blocked by one of Bob's shutters.

"Cady?"

"I'm here," she said. "We lost power." Sandwiching her phone between her ear and shoulder so she could keep both hands on the railing, she continued her descent. After what seemed like an eternity, her socked foot hit the linoleum at the bottom of the stairs. Cady shuffled along with one hand out, feeling her way to the shop's alley-side entrance.

"Where are you now?" Fox sounded like he might be on the move too; his voice was modulating in time with crunching footsteps.

"I'm at the side door to the shop."

"Take a deep breath for me."

Cady closed her eyes, adding voluntary darkness to the involuntary abyss. She breathed, found the handle, and allowed muscle memory to take over.

Click.

The lock opened.

"I'm in."

Anchored by the familiar scent, her heart began to slow.

How many times had she counted these steps on days when it was bad? On days when it was the worst. Measuring time not in minutes, but in the distance between her and relief.

Just a few more.

The side door to the oversized leather reading chair where arthritic Myrtle always sat to record their BNBC minutes.

Five steps and I'm there.

From the chair to the railing by the register.

Three more, and we're done.

One...two...

Her foot kicked something where the last stair should be. She grabbed for the railing and caught the edge of it, but her clammy fingers slid off and the phone clattered to the floor as she went down hard with a startled cry.

"Cady?" A hot wire of hysteria had crept into Fox's voice. "*Cady*," he roared. "Answer me."

Vertigo smeared her vision, blurred her senses. The various stimuli were profoundly disorienting in the inky dark.

His voice was so loud. Loud enough to create an eerie echo shattering into shards off the buildings outside.

Outside?

Couldn't be.

Cady struggled to her feet and steadied herself against a bookshelf, her head reeling. She blinked at the faint rectangle of light spilling across the floor, a dark shape spreading within it. A silhouette.

There, at the back door. A man.

A man calling her name.

A man with Fox's voice. A man with Fox's voice and Bob's face.

The world shifted on its axis.

Fox.

Steam rose from beneath the collar of his sodden jacket. His deep chest heaved as white clouds escaped into the downpour. Water hung in droplets from the dark hair stuck to his forehead and glued his long lashes into clumps, beaded on the prominent cheekbones and dripped from his nose.

Their eyes locked.

The questions asked with hers were answered in his.

Yes, he was here.

Yes, he was real.

Yes, he had lied.

Yes, this was the truth.

Yes, he had come for her.

Yes. This was happening.

Her fingertips floated up to the translucent barrier separating them. Her tongue broke free from the cement binding it to the bottom of her mouth.

"Hi."

FIFTEEN

Conquorer

(KŎNG'KƏR'OR) NOUN. TO OVERCOME OR SURMOUNT MENTALLY OR EMOTIONALLY: OR TO SEDUCE.

Hi.

Fox had stared into the eyes of innumerable dying men. Of people begging for their lives. Of people begging for death.

But he'd never witnessed someone *coming to life*.

The recognition sparked first. The confusion. The anger. The threading together of her relationship and conversations with the two monosyllabic-named men in her life.

His breathing became a prisoner of her expression, unable to move until she did.

He waited for feminine rage. For fear. For recrimination and rejection.

For all the shit he deserved.

A coward would run. It was what he yearned to do. Melt into the shadows and hope his lies hadn't done too much damage to her kind, trusting heart.

But the only way he'd protect her from pain now was to take whatever whipping she thought he deserved.

If only the thought of her whipping him didn't send all his available blood to his cock.

She looked like a Valkyrie. Blue eyes shot through with electric silver. Golden hair barely secured back. Chest heaving with violent emotion.

She could spill his blood with a knife, and he'd thank her for the intimate penetration.

Darkness gathered like energy in the storm, preparing to strike. The demonic need to claim her whispered devilish thoughts through his broken brain. He wanted to fuck, and fuck, and fuck until oblivion was his only physical option. He wanted to pound into her all the pain and loneliness he'd suffered. The loss and shame. The desire and devotion.

Without breaking eye contact, Cady undid the deadbolt.

He shook his head with wide-eyed warning as pelts of rain flowed from his hair down his neck and cooling veins sweltering with lava-hot lust.

The rage and fear and adrenaline transformed into something even more powerful and ultimately perilous to them both.

Violent need.

The second lock clicked.

The door opened.

Only the storm stood between them.

She'd done it now.

In a last-ditch attempt to escape the inevitable, he stood for a moment in his twitching, straining body and drank in the sight of her like an addict taking the first tongue-stinging sip of liquor in years.

He shouldn't.

But it was too late for that now.

"Fox—"

Neither of them realized he'd moved a muscle until he exploded forward, snatching her up and molding her warm, soft body to his hard, wet one, swallowing what he hoped was a sound of shock and not distress.

The kiss was flavored with rain and skin and urgent, ardent hunger.

Immediately she responded, matching his hunger with need of her own. Tongues tangled with wet, penetrating thrusts.

Sometimes passion was a whisper, other times a roar. This time?

It was a storm.

His, a white-hot flash of lightning. Hers, the answering thunder.

It snaked through the room as intangible as the air and yet destructive as the tempest when whipped into such a frenzy.

This was happening. No more words. No more yearning.

Everything burned to ash. Panic. Anger. Restraint. Hell, *common sense.* It'd all been swept away with a flood of carnal, primal, animal need.

He did his best to kiss the questions and the thoughts of tomorrow out of her, letting her meld to his body with the pliancy of warm honey over granite. Filling his rough spaces with smooth, sticky sweetness. Surrendering to his dominance.

He was in the driver's seat. Driving his tongue deeper. Driving her against the credenza and crowding her up onto it with his big body, letting her feel the totality of his strength. Warning her that, even though they were the same species, he was a different animal.

A beast.

He didn't speak, and neither did she. Somehow it felt like it would cheapen the moment and profane the purity of what flowed between them. Language was not meant to contain such phenomena.

No more words.

Fox fused their mouths, letting the storm rage on, blowing their pain and fear and sorrow away like it was built on fragile foundations.

What stood was what they felt for each other. What they needed. What they were willing to give.

He palmed her ass as he'd been dying to do since the moment he'd followed it up those spiral stairs. She purred against his mouth, her sibilant sound of surrender having the opposite effect than he'd expected.

His snarl vibrated against her teeth, a threat of what was about to come.

Bodies melded together as they were, his erection ground against the zipper of his jeans with a painful insistence.

Their breaths were short and swift, fanning the flame between them, providing much-needed air, as neither of them would separate their mouths long enough not to drown in each other.

He didn't bother with her shirt, but her yoga pants disappeared. Her panties disintegrated.

A tremble rolled through her, but her mouth was strong against his, returning his kiss with equal force. He'd been right when he thought those lips were made for sex.

Not remaining compliant, she pushed his wet jacket off, then his shirt and tank, and her fingers found the warm, tight muscle of his smooth chest.

He watched her lashes drift down over the soft curve of her cheekbones before he splayed his hand on her chest and pushed her back to lie on the desk. Watching her with uncompromised dominance, he wrenched her pale thighs wide enough to accommodate the broad expanse of his shoulders.

Breath abandoned him as he exposed her. Pink and pretty, weeping with want and glistening with desire.

She was so wet.

He couldn't die without a taste.

Since his tight throat could make no sound, he hit his knees, securing her thighs open with his strength and draping her legs over his shoulders.

He yielded for no ceremony as he split her with one long, sinewy lick with the flat of his tongue, lapping up her body's lubricant like the dog he was. Her body clenched and she made a strangled sound that sang like a benediction through his blood.

He did his best to subdue his strength. He really did. But his restless, relentless tongue slipped and slid through the delicious ruffles and pleats of her pussy with relish.

Somehow, he'd known how she would taste. Would have ordered this for his final meal. The texture of her. The flavor. The pheromones plying their alchemical trade with his olfactory senses. Fusing with his DNA, then deeper. Into the spaces between his molecules. The places unexplored by the most ingenious of quantum physicists.

This was where the soul lived.

And she'd fucking reached in and reanimated his.

The sounds she made ratcheted his lust higher. His cock fuller and heavier.

More insistent.

Not yet. First, she was going to come in his mouth.

He focused just below her clit, bearing down with unrelenting pressure, even as her raspy sounds became almost plaintive as she surged against his mouth.

Grappling her back to the desk, he pinned her with his face and forearm pushing her higher. Further. Until she gripped the back of his head and tugged on his hair with such ferocity that he could hear some of the strands separate from his scalp.

The pain nearly unmanned him right there.

With a sob, she trembled and bucked, writhed and wriggled as the release became so powerful, she now sought to escape it.

Fox granted her mercy by standing, allowing her legs to melt down his shoulders and arms until they rested in the crooks of his elbows. He tugged her closer, bringing her round ass to the very edge of the desk.

When he wrenched his zipper down, his knuckle brushed against her sex. Soft hair tickled and moisture coated the rough skin.

Which broke the last vestiges of his humanity.

He thrust with such power that her body resisted halfway. When he might have panicked, she arched and whimpered, letting her legs fall completely open, placing their weight directly on his arms.

Their eyes locked and held. A low sound of demand vibrated in the air between them.

His? Hers? It was impossible to tell.

It could have been a millisecond or an eternity before he allowed her to adjust. But before he could stop himself, he was drilling her into the desk, hungrily watching what the motion did to her tits beneath her shirt.

For a man so constantly on the edge, he exercised unnatural control and precision. Once he found what made her gasp or squirm, he never altered. He reveled in her pleasure. Became a student of her responses.

He vibrated with rigid intensity. Thrummed with all the unspent lust of a stag in rut. His body took over.

He cursed.

She arched.

Then they were surging against each other, the connection going deeper than their thrusting flesh. Deeper than their grinding bones. Until this, too, found that space. The part of the construct built and unraveled by forces unseen.

He'd lost track of every *yes* she uttered. A thousand at least escaped with each powerful impact of their bodies.

For a moment he became somehow detached from his own long, brutal strokes by a reverent disbelief. A tender awe that both soothed him and seized him with unfathomable dread for when this moment ended.

Fuck that. Fuck everything. Fuck. Fuck. Fuck.

He spoke then, demanding explosions of vulgarity that he'd never remember. Even if she repeated the words.

When she came, he'd expected her to throw her head back and arch forward. But she surged up, clamping her arms around his shoulders and clinging on for dear life as her intimate muscles clenched and pulsed. Growing tighter. Wetter. Infinitely sweeter.

Yes. The victorious word hissed through him as he fought the sweet release gathering in his spine, threatening to blow his entire world wide open.

No. Not yet. It couldn't be over yet. They might never get the slow, long, all-night fucking some lovers did, but dammit, he wasn't finished with her.

He couldn't stop a growl rising from the deep. Threading his hands in her hair, he curled his fingers into claws, imprisoning her to his will. He pulled her head back, exposing her neck and falling on it like a fucking vampire.

Down her jaw. The column of her throat, using his teeth in little bursts, tasting her skin. Inhaling the fruit and feminine scent of her deep into his lungs as if he could make it a part of him.

Burying his face in the cove where her neck and shoulder met, he locked a leg around his thrusting hips and then reached between their bodies to flick his thumb against her sensitized clit, making controlled but insistent circles around the tight, smooth bud.

Her sound of delighted astonishment gave him fucking life as she wordlessly but ecstatically convulsed around his cock. Once, twice, then again, suffused with the tremors of another climax and a smaller one right on its heels.

Through her mewls he noted a pinch of desperation between her brows. A sheen of moisture on her skin. She was done. Tired. Spent.

He should be too.

A generous woman made a man like him greedy. And with the stamina he'd summoned over the years, he'd not even broken a sweat.

Surrendering to the frenzy, Fox finally allowed himself to follow her into that place where dark prayers and little blasphemies accompany a mire of inescapable bliss.

This. This is what you were missing. What you always wanted.

He crushed her body to him, wrapping her legs about his waist until she clung like a barnacle to his straining, bucking body. Never. Never had it been this good. This strong. This sweet.

She's yours if you ask her.

But he knew he never would.

To cuff her to his side would be like putting a bird in chains.

And to a free spirit like Cady...he could never do anything so cruel.

SIXTEEN

Furious

(FYO͝OR'Ē-ƏS) FULL OF OR CHARACTERIZED BY EXTREME ANGER; RAGING.

RAGE WAS A SERIOUSLY UNDERRATED MOTIVATIONAL agent.

Not even nine a.m., and already, Cady had emptied the dishwasher, done her laundry, put away all the boxes outside of Aunt Fern's office, and was halfway through cleaning out the much-dreaded walk-in closet.

She might have been all the way through, were it not for the Sally Fields *The whole time?* sound bite loop playing endlessly in her head, and questions being shot at her from Gemma, Vivian, and Myrtle.

Having responded to her All Hands on Deck text to Gemma, they were seated at strategic points around Aunt Fern's room, wrangling the particulars of the whole Fox/Bob imbroglio like a panel of Harvard scholars.

"All I'm saying is, that's some next-level catfishing." Gemma set her needles aside to accept a stack of books Cady handed out to her with a quiet "keep."

"I thought catfishing is pretending to be someone else," Myrtle said, nudging the brimming box out of the way with the toe of a sturdy work boot. "Not pretending *not* to be someone who you *are*."

"But Bob wasn't pretending *not* to be Fox." Vivian set her teacup down on the saucer and picked up the permanent marker to label another empty box before sliding it back in the "keep" spot. "You'll recall that Gemma was the one who provided him with a handy nickname. He simply didn't disclose his true identity."

"It's the not disclosing part that's the problem," Gemma pointed out. "Here he was, lurking around her shop, knowing all this intimate shit about her and not saying a damn thing. It's fucking creepy, if you ask me."

No one had, but this never seemed to be a source of demotivation for Cady's best friend.

"This is where you and I part ways, Gemma," Vivian said. "Were Mr. Fox pretending to be someone else to gain Cady's trust for the purposes of sexual gratification, I may be inclined to agree with your assessment. But he went to great lengths to make himself sexually undesirable."

"For, like, five minutes," Gemma said, her knitting needles clicking furiously. "Then it's shave and a haircut"—she stomped her chunky heel on the wood floor in time with the old earworm —"fuck me."

"But they didn't have relations until *after* he had revealed himself as Fox," Vivian pointed out.

"Revealed by *accident*," Gemma argued. "Before he unintentionally outed himself, we have no idea what his plans were."

Cady had an idea. Many ideas, in fact.

All of them getting darker the higher the sun rose.

The whole time.

When he'd showed up to haul her broken bookshelf away. When his finger had brushed hers as she handed off a half-eaten burrito. When he'd stacked books and listen to her prattle on about her penchant for bad taxidermy. When he'd made a paper-clip monocle for her raven. When he'd been naked in her shower and sat across the table eating curry. When he'd fixed her roof and broken her heart.

He'd been Fox—her Fox—the whole time.

"Accident or no, it's his exit that chaps my saddlebags. What the shit does *leave my loneliness unbroken mean*, anyway?" Myrtle squinted at the scrap of paper they'd all taken turns examining, as the sunlight streamed through her wispy white hair above a retina-frying neon-pink headband.

Cady blew hair out of her sweaty face as she dumped an armload of old magazines into the box Vivian had labeled *charity shop*. "It's a quote from 'The Raven.'"

A quote from "The Raven" that she'd discovered on the pillow next to hers when she woke in the gray light of predawn to find Fox long gone. So long gone, his side of the bed held no trace of warmth.

Somehow, that had made it all worse. That she'd been alone for much longer than she knew.

"Still, you have to give him points for working on a theme." Myrtle set the paper aside and took up her plastic cup of swamp-water-colored sludge that she called her go-go juice for reasons Cady didn't need to guess. "I once had a man break up with me on the check from a Denny's."

"Get the fuck outta here," Gemma said, lowering her wrath scarf to her lap.

"True story," Myrtle said. "Five months we're dating. I excuse myself to powder my nose. I come back and all that's left of him are two one-dollar bills and *it's not working out* on the back of our brunch ticket. This from a man who ordered the Moons over My Hammy and didn't even take his socks off during coitus. Is it any wonder I had my bisexual awakening at sixty-five?"

They all agreed that it was not.

"Maybe that's what I'm doing wrong," Cady muttered, turning her attention to a shelf of vintage Johanna Lindsey hardbacks with their dust covers still in mint condition. Reverently, she pulled *Love Only Once* from the shelf.

Her gateway drug. Snuck from Aunt Fern's personal collection the summer of her seventeenth year, when words were the only thing that could distract her from the pain. She carefully opened the front cover as she had all those years ago, and was already searching for the looping autograph when a tri-folded paper fluttered to her feet.

Cady stooped to pick it up, wincing at the dull but not entirely unpleasant ache of her inner thighs.

"Your back?" Gemma asked.

Cady felt her cheeks flood with heat. "Uh...yeah." She unfolded the paper, her pulse beginning to pound at the words *To Fern Bloomquist.*

Cady's eyes sped down the page, chewing up the words in giant bites. *I hereby deed the Townsend Building... until such a time as my will can be updated... shall serve as legal notice... a token of my love...*

Ethan Townsend III.

A high-pitched buzzing invaded Cady's ears as she folded back the book's dust jacket to reveal more of the same angular, masculine script.

My love, my heart is yours, as is the place where you first stole it. Nevermore will we be separated.

-E

"Holy shit," Gemma murmured over her shoulder. "Is that what I think it is?"

Cady turned mechanically, took three robotic steps out of the closet, and sat down hard. "Uh-huh."

"But I thought Aunt Fern *bought* the building from the Townsends."

"So did I," she said, her brain spitting out thoughts at warp speed.

Aunt Fern and Ethan's father? But...how? When? For how long? Glancing back down at the deed, she found one part, at least, was confirmed. It was dated July of three years ago.

"But this is good, right?" Gemma asked brightly, crouching down next to the chair. "With this, and your being Aunt Fern's legal next of kin—"

"May I see?" Vivian's signature lemony-floral scent wafted over Cady as the older woman sat down on the arm of the chair. Her eyes were wary when she glanced up from the paper. "Helpful to have, perhaps, but not proof sufficient for a probate court, I'm afraid."

"A philanthropist *and* a philanderer," Myrtle said. "He sure did like spreading it around."

Cady could feel her heartbeat in her eyelids. Her lips. Her fingers.

"Motherfucker," she said, launching out of her chair.

"Daddy Townsend?" Gemma asked.

"Fox," she bit out as she stomped back into the closet.

"I'm glad I'm not the only one who's having trouble following this," Myrtle said.

"I want answers." Cady jumped for the black nylon handle of Aunt Fern's old hiking pack, but missed. "About his identity, what he found out while he was here, all of it." She closed her fingers over the strap, bringing down an avalanche of sweaters and a hatbox as it slid off the shelf.

Gemma filled the doorway, arms folded across her breasts. "What do you think you're doing?"

"I'm going to go find him."

"Where?" she demanded. "In the goddamn *wilds*?"

Cady marched past her into the bedroom, grabbed her pills off the nightstand, and slammed them into one of the pockets. "Yep."

"But you don't even know where to look," Gemma protested.

"Cy might."

Gemma shot Myrtle a dirty look.

"Cy the Tree Guy?" Cady asked.

"Yes indeedy. I ran into him on the way over this morning," Myrtle reported, picking up the hatbox. "Big branch came down on the Uptown stairs. Said it was lucky the big, scruffy fella he'd seen hunkered down there a time or two had moved off or he'd have been wearing his brains like a bib. Said he saw the fellow near the clearing on the edge of the national forest land by his family's lake."

Ice water ran down Cady's spine.

Anyone at the base of that oak would have a straight eyeline to the Townsend Building.

And to her room.

"How far of a hike from the lookout point is the clearing?"

Myrtle chewed the inside of her papery cheek. "That's gotta be two miles at least."

"Two miles," Cady repeated. "I can do two miles."

"Around the coastal trail, maybe," Gemma said, following her into the kitchen. "But we're talking about a *hike*. Like, up a mountain and stuff."

Cady opened the pantry and began adding components to her pack. Water, trail mix, granola bars, emotional support Oreos. "The way I'm feeling right now, I could cartwheel up that mountain and kick his ass when I get there. Twice."

"You say that now, but—"

Cady turned to look at her friend, reading the clear concern in her glass-green eyes. In that moment, their entire friendship elapsed in a ten-second highlight reel. All the crazy shit they had done together. The terrible ideas. The unintentional adventures. The individual triumphs. The shared defeats. Their friendship was the longest relationship either of them had ever been in, and the platform from which she felt comfortable enough to make this kind of leap.

The crease between Gemma's dark brows smoothed out and the corners of her siren-red lips curled.

"Take these," Gemma said, reaching in her pocket to produce the same extendable knitting needles she'd brandished the first time Cady went to give "Bob" her burrito in the alley. "In case you run across any *Bob*cats."

Cady surged forward and wrapped her friend in a hug. "Thank you, Gem."

Myrtle wandered in with her cell phone pressed against her

bony sternum, the bejeweled case winking like a disco ball. "You want Cy to take you up to the ridge?" she asked. "He says he's free from now until two. Should give you plenty of time before it gets dark."

"That would be great," Cady said. "Tell him I'll meet him down front in fifteen minutes."

"Roger that," Myrtle said with a wobbly little salute.

Vivian hung back in the doorway, a strange little smile on her serene face. She winked at Cady over Gemma's shoulder, mouthing a familiar sentence.

Go get your man.

If Cy Forrester had one unforgivable flaw, it was his annoyingly calm, ridiculously soothing presence.

Cady had hopped into the arborist's old truck hoping for conversation to distract her from the many doubts beginning to creep into her subconscious. But what she received instead was a spa-like atmosphere inside a circa 1980s Dodge extended cab. Ambient new-age music. A faceted crystal dangling from the rearview mirror. And was that eucalyptus and sandalwood she smelled?

His profile looked as indestructible as the russet desert rocks. His arms steady as the steel cables that held the Bridge of the Gods aloft. His powerful thighs like roots anchored to the bench seat, his boots gentle on both the gas and brake.

He greeted her warmly, ensured that the cabin was a comfortable temperature for her, then gave her entirely too much time to think. All the way out of town, he steered them along roads curtained by trees on either side. The thick forest itself held a silence for her thoughts to fill.

And fill it they did.

Flashbacks of Fox's eyes burning into hers through the glass door. The feeling of his feverish lips, his silky tongue, his hands, his cock. The wicked, worshipful words he had mumbled into her ear as he joined their bodies and drove into her right there on the credenza by the phone that had become a talisman to the only joy she'd known in the last several months.

The truck's substandard shocks were no help whatsoever, mimicking a very particular hip-jiggling rhythm that made her develop a second pulse against his blanket-covered bench seat. Fox's touch haunted her entire body. The discreet twinge of the bruises his hipbones had left on her inner thighs. Her over sensitized nipples hardening against her bra with every bounce and sway.

"It's a pretty straight shot up the trail," Cy said, his voice as soothing as the leafy climes where he spent his summer days.

"Oh, uh-huh." Fox's mouth, plying her apart. His clever tongue splitting her—

"About half a mile up, you'll run into a scramble, but that's the only one. The handholds are pretty clearly marked."

The only scramble she wanted to run into at this particular moment would include at least two animal products and a side of something that hot sauce would improve. "That's good to know."

"The rangers keep it pretty well maintained overall, but with those shoes you'll need to be careful on rocks especially."

Cady glanced down at her canvas Chuck Taylors. She didn't own a pair of hiking boots, but to her credit, she'd grabbed the newest pair with the best traction.

Traction being a relative term for the brand.

The truck's engine whined as Cy geared down and they rounded a turn that made Cady's stomach drop toward her ill-suited shoes.

She tried to summon the rage that had gotten her this far and quailed until she remembered what Myrtle had tucked into the front pocket of her pack. She unzipped it, her fingers brushing the paper. The grooves of her fingerprints sensed the minute depression of the pen's ink under Fox's heavy hand.

Leave my loneliness unbroken.

Like fuck she would.

He'd better hope she left his stupid, beautiful, craggy, kindly face unbroken by the time she was done.

"Here we are." Cy pulled the truck over into the scenic lookout area, and the tires crunched and popped on the gravel. "You want me to come back in a couple hours?"

"That's okay," she said, unbuckling her seatbelt. "I appreciate the lift, though."

"Tell you what," he said, leaning a forearm on the well-worn steering wheel. "I can come back with Rowan and leave a Gator for you. That way, you can come down when you're ready."

"That would be great," Cady said, somewhat relieved. She had absolutely no idea how this was going to go.

"Gotcha covered," he said, reaching across her lap to open her door. "You be careful out there. Those rocks get wicked slippery."

"Will do." Cady slid down from the seat and waved as his truck pulled away. The trees seem to have grown thicker, the rise steeper, the rock...rockier, purely out of spite.

Pulling in a lungful of air tinged with rain and pine, she yanked her hood over her ears and set off in search of a ghost.

SEVENTEEN

Informant

UH-OH…

"It's Fox."

Silence. "Okay."

"You were right. I should leave."

Ethan Townsend paused, a big question mark no doubt hanging above his head. "We both know you didn't call this late to tell me I'm right."

"Cady. I need her to be safe. There're cameras at every access point, but the one in the raven no longer operates. She needs someone…someone else to keep watch."

"Why not tell her who you really—?"

Fox hung up.

EIGHTEEN

Defector

(DIˈFƐK TƏR) NOUN. TO ABANDON A POSITION, PERSON, OR ASSOCIATION.

It took hours for the panic attack to fade.

Fox had done everything in his power to fight it. Biofeedback. Grueling physical labor. Reading. Meditation. Rubbing one out because the memory of being inside Cady wouldn't leave him the fuck alone. Hunting. Cleaning and recalibrating all his weapons and gear.

The war was over, but here he was...sweating and shaking. Standing in the bottom of a pit dug years ago with no handholds to climb out of.

Finally, he'd done what his ex-wife, Jenny, had often screamed at him to do, and jumped in the lake.

That did the trick.

He felt some type of way about scrubbing Cady off his skin, but it had to be done.

The sight of her, tucked away in her aunt's ancient bed, where he'd carried her after, proving, once and for all, that he was strong enough to.

The vibrations of anxiety had thrummed through him even then, but he'd allowed himself to hope that the enormity of what they'd just done—of what he felt for her—would be enough to withstand the onslaught of mind-melting, ball-shriveling, soul-shrieking dread that captured and imprisoned him.

With no hope for escape.

Until he was nothing but an animal with no hope of escape. A creature *not* of dominant lust, but of pure, adrenaline-fueled panic.

She'd wanted to talk after. Had so many questions. Questions he'd promised to answer in the morning as he brushed her eyelids closed with the last kisses his lips would take from her.

He'd made it two hours watching her sleep before the flashbacks and waking nightmares drove his sweating, trembling body out into the night and back to his mountain. A place he never should have left to begin with.

After bathing, Fox swam until his skin turned an alarming shade of iridescent blue and the bone shivers had begun.

Hypothermia stage one.

Maybe he should just float here, wait until his heart became as frozen and heavy as it felt, weighing his body down until he sank like a stone. His breathing would slow so he could no longer be tormented by the scent of her. He'd forget the anguish of knowing what it was like to be inside her as confusion set in. He'd give his despair over to the sleep that would come for him.

And just not wake up.

What if someone comes back for her?

The thought peeled his eyes open and sent him toward the shore with long, sure strokes.

Shivering out of the water, he made his naked way toward the base camp tent to snatch a heavy blanket he'd left warming on the stones by the fire.

Cady would be safe.

Fox's antipathy for the man aside, the sheriff was someone with a commitment to his job, and he cared for Cady.

It'd been weeks since a break-in, and, Fox had to admit, when it came to petty crimes such as this one, the likelihood of another was slim to none. He couldn't stop lying to himself about how much she needed him. How much he was enjoying being needed. How much having a purpose had meant. And, for a moment, he'd allowed himself to imagine that he could be a part of her world and not live in it.

What a fucking dumb ass. What did he think he was going to do, sleep on her porch like a dog? On her busted-ass roof?

At least that was taken care of. He'd seen to it. It was the one thing he'd done right.

That and leaving. She was young and beautiful, kind and unique... She'd easily move on.

It was time he did the same, though every mile between them was another weight around his heart.

A branch snapped in the distance. Disturbed birds took to the sky, warning him with their percussive wing beats to get ready or get lost.

A predator approached.

Crouching low, Fox retrieved his knife from its sheath in the belt he kept looped in the pants that'd almost dried by the fire.

"Mother of—" The words burst from the north, along a tree line where evergreens crowded ash and elms with the final stubborn fall leaves shivering on their empty branches.

Was he hallucinating?

"Shitballs."

No. *No*, he must be having a cold-induced hallucination. Or some sort of stroke. That couldn't be—

Cady burst from the trees, a walking stick clutched in her hand as she disentangled some sort of dry weed from her hair and bright, puffy jacket.

"Ugh. Finally!" Breathing as if she'd just summited Everest, she leaned—more like collapsed—against a tree. "Son"—*pant*—"of a"—*gasp*—"bitch!" *Wheeze.*

His first thought: How was it a woman with hair sweat-slicked to her neck and round cheeks flushed red with exertion could look so goddamn tempting?

His second thought: *Fucking glad I got out of the freezing lake before she got here and saw me naked.*

Followed by: *Did she just call* me *a son of a bitch? Or was it just a general expletive?*

And finally: *What the fuck is she doing here?*

"What the fuck are you doing here?"

The look she leveled at him was so full of scorching condemnation that he almost took a step in retreat.

"What does—it—look like?" she managed, bending at the waist and resting her forehead on her walking stick while digging one hand into a stitch in her side. "I'm dying."

"Come by the fire." Instincts kicking in, he almost offered her his blanket, but realized what a mistake that would be. "You need to sit down."

She shrugged off his hand on her elbow. "*You* need...to fuck...off."

His hand dropped to his side, shoulders slumping. "Cady...I *did*. This is me fucking off. I—"

"*Hup*." She hushed the shit out of him by holding up one finger and directing a death glare the heartiest of warlords would be wise to fear. "Listen. I'm going to...kick your ass...just as soon as I'm done exhaling lung tissue...probably."

He couldn't help but smirk, despite his freezing heart. And feet. "That right?"

"Yeah."

"How?" he breathed.

"Oh, I took ass-kicking classes," she said, finally able to speak in sentences, though her breathing remained labored. "What's that...Brazilian ground karate?"

"Jiu-jitsu?"

"Yeah. That. I can do a rear-naked choke." She demonstrated a terrible choke-out.

And here he thought he was too frozen to get a boner.

"It's not exactly karat— You know what? Doesn't matter." He shook himself, hating that she was so adorable, even when quite obviously furious. She was probably the only person in the PNW without hiking gear, and very definitely the only one on the Olympic Peninsula to wear Chuck Taylors up a mountain.

Finally, his brain turned over as if he'd yanked on the cord hard enough. He reached for her, his instinct to check her for injuries. "Tell me what's wrong. What happened? Are you in trouble?"

She slapped his hands away and continued fighting for breath. "No. *You are.* Big trouble. Big *fucking* trouble, Fox." After sloughing her backpack, she dropped to her knees and yanked it open, diving in for three separate bottles of pills.

He stood there like a dope, watching her pour one of each into her palm.

"You came after me?" His heart shattered into pieces, some of them taking off into the stratosphere, and others sinking into the depths of his personal abyss.

"Yup."

"Cady. Why would you do that?" He wanted to gesture wildly, but that would mean letting the blanket drop, and a lecture just wasn't as profound with your dick out. "Let me rephrase. Why *the fuck* would you do that?"

Ignoring him, she dug into her pack. "Where is my water bottle?"

Stalking to the tent, he grabbed one of his glass growlers he'd dipped in the fresh spring and treated. "Here. I have water. Drink."

"I don't need your drink." She'd found her water bottle. It crinkled in her hand as she gulped her pills down.

She was being obstinate. Angry. He deserved it.

Never in a million years had he thought she might follow him up a mountain to dress him down. He must have hurt her more than he'd thought...

He wished that didn't feel as good as it did awful. It meant she cared more than he realized.

Shit.

"Cady." He stood over her, as close as he could get without touching her. "It was reckless and dangerous coming up here. It's at least three miles down to the road."

"You don't have to tell me that. I just climbed that far up this godforsaken mountain." Again, her facts escaped as accusations. "I need you to come back with me. If we leave now, we can be back to town by dark. It's three miles downhill, and Cypress Forrester said his sister, Rowan, left one of those Gators or Alke's in the Salish Meadow to take us back to town. Come on. We'll talk on the way. Well, *I'll talk*. You can stay in your monosyllabic and terse and emotionally constipated comfort zone if you want to."

"No."

"What did you just say to me?" Her eyes darkened from cerulean to a stormy sea gray.

"I'm not going back to town. And you shouldn't have come here." His voice had hardened against her anger.

"How the hell else am I supposed to talk to you?" she demanded, using her stick to stand after refusing his offer of help. "You won't pick up your sat phone."

"I threw it in the river..." he muttered.

"What?"

"Nothing." He looked at the sky, at the treetops becoming shadows. "Come on," he said, resigned to a night of utter misery. "Let's get you by the fire."

"No!" She again resisted his leading hand. "No, I'm not leaving you here to sleep in a tent in November. You just said there isn't much time left." As she stepped forward, some of the fury leaked from her eyes, replaced by pleading. "Please. Come home. We'll—"

"Townsend Harbor is *your* home, Cady, not mine."

Her expression nearly killed him. An amalgamation of hurt, anger, surprise, and regret.

Great, another thing to feature in his nightmares.

"Cady, if you don't get warm and dry, your sweat will make you colder and possibly give you hypothermia."

"Don't be patronizing," she said, suddenly all spikes and barbs. "You don't have to mansplain the woods to me, asshole—I've lived here longer than you. I know what's dangerous and what risks *I* decide to take." A shiver coursed through her, and she winced as if it'd hurt her bones. "*I* decided *I'm* going to sit by the fire. But not because *you* told me to." She marched toward the glowing coal bed, and he followed, picking up a log to drive the flames higher.

Jesus, she was more beautiful by firelight. Last time he'd seen her, she was covered in a similar sheen. An afterglow of pleasure that turned her into a living seraph.

The blanket fell open, and he felt the autumn chill on his nuts. He needed to get dressed before something bad happened.

Before something *amazing* happened.

"Stay here—I'm going to get dressed."

"Why are you undressed?" She swallowed, pretending not to sneak glances at him from beneath her lashes.

"I just took a bath." He pointed to the lake.

"You are crazy," she said, staring at the unfriendly water beneath a sky threatening to bring winter any moment.

"That's what I've been trying to tell you..." he said with the kind of gravitas he could see hit her hard. "Now come on and get warm while I dress, and I'll take you back to the vehicle." He shouldn't, because then he'd want to take her home. Follow her in. Fuck her again.

Dammit. It was a cycle he refused to perpetuate. He would get her home and disappear.

Suddenly he knew that would do him all the way in.

"I'm not leaving until we talk," she said, blocking his way with her body.

Instead of backing down, he stepped up. "I told you from the start—I'm not the kind of trouble you need."

She snorted, undeterred by his intimidations. "I know you

think you're some kind of big, strong hermit who's too broken to love, but you don't get to decide that for me. I'm sorry, but you can't just show up and make me...make me care for you and then fuck my brains out and bounce. Who do you think you are?"

"A piece of shit, Cady," he shot back, injecting his voice with the frustration he felt as he stepped around her and offered her his back. "I'm the kind of man that does that kind of thing. Surprise —I'm an asshole."

"No, you're not."

"You just called me—" Whirling, he stabbed his free hand at her. "Know what? You don't know the first thing about me, Cadence Bloomquist. You don't even know my name."

"Not because I didn't ask! *You* keep giving me fakes." She gestured wildly, and her puffy peach coat made swishing sounds with her movements.

"Then take the hint!"

"This wasn't a hint!" Her voice rose two octaves from crunchy to pissed as she reached into her pocket and pulled out his note. "It was a fucking cop-out. You got scared and you ran, and then you decided that I shouldn't chase you." She carefully unfolded the note that had been obviously read many times it was like a piece of tin foil trying to be reused. "I mean, what—and I cannot stress this enough—the absolute fuck were you thinking? How dare you treat me like that. You call me and seduce with your stupid deep, sexy voice and your brilliant dumb fucking man brain who reads stuff other than novels about various Jacks that kill people in combat boots."

Her features pinched into something that lanced him all the way through with self-hatred, her eyes large and swimming with emotion. "You quoted fucking Shakespeare, Poe, and Plath to me. And then you come to my house, to my business, and protect me and help me and make yourself an indispensable part of my life until I'm so seduced, I can't see straight."

"Cady, that's not what I meant to—"

She cut off his apology with a violently expansive gesture.

"And then? *And then* you fuck me within an inch of my life, give me three orgasms in less than twenty minutes, and tuck my ass into bed as I'm thinking maybe..." She let that thought trail off. "I wake up to this piece-of-shit note? How could you? Are you some kind of sociopath?"

A sociopath couldn't hurt this much. "Maybe."

She rolled her eyes so hard he was worried she'd sprained something. "It's called hyperbole, look it up."

"There are days I'm dead inside, Cady. Just waiting for my body to catch up."

"Oh please, we've all been dead inside since the pandemic." She threw up her hands. "You are one of the most vital men I've met. And I know you love it here in the woods with your perfect lake and your tent and the fucking coyotes and deer to keep your damage company. You are *capable*, Fox. You're broken, but so is everything else I love. So am I. You just have to want *this* enough to fight for it." She gestured between their bodies, and he actively hated the space between them.

"I won't fight for it." The words fell like razor blades from his mouth, cutting deeper than he'd even expected.

Her jaw went slack.

The look in her eyes made him want to tear his own out. It wasn't that he wouldn't fight to keep her. He *couldn't*. He wasn't just broken—he was ruined. Beyond repair.

"You need to forget about me, Cady. I was cruel to foster something between us. I was selfish and mean, because I knew the whole time, I couldn't keep you. And I still allowed myself to get close... But Cady, you need to find someone else. Someone who can take you to movies and restaurants and dinner parties at friends' houses. Someone who can sleep next to you. Someone who is capable of loving you the way you deserve..." His throat closed, as he could say no more on the subject without swallowing a bullet immediately.

For a second, she looked as if he'd slapped her. "Literally? Who would you suggest? You don't think I've looked? The men around here either hoard guns or spooge kombucha. What am I supposed to do with that?"

"There's Ethan." He deserved another medal of valor for not puking on the spot.

She pulled a face. "No there isn't."

"He likes you. He wants you."

"We respect each other. That's different."

Fox turned away as every awful thing he'd ever witnessed men do to a woman became some sort of morbid, infuriating PowerPoint in his mind. "I've seen what's out there in the world, Cady. You could do worse than a handsome man who would protect and respect you with the security of family money and a good name in the community."

"Ew, what is this, the 1800s?" She stared at him as if he'd tried to sell her laudanum or some shit.

"I'm just saying."

"*You* think he's so great? You end up with him, then."

After taking a deep breath, he tried again. "I've been through this before, remember? I was married. I saw what a man like me can do to a woman's life. I know why I'm— Why do you keep making that expression?"

"Because you keep saying stupid stuff with that hole in *your* face!" she hollered.

"Because you won't listen!"

"Because why should I? You're talking nonsense."

"I'm speaking the truth."

She'd fully recovered her breath, though her chest heaved for a different reason now, and her eyes and color were no less bright. "Your truth isn't mine. You don't get to tell me what my truth is."

"My truth is that I cannot live in town. And you can't live like this." He thrust his hand toward his tent, the one in which he slept with the window unzipped to the mesh.

Her jaw jutted forward. "Watch me."

Stomping over to the fire, she punched open the tent flap and tossed her bag inside.

"Cady—" He moved to stop her.

"Nope. Nope, you said it'll be dark soon, and I'm not driving down the mountain in the dark without you, so..." She ducked into the tent, leaving him with a sight of her ass in those tight jeans before the flap fell back over the door.

Silently screaming just about every bad word, Fox considered his options.

Other than this super-insulated blanket, he had an all-weather sleeping bag. The night was chilled, but not freezing, as the temp rarely dropped that low in the PNW, even in the dead of January.

However, she wasn't a woman used to the hard ground. Or sleeping bags. Or life without her pills to make it bearable.

Maybe he should encourage her to stay. Let her learn how inhospitable and uncomfortable his life could be.

He checked the sunless sky, too aware of his own nakedness. Bad idea. He needed as many layers as possible between him and the woman with whom he'd had the hottest sex of his life.

"Can I at least have my clothes first?" he requested through his teeth.

"It's your tent. I'm not keeping you from it," came the salty reply from within.

"Can you hand them to me?"

"It's too risky and dangerous for li'l old me out there. Probably have to get them yourself."

"You're acting like a brat," he muttered.

"And you're being a selfish ass. So we're in great company."

She was making this harder than it should be. Both figuratively and literally.

His heart threw itself against its cage a few times, trying to drag the rest of him into that tent with her.

She came for me.

What the fuck was he supposed to do with that?

Dammit. He punched the abused flap aside as well, unveiling her prone form resting on her elbows and stretched out on his bedroll. "It's not so bad in here." She looked around as if sizing up real estate. "Actually kinda roomy."

He ducked inside and let his sheer mass take up most of the room. And noticed she suppressed a shudder.

"You're cold," he said, wisely leaving out the *I told you so*.

"*You're* cold. I'm dressed."

His irate sound grated through the gathering evening. "Cady, you're shaking."

"Because I'm *that* mad," she said through trembling teeth. "Those are the mad shivers. I'll shiver until we hash this out."

He ached to hold her. To pull her close and share their heat. To slide against her body and...

"Listen, woman." He used his commanding soldier voice. "You're going to climb into that sleeping bag and zip it up until you are either dry or your core temperature rises, and you stop shivering. Got that?"

Squinting at him, she showed no fear, though she chewed the inside of her cheeks as she contemplated her counteroffensive. "Fine." She grunted, squirmed, and wriggled into his bag, eschewing all help from him. "I'll sleep over here."

"Fine. I'll take you back in the morning."

"Fine." She stared at him a moment, her eyes begging him to say something. Anything else.

"Fine." He turned away from her, not bothering to change into anything but the fur blanket in which he was now ensconced.

"Fine." She turned to face the opposite wall, sniffing suspiciously.

Don't cry, he silently begged.

Fine?

Nothing was fine. Nothing would ever be fine again.

KRAAA

NINETEEN
Passionate

(PĂSH'Ə-NĬT) CAPABLE OF, HAVING, OR DOMINATED BY POWERFUL EMOTIONS: OR MARKED BY STRONG SEXUAL DESIRE; AMOROUS OR LUSTFUL.

CADY WOKE WITH A STIFF BACK, A FULL BLADDER, AND an empty stomach. In her high-handed insistence on proving just how capable she was of sleeping in a tent in the wilderness, she had neglected to consider the fact that: A. Her body hated her even when given a down mattress pad to sleep on. B. She hadn't eaten since the pitifully small granola bar she had awkwardly inhaled while in Cy's truck, and: C. She hadn't bothered to scout out the toilet situation.

As she lay staring up at the tent's ceiling, she had a sinking feeling that the "situation" for her involved squatting behind a bush.

Unlike Fox, whose unfair biological advantage would allow him to just unzip the tent flap and hang out a hose.

Shifting within the cocooned warmth of her sleeping bag, Cady turned her stiff neck toward the deep, heavy breathing that had doubled as a sound machine while she slept.

Sometime in that interval, Fox had rolled toward her, one massive forearm pillowed beneath his head, the fur blanket sliding down the powerful slope of his torso to barely cover his hip, and—

Speaking of hanging out a hose.

Only, it wasn't hanging so much as poking out from beneath the fur like a curious cave creature, its cyclopean eye staring straight at her.

"Oh no you don't," she whispered, gently lifting the fabric back over his erection. This proved to have quite the opposite of her intended effect when her mouth immediately began to water at the sight of its full length and girth in high relief beneath the caveman skirt.

Of all the times for the clouds to fuck off under a full moon.

Cady bit her lip and squeezed her eyes shut.

If she could only fall back asleep...

She conjured a peaceful green field and invited the sheep therein to leap over a fence behind the screens of her eyelids.

One. Two. Three.

Four caught its hoof on the post and face-planted in a cow pie when Fox moaned in his sleep.

A soul-deep, rib-cage-vibrating, abdominal-tightening, ovary-stimulating groan that sent moisture flooding much further south with a bonus involuntary clench.

Which only reminded her that she had to pee.

With a beleaguered sigh, she began the painstaking process of wriggling her arms out of the quilted fabric with as little rustling as possible.

Fox, gods be thanked, appeared to be a heavy sleeper. And, gods also be thanked, she still wore her coat, jeans, socks and shoes. Purely for practical reasons, she unzipped the top twelve inches as quietly as possible before peeling it back from her torso.

She immediately missed the warmth.

Were it not for shame and the memory of the Oreos in the side pocket of her pack, she might have been tempted to stay there and let nature take its humiliating course.

The real trouble came when it was time to sit up.

Her back seized up, sending radiating pain through her hips and fiery arrows into her muscles.

Cady gritted her teeth and mentally taco-kicked the version of herself who had foolishly boasted about her ability to handle a two-mile hike.

After an eternity of painfully minute progress, she had freed her lower extremities, a thin sheen of sweat on her face. Her palms boasted several indentations from the uneven ground of the tent's floor. Her bladder was quickly becoming a waterbed for her lungs.

Rocking onto hands and knees, she crept toward the mouth of the tent and the dark splotch of her pack near the entry flap.

"Don't."

Cady froze with her fingers a hairsbreadth from the zipper, glancing back to see Fox's eyes firmly shut and his hands balled into fists at his sides.

Still sleeping.

Altering her intended route, she reached for her bag instead.

Fox emitted a low growl, his long leg kicking out and rolling him onto his back. The blanket slid off him once again.

Cady whimpered, unable to tear her eyes away as she frisked her pack for the familiar shape of sandwich cookie.

Jackpot.

Sustenance in hand, she crouch-walked her way to the exit and slowly created a Cady-sized opening in the zipper before nearly somersaulting out.

A damp, pine-scented blast turned her sweat into a thin candy shell of icy cold. Without her glasses, the moon was a half-melted lemon drop, turning the landscape iron gray. Her options for cover were—quite literally—few and far between.

The charcoal smudge of the tree line might as well be a league away, given the urgency of her need. Stalking past the firepit, she rounded to the side of the tent without a window and quickly unbuttoned and unzipped her pants.

Sinking down into a squat, she retracted her earlier thanks and went so far as to curse the old gods and the new for the six years it required to relieve herself.

"Who even invented quads?" Cady unceremoniously

bounced to finish her transaction and felt panic grip her chest when her legs refused to straighten.

Okay, she told herself. *Don't panic. Air drying is a thing. Just give it a minute.*

Only, she wasn't sure she had a minute. Magma coursed through her quads, and the frigid wind across her nether bits was waking the chill the sleeping bag and the radiator of Fox's body had chased away.

Let's try this again. Slowly.

Planting her hands on her knees for leverage, she breathed in, breathed out, and attempted to stand.

Nope.

She got about halfway before she locked up like a rusty hinge.

Shit. Shit. Shit.

Motherfucking Astrid and her extra-salty bullshit.

Cady watched the white clouds of her breath disappear into the wind, contemplating desperate options.

Call for Fox?

Because that was *exactly* what this day needed. The man who'd bounced after bestowing a triple-orgasm combo that altered the space-time continuum to find her stuck with her pants around her knees and a pack of Oreos in her pocket.

She could do something about one of those items, at least.

And anyway, as she seemed to be burning sugars in her thighs, she really ought to replace it with something, right?

Careful as she was, the telltale crinkle seemed to echo down the valley to the sleeping town below.

How the ever-loving fuck was it possible to have an AI entity in your phone capable of drafting articles of confederation for an interplanetary treaty, but no one had managed to invent Oreo packaging that didn't sound like a badger fight in a cellophane sack?

She'd managed to liberate a lone cookie and get it halfway to her mouth when she heard a rustle. Then a jingle.

The night wind disappeared below the primal rushing of her pulse in her ears.

This cannot be It. Not the woman who collects terrible taxidermy being mauled by an actual bear.

"I'll take the cross-eyed puma out of my Etsy shopping cart the second I have cell reception, I swear," she whispered to Whomever It May Concern. "Just please, please let me get out of this alive."

Blinding light blasted her irises. Cady's arm flew up to cover her eyes, a hand held out to shield her sizzling corneas.

Wasn't that supposed to happen *after* you died?

"What the fuck are you doing?" The deep, rumbling voice was not, in fact, the Prime Creator, but Fox, his rumpled silhouette barely visible behind the sunburst.

"Well, I *was* trying to go to the restroom without disturbing your sleep, but now I'm praying for death to end my humiliation. You want to turn that off?"

Being Fox, he didn't.

What he did was *lower* it.

"Jesus fucking Christ, woman," he growled. "Pull your pants up!"

"Put your pants *on*!" Even when she blinked blue spots and squiggles out of her vision, the light bouncing from the frost-covered earth was sufficient to see that he was still naked.

And at half-mast.

Impressive at this temperature, she thought, wondering if she might be depraved.

"Why aren't you moving?" he asked with a measure less middle-of-the-night irritation in his sleep-thickened voice.

"My back locked up." A phrase altogether inadequate for the agonizing involuntary paralysis.

"Fuck, why didn't you say that?" The beam shifted as he tucked a fire-hydrant-sized flashlight beneath his arm and stalked over to her.

"It was next on my agenda."

He approached her from the side. "Hold still."

The pain lashed through her body and out of her mouth in a fierce pulse of irritation. "Like I have a fucking choice, you dick-hole. I'm sorry," she mumbled. "I'm so sorry. I didn't—"

"I know," he said. Warm, rough knuckles brushed her knees as he located the lacy edge of her panties and gently skimmed up her goosefleshed thighs.

"Oh, God, this is humiliating."

"I once got food poisoning and shit myself when we were on a thirteen-hour convoy to Arghandab, if it helps."

And weirdly, it did.

Fox set the flashlight down on the ground, and in its ambient glow, Cady saw his big, bare foot step parallel to her poorly chosen sneaker.

"I'm not going to pull your pants up until I fix you."

Cady rotated her head at an owlish angle to try to find his eyes. "Fix...me?"

Fox nodded his shaggy head. "You're going to hinge forward at the hips. But keep your back as straight as you can. Got it?"

She nodded.

His hand hovered close enough to the small of her back for her to feel its warmth. "Good. Now stick your arms straight out to the sides like you're flying."

Cady did so. An inopportune moment to remember that one of those hands still held an Oreo.

Fox made a sound somewhere between a snort and a chuckle. "No wonder Momma came."

"Momma?" she asked.

"One of last season's yearlings. Junior is her first fawn," he said. His hair-roughened thighs pressed against the backs of hers as his hands braced her hips. "So far, so good?"

Under different circumstances, it would be fucking fantastic. "Mmhmm," she grunted.

"I'm going to wrap my arms around your rib cage and lift you. Just let your legs hang heavy."

"That's pretty much what they always do."

His torso folded over hers, his forearms anchoring her to him, pelvis to pelvis. "Not always." The husky note of his observation further heated her cheeks.

Okay, so there was that one time after orgasm number two that they'd started to shake like they were hooked to a generator, but thinking about that with his partially inflated cock nudging her ass would do her absolutely no good whatsoever.

And yet...

"Ready?"

"Yep."

The ground disappeared from beneath the soles of her sneakers as he lifted her. Back flush to his chest, she felt herself gradually approaching vertical.

A pop, a tingle, and her legs dropped limp as a clubbed fish.

Her body still felt like she'd been hit by a truck, but only a medium-sized one as opposed to an eighteen-wheeler.

"What did you do?" she asked as she slid down his body and touched down on the ground.

"Called the Hicks maneuver. One of the guys in my squadron showed me after I fucked up my back during a CASEVAC operation." His chin dipped near her shoulder as he helped wiggle her jeans up her hips.

"That's unbelievable," Cady said, taking a few exploratory steps.

"That your back is better?" he asked, reaching down to grab the flashlight.

"That anyone could lift you."

He grunted something that may have been amusement or annoyance as he walked back toward the tent.

Cady shoved the cookie in mouth, hoping to distract herself from the sight of his perfectly formed ass in the bluish light of early dawn.

He illuminated the tent's interior like a lantern with the flashlight. "Coming?" he asked.

Spontaneously, if he kept this up.

Once safely inside, she took the maximum dose of the pain meds that made life somewhat tolerable and washed them down with several gulps from her water bottle. This time, she removed her shoes before carefully crawling back into the sleeping bag.

Fox already lay on his back with his blanket covering him, his eyes closed and his *brute*-iful face aimed up toward the tent's pitched roof. The corner of his mouth curled.

"And you said I couldn't carry you over the threshold."

Had she said that? A million years ago, maybe.

He clicked off the light, and whether because of her medicine's absorption in her empty stomach or some magic post-panic elixir, she dropped off to sleep.

She woke a little over an hour later.

The muscle relaxers had been hard at work while she slept, and though her back held a memory of her earlier agony, she was able to sit herself up with almost minimal profanity. With eyes stripped of their dulling veil, she saw her surroundings as if for the first time.

Fox might have been in this very tent when he called her.

The jingling she'd always fantasized into a butler for him was an alarm for wild animals. The state-of-the-art multi-head shower, an icy lake. The four-poster bed with brocade coverlets, a heavy-duty sleeping bag on the ground. The library—complete with rolling ladder—a cardboard box lined with an oversized vacuum bag to keep out the moisture.

This was how he *lived*.

This was how he lived while simultaneously keeping her shop afloat.

Fox grimaced in his sleep, his lips peeling back from his teeth as his body began to twitch. His fingers tightened into fists, and his eyeballs rolled beneath the thin skin of his lids. What she had mistaken for a groan of pleasure before now sounded completely different from this new vantage.

Pain.

His chest rose and fell in rapid puffs. The rounded globes of his eyes began to roll beneath the thin skin of his lids.

"*No,*" he said through a clenched jaw. The scar on his ribs puckered as he flinched.

Cady's own heart had begun to accelerate.

She'd heard of night terrors, but had never witnessed one in real time. Nor could she remember what kind of traumatizing dreams it was okay to wake people up from, and which should be allowed to run their course.

Either way, being woken by touch from a dream where he was already being touched in a way he didn't appreciate seemed like a distinctly bad idea.

The answer hit her in a flash of inspiration.

Reaching into the pocket of her coat, she pulled out the packet of cookies and opened it as aggressively as possible.

Fox sat bolt upright, breathing hard, his eyes opening on the world but still reflecting the shock of the one he'd left.

"Bad dream?" she asked.

He flopped back onto his bedroll, pectorals flexing as he lifted his forearms over his head to cover his eyes. "Yeah."

"Wanna talk about it?"

"No."

"Midnight snack?" She took a cookie for herself and bit into it. "The filling is the perfect temperature from being in my pocket."

"It's four a.m.," he grumbled.

"You don't have any yak's milk or anything, do you?" she asked, swallowing a grainy mouthful.

"Huh?"

"With the hunting and the gathering and whatnot, I just thought you'd have figured out how to milk something out here." She shrugged.

Fox sat up again and leaned forward to hook a finger through the small glass loop on the growler's neck and heft it onto his shoulder with a practiced swing. Lifting his bicep brought it directly to his lips.

"Is that what those are for?" she asked, already on her second Oreo. "I'd always wondered."

A droplet disappeared into his beard and reappeared on his stubbled throat. He offered the jug to her, and she washed down her cookies with water that tasted better than anything that came with *artesian* prominently featured on the label.

Maybe it was madness.

Maybe the pheromones radiating from his naked skin. Maybe it was the memory of him hard while he slept next to her. Maybe it was the sight of a single battery-powered reading lamp clipped to a piece of carboard he'd duct-taped to one of the tent's inner pockets.

Whatever the case, Cady scooted toward Fox's reclining body like a spastic caterpillar, not stopping until she was nestled into his side.

Fox cracked an eyelid. "What are you doing?"

"Sharing body heat?"

"That works best skin to skin."

"In that case..." She unzipped the sleeping bag, then her jacket, and was already reaching for the button on her jeans before recognition dawned on Fox's sleep-creased features. His large, warm hand covered her cold, stiff fingers.

"Bad idea," he said.

"So, you're the only one who gets to be naked?" she teased. "That doesn't seem fair."

"'Fair' fucked all the way off a long time ago, where you're concerned." The tendons on his neck stood out as he lifted his head to look her in the eye. "It's hard enough to keep my hands off you as it is."

"But your hands *aren't* off me." She flicked her eyes down to the tips of his fingers just above the waistband of her jeans.

He yanked his arm back like her skin was lava.

And it was damn near the truth. She burned for him. Embers

smoldered everywhere he'd touched and everywhere he hadn't, tinder waiting the smallest spark to ignite.

"Nothing good can come from our being together again, Cady." He brushed a lock of tangled hair away from her cheek.

"You're wrong." She pressed her palm against his knuckles to mold his hand to her cheek. "I don't know how my body is going to feel from one day to the next. From one hour to another. When the misery will set in, and it's everything I can do just to open my eyes on another day." A hot tear leaked from the corner of her eye and trickled into her ear. "Because this *is* good. Right here, right now. Your skin on my skin. I'll take good, even if it's just for this minute. And the next. And the next."

A piece of his soul tore loose and exited on a groan that brought his mouth to hers.

Their kiss was not a reunion, but a revolution, their bodies changing what their minds could not. Lips and tongues and teeth transmuted the bitter words that had separated them into the simple truth of mutual need.

Fox's fingers tangled into the hair at her nape while she slipped hers beneath his blanket, greedy for the parts of him she hadn't gotten to touch in their frantic first time at Nevermore. The taut muscles of his lower back, the muscular curve of his ass, and the dangerous ridge where his abdominals narrowed to the base of his cock. He sucked in a breath against the sensitive skin of her neck as she wrapped her hand around him.

Already, he was thickening, pulsing under her touch as he peeled her out of her coat, her sweater, her t-shirt.

"You're so fucking beautiful," he breathed into her hair.

"So are you." Pushing up on her elbow, she wriggled free of the sleeping bag and sat back to shimmy out of her jeans. Fox helped pull them free of her tired feet, capturing her ankle and pressing a kiss to one instep, then the other.

Cady tried to squirm away, but he held her fast, pressing the thick tips of his fingers to the soles of her feet, which sent strange little shocks curling around the base of her spine by way of her sex.

"What are you doing to me?" she said, her head falling back.

"Reflexology." He moved his thumb to a place that made her pelvic floor contract.

Her toes curled as her hips arched of their own volition. "If you're an incubus, just say that."

"What I am is a man who loves your body." Fox trailed his fingers up her leg and inner thigh, but Cady caught him before he could reach the part of her aching for his touch.

"Not yet." If she allowed him to work his probably demon-bestowed magic already, her brain was likely to leak out her ears before she could do the things *she* wanted while the half-light still made her bold enough to do them.

"Lie down," she ordered him, sitting back on her heels.

"Yes, ma'am," he said, lips quirked in a sardonic smile.

Releasing her hair from its hasty braid, she ran her fingers through it, letting it trail across his skin as she lowered her mouth to the part of him darkened with blood and twitching with need.

Cady took her time, rubbed her cheek against his belly, grazed his hip crease with her tongue, breathed down the length of him before dragging her lips back up again.

Fox's stomach muscles jerked when she reached his taut, silky head. She parted her lips to flick her tongue over the delicate seam, earning a curse that felt like a badge of honor.

She repeated the process, mapping him with her mouth. Studying what made his hips jerk. His fists tighten. His jaw clench and his breathing quicken.

Only when he was panting and sweating like an overworked horse did she close her lips over him.

Fox hissed out a breath and uttered a grunt that hit her squarely between her belly button and spine.

His hips surged upward, driving him deeper into her mouth and her tongue over every ridge and ripple. When she had him coated and slick, she added her hand to the efforts, creating a syncopated rhythm that spurred him on.

She waited until his hips began to thrust him in and out of her grip to ask her question.

"Did you watch me from the hill?"

Fox froze, his entire body tensing.

Cady looked at him from beneath heavy-lidded eyes. "While we were on the phone that night," she said, "were you watching me?"

The ravening, hungry part of him she had glimpsed the night of the storm swam to the surface once again. His pupils dilated, and his mouth turned down at the corners.

"Yes," he said.

Cady grazed his head with the flat of her palm. "Did you like watching me?"

"I fucking loved it." If she had expected him to be abashed, she was sorely mistaken. Challenge lived in his eyes, daring her to admit that the only thing about that night she would change was wishing she could have watched him return.

"What did you see?" she asked in a breathy voice she almost didn't recognize.

"Not enough," he said.

"You didn't watch me touch myself?" she asked, moving her other hand over the dampening patch on the front of her panties.

"No." The cords on his neck stood out as she slipped a finger below the lace.

"Do you want to watch me now?"

His eyelids fell half-closed. "Gods, yes."

Keeping her right hand on him, she widened her knees and slid her left hand beneath the silky fabric.

"Pull them to the side," he ordered her in a voice that made her clench.

"We have the same problem that we did that night," she said. "There's only so much I can do with one hand."

Fox sat up. Sweat ran down the ridge of his stomach as he lifted her hand from his cock and placed it on her own sex.

A sound like a purr rumbled from him as he slid his fingers between hers, coating them with her moisture and bringing his slick hand back to his cock. Matching her rhythm, he began stroking himself, his eyes fixed on her the whole time.

Cady could feel it building, the first flutters of her release quickening within her.

Fox bit his lower lip and gripped the base of his cock, ceasing all other motion on a long exhale. He beckoned to her with the other hand, guiding her to straddle his hips.

"Kneel," he said, borrowing a line from her fantasy.

Only, he wasn't standing in front of her. He was lying below her.

"Oh, no, no, no, no," she insisted, once she understood what he intended to do. "You don't understand. I don't— You can't— A hike happened between me and my last shower."

A wicked light danced in the depths of his eyes. "Good. Spread yourself for me." His dark gaze burned up at her from beneath his lowered brows.

Cady could scarcely keep the breath moving in and out of her lungs, but slid her hands downward to reveal the very heart of her aching, intimate flesh.

Fox hummed in appreciation, dragged the straps of her bra down her arms, and moved the cups aside to free her breasts. He captured the pearly peak of one nipple between his thumb and forefinger and brought his mouth to the other, flicking and teasing her with the tip of his tongue.

Cady's stomach began to quake, and her inner thighs were tight as bowstrings.

"Please," she said. "I need—"

Palming her ass, Fox hoisted her up to his mouth, and the world ended.

The sounds she made could no longer be classified as human,

and for once, she didn't care. Didn't care who or what knew she had taken this pleasure for herself.

"Come here," he said when her tremors had ceased.

Cady glanced at his outstretched legs and extending arms, reading the invitation to be on top.

"My back... I can't—"

"Yes, you can." His long, sinewy arms stretched around her hips, his forearms beneath the backs of her thighs and his hands cupping her ass. "Put your hands on my shoulders and rest your weight on my hands."

"I really don't think—"

Fox delivered a lightly stinging slap that vibrated straight through to her core to one side of her ass. "Do it."

She did it.

Angling his hips back, Fox lowered her until he nudged her opening. She felt him there, hot and throbbing and alive for her.

"Tell me when you're ready for more."

"More," she breathed.

His muscles flexed beneath her palms as he lowered her.

By degrees, Cady's body relaxed around him, and she sank until he was buried to the hilt. They stayed that way for an immeasurable stretch, breathing together. To have him physically inside her body when for so long he'd been just a voice in her head...

Cady began to move. The heat of their joined bodies burned away the last scraps of her self-consciousness, her fear that her body may not be capable of making love to him this way.

"I love...how you feel."

She rolled him inside her, feeling him with every part of her most secret self.

"That's it," Fox coaxed, supporting her weight through every rise and thrust up to meet her every descent. "Take it all."

They slipped into a rhythm that became a dance of sound, sweat-slicked flesh colliding in time with their ecstatic call and response.

"Fox." His name escaped her on a plaintive note, her second undoing looming like a summer storm, hot and electric.

His thumb found her engorged flesh and circled it once before oblivion took her in a thunderclap. Fox drove into her as she contracted around him, following her down with a roar that elicited a cry from the forest beyond.

She collapsed against him, torso to torso, her cheek resting at the base of his neck.

Drowsiness injected her exhausted limbs with lead, and for once, she didn't try to fight it. Didn't try to prove her capability or offer assurances that this hadn't cost her dearly.

It had.

It would.

But until then, Fox became the place she could rest.

If only for a chapter in her life's long story.

TWENTY

Martyr

(MÄR'TəR) NOUN. A PERSON WHO UNDERGOES SEVERE OR CONSTANT SUFFERING.

"They call you Fox, but you are not so hard to hunt," taunted the dusky-faced guard as he tested the pad of his thumb against a wicked blade.

Fox's heavy limbs strained against his bonds with such animalistic frenzy that his veins felt like ropes beneath skin stretched taut with restrained rage.

He *was* hard to hunt.

Impossible to find...

They'd been after him and his intel for months. Which meant someone had talked.

But who?

A dead man, that's who.

"It is permissible to show fear," continued his captor, a meticulously clean and gentle-voiced man who could have been thirty-five or fifty—it was impossible to tell behind the trendy glasses and traditional garb. His dark eyes held unholy knowledge, and his smile a tinge of genuine admiration. "I'm called the Creature in my language. I've ripped open a dozen men. I've bathed in their blood and tanned their flesh in the desert sun... I've—"

"Fucking please." Fox snorted, remembering too late his sinuses were already filled with blood from his broken nose. "That supposed to impress me? I kill dozens of you fuck-knuckles before breakfast." Just to be a dick, he horked up something intense to spit on the Creature's expensive shoe. "Fact that you have me tied up and still guarded by five..." He threw as much sarcastic disgust into his expression as his broken orbital bone would allow. "I'm gonna call them *soldiers*? Well, my dude, it shows your ass, is what it does."

"I do not recognize this idiom. Show my ass? I am quite clothed."

Fox sighed the sigh of an older brother having to explain the fucking obvious to his naïve sibling. "Your overkill of my incarceration is a testament to *your* fear of *me*."

The flare in his eyes made Fox bare his teeth. It was supposed to be a smile, but whatever—he couldn't remember the last time his face was such a mess. Maybe never?

Fox didn't pay attention to fear. He'd been that way since his first slippery, tight-fisted squall. And his rancher mother would have it no other way. If she were here, these bitches would be shitting down their legs before she took away their birthdays.

Oh man, he'd pay to see that.

He'd give just about anything to see his mom.

"Let's do this," Fox hissed, clenching several loosened teeth. If he gave in to any thoughts of home, that was when the despair set in. When the fear of loss fought the strength of will. At a time like this—in the hands of the enemy—a man couldn't be at war with himself. "Untie me and let's meet, Fox to Creature."

What he saw in the Creature's returned smile touched something dark in him he hadn't known was there.

A twinge of doubt.

This man enjoyed his job. He didn't hate Fox, as so many enemies did. He didn't feel anything in particular about him.

Fox had been right. *Psychopath.*

"I hope you have filled out your advanced directive, Fox, because if you make it out of this alive, you're going to wish you had not."

"I mean, after this conversation, I may be in need of some resuscitation." He faked a yawn that got him kicked in the face. Fox met the ground with bone-jarring force and had to blink several times before he could shove air into his lungs.

"My 'soldiers' like you, Fox," the Creature informed him with a slight smile of anticipation as he crouched over him, still holding the blade as some sort of terror prop. "They want me to leave you alone with them for a while...before I start my own work. Can you give me a reason not to?"

The Creature slid the dagger into the sheath strapped to his calf disappearing into his boot before he stood to look down at Fox like an insect he was about to squish beneath his heel.

Fox needed that knife.

His heart kicked into overdrive. His rib cage became a prison, as he'd been unable to even use his easily disjointed thumb to slip his bonds. Whatever horrific substance covering the concrete floor melded with his cold sweat to create a layer of unthinkable filth. "Which one is your favorite?" Fox asked, spitting out more blood. "I'll make out with him first."

I need to get that knife. Or I'm fucked eight ways to midnight.

"Look at the sky, Fox," his captor implored in a velvet voice. "Feel the sun on your face. Breathe the air rich with desert spices and radiant heat. Give thanks to Allah for this moment, and then make your peace with the dark."

"I'm not afraid of the dark." Fox laughed until a soldier's boot on his neck silenced him.

"You will be."

A pain in his jaw startled Fox from the dream.

He almost didn't believe the sunlight illuminating his reality. Well... daylight, anyhow. The soft patter of a gentle rain fell loud against the flexed roof of his tent, running down the clear plastic of the window, beyond which he could see the forest shrouded in morning mist.

He never slept through dawn.

The dreams always dumped him, fighting or flying, into the dark, where he immediately had to prove to himself that he was not underground. That the pain in his jaw was not another kick to the face. Just the molars he'd ground to dust.

He had a carousel of nightmares to select from, and somehow this was the worst. Because the person he hated in it the most... was himself.

He was such a fucktwat back then. Twenty-seven. Whiz kid. Tall as his six-six father. Tough as his dense-boned, practical black Irish mother. Faster and more efficient than most of his fellow soldiers. Smarter than his commanding officers. Stronger than any challenge he'd stood against. Braver than some battle veterans he knew. Crack shot. Unbeaten grappler. Stone-faced liar. Great with accents, languages, and storing shit in his mind palace for later use.

All that and blessed with a dick that made insecure men pick another shower tree.

The most legendary thing about him?

His ego.

Come to find out, his bones broke first...

His legs involuntarily stretched, and his morning wood ached as it rubbed against the soft skin on the inside of a woman's thigh.

Cady.

She held him a most willing captive beneath her soft weight. Cheek crushed to his chest, hair tickling his arm.

Never had the nightmares vanished so suddenly, replaced by instant reality.

A reality that, for once, didn't remind him how cold and alone he had to be.

Remembering the previous night, he lifted his free arm and brushed some of the hair away from her face. She was everything. Just everything. A warrior. A boss. A lover. A survivor. A woman who clutched her compassionate humanity with both hands and refused to let the world turn her bitter.

Not that she didn't have reason.

I can't be another thing she has to survive, he thought. *I can't be another burden on her shoulders.*

He knew what was right but couldn't stop touching her. Not even while she slept.

He trailed mischievous fingers over her shoulder, enjoying the goosebumps lifting her fine gold hairs. The hard-earned calluses on the pads of his palm barely caught on skin smooth as hers.

He knew a few women who'd commit murder for the name of whatever demon she'd sold her soul to for her perfect peaches-and-cream complexion.

Fox ran his fingers down her arm to her elbow, then charted a course to her ribs and down the naked waistline, hip, and the thigh she'd thrown over his own.

Stirring against his body, Cady shifted her leg lower, and the warm places where their skin had met missed her instantly.

However, it gave him some room to work with.

Fox smiled in impish victory, as now he could now caress down her belly and tease the line of soft hair on her mons.

"*Nooooo,*" she moaned grumpily. "Mornings are bullshit, and you can't have any more."

A smile touched his lips, and he dropped his head to kiss her hair. He'd had plenty.

He'd never have enough.

"Good morning." His exhale against her skin warmed his own face as he nuzzled closer.

"No such thing," she groused, digging her face into his chest to cover a sneeze.

He wiggled the fingers still trapped against her body and she rolled away... Well, the two inches the sleeping bag would allow.

Oh, hey. More access. Score.

"No means *noooooo,*" she complained with a short bark of laughter. "Besides, I'm all, like...gross from last night, and unwashed, and also I didn't think I'd be having sex at all, so I'm super *not* groomed, as you may have noticed. Allow me some dignity."

"I'm not making a move," he said in a sleepy voice he'd not heard in a million years from his own throat. Smooth. Relaxed. Sated. "I'm just petting you. I like it."

Squirming uncomfortably, she covered her eyes. "How can you like it? It's like I have Colin Kaepernick in a leg lock down there."

A chuckle escaped as he threaded his fingers closer to the warm inlet of her sex. "It's soft," he murmured appreciatively.

"It's...crispy."

Fox looked at her askance, brushing his fingers through it. "Nuh-uh," he argued convincingly.

"Like, crisper than the hair on my head," she said, rubbing the sleep from her eyes.

If she were any more adorable in the morning, his heart might explode. "Well, trust me, compared to most women, yours is soft."

Her snort accompanied a look so wry, it might have been interpreted as exasperation. "Tested the texture of lady pubes the world over, have we, James Bond?"

An aggrieved tinge of warmth burned his skin. "I mean, I'm a hermit, not a Boy Scout," he muttered. Jesus Christ, when did he learn how to blush?

"Well...I suppose if you prefer a 1970s muff, you'll be saving me a bunch of money on personal grooming," she said when a jaw-cracking yawn had died down enough to speak.

"Just wait until you hear my views on the evils of underwire," he teased.

"What even *are* you?"

"I'm a creature," he murmured, a sense of gravity smothering his enjoyment of the moment. He was what *the* Creature created.

She pushed back from where her head had been cradled in the crook of his arm, her cheek resting on his chest. When she looked down at him, her eyes seemed to touch every part of his face. The scar in his hairline, his twice-broken nose, his tightly drawn mouth.

"What are you?" she repeated, the creases next to her mouth deepening. "I mean it."

Smothering a yawn with his knuckles, he made a surreptitious sniff to check for morning breath. "You mean, other than a cisgender, straight, masculine-presenting, neurodivergent white man?" He thought that was how he was supposed to say it these days.

She scoffed. "You are this and—survivalist mountain man with Liam Neeson skills and almost no possessions except for a huge pack that looks like the leftovers from John Wick's basement. What *are* you, Fox?"

He was nothing to write home about, that was for sure. "I told you, I'm army...was army."

She rolled her eyes so hard, her lashes fluttered. "I've met men in the military. We have a naval base, air base, army base, coast guard, and border patrol offices all within an hour or so. *You* are something else. Someone special."

There were many ways to interpret that word, *special*, and none of them were sexy. Closing his eyes, he pulled her closer, hoping to distract her with a searing kiss.

It worked for a second, sealing their mouths, and his body responded immediately.

"But, like, what were you in the army?" she asked against his lips.

Pulling away, he allowed his boner to die with his hopes of avoiding this conversation. "I was a ranger."

Her eyebrows lifted. "Ohhhh, the bad-ass ones. What was your specialty...survival?" She took time to glance out the mesh window. Whatever she saw out there made her burrow deeper into their shared warmth.

"Oh, bit of everything. Some intelligence. Some coms. Some support missions. Some—uh—tactical resource infiltration and surveillance. Urban warfare. Bunch of EOD." *All killing, all the time.*

"EOD?" she queried.

"Explosive ordinance disposal. We worked closely with the Air Force on that one."

"OMG, bombs? That sounds terrifying! I'm glad you're okay." She hugged him closer.

"Bombs, missiles, trip mines, IEDs, and..." She didn't need context, he realized. "But yeah."

"Did you disarm them?"

He closed his eyes against the gentle curiosity in her gaze. "No. No, I didn't disarm them."

"Oh..." The gentle understanding almost glowed through the conflicting disconcertion in her voice.

"Yeah. I activated, or armed, or aimed," he confessed. "And then...cleaned up after."

They were doing this, then. He'd known they'd have to. Especially after last night. A bleak, black chill snaked its way around his spine like the fingers of the devil.

"Where did you...um...serve?" she asked, repeating the question she'd asked Bob what seemed like a lifetime ago.

This time, he felt he owed her the truth. "Officially, Afghanistan. Syria. Supporting allied troops in the Middle East in general. The usual suspects."

"And unofficially?"

He opened his eyes, confused—relieved—not to find the censure he'd expected in her expression. Much as he and Cady had in common, she didn't have SUPPORT THE TROOPS stamped anywhere in her insular, academic life.

Why would she?

"Unofficially, I've been just about everywhere else. The other usual suspects. Russia. China. Gaza. South America."

"What did you do...unofficially?"

Suddenly restless, he slid his leg from beneath hers, already regretting he was about to sit up.

She rolled off him and slowly levered at the hips, squirming around until she found a comfortable spot from which to see him and also keep the blanket over her.

Fox mourned the absence of her heat, but this wasn't a conversation you had while cuddling.

It could get ugly.

"Same thing I did officially—Cady, I killed people."

She blinked, but her expression didn't waver—she kept it carefully blank.

Which meant she was falling apart on the inside.

So it began.

"People who would have killed you?" she asked.

He shook his head, his gaze steady. "Yes. And people I was ordered to kill. Sometimes in open battle. Sometimes alone. Sometimes with explosives. Or firearms. Knives. Shoelaces. My bare hands. Fucking name it."

A gentle hand rested over the knuckles of the fist he'd buried in their covers. "I'm not trying to bring up painful triggers. I-I want to understand you better. I've learned we all have a few skeletons in our closets, and I think yours take up more room than most. Maybe they keep you from joining the rest of us?"

Her sweetness threatened to unstitch the fibers of his makeup until he was as unraveled as one of Gemma's discarded balls of yarn.

"I don't have skeletons in my closet. I have *mountains* of bodies. Do you understand? I've done things...things that would disgust and repel you, and I don't want to give you any of that to chew on. To imagine. Because the reality is something I would sell my left nut to forget. Look, if you run into a soldier that is telling war stories, he's either a psycho or a liar. The things we had to do, the things done to us... It's part of what we sign up for. What we sacrifice. Our ability to be as human as everyone else. Because at one point or another, they had to deprogram our humanity a little so we could survive what they asked us to do."

"I'm sorry that was done to you." She ran her fingers up his arm, tracing the latticework of veins, her face a mask of sorrow on his behalf. "Is it a sense of...of guilt that keeps you from being inside for long?"

He shook his head, fighting back down the plethora of anxiety, anguish, anger, and agony that accompanied this subject. It made him wild.

Not untamed.

Unhinged.

"I was undercover in Kandahar as a mercenary arms dealer playing both sides. A Taliban warlord employed a caliphate leader named Makhlooq. Technically, The Creature. He'd been hunting me since a previous deployment, and I was taken before I could complete the objective."

"Taken? Like...as in...prisoner?" Her eyes were wide as an owl's.

He nodded, his jaw working over some overwhelming emotion.

Nostrils flaring, Fox reminded himself not to gulp air. He was free. Outside... Even if this tent were to collapse, he could rip it open at the seams. Cut it with his knife.

He wouldn't be trapped.

Staring into the middle distance, he allowed the shape of her face to distort and blur, focusing on the sounds of her breath. The quiet rain.

So he wouldn't hear the yawning silence of the void inside of him.

"Three months." He remembered. "Three months in a sandpit beneath an old temple so deep, there was no way out."

"Holy..." She couldn't seem to land on an expletive, and he didn't help.

He didn't even look at her.

"I put myself there," he confessed. "Me and my big mouth. I thought I was king shit of fuck mountain, and I pissed in the wrong psychopath's Cheerios."

"Oh, Fox. I can't even imagine..." The pity in her voice stung, but she'd work through it...get to the disgust and disappointment eventually. "Were you there all alone?"

"Eventually. It was like a hundred-and-six-degree human litter box with little to no ventilation. Four other men started down there with me. Other prisoners. None of them spoke English. One by one, they'd be summoned out with a rope ladder, and climb out." He had to stop for a moment to swallow the bile threatening to climb the back of his esophagus.

"And...you never saw them again?"

"I wish I could say that...but it was my job to bury them. When they put the ladder down the pit for me, I didn't know if it was for my execution, or just because I was the strongest man to dig another grave."

She gave a suspicious sniff, and if he saw her tears now, he'd be lost.

"So they left you there for three months? You never knew if you'd see the daylight again?"

"I was beaten a few times. Interrogated for information on strategic points. They liked to make me think a diplomatic exchange was being discussed. That tomorrow I would be released. Or the day after that. Once they bathed, shaved, and dressed me in my own uniform—only to march me in a mile-long circle of tunnels and dump me back in my cell to laugh at my rage."

His breath had become so harsh that he had to stop talking and focus on slowing it down.

Her hands bracketed his face, and finally he brought himself to look at her azure gaze.

What he saw glowing there had nothing to do with tears. It was something deeper. Longer.

Possibly eternal.

It terrified him the most.

"You survived." Her tender expression was tinged with a bit of awe. "You made it back."

"That's where you're mistaken." He retreated from her touch.

"I died in that pit. Parts of me that I'll never get back were cut out. I tried the meds. The techniques. The self-help books. PTSD isn't some disease. It's learned behavior and reaction to stimuli. It's knitted into your DNA and is almost impossible to root out."

Lifting to her knees, Cady moved closer, not allowing him to withdraw. "Thank you for telling me. I understand better now, and Fox, I'm glad." Both her hands clutched his. "I'm glad because this means we can work on it together, you and me. You don't have to be better—you can just be. Be here. And I'll come to you."

Drawing his brows down, he shook his head violently. "That's not sustainable in your condition, and you know that."

"Pssh. Not *here*, but we could figure something out. Some place that gives you plenty of open sky and escape routes, and gives us a place to spend time together. You seemed to take to the bookshop okay, so long as all the windows and doors were open all the time."

"You're not hearing me, Cady," he snapped. "I'm not safe for human consumption. I'm reactive. Prone to temper. Violence. I live with the morality of the wild. Kill or be killed. How am I going to live life alongside normal people like Myrtle and Gemma?"

She wrinkled her nose. "I wouldn't call Myrtle and Gemma *norm—*"

"The fucking point is, I can't come back with you. You're going back down this mountain, and that's the end of things."

"Things?" She flinched as if he'd slapped her. "You mean...us?"

"There is no us." It killed him to say the words. Literally stopped his heart several times. "There never was, and there never will be."

N*ormal people.*

Of all the things Fox had said, that was somehow the most insulting. As if she, Gemma, and Myrtle belonged to some homogenous group of negligible extras in the disaster movie where he was the flawed but rugged hero.

No, the villain.

That was clearly the role he was attempting to cast himself in. The initial shock of what he'd revealed had already begun to burn away, replaced by a small blue pilot light of anger. Even after what they'd shared last night, Fox was still attempting to talk himself out of this. Only, the talking had stopped as well. Having dismissed her with his dramatic pronouncement, he'd apparently resorted to chopping wood *at* her continued presence.

Still stiff from the sleeping arrangements and sore from the sex, Cady was too pissed off to care.

"You're full of shit, you know that?"

Whack.

The squat log fell in two perfect halves on either side of the blade-scarred stump where Fox had placed it.

"There *is* an us. And you had a direct hand in helping build it from the ground up."

Fox bent at the waist to retrieve one of the logs and place it back on the block for further refining.

Whack.

"You were the one who called my store. And you're the one who called back a second week, and a third. On the same day, at the same time. Almost like you *wanted* it to become a pattern."

Whack.

"You were the one who came down from the mountain. You were the one who came up with this insane idea of disguising yourself as a drifter so you could stick around and keep an eye on me."

Whack.

"You were the one who watched me through the window—"

Whack.

"The one who spouted poetry—"

Whack.

"Made love to my mind—"

Whack.

"The one who protected me—"

Whack.

"Kissed me—"

Whack.

"Fucked me—"

Whack.

"Left me."

Whack.

"You made *sure* there was an us, and now you want to pretend like it's fiction and that I'm the author." She took a step toward the stump, doing her level best not to notice the way his gray thermal darkened with sweat in a ring below the powerful cords of his neck. "At every single step, you've been the one driving the narrative. You just don't like that the best ending to this story is the two of us ending up together."

Fox kept his eyes on the growing pile at his feet. His entire body radiated hostility like a blast furnace. Cady could see the man he had been, could imagine how terrifying it was to end up on the wrong side of his hands or weapon.

His jaw flexed as he gave her his brutal profile. "No."

"Yes," she insisted. "What you did for me last night? You know how many men would be capable of not only understanding that kind of pain, but also what the hell to do about it? You think there are men lining up to sign on for a lifetime of a partner with my difficulties?" She dared take a step closer. "They're not, Fox. So, this imaginary life you've created for me with this imaginary man who's going to give me all these amazing things you can't, whatever it is you're telling yourself to make you feel better about running away, you don't get to keep that. You don't get to tell yourself you're doing the right thing. You're doing the scared thing. Because it's easier to wall yourself off than face the truth."

Fox shouldered his axe and bored the full force of his gaze into her. "And what is the truth?"

"The truth is, I fell for you before I ever saw your face, and you know it."

A raven's harsh, hectoring call broke the silence of the still morning.

Fox's knuckles whitened around the axe handle. His nostrils flared on quickening breaths.

"You already know it, but you're afraid you're going to hurt me like you hurt them."

"Cady—"

"Let me spoil it for you right now," Cady continued, afraid she would lose her nerve if she stopped now. "You *have* hurt me, Fox. You're going to again. I'm going to hurt you, too. But you can't hurt me any worse than my own body does. You can't hurt me any worse than life already has. I'm not afraid of pain. I'm afraid of letting it keep me from living."

Tears stood in her eyes, blurring the tree line into an inky smudge.

"This is the only way I know how to live, Cady. That isn't going to change."

"Neither is the way I feel," she said. "And I'm not going to make it easier on you by pretending it will." She was close enough to smell the mix of sweat and soap rising from his heated skin, cementing it in her memory against the ache already waking in her chest.

"After everything I've done—"

Cady reached up and put her fingers on his lips. "My mom is in prison, Fox. At the Topeka Correctional Facility. That's why I came to live with Aunt Fern."

She watched the shock roll over his stormy features like thunderheads.

"My father left when I was still in diapers, and she had a string of terrible boyfriends. One of them stole a car from the auto shop where he was working, and my mom hid it for him at our trailer park. She was charged as an accessory and sentenced to eight years."

It had been so long since Cady let herself think of those days that the memories were as weak as watercolors.

"I didn't even know I had an aunt until a social worker told me because my mom had alienated everyone by the time, she became pregnant with me. And you know what happened after I moved in with Aunt Fern?"

Fox's eyes burned a hole into the chopping stump.

"Aunt Fern reconciled with my mom, and helped me forgive her too. I talk to her twice a month now. She hurt me, she made terrible decisions, but we've learned how to move on from that together."

Cady stepped in closer, feeling the heat baking from his skin.

"You once told me that if I knew you better, it would matter to me where you'd been and what you'd done. You're still wrong. Just like you were wrong in thinking that I'd run screaming down the mountain after you told me. I think what you really were hoping is that this wouldn't have to be *your* choice." She dropped her hands, carrying the ghost of his kiss there. "This *is* your choice, Fox. That weight is yours to carry. So, if you decide to stay up here, you're going to do it knowing that you could be down there, with me. You're going to do it knowing that my door is always open and that I'll be waiting."

She made herself turn away and retrieve her pack, lest she give in to the overwhelming urge to wrap her arms around him and never let go.

"I brought you a book," she said, opening the flap and handing him what she'd unearthed in her aunt's closet.

Fox stared down at the couple dramatically embracing on the vintage dust jacket. The raven-haired woman spilling out of a foamy gown, her gloved hand cupping the head of her bronzed, shirtless, sandy-haired lover. Cady had spent a considerable stretch of her hike up wondering if the physical resemblance to Ethan's father and Aunt Fern had had any bearing on why he selected it as a gift.

"I know it isn't your usual genre, but I thought you might like it," Cady said.

Fox took the book and lifted his eyes to her after a long, slow exhale.

Cady shrugged her pack on her back and wiggled the straps into place with her thumbs.

"Maybe you'll call me, and we'll talk about it. Maybe you'll understand why happily ever after isn't always the point."

Alone, she set off toward the trail, grateful her tears held until her sneakers pointed down the mountain.

TWENTY-ONE

Devestation

[ˌDEVəˈSTEIƩəN] NOUN. AN EVENT THAT RESULTS IN TOTAL DESTRUCTION

One month later...

Historic or no, Cady was convinced that all government buildings smelled the same.

Paper, warm ink from recently processed photocopies, dusty seats that had held a thousand asses, and an earthy undertone she decided must be sweat.

She was certainly manufacturing enough of it as she sat in the second row of the amphitheater-style hearing room in Townsend Harbor's city hall.

Dead ahead of her, set away from the problematic plebes by a wood-paneled riser, was a long bench where the officials conducting the hearing were privileged to sit. Today, it held Mayor Stewart, Caryn Townsend, several suited county officials, with a sprinkling of representatives from the Washington State Department of Historic Registers.

Water had been poured in the glasses and placed in front of each of them, insulated carafes dispersed throughout for ease of access.

They were expecting a long meeting.

If the buzz rising from the bodies filing into the room behind her was any indication, they were correct.

Cady's knotted stomach tightened another notch. The manila folder of paperwork she held had begun to soften where her damp fingertips death-clutched the cardstock.

Gemma, as if having sensed the spike in her cortisol, placed a warm hand over Cady's. "It's going to be okay," she said, even though they both knew she had zero ability to ensure this.

"How many?" Cady asked.

Gemma lifted her eyes and turned over her shoulder, a knitting needle bobbing along as she counted.

"No, don't tell me," Cady said. "Okay, tell me. Wait, never mind. If I have to nervous-pee again, my bladder might permanently collapse."

Had she known exactly how many times she'd have to sprint to the restroom and wrestle herself out of the control-top pantyhose that she had made the mistake of donning in the misguided belief that they made her look more capable, she'd have stopped all liquids twenty-four hours ago.

"It's really not that bad," Gemma said. "Twenty, maybe twenty—*holy shit!*"

"What?" Cady's neck wrenched as her head involuntarily swiveled toward the back of the room and whatever it was that made Gemma's jaw drop to her plaid skirt.

Ethan Townsend.

Ethan Townsend in a killer suit.

Starched white collar, vest, tie, and all.

Even in her current condition, Cady had to admit that the granite jaw and narrowed eyes gave him a distinctly James Bond-ian air.

"Why didn't you tell me he looks like fucking Daniel Craig when he surrenders the khakis?" Gemma asked.

"Because I've never seen him in anything except those, his uniform, and jeans."

They watched as he worked his way down the aisle, stopping to shake the hands he was offered and supply curt nods of acknowledgement. He took a seat at the end of the first row on the side of the aisle that mirrored his mother's position on the board table. Cady couldn't help but steal a glance at Caryn, incredibly chic in a designer suit, who visibly swelled with pride at the sight of her dapper son.

The familiar scent of the stout floral perfume Myrtle favored to offset any lingering aroma from her chosen vocation reached Cady before she heard the "*pssssst!*"

She and Vivian slid into the bench behind theirs, taking the seats behind and just to the left of Cady.

"How are you holding up, honey?" Myrtle's bony but surprisingly strong hand squeezed Cady's shoulder.

"I'm okay," Cady lied.

"If you need a little something, I'm packing," she stage-whispered on a peppermint-scented breath.

For a very strange moment, Cady thought she might be talking about a firearm. In fact, even after the strange moment, it lingered as a distinct possibility. It wasn't like Townsend Harbor had metal detectors in their government buildings, and there wasn't much she'd put past Myrtle.

Who must have read Cady's confusion, because she fished in her giant bag and came back with several pill bottles. "Leftover from my hip replacement," she reported. "Got me a doctor who understands how emotionally taxing having your parts replaced can be."

"Oh wow. That's so kind of you to offer, but I'd better keep my wits about me," Cady said, tapping her increasingly sweat-damaged folder.

"Just know they're here if you need them." Myrtle gave her another squeeze. She sat back in her seat, placing her enormous bag at her feet while Vivian took her turn in the emotional support position.

The older woman's steady, sane voice rolled over Cady's heated, twitchy person like the cool London fog. "We're with you, my darling. It will all come right in the end."

The temporary burst of hope Cady felt evaporated the second the thunk of a gavel echoed through the room.

"If all council members could take their places," Caryn said crisply.

"That's my cue." Gemma's eyes flicked toward the empty chair at the opposite end of the podium from Caryn. Tossing her knitting in her bag, she peeled Cady's hand away from the folder and held it in hers.

In her best friend's golden-green eyes, Cady read the resolute stubbornness that had seen them both through so many impossible situations. "After this shit is over, we are going directly to my place, where I'm going to get you shamelessly day-drunk before we marathon *The Punisher*," Gemma said.

Gratitude made Cady's throat ache with tears she'd so far managed to keep trapped in their ducts this morning. "Deal," she said.

Another insistent crack killed the remainder of restless chatter.

"She brings the gavel from home you know," Gemma whispered from the side of her mouth before rising.

Cady covered a burp of laughter that may have passed for dismay, given her current circumstances.

"We'd like to thank everyone for coming today," Caryn said, shimmering into her former-first lady-hostess voice. "As you are all aware, the primary reason for this special joint meeting of the city council and Historical Preservation Society is to address the renovations on the *historic* Townsend Building."

A murmur of appreciative agreement rose from the assembled crowd.

"As I'm a member of both committees, Mayor Stewart has asked me to preside over the proceedings," she said, sending a syrupy little smile in his direction.

"You think they're doing it?" Myrtle whispered, leaning forward.

Cady nearly aspirated a sip from her water bottle, which resulted in a very loud, very distracting coughing fit.

Caryn waited until the very last rasp to continue.

Sorry, Cady mouthed, her face hot from a mix of shame and forcefully exhaled breath.

Caryn sipped her water, cleared her throat, and continued.

"Regarding the renovation, there are several items of concern at stake. First, the validity of the International Building Code review with regard to the additions. Second, the question of whether the proposed plans warrant vetting by the Washington Department of Archaeology and Historic Preservation, and finally, the ongoing question of the building's ownership, pursuant to claims made in Fern Bloomquist's probate court."

As hard as Cady tried to hold the parade of words in her head, they converged into a common soup between her ears. Her mind suggested an altogether different list of items for Caryn to consider.

Did you know your husband was having an affair with my aunt?

How did it feel when you found out?

Did you ever talk to her about it?

Why would my aunt choose a man like your husband?

"Miss Bloomquist?"

Cady snapped to attention, pushing her glasses up her nose and aiming her face toward the council bench. "Yes?"

Caryn shot an *I told you so* look toward one of the state code office employees whose name Cady couldn't remember for the life of her.

"Council Chairperson Townsend invited you to provide your evidence that the appropriate paperwork was filed with the city planner's office," Mayor Stewart said, managing to work in his trademark *a vote for Stew is a vote for you* grin.

Cady's nerves jolted as if hooked to a car battery.

"Yes, of course," she said, flipping open her folder and paging through the paperwork with shaking hands. Panic made the black letters swim on the page, and she was already finished with her third time through the stack when Vivian's hand snaked over the back of the bench.

"It's that one, love," she said, giving Cady an encouraging smile before resuming her seat.

Ethan, who hadn't managed to stick to his, loped over to her from the aisle to save her the trouble of having to scoot all the way down in order to carry the paper up to the podium.

Their eyes met for a split second during the hand-off.

Cady tried to load her end of it with as much gratitude and apology as she could, but was met with blank indifference.

He handed the papers to his mother, whose lips twitched at one corner.

Caryn glanced at them for approximately a millisecond before handing them down the row. Cady hadn't realized she'd been holding her breath until Caryn announced that the papers would be filed officially with the city council matter in question.

"I also have receipts for the licensed and bonded contractor from the historical society's list of accepted vendors. They've been filed with the records department as well as—"

"That won't be necessary," Caryn interrupted. "The council was already aware of this fact. At issue is whether you had the legal right to engage in those processes in the first place."

Her statement was thick with the suggestion that, in using the established pathways, Cady had purposely circumvented the unspoken expectations of Townsend Harbor local politics.

She absolutely had.

The infusion of her aunt's life insurance policy had been such a financial relief that she might have gone just a little crazy in her plans.

Heartbreak would do that to you.

An entire month, and not a word from Fox. It had been an exquisite form of torture to watch the physical aftermath of their joining slowly fade from her body while his mark remained on her soul. With the construction, she'd at least had other humans around her living quarters for some of the day. Undertaking the renovation had been the only thing keeping her sane since the day she'd come down from the mountain alone.

"Is there specific evidence that Councilperson Townsend would like to introduce into the record?" Mayor Stewart asked in the perfect layup.

"There is, Mr. Mayor."

"*Mr.* Mayor," Myrtle whispered. "I got twenty dollars says she calls him that while wearing nothing but his tie and a smile."

Cady bit the inside of her cheek hard enough to taste copper.

"I have here letters from several concerned citizens regarding Miss Bloomquist's previous use of illegally contracted employees." Caryn lifted a manila folder of her own. "Prior to her use of Miller and Sons, she engaged the services of a local drifter our own Sheriff Townsend is seeking charges against for impersonating a contractor."

The bottom dropped out of Cady's stomach.

This was news to her.

She glanced over to Ethan, whose gaze remained fixed on the council, his expression stubbornly impenetrable.

"But he didn't," Cady insisted. "He was only helping me with temporary fixes to prevent further damage to the building. He never claimed to be a licensed contractor."

"Sure did with me," Ethan said. "Made a verbal statement to that effect."

Caryn's lips flattened into a fuchsia line. She may be grateful for the information, but not for the timing or manner of delivery.

"I think the fact that we are all attempting to politely dance around here is that it has not been established that Miss Blomquist is the rightful owner of the building."

Cady found that thick sheaf of papers by feel alone and held them up like a truce flag. "I have a copy of my aunt's will right here," she said. "As the councilwoman has so helpfully pointed out, it hasn't yet completed probate court, but the will explicitly states Aunt Fern's intentions to leave me the Townsend Building, the bookstore, and all its assets, in addition to the living space associated with the property."

"I understand that the late Mr. Townsend's will contradicts this?" Mayor Stewart asked.

"That's correct, Mr. Mayor," Caryn said, stabbing an icy look at Cady. "Being a consummate businessman and a pillar of the community, my late husband made very careful provisions for his family and other beneficiaries. I would be more than happy to furnish copies of his will, which clearly states his intention for the building to be left to his son, Ethan Townsend IV."

Cady felt her jaw unhinge.

Had that been the reason Ethan was so keen to change the locks? To install security cameras on the inner and outer areas? Because he had intended to take possession of it all along?

"I assume if Fern Bloomquist had a legitimate claim to the building, she would have produced the evidence while probate court was settling my late husband's estate," Caryn continued. "As she didn't, ownership was awarded to my son, who then deeded it to me. And if the building never belonged to Fern, that would necessarily invalidate her niece's claim to its possession."

"If this is true," the mayor said with a contrived expression of thoughtfulness, "why is it you've permitted Miss Bloomquist to remained as a resident of the building?"

Caryn's face softened, and she turned toward the other members of the city council. "I was very aware of the"—she paused as if searching for a word—"*challenges* Miss Bloomquist faces. With her aunt's recent passing and the erratic behavior she's displayed since, I thought it would be best not to add to her stress. My son, who was briefly romantically linked to Miss Bloomquist, held a similar opinion. Blessed as we are, I was happy to be of assistance in making sure she had the opportunity to keep running the little bookshop. As a mother, I confess I'd thought that perhaps it might take a load off my son, who was doing his best to help as well. But it seems our efforts weren't sufficient to prevent Miss Bloomquist from developing *other* interests."

In one fell swoop, Caryn had painted Cady as a burden, an unstable charity case, *and* a gold digger. You had to hand it to her. It was basically a passive-aggressive masterwork.

"Sex, drugs, and rock 'n' roll!" a grating, metallic voice croaked out from the back of the room. "That's what she brings to the neighborhood."

"Roy," Caryn said in a tone generally reserved for scolding puppies, "we know you have very strong feelings about this topic, as your proximity exposes you directly to the kind of clientele she attracts, but we'll have to ask you wait to be recognized to speak."

Roy's beady eyes blinked out from behind his thick glasses as he obediently raised his hand.

"Yes, Roy," Caryn said. "Please proceed."

Clearing a throat constantly roughened by cigar smoke, Roy stood. "We've all seen the kind of people she has hanging around at her shop."

"As opposed to the actual toilets you have outside of yours," Gemma muttered just loud enough for the microphone to pick up.

"While you make an excellent point about the privilege of being entrusted with a business on Water Street, I'd suggest we table this point until the tourism council can join us to weigh in," Caryn suggested.

"I'd agree with that suggestion," Mayor Stewart added before turning his attention back to Cady. "Miss Bloomquist, to Councilwoman Townsend's original point, are you able to furnish any evidence that your aunt was the legal owner of this building?"

Cady's heart started an impromptu slam dance against her ribs. Her mouth had gone dry and sour. Her palms clammy and cold.

Gemma caught her eye and lifted her eyebrows.

They'd been of very different minds when it came to bringing up the evidence of Aunt Fern and Ethan Townsend Senior's affair. Cady's opinion being that lambasting Caryn at the expense of revealing Aunt Fern's affair should be avoided if there was a way to get around it through other mostly legal means.

Gemma's was that they should rock Caryn's shit with a nuclear war hammer and dance around her radioactive ashes.

"Miss Bloomquist?" Mayor Stewart repeated.

"I do," Cady said. "But it's of a nature that I would prefer were reviewed privately, if possible."

The pin-drop-silent room began to hum with whispered conversations.

Caryn grabbed her gavel and thumped the block decisively as she and Cady locked eyes. "We have not been made aware of any such evidence."

"It was recently uncovered within my late aunt's *private* correspondence," Cady said.

"I am certainly not aware of any private correspondence that happened between my husband's estate and your aunt," Caryn countered.

"I would be happy to let you review it in a more confidential setting."

"I think everyone has had quite enough of matters being handled privately when it comes to such a public and treasured town asset."

Cady and Gemma traded another look.

Did Caryn legitimately not know? Or was she going to try to spin it as a desperate attempt on Cady's part?

Fuck it. She'd tried.

"Based on items found in my late aunt's effects, it's my belief that the late mayor left the Townsend Building to her as a token of his love."

An audible gasp roared through the room like a riptide.

Caryn paled beneath her perfectly applied makeup. Her rouge stood out in harsh blocks on her prominent cheekbones. Her lips were a garish slash across a mask-tight face.

"And do you have that evidence with you?" Gemma asked, giving Cady a not-so-subtle nudge.

"I do," Cady said.

Collective gasp, round two.

"Please present it to the council," the mayor said with about eighty percent less swagger.

Returning to her file folder, Cady pulled out the page in the very back—a color copy of the note from the front of the book that she'd made before she gave it to Fox. She had selfishly hoped it might trigger his interest enough to want to return and stay by her side through this fight, but her giving the book to him had been down to other motives too.

If she really was being targeted by somebody with the power to access her building, rearrange her taxidermy animals, and create havoc with her book stock, she didn't want this one within their reach. Next to Fox was about the safest place she could possibly think of.

She tried to catch Ethan's eye as he came to retrieve the paper, but he kept his gaze stubbornly fixed on inanimate objects in the vicinity.

He walked the paper up to his mother, and this time, Cady didn't miss the beat that passed between them.

Caryn's eyes fell to the paper, and in that fraction of a second before her control snapped into place, Cady saw fine blue veins pulse at her temples. The moment was there and gone again, replaced by a breezy laugh that ended up an amused but pitying smile.

"It's adorable that you thought a handwritten note would be any kind of evidence, but even if my husband would lower himself to be with Fern Bloomquist, *not one other person* knows about it or witnessed a *thing*."

"Yes, they did."

Every single hair on Cady's body stood on end. Her cheeks prickled as blood drained from her face. Her pulse moved from her chest to her ears, her lips, her neck—even her eyelids, it seemed.

The old wooden pews creaked as every single person in the

meeting hall turned toward the back of the room to see who it had come from.

Cady turned with them, even though the imprint of the specific timbre, texture, and pitch had been forever burned into her brain.

Time slowed. Faces blurred like a funhouse mirror as she searched the rows of spectators for the planes and angles of a visage she met nightly in her dreams. Once, then twice, she swept the crowd and came up empty.

Then he stood, and her heart stopped.

Fox.

His dark hair had been cropped into a military-precise Irish gangster fade, his face and neck clean-shaven for the first time since she'd met him. The grubby flannel and long-sleeve thermal had been traded for crisp dress blues, complete with an array of multicolored badges, ribbons, and embroidered patches she couldn't begin to guess the meanings of. He stood and stepped into the aisle, revealing tapered slacks of a lighter blue embroidered with gold stripes narrowing into charcoal-black combat boots. Gold buttons winked from his chest as he stepped to the side to make way for a small, squat figure shoving past him.

"Ho-lee shit," Myrtle said from behind her. "Is that Judy?"

TWENTY-TWO

Hero

(HÎR'Ō) NOUN. A MAN DISTINGUISHED BY EXCEPTIONAL COURAGE, NOBILITY, FORTITUDE, ETC

ADVANCE OR RETREAT.

Two equally intolerable options.

But he couldn't listen to this shit any longer. Couldn't sit here and see the distress curling Cady's shoulders forward as if they could shield her heart while this fucking harpy tried to take her entire life away from her.

Fuck that.

For this—for *her*—retreat was not an option.

He advanced.

Sort of.

Hard to charge into battle behind a woman as wide as she was tall and had to wear shoes two different heights for very obvious orthopedic functions.

"The chair does not recognize Judy Miller at this time. In order to speak, you have to petition to the council or wait until the floor is opened." Caryn banged her gavel on the semicircular podium where the six city council members had attempted to preside with the gravitas of a military tribunal.

Except for Gemma, who'd paused in her furious knitting of a giant squid to gape at him like everyone else. "Holy fuck me sideways," she breathed, just close enough to the microphone to have the whisper caress the ear of everyone present.

"Um...do I put that in the notes?" asked the recorder, a fluffy-haired, apple-cheeked woman with pleasant ochre skin and a cornea-melting fuchsia pantsuit.

"*No,*" Caryn barked, as Vee simultaneously purred, "Please do."

The place was packed, everyone breathing the same air. Taking it. Transforming it. Holding it hostage so there was none left for Fox.

As he fought for breath, he realized it was packed like a wedding, in a way. Pro-Cady on one side, pro-self-interest and bureaucratic bullshit on the other.

He'd been glad to see the townspeople, in general, were firmly in Cady's court, supporting the small business owner against America's version of landed gentry.

An Orwellian scene but fucking weirder.

Unfazed by Gemma's profanity or Caryn's propriety, Judy waddle-sprinted down the aisle with the self-importance of a wronged female plaintiff in the eponymous Judge Judy's televised court. "Don't be such a *Karen*, Caryn." She cackled as if that joke hadn't probably been made at least a trillion times in the past decade. "Surrender the floor to me or read what I have to say in the *Townsend Crier* on Sunday in time to ruin your fancy brunch."

Damn. Judy was not fucking around.

Caryn's eyes narrowed on Fox. She clearly did not recognize him at all. "Who do you bring with you, and what does he have to do with the situation?"

"*I* didn't bring him." Judy threw a lascivious look over her shoulder that would have been a possible #MeToo crime if their genders were reversed. "I *came* because of him."

"*Yeah,* she did." Myrtle's gravely whisper into Vee's ear made use of the room's hundred-year-old acoustics, and several chuckles competed with the groans of the perpetually offended.

A bead of sweat trickled from Fox's orderly hair down the column of his spine beneath his dress blues. He'd done this a million times in a million different rooms. Addressed someone who had a title that commanded respect, or maybe a superior rank, but who couldn't best him at anything but paperwork.

Just...most of those rooms were built in the last century.

And had windows.

Or more than two doors.

And the attendants were... Well, this crowd was probably equally as full of old, officious white guys as any the military could threaten. And this crowd was just as grumpy with the additions of their bitchy, bureaucratic wives. Basically, this was Hell's waiting room, and Fox wasn't going to take a number. He'd force himself to the front of the line.

Curling his shaking hand into a fist, he decided he'd waited long enough for Judy to get a head start so he didn't bowl her over and make an ass of himself.

"Madam Chairperson, Mayor Stewart, members of council and committee." He offered a clipped nod to each, measuring his eye contact with respectful precision. "Major Roman G. Fawkes, 75th Ranger Regiment, Second Battalion, formerly of Joint Base Lewis-McCord, requests the floor."

There. At least he'd have most of the Boomers, veterans, law enforcement, self-proclaimed alpha males, and Karens of the figurative variety more likely to lend credence to his word.

How he looked in a uniform didn't hurt in picking up a few more favorable opinions.

Not that he was cocky, just working with the tools his meat suit and hunter/gatherer lifestyle provided.

"Get it? F-A-W-K-E-S!" Judy gleefully spelled, apropos of nothing. "You're thinking the animal at first, and *then*—"

"Request denied." The literal Caryn banged her gavel against the wave of murmurs in the room, spearing him with a perfectly lined glare of antipathy. "While we thank you for your service, the council doesn't recognize you as having a stake in this issue or a claim on the building in question."

Finally gaining the intestinal fortitude, he turned to where Cady sat in the front row and let himself drink in the sight of her face—vibrant eyes muted, a little sunken and bruised from lack of sleep, lashes heavy with unshed tears, lids puffy from the ones already wept in anticipation of today going badly. Her cheeks glowed crimson with emotion, the skin below ghostly pale from shock.

And still...she was flawlessly beautiful, even beneath the harsh tube lights installed by the energy-conscious.

How many tears had fallen on his behalf? Every single one was like acid to his skin. And the only thing he could do was this.

"I have nothing to lose," he admitted to her. "Everything's at stake for Cady Bloomquist, wouldn't you agree?" he asked the room. "Doesn't she deserve to have all witnesses heard?"

"Sit down, Mr. Fawkes," Mayor Stewart ordered him, waving his hands as if that'd do anything to restore the silent expectancy of before.

Fox knew what to do, but still he fought what he yearned to do—stomp and snarl. Threaten and throw things. Break stuff with his bare hands. Bones sounded fun.

But if he could spend four hours talking a caliphate warlord into selling him illegally gained U.S. munitions at a loss, he could keep his cool against the rat-fink mayor for a few minutes.

"I will stand, and I will be heard, *Mr. Mayor.* But, with all due respect, it is correct to refer to me as Major Fawkes—"

"*Yeah,* it is." All eyes turned for a second to Myrtle, who wiped (what he hoped was) pretend drool from her deeply grooved lips.

Vee put a hand on her—girlfriend? common-law spouse?—and whispered something unintelligible in Myrtle's ear.

"Oh, come on," she said to the assembly at large gesturing toward him with gnarled fingers. "That one set *itself* up. I mean, look at him. A *major fox.*"

"Myrtle, enough." Ethan kicked his hip away from the wall against which he'd been leaning, fair hair kept in place by the exactly measured teeth of a basic black comb and the favored gel of Boy Scouts everywhere. "This isn't a court of law, major. If the chairperson tells you to sit down, you do it, or we have a problem."

If Superman-punching a cop wouldn't ultimately hurt Cady, Fox would have cheerfully gone down for it.

"Oh, we have a problem, you and I," he said evenly, not completely masking the violence in his stance. "And we're about to find out just how big it is and what I'm going to have to do about it."

Ethan stomped closer, stopping in front of the first church-pew-style bench, and its seven occupants were all that separated the two. His ice-blue eyes glinted with aggression. "That a threat?"

Uh-oh, someone had their enormous feathers ruffled.

Buckle up, big boy, Fox thought. *Your day is about to go to ripe shit.*

"Fox?" His name finally escaped from Cady's mouth, melting some of the malice from his blood.

He took a pause from eye-fucking-up the sheriff to glance in her direction.

A whole month.

Four quiet, bleak Thursday nights. Forty-three-thousand-eight-hundred eternal minutes since he'd last heard her voice. Two-point-seven million seconds since he'd bathed in the glow of her smile.

And counting, as her generous mouth currently trended downward into a perplexed grimace pinched with concern.

He forced himself to look away, or he'd never accomplish what he'd come here to do.

Drawing strength from his purpose, he faced the raised dais on which he found only one friendly—if skeptical—face. "You are aware Judy is not only the night dispatch for the county, but also one of the only notaries public for probably twenty miles."

"That is correct," Judy announced, with the importance of a star witness on a primetime court drama. "I know every divorce, affidavit, mortgage, and et cetera filed in Townsend Harbor and the surrounding communities."

Dangerous job for the town gossip to have.

Caryn's gavel became more insistent. Sharper. Her voice inched from authoritarian to shrill. "Judy, might I remind you of confidentiality and your duty to your community. You will wait to address this council until you're invited by the—"

"I submit to you, *et cetera*." Judy open-palm-slapped a piece of paper on the long oak table reserved for people making their case to the council. "If it please the court, I would like to enter into the record this irrefutable evidence of Cady Bloomquist's innocence of the charges brought against her."

Ethan strode toward Judy's table to examine the document. "Again, Judy, this isn't a court of law. This is a city council meeting. No one is on tri—"

Wide brows knitted together as he looked down to read the document, scanning it again and again as red crept from beneath his collar. When he looked up, he turned to where Cady was frozen in place. "Cady. I'm sorry for all of this."

She went impossibly paler. "What is it?" she asked, looking from Fox to Judy to Ethan and back. "What's going on?"

"That there is a copy of my notary record book from five years ago," Judy answered before the question was finished. "From the night Ethan Townsend III signed a Deed on Death, granting Fern Bloomquist ownership of the Townsend Building and enough cash to cover the inheritance taxes upon his demise."

Her pause for dramatic effect was surprisingly effective, as the entire room erupted into chaos at the politest possible decibel level.

Caryn's gavel did nothing to quiet the room, and she had to turn the volume on her mic up to be heard. If she wasn't Satan's own secretary, Fox would feel kind of bad that her husband's affair had been so publicly revealed.

Even though his own marriage had disintegrated, it could have been worse. They could have stayed together.

"Wait." Cady raised her hand like a kid at school, though she didn't wait to be called on. "Are you saying that's the document that proves Nevermore and the Townsend Building belonged to Aunt Fern?"

"That's exactly what I'm saying," Judy replied.

"Outrageous!" Caryn shrieked as she thrust her hand out to her son. "Give that here."

Ethan strode over, handing the paper up to her. "It's right there," he said, face a mask of regret. "In black and white."

Caryn's hand trembled as she looked at the document, but her features didn't crack.

She had a big old set of lady balls—Fox had to give her that.

"This is a copy of your handwritten documentation, not the document itself. I'll see proof of that before I believe a word of this farce," Caryn said coldly.

"I don't keep the docs, I just watch people sign 'em," Judy announced. "But I did pass the paperwork on to be filed with the court."

"I requested all such documents!" Cady insisted. "Who did the filing?"

"The Townsends' lawyer, of course." Judy turned her pointed condemnation toward the dais. "Mayor Stewart."

A theatrical gasp echoed through the congregation, and the mayor surged to his feet, though his response was lost to the din.

Caryn Townsend lifted her gavel, but Gemma snatched it away before it could come down.

"Give that back!" Caryn barked, abandoning her self-containment altogether. "Everyone clear out! I'm declaring a close to this council meeting until further investigation can be—"

"I gave the Deed on Death to you!" Mayor Stewart hollered,

pointing an accusing finger at none other than Caryn. "You were the one who told me to forget it ever existed."

"Libel!" Caryn was the last to gain her feet. "You have no proof! You will find no documents. Get ready for a lawsuit to end all, Stewart, you toad!"

"Strange way to word that, Madam Chairperson."

As often happened, when Fox spoke, the room quieted.

All eyes turned to him, but he'd lasered away everything but the fire covering the fear in Caryn's eyes.

"You deny that the documents would be found," he repeated. "Not that they exist."

Caryn affected an obviously practiced imperious look down her literal nose at him. "My husband would never have taken the Townsend Building away from our son's legacy."

"Except he did." Fox fought the urge to straighten his jacket and tug on his collar. It was infinitely easier than not snatching Cady and dragging her back to his Neanderthal cave.

Just don't look at her, he reminded himself. *Focus. You are no stranger to suffering. This moment will be over. Do your worst to it.*

"Let me ask you something, Madam Chairperson." He drifted closer, drawn in for the kill by the flash of apprehension in her dark eyes. "Do you have your husband's keys to the Townsend Building?" He turned to Ethan. "Or do you?"

"I haven't touched anything of my dad's since his...loss." Ethan looked up to Caryn for verification from her.

"I wouldn't know where he kept the keys." She shrugged airily. "I'm sorry, I don't understand why this is relevant."

Fox lifted a skeptical eyebrow. "It's relevant because someone broke into Nevermore Bookstore on Thursday before Halloween and ransacked the place. Nothing valuable went missing, but the content of the front end of the store and paperwork was not only disturbed but strewn all over the floor."

"And?" she asked impatiently.

"And no one could figure out why. No windows broken. No sign of lock tampering. No helpful fingerprints." Fox leveled an assessing look on Ethan. "Fruitless investigation done by your son, who not only has an interest in Cady, but also in the building."

"Don't you dare bring Ethan into this," Caryn hissed. "I don't care who you are—"

"This Ethan?" Fox jabbed a finger toward the scowling sheriff. "The one who replaced the locks after the break-in? The one who installed security cameras on the exterior of the building?"

"Oh, that is *sus*." Gemma skewered her dark hair into a bun with a knitting needle, as if preparing for battle as she pointed at Ethan. "Sheriff, you'd be the first person to preach that officers need to be accountable for what they do. Especially while operating in the capacity of their job. What do you have to say for yourself?"

Sheriff Ethan Townsend IV wasn't a complicated or conflicted man. He knew right from wrong, and he enforced it. He opened his mouth to address Fox. Closed it. Turned to Cady as if to speak to her. Changed his mind, then spun to look at his mother for a full three breaths.

As Fox's own mom used to say, it was so quiet in the crowded room, he could have heard a tick fart.

"In the hook cupboard by the garage." Ethan's admission astonished everyone, but only Gemma said the one word everyone was thinking.

"What?"

Ethan's gaze never wavered from his mother's. "All Dad's keys. To any of his properties, his cars, storage—even the gun locker—are kept in the key cabinet by the garage. Labeled. Alphabetized. Has been that way for the thirty-five years I've been alive."

"Ethan." His name escaped his mother's expertly glossed lips on a plea. "Ethan, we'll talk about this—"

"What did you do?" he asked his mom.

"Look," Vee stage-whispered. "His dad used to have that same vein in his forehead when he was cross and trying not to hit people."

"She didn't do anything." Roy stood with all the alacrity of tree Ent. "It was me."

With eerie syncopation, the entire room turned to watch him knock the knees of the other people on the bench as he scootched past on his way toward the middle aisle.

"Why am I not surprised?" Cady spat at him. "You want Nevermore so much, you broke into my home and went through my things? Were you trying to hurt me when you caved in my roof?"

"Not *your* roof—Mrs. Townsend's roof," he said through his *Duck Dynasty* beard, then cast Caryn a sheepish look. "But no. That was an accident." Crossing beefy sailor arms over his barrel chest, Roy finally allowed his condemnation to rest on Fox. "Besides, if this idiot carpenter didn't fu—er, foul up the ceiling joists so bad, it wouldn't have collapsed by me just poking around."

"I didn't touch the joists." Fox's arms tensed, his short nails making indents on his palms as he grabbed his temper with both hands. "They'd clearly been 'fouled' up by the shoddy carpenter the Townsends approved to do the initial restoration work through this very Historical Preservation Society."

A contingent of Q-tip heads lost their shit, the core of the Historical Preservation Society quite obviously feeling more bereaved about the building damage than anything else going on in the room.

Like cat people, but for architecture.

"The pertinent question is why you were poking around the roof without permission in the first place," Cady admonished Roy.

"I had the permission I needed," he said, approaching her. "Your Aunt Fern, God rest her, usurped what was rightfully Mrs. Townsend's by way of her questionable conduct with a married man. Now, I'm not here to speak ill of the dead, though we both had little good to say about each other when Fern was alive, but that wasn't right."

Fox grabbed the gorilla-sized man's shirtfront, nerves stretched to the limit. "Were you the one who disabled the register surveillance camera the night of the break-in? And I'm begging you to lie to me, old man. To give me a motherfucking reason."

"Hands off, Fawkes." Ethan immediately turned from son to cop in the space of a blink. "I'll warn you once."

Cady stepped forward, putting her hand on the forearm of Fox's jacket. "Hey, it's okay. I've never had a surveillance camera inside the store."

Fox scowled down at her, keeping one eye on Roy. "The one in the raven."

She shook her head. "No. That's just a googly eye I put on it because it only had a filmy glass—" Stiffening as if struck by a thought, she turned to Ethan. "You gave me the raven. When you asked me on our first date, you told me you wanted to bring something more meaningful than flowers. Something relevant to my interests."

"I did." Ethan nodded, his back to the dais, arms stiffly folded as his jaw twitched in time to the vein pulsing in his forehead.

"What else did you do, sheriff?" Myrtle demanded. "What the hell is going on here?"

Ethan's inhalation lasted longer than should be physically possible as he looked from Fox, to Cady, to Roy, to survey the gathered crowd with something bordering on contempt.

His proud shoulders and jaw dropped a notch as he did an abrupt about-face and mounted the five stairs of the dais in two swift strides.

Gemma jumped out of his way, as did another councilman, clearing a path to his furious mother.

In a flat voice, Ethan said, "Caryn Townsend, you're under arrest for illegal surveillance, unlawful trespass, and fraud. You have the right to remain silent; anything you say can and will be held against you..."

Caryn's infuriated protests drowned out her son's monotone recitation of her Miranda rights, but didn't make him pause in the least. "Ethan? Ethan! What the hell are you—? I can put up cameras in my own building. I don't care what— Ethan, put those handcuffs away this minute! I am your *mother*."

The only deference he showed was to cuff her wrists in front of her rather than behind her back. "You bought the cameras, Mother. You had the raven 'restructured' before I gave it to her. And when the"—he broke off, as if he couldn't pry his teeth apart enough to bring himself to say the next words—"the *googly* eye covered your hidden camera, you sent me with a houseplant. You made me complicit in a crime."

Fox remembered the weight of the plant landing on his head, wondering what was sharp enough to have cut his head when the insubstantial plastic holding the roots together crumpled when you looked at it too hard. The mess of wires he'd chucked into the dumpster. A camera, perhaps?

"All we'd have to do is search the construction dumpster for what was hidden in that plant," he said.

Caryn gasped. "You threw the plant away?"

"Immediately," Cady said coldly.

Roy lunged for Ethan, but had forgotten about Fox's unyielding grip. "You can't arrest your own mother."

"You shut your mouth, Roy," Ethan snarled. "You and Mayor Stewart are next."

"Just take me in for everything," the older man demanded. "Caryn doesn't belong in jail."

"Wait!" Cady held out both arms in a T as if refereeing an MMA match. "Wait. Everyone wait." She addressed Caryn, specifically. "I know you could be in huge trouble for not filing that deed. Let alone for what you commissioned Roy to do after you knew the building should be legally mine."

"It isn't right." Caryn's face crumpled, and she lifted her cuffed hands to cover it. "It isn't fair that she took him from me, and then he humiliates me further by making it obvious that he gifted it to his mistress."

"You should have brought it to me," Cady said. "Because I

agree—it isn't fair, and it isn't right. But neither of them are here now, so let's do this. You find that paperwork and file it, handing the deed to me free and clear, and..." She looked at Ethan. "And I press no charges."

Caryn opened her mouth, but Ethan spoke first. "Done."

"How about you settle for what's rightfully yours, *and* let these criminals rot in jail for a bit before you file a lawsuit against them for using their political offices to cheat you?" Fox said, offering Cady his favorite alternative. "All I ask is you give me five minutes alone with the asshole who made you fear for your life."

He gave Roy's collar a shake, and the man at least had the decency to look abashed, if not afraid. "I didn't hurt a hair on Cady's head."

"She was in a sling because of you," Fox reminded him. "Want to know what that feels like?"

"Ummmm..." Cady's drawn-out word was several octaves too high. "To be fair...I pulled that bookshelf over on myself."

Roy put his hands up as if Fox's glare contained live rounds. "Cady was supposed to be at Myrtle's party—I was going to be in and out before anyone came back. How was I supposed to know she was chatting on the phone in the dark?"

"By not breaking in there in the first place?" Gemma suggested.

Roy closed his eyes and let out an eternal sigh. "The day of the festival, I couldn't use the key Caryn gave me due to the lock change, so I was trying to get in through the hole in the ceiling, is all. Seeing as how there was one no one in a hurry to fix the damage."

"Don't press charges against Roy," Caryn had the audacity to ask of Cady.

Ethan had her upper arms shackled in his bear-paw hands as he marched her down the aisle, but he allowed her to pause to entreat her nemesis.

"I'll give you back your copy of the deed and file it properly," Caryn said, frigid eyes pooling with panic and emotion. "I'll do whatever else you ask. But Roy didn't know what I asked him to do could get him in trouble."

"Ignorance isn't innocence," Fox spat. "Anyone should know not to break into a woman's home."

Roy nodded, coloring as he looked at his feet like a chastised child. "I knew it was wrong," he muttered into his overgrown mustache. "Just...couldn't say no."

"What's that?" someone asked from the peanut gallery, apparently perturbed at not being able to hear the entire drama as it unfolded, which started a new set of complaints.

"Yeah, speak up!"

"I can't hear what's going on."

"Who's the hottie in uniform?"

What Fox recognized in Roy's eyes as he looked at Caryn made him disengage his fingers from the man's collar.

"I believe him." A presence at his elbow caused his skin to prickle in awareness. Fox smoothed the fine hairs on the back of his neck before looking down at Cady. "What's the move?"

She searched his face for a moment too long, and apparently did not find what she was looking for. Her smile deflated incrementally before she turned away. "I don't want anyone to go to jail. I just want my bookstore and to be a part of that building's story. Just like Aunt Fern was. Just like the Townsends were before it."

This time, no one—not even Caryn—objected to a thing.

The gavel fell once again, startling everyone and pulling the attention back to the front of the room, where Gemma held it like a battle ax. "Regardless of criminal status," she said, "I move to relieve Mayor Stewart and Chairwoman Townsend from all public service immediately and furthermore..."

Fox used the absolute attention commanded by Gemma to slowly melt backward by allowing others to step in front of him. The retreat was slow and painful, and for a man lauded for his dexterity, he was weak-kneed as a two-legged tripod by the time he was able to tumble out the door and into the daylight.

Immediately, he loosened his tie so his trachea stopped closing off, and dabbed at his drenched forehead with a handkerchief as he ate up the concrete in long strides.

The crisp autumn wind caressed him like a lover, and he truly breathed for the first time since he'd descended into the city.

He'd done it.

If he was nothing else, he was the architect of Cady's happiness, and that was what mattered. There were many stains upon his soul, and many times he'd made the wrong call.

But sometimes seeing the good side win was better than any drug. It happened too seldom these days, and too many people were starting to realize the good guys weren't whom they'd initially assumed.

Cady, though...

If the world fostered more people with hearts like hers, men like him wouldn't have to exist.

Aiming toward the Uptown steps, he figured he could calm himself in his old clearing and wait for night to descend to comfortably travel.

He'd been stretched to the limits of his masking capabilities, and the veneer of humanity was beginning to crack, uncovering the beast beneath.

If he was lucky, he'd be able to watch Cady enter her building, secure in the knowledge that no one could take it from her for the first time since her aunt died.

He could allow himself that, at least. One last look at—

Fox crested the top of the staircase and had to grab on to the railing to keep from taking a dive down all six flights of stairs because of what had changed. Weak knees became jelly. Sweat dried in the breeze and locked shivers into his guts, amplified by the quaking of his own bones.

The roof of the Townsend Building was not only being restored and remodeled, but rebuilt.

As a conservatory.

Iron and steel secured panels of reflective glass storm windows in place to form a Victorian-style dome that Covent Garden would envy.

It took his breath away. Not just the beauty of it. Not the incomprehensible cost. Not just because it improved upon the already unparalleled skyline of the Townsend Harbor Downtown, but because...

Because he'd told her they might never see each other again...

And she'd still built him the perfect home.

Why?

"Because I know you, Major Roman G. Fawkes," Cady said from behind him. "Even though I was today years old when I learned your actual name, I realized I knew you well enough to be certain you wouldn't stay away forever. And I could think of no greater idea then for you to have a place to shelter from the storm, but also not feel trapped."

Swallowing profusely, Fox didn't allow himself to turn around. If he saw her, he'd have to touch her. To hold her.

If he did that... Well.

He'd never let go.

Instead, he'd bury his face into her fragrant hair and wash it in tears he'd never allowed himself to shed.

"Nothing's changed," he lied, his voice tight with barely leashed emotion and the agony of the past five torturous years threatening to break his resolve.

"I don't believe you," she said, her voice measured but firm, underscored by a note of something he didn't dare analyze. "You seem...different. Something has changed, other than the obvious." She made as if to reach for his newly shaved face, but pulled back at the last moment.

If disappointment could do bodily damage, he'd be a corpse.

"I'm ah—taking advantage of some of my military benefits. You know, meds and"—he cleared his throat—"therapy and whatnot." Fighting the urge to kick at loose gravel like a child, he remained perfectly still. "Figured I needed to give it another shot."

She made an impressed noise. "You spent so long in the

council chambers today. I, alone, know what that cost you. And I know you wouldn't have done it for me if you didn't...if you didn't care. If there wasn't hope."

Finally he spun to face her, prepared, at least, for the sucker punch in the gut at the sight.

She glowed with an ethereal luminosity that had to be divine.

"Cady...I came back to finish the job. That's it. I had to do the right thing." His eyes already skittered away, and he forced them back to her face to suffer the punishment of her displeasure.

What he found was a teasing sort of smugness dimpling her cheeks. "You're saying you came out of the mountains right before Christmas, retrieved your dress uniform, colluded with Judy freaking Miller, and *this-is-Sparta*-kicked open the door to the council meeting to Mr. Darcy-style save the day, because you *don't* have feelings for me?"

"Don't have—" His jaw unhinged as he struggled to process the absurdity of what she'd just said. "Let me make something perfectly clear. I went into those mountains to eventually die, Cady. I'd gotten used to the darkness. I'd given over to it. And then *you* picked up the phone, and I felt my heart beat for the first time in ages."

Her lip disappeared between her teeth as if she had to bite it to stay quiet.

"That's when I'd vowed never to call again. And I made that same promise every time I couldn't help myself. I should have cut all sense of attachment earlier. Before I could want you so much."

He clamped his mouth shut, feeling his heart pounding like a jackhammer, ready to shatter into a million unrepairable pieces at his next revelation.

"When I say nothing has changed, I mean it." He snatched the hand she pressed to his chest, meaning to thrust it away, but found himself clutching it instead. "I'm still...me. I can't do what other men can. Can't provide the simplest pleasures in life. I wouldn't be able to share with you. And this isn't me being some altruistic martyr, here. Because, dammit, my worst fear is watching the love you think you feel for me drain from you as the reality of life with me replaces this intensity between us. Do you understand? I can't put myself through that. But don't you ever believe I don't have feelings for you, Cadence Bloomquist, because you're the love of my fucking life."

TWENTY-THREE

Elation

(IˈLEIΣƏN) NOUN. JOYFULNESS OR EXALTATION OF SPIRIT, AS FROM SUCCESS, PLEASURE, OR RELIEF; HIGH SPIRITS

You're the love of my fucking life...

Every time Fawkes' words echoed through Cady's head, her knees liquified all over again. How they'd gotten to Nevermore from the town hall, she couldn't be sure. She hadn't felt the earth beneath her feet for a single step.

Running on a curious mix of exhaustion, elation, and relief, she'd floated down Water Street with Roman Fawkes at her side, her heart swelling as the building that was *hers* came into view. This knowledge made the bell's jingle sound brighter, made the lamps glow warmer, sparked from her fingertips as she ran them over the spines of books as she passed, greeting them like old friends.

Hell, even her critter menagerie seemed to be grinning right along with her.

Which, admittedly, should have been creepy but wasn't. Not on a day like today.

Today, her hip's bark of protest at the two-story climb had been dialed down to a mild yelp. Her back's objections to the barely padded meeting room pews was quickly forgotten as they stepped out into the conservatory together.

Cady stood with her back against the bricks of *her* building, silently swooning as Fawkes walked the perimeter of the ongoing construction, his beret tucked beneath his arm against his pristine dress coat. How strange, and wonderful, and deeply weird it was to see this man in the space she had designed with him in mind—given the version of him she'd imagined here hadn't been dressed like a panty-melting army badass straight out of a Tom Clancy military thriller—but she was more than willing to make the necessary mental adjustment.

Keen as ever, Fawkes' eyes moved from the dark aluminum framework to the glass panels beaded with the morning's rain. Any minute now, she'd figure out how to tear her eyes away from him and say what she'd brought him here to say.

He was humoring her. Honoring her request that they finish here the conversation they'd begun on the Uptown hill.

Here, where they had spent the first hours in each other's physical presence. Here, where she first knew the feeling of his body on hers. Here, where the sea and sky could conspire with her to convince him to stay.

"So what do you think?" she asked at last.

Fawkes glanced at her over a gold-embroidered epaulet on his shoulder. "I think this is fucking incredible."

"Wait until you see the freshwater fishing pond and the infrared sauna," she said, pushing off the wall.

His eyebrows shot toward his newly shorn hairline.

"Kidding." She laughed. "About the freshwater fishing pond, anyway. Infrared light therapy is actually supposed to be helpful for *both* our conditions. At least, I read that it's supposed to improve the homeostasis of the autonomic nervous system. Which can't be a bad thing, right?"

"You read?" The corners of his clean-shaven lips curled up in a smirk.

She nodded. "Every now and then. Which is why I'm also putting in an herb harden," she said, gesturing toward the south-facing corner of the glass panes. "Moxibustion works better if you grow and dry your own."

"Moxibustion?"

"Burning mugwort," she explained. "My acupuncturist says it's supposed to help the treatments be more effective, and it's a personal life philosophy of mine to never disagree with a man who's sticking needles in my face."

"Solid logic," he said. "Infrared light therapy, face needles. Sounds like you've been a busy girl."

"I have. That's kinda part of what I wanted to talk to you about," she said, hating the sound of her awkwardly obvious transition. "I was doing that thing I do where I learn everything about a topic of potential interest, and in my CPTSD deep dive, I had this very unwelcome realization that...um...I'm an asshole."

"An asshole who built out an entire human terrarium and has been researching treatments for a debilitating mental illness?" he said, sweeping a hand toward the view.

Cady took a deep breath and walked to the wall of glass facing the shoreline. "When we were up on the mountain, and you were trying to explain to me why you didn't feel you could be in a relationship with me, I dismissed your concerns."

She glanced at the flickering reflection of him over her shoulder in the glass panel.

"I talked about how I'm not afraid of pain, and I don't let it keep me from living, but in the process, I ignored and invalidated how yours might be affecting you. I tried to convince you that your issues weren't issues for me. But I didn't acknowledge my own problems, or the fact that I had things I needed to work on before I could be a solid partner for anyone."

That there had been a first-class mindfuck—riding home on her tidal wave of righteous indignation, basking in the glow of self-congratulatory romantic bravery as she recounted the details of their conversation to the girls over many mimosas, only to have Vivian ever so gently point out that she'd been doing to Fox the very thing she hated.

Stupid bullshit self-actualization and motherfucking emotional honesty.

"Cady, you don't have to do this." His boots shifted on the brand-new masonry, still coated with a fine layer of dust from the grout.

"Yes, I do." She turned to face him. "I need to say this, and I need you to hear it, Fawkes. All I talked about is what you did for me. How much you helped me. And you did. More than you'll ever know. Your calls were my life raft. My escape. But this," she said, lifting her eyes to the gunmetal-gray sky overhead, "this isn't about escaping. It's about staying."

Up until now, she'd been able to resist the mysterious, magnetic pull of his body. She'd spent the last four weeks both longing to find her rest against the solid wall of his chest, and preparing herself for the possibility that she might never again know the kind of peace she felt with the steady thrum of his heart in her ear. But now he was so close, she found herself drifting into his orbit, drawn by a gravity that was all their own.

"This place is yours to come to. Whenever you can. However you can. For as long as it helps. Whatever healing looks like, we can do it together. You and me."

Fawkes gazed down at her from beneath the structure that blurred the lines between inside and outside. Up and down. Day and night. Him and her. "You also said I was full of shit."

Cady looked into eyes she'd spent so long dreaming into life that they almost didn't seem real. "I stand by that statement."

"I'd expect nothing less." By degrees too small to measure in anything but time, they found each other. Breath to breath. Mouth to mouth. Body to body, various scars and all.

Cady felt herself melting into him, strangely touched by the unfamiliar shapes of ribbon bars and medals pressing into her skin. This part of his life she hadn't known now becoming part of hers as well. Their past, their present, and their future fused with the heat of their kiss.

The sweetness of their reunion quickly burned away, replaced by something hard and hungry.

Fawkes smiled against her lips as she wobbled in the steady circle of his arms.

"You okay?" he asked.

"So good. It's just that these stupid pantyhose are cutting off the circulation to my brain." She wriggled to move their stranglehold further down her liver. "Whoever decided underwear needed built-in mesh socks can kiss my whole ass."

"Allen E. Grant, and it's a good thing he's long dead, because if he tried to kiss even a part of this ass," he said, giving her cheeks a firm squeeze, "I'd have to shove his jaw down his neck."

"Only what he deserves for inflicting his bullshit misogynist torture device on generations of women."

Fawkes' hands migrated up toward her waist, releasing a tide of goosebumps down her neck and arms. "It just so happens I'm an expert at disengaging misogynistic torture devices."

"You're a man of many talents, Roman Fawkes," she said, stepping out of her sensible heels. "That reminds me. What should I call you? Now that I know you have a first name and you're a Fawkes as in *Guy* rather than as in dumpster fire news media or cunning woodland creature, it feels weird to keep addressing you by a three-letter call sign."

The Man Formerly Known as Fox found the zipper of her skirt and released it from behind. "Call me but love, and I'll be new baptized," he whispered against the ticklish skin of her bare neck.

"At least you chose a thematically appropriate Shakespearean character to blatantly thieve lines from," Cady said, catching his eye over her shoulder. "Romeo totally had a thing for watching as well."

The hem of her skirt began to rise up her thighs under the power of two large, warm hands. "Please," Fawkes said. "Juliet was the one on the balcony talking about names and man parts."

Speaking of...

A familiar and very insistent shape nudged up against her ass he began rolling down the elastic band that had been slowly dissecting her internal organs. Cady's body proved embarrassingly Pavlovian in its response.

She blamed the beret.

His fingers skimmed the hosiery over her hips, down her thighs, her knees, her calves.

"Put your hand on my shoulder." Crouching down, he slipped the stocking from one ankle and foot, followed by the other.

"Just like Willoughby when he found Marianne on the moors," Cady said dreamily, gazing out at the pewter-bellied storm clouds rolling in.

"As if. I'm an officer and you have daddy issues," he pointed out. "We're solidly in Colonel Brandon company."

"That may the sexiest thing a man has ever said to me."

"I could say more." His fingers flexed against her pelvis.

"What would you say to baptizing that chaise over there, Colonel Brandon?" she asked.

Fawkes slipped his arms around her torso, pulling her against the warm, solid wall of his body. His chin rested on the crown of her head, anchoring them in this one moment of time and the question whose answer made sense in a story only they knew.

"I'd say hi."

Epilogue

Morning in the PNW could vary widely. In the winter, the sun might not rise until eight or so. Around the summer solstice, it often came up before four a.m.

Either way, Fox was usually awake to see it.

And every time he woke before the silver light of predawn kissed the bank of clouds or a clear horizon, he'd spend a moment in gratitude for another day.

With Cady.

The dome she'd built him had been financed by the overcalculation of tax costs Mr. (he called no man Daddy) Townsend had left to Aunt Fern alongside the money provided by insurance and a generous reparations payment from the Townsend Endowment to the Historical Preservation Society for the express purposes of the care and upkeep of the Townsend Building for decades to come.

Whether the world ceased buying paperbacks or not, Cady would be able to surround herself with them, and create a place for creatives to gather and read about their own passions.

On top of that, Fox's officer pension hadn't been spent in a handful of years, and to say he had a nest egg was a bit of an understatement.

The money, of course, was all Cady's.

Everything he had was hers. His blood, sweat, and tears. His damage and his skill. His heart, his strength...his very life, if she wanted it.

And, apparently, the razor he'd specifically bought for his own thick beard that she pretended she didn't use, his toothbrush when she couldn't find hers (who loses a toothbrush?), and any leftovers he abandoned to the fridge for more than a cursory twenty-four hours. Her moral standpoint where others' food was concerned was from the you-snooze-you-lose college of thought.

Life shouldn't be this sweet. He didn't deserve it.

The errant thought threatened the supreme peace of the moment, and he chased it away by wrapping his arms around the woman nestled in next to him. Sleeping always turned her a bit pink, and if he took a photo of her now, all she'd do was demand he delete any evidence of a double chin as her jaw relaxed at the most adorable—if not exactly flattering—angle.

Beauty.

There could never be an angle he didn't find exquisite. Because Cady was the sum of her pretty parts and the whole of his heart. She'd breathed new life into him over the past handful of months. Had been understanding of his bad days and slowly allowed him to help alleviate hers. Patience came easily to them both, as they were each intrinsically compassionate toward the other's struggle and diagnoses.

The willingness to love and heal and forgive outweighed all other difficulties.

In fact, it astonished him what came easily. Things he thought never to hope for again. Laughter. Passion. Pleasure. Comfort. Rest. Sleep.

Trust.

All because of the open heart of a gentle soul.

A lead weight landed on his balls with a rude sound, and he jerked in pain.

"Goddammit, Kevin Costner." The gigantic bastard leapt off

him, narrowly avoiding the decorative pillow that sailed in his direction. "Next time I won't miss."

That not-so-little little fucker hated Fox. They were locked in a now-indefinite battle for Cady's ultimate affections.

Because Mr. Henery went into a home after his hospitalization, Cady had easily taken on Kevin Costner to be Nevermore's unofficial mascot. This after her recently becoming wary of raven figurines, turning the googly-eyed one to face the corner, even after the camera had been removed.

Poor Edgar was in perpetual timeout.

"You okay?" She yawned the unconcerned question into her hand and succumbed to an involuntary stretch before nuzzling into the cocoon of his body.

"Kevin Costner tried to re-circumcise me," he griped. "If he's not careful, I'll be giving you a taxidermized cat next Christmas."

"Don't even joke about it!"

A dull *whump* sounded as she swung her pillow against his face, and he used her momentum to enfold her and roll her over. Pinning her down with his body while controlling his weight with his arms, he buried his scratchy beard in her neck and rooted for places to kiss her.

"No! I have morning breath!" she croaked. "No sex before coffee."

It was a rule he'd enticed her to break on occasion, but he had the feeling today wasn't that day.

Nibbling up her throat, he nipped at her earlobe.

She shivered and purred, the vibration landing in his cock.

"You sure you don't wanna—"

"It's now, or after I go shopping at Vee's Lady Garden." She gave him the ultimatum while rubbing the sleep crust from her eyes.

"Let's get coffee." He bounced—*bounced*—from the bed and rushed through their morning routine. She lay there and scrolled through mysterious media while he found her coat, her fuzzy socks, her boots, and the bra-that-wasn't-really-a-bra that she liked to wear in the morning.

By the time her feet swung over the side of the bed, he'd showered, dressed, shaved his neck, trimmed his beard, combed his hair, and remote-started the car to heat up.

By the time she'd wrestled herself into the morning spring garb, he was waiting at the door with lemon water and an entire handful of pills, supplements, and vitamins.

"You've got to stop," she bitched as she tossed the pills back. "I'm going to get used to this, and then you'll get tired of this, and I'll have to go back to being a plebian who does all of the drudgery herself."

"I'll never get tired of taking care of you," he said, placing a kiss on the corner of her mouth and holding the door open for them both.

"Challenge accepted," she snarked, booping him on the tip of the nose before walking through the door.

"We're taking my car to work this morning," he called, grabbing the fob. Tourist season was coming, and his new position as trailblazer for the forest service would keep him occupied until then...

This time of year, it was quiet and still, even misty when he arrived to the place where Cady dropped him off at the base of the mountain. Not a hiker or biker in sight.

Which meant when they got coffee on the way, there was still hope for sex in the car, and his had more headroom.

Hope, he realized with a dopey-ass grin, had gotten him this far...

Author's Note

Kerrigan

Growing up I was forbidden to laugh.

It sounds stupid. It *is* stupid. But there are some stupid commandments in some stupid, old-timey books that mention being light-minded or indulging in loud laughter is a sin.

And so I could not do so without intolerable punishment.

Being a polygamous cult-raised, homeschooled kid—until a well-timed, post-Waco raid by local and federal law enforcement scattered the rats—let's just say I wasn't surrounded by folks known for their senses of humor.

Fast forward almost thirty years?

I'm addicted to comedy.

I'm addicted to reading, streaming, video games, audiobooks/podcasts, work, food, my phone, coffee, the devil's lettuce, and online shopping, but mostly comedy.

Comedy is *so* important, you guys. Because laughter (like crying) is a hysterical response. A release. A producer of chemicals in your brain that are no less than the magical—alchemical—components of joy. And joy is something in precious short supply these days. Not only has comedy always been used to subvert authority, but it can break down social barriers, lower defenses, illuminate our compatibility, change our minds, teach us empathy, help us cope with tragedy, and will often stimulate sharing and discussion.

So, this was my first stab at being funny on purpose.

You see, distraction and escapism is how I cope. It's how I disassociate from several diagnoses, including: c-PTSD, ADHD, Autism Spectrum Disorder, Generalized Anxiety, Panic Disorder, Attachment disorder, Ehlers-Danlos syndrome, dissociative disorder, and a few other physical/mental ailments that would be as tedious to list as they would be to read.

I've never been to war, not in the literal sense, though I have four siblings and several in-laws in the service or retired from a military career. Many of them with similar diagnoses.

Their struggles (and mine) inform my characters, especially Fox/Fawkes, and I wanted to use his story to illuminate the fact that tragedy and comedy are *not* strange bedfellows. Hell, they're best friends. Not only does comedy=tragedy+time, but in my opinion it can appear in the midst of tragedy, tension, or trouble to lighten the moment. To lighten everyone's mind... Everyone's load. (hehe)

What I am not doing, however, is making light of heavy things.

I see why a light mind and a loud laugh could be terrifying to people who write commandments. To people who decide what it means to sin. When women or children suffer, it is often because they laughed at the wrong man or at the wrong time.

I am aware comedy is subjective. That laughing at someone's expense is cruel. I am also aware that so much absurdity surrounds us that sometimes laughing is the only way to continue to live in a cruel world. That sometimes you're staring into the snarling, open maw of your demons (or someone else's) and you have no weapon and no choice but to laugh in their faces.

So do it.

Fucking giggle, chuckle, guffaw, cackle and laugh at those who would try to keep you quiet and afraid. And ABOVE ALL, learn to laugh at yourself. Life is just easier if you do. Trust me. We are all a little ridiculous. That is our gift. Learn to fall in love with laughter and with people who make you laugh!

That is what the Townsend Harbor Series is to me.

It's not only a love letter to the town that has become my home far away from the oppressive boundaries of my former life.

It is a love letter to laughter.

Written by someone who learned to laugh far too late...

And her best friend who taught her how to truly giggle.

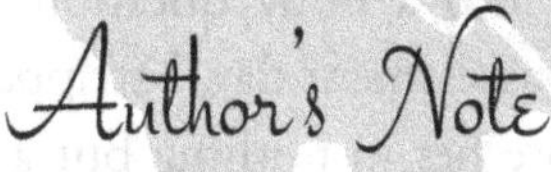

Cynthia

I have what you might call a combative relationship with my body.

You wouldn't necessarily know it to look at my social media, but I've not found a very comfortable home in the meatsuit on loan to me from the Universe.

Mostly, because it hurts a lot.

It's a thing I've joked about frequently—because self-deprecating humor is the comedic heritage of the X bit of my generation—but the truth is that chronic pain of the kind that Cady suffers is a reflection of my personal flavor of hell.

It begins with mild scoliosis.

I discovered this was a thing the same way lots of Xennials did: by being palpated and posture-shamed by a wildly unenthusiastic nurse with cold hands and coffee breath in the junior high gym.

It wasn't until Nurse Frozen Fingers asked me how I stand when I'm not slouching, that I realized I *was* slouching. Having shot up about eleventy-seven inches in one summer, I developed the habit of curling my head and shoulders forward so as to blend in with my frequently shorter friends. A goal which began to inform my eating habits as well. Spoiler alert: making myself smaller has been kind of a theme.

I was so good at it that by the time I was thirteen, I had basically turned myself into a bony question mark with no good answer. On scoliosis assessment day, I stripped off my oversized t-shirt and stood before her in nothing but a training bra and my standard-issue gray gym shorts. I remember that the nurse was quiet for what seemed like the very long time, and then she asked me what I liked to eat, and whether my back ever hurt. Coming from a long line of comedic deflectors, I reported that my back *sometimes* hurt even though *pretty much always* was closer to the truth, and that Mountain Dew was a vastly overlooked food group.

She was not impressed.

She then made the mistake of asking me what I did for fun.

"I read."

Like Cady, books were my escape. Summers especially, I'd sometimes plow through more than one a night as I was slowly training myself not to live in my body (because why would I even want to)? The trouble with this philosophy is that things were slowly getting worse without my realizing it, and by the time I was in my mid-twenties, arthritis had basically invaded the lower quadrant of my spine. In addition, several of the cartilage disks separating vertebrae decided to rage quit, and the sciatic nerve responsible for messaging many nerves in my left leg got crushed in the fallout. Five surgeries, two rods, six screws, and a nifty titanium cage later, and I could maintain feeling in my left foot—which I very much appreciate, for the record—but the pain that all these surgeries promised to address had only gotten worse. As is so often the case, lack of control in one area resulted in my doubling down in another.

I wanted better for Cady.

Writing her was my shameless attempt to try and give a

younger version of myself, and anyone who might relate to her struggles, the support I wished I'd had when navigating the daily realities of a body that I couldn't count on. The kind of best friend who, say, might make you laugh so hard you forget to hurt, or take on an eight-hour road trip to nurse you back to life after a terrifying spinal staph infection <cough> Kerrigan <cough>. Or the kind of partner who sees you not as a burden, but a blessing, and is more than willing to be your legs, your hands, or even your heart <stares in Ted>.

But I also wanted to leave room for Cady to see past her own pain. To understand that, like love, few people escape this life without feeling or earning their share. That perhaps, vulnerability —not—positivity—is the ultimate healer. Even when the wound is permanent.

Please enjoy this excerpt from Brewbies, the next book in the hysterical Townsend Harbor Series!

EFFORTLESSLY FUNNY!"
– PENNY REID

Brewbies

USA TODAY BEST SELLING AUTHORS

KERRIGAN BYRNE

& CYNTHIA ST. AUBIN

Sneak Peak at Brewbies

TOWNSEND HARBOR BOOK TWO

Darby Dunwell stood before the window of her vintage camper turned coffee truck, staring at her one-night stand and bargaining with a God she hadn't believed in since the tenth grade.

Her official break-up with a higher power occurred when Sister Mary Mildred broken a paddle over her ass after she'd stolen from her reform school's bake sale proceeds to buy cigarettes off an older co-ed. As it had been Darby's mocha-nut cupcakes that brought in the lion's share of confectionary proceeds to St. Vincent Academy, she'd reasoned that she was due at least a slim margin of the profits.

Sister Eminem (as Darby had not-so-affectionately called her) hadn't shared Darby's financial assessment.

Still fizzy with her first nicotine high, Darby had flipped up her uniform's plaid skirt, planted her hands on headmistress's moat of a desk, and invited The Hand of God—Sister Mary Margaret's paddle—to do its worst.

The resounding crack—the paddle's, not her backside's—echoed through twelve years of her memory as she looked at *him*.

Not God, but a man who'd made her howl His name to the heavens *very* enthusiastically.

Last in the line of customers waiting for her to part the Barbie-pink curtains and begin dispensing the life-enhancing elixir she'd become semi-famous for since she opened a month ago, he glowered like he wanted to dick-punch the sun just for rising.

Hungover, she guessed, if he'd necked as much whisky the evening previous as he had when she'd seen him last.

But there wasn't *supposed* to be a last.

Because she was never supposed see *him* again.

This could not—should *not*—be happening.

For once in her life, Darby had done everything right.

She had driven two hours away from the tiny coastal hamlet of Townsend Harbor. She had taken a room at the shittiest of motels next to the shittiest of dive bars. She had selected her quarry carefully after hours of observation.

Of all her one-nighters, why did it have to be *him*?

The man who'd had her recalibrating her walk for days afterward.

The man who'd left her stretched, abraded, satiated, and in such a manically good mood, her colorist asked what kind of meds her psychiatrist had her on.

The man whose name she didn't know despite the fact that he'd been inside her.

Deep, deep inside.

'He sees everything you do, even when I don't,' Sister Mary Mildred whisper-hissed in her head.

Whack.

'His justice will be swift and sure.'

Crack.

Was that what this was?

Justice?

Some kind of karmic one-upmanship in her life-long game of chicken with the Universe?

One thing Darby knew for sure.

She really had to stop inviting wood to come at her as hard as possible.

"To Whomever it May Concern," she began, fastening her eyes shut. "I solemnly swear I will never have another one-night stand so long as I live if you could kindly make the lumber-snack-looking guy with the icy glare decide to leave in the next thirty seconds." Her throat worked over a gritty swallow. "It doesn't have to be anything super bad. Maybe a mild case of diarrhea? There's a gas station just up the road and they keep the bathrooms pretty clean I hear. Thanks. Oh. Amen and stuff."

Feeling completely foolish for hoping *he* might have magically evaporated, Darby gently widened the narrow slit between the fabric panels.

If anything, he looked more solid from this angle, his broad shoulders juxtaposed against the backdrop of pine trees across the interstate. The sunrise gilding the crown of his head like the molten halo of an avenging angel.

In flannel.

A shirt very much like the one he'd worn that night.

A shirt very much like the one she'd worn home the next morning.

After what he'd done to her dress, he'd insisted.

A rather gentlemanly thing for him to have done after an encounter that had been anything but.

Darby cast a guilty glance back to the living area of her vintage trailer, where, at that very second, in a cupboard above her bed, the souvenir in question whispered from the confines of a gallon-sized freezer bag. Not to preserve the scent of fabric softener, soap and a cologne that reminded her of a meadow after a summer storm, but to protect it against the moths that held nightly mixers around the light on the outside her camper.

Or so she'd told herself every time she cracked the zipper to inhale a heady hit of *eau d' deep dicking*.

Darby bit the pointed tip of her nail as the man who'd renovated her pelvic floor glared at a passing police cruiser.

Maybe he wouldn't recognize her.

Right. Because it wasn't like she had branded her entire fucking business to her two most recognizable features or anything.

Brewbies.

Townsend Harbor's first and only sex-positive, body-positive, bikini coffee camper.

She glanced in the full-length mirror she'd mounted on the door leading to her tiny living area at the camper's rear and let out an anguished groan.

Showgirl tits and hot pink hair present and very accounted for. Hell, an only slightly exaggerated caricature of her glowed from the top of the camper this very second, blinking neon Las Vegas showgirl leg kick and all.

Christ, did she have to strangle every single theme to literal death?

The sound of boots crunching on gravel yanked her out of self-speculation and cattle-prodded her into motion.

Her regulars were growing restless.

At the front of the line, the hulking dark-haired dude who looked like he just stepped off the set of a movie with *destroyer* in the title. Tucked protectively against his broad chest, the buxom, blond bookstore proprietress who reminded Darby of Botticelli paintings she'd sit in front of for hours when she cut school and took the train into Manhattan to sketch at the Met.

Him: D cup Slow Grind, extra sweaty—Pour over coffee, black, 180 degrees.

Her: C Cup Vanilla Pump and Dump—regular Italian roast with house made Madagascar vanilla syrup and extra half n' half.

Darby rummaged through the various shelves and cupboards to pull out the necessary accoutrements and scooped a healthy shovel of spicy, cocoa-scented grounds into the compostable paper cone before dispensing the appropriate amount of scalding water. While it brewed, she shimmied through the small door to her dining room /lounge/wardrobe/craftroom/library.

Yanking open her "closet," she double-fisted the contents and flung them over her shoulders like a cartoon strumpet, furiously searching for anything to cover her hair.

How could she condense an entire Etsy vintage pin-up boutique into a repurposed broom cupboard but still not own a single hat?

Desperate, she snatched up the baggy Betty Page t-shirt she'd slept in and hauled it over her bikini top before grabbing another and twisting it around the chignon and victory rolls she'd so painstakingly assembled earlier that morning.

She'd sooner scrape her entire face off with a cake spatula than re-contour, but wiped off her signature siren red lipstick as tribute.

Glancing down at the smeared crimson rings on the make-up wipe, her staggeringly unhelpful brain idly wondered if Deep Dicking had seen something similar when he took a washrag to his cock the morning after their anonymous feral fuckfest.

Spontaneous under-boob sweat broke out beneath her bikini top at the thought. Darby grabbed a silk fan and beat it against the close air of the camper to cool her furiously flushed cheeks as she lunged the four steps back to the coffee cubby.

Go time.

Allowing herself one last breath, she shoved the curtains aside and slid the pocket window open.

The cool, pine-scented air of an early Pacific Northwest summer felt delicious on her heated skin as she leaned out the window to prop up the cotton candy pink mini-awning over the small, brushed steel service counter mounted on the camper's flank.

"Morning," she greeted with considerably less volume than she normally employed. "Sorry about the wait. The grinder was being an absolute dickhole."

Cady Bloomquist met her with a beaming smile. "No worries whatsoever."

If Darby had a six-and-a-half-foot search and rescue team/personal space heater following her around town, she suspected she might not have any worries either.

Turning back to her barista nook, Darby quickly finished their drinks, and fitted the cups with lids, insulation sleeves, and sip hole stopper topped with a tiny—but remarkably perky—pair of tits.

Punching the order into the iPad, she swiveled it on the lazy Susan base to face them.

Cady's Viking escort forward and held his iPhone up to the screen to complete the transaction with a tip far more generous than she deserved.

"Have the breast day," she said, handing their drinks over.

"I will when you actually come to the Barenaked Book Club like you promised," the Cady teased with an arched eyebrow.

"Next Thursday, for *sure*," Darby said, hating herself a little for what she already knew was a lie.

Cady's smooth cheeks lifted in a serene grin. "I'll save you a seat."

They walked off together toward a black SUV big enough to be army issue if not for the uber-tinted windows, Darby's heart squeezing as Conan hooked a finger through the belt loop of Cady's wide-legged denim trousers.

The next three customers were drive through interstate traffic that represented the bulk of her business. The fourth, a sight that made her face grow longer on her tired skull.

"That timer says twenty minutes," he said in a congested voice dripping with sinus infection. "Your website promises that you never serve coffee that's been sitting for more than fifteen."

On a normal day, when she wasn't having mild regret-based panic attacks about a man who'd had his mouth on her lady lips lurking at the back of her line, she'd have remembered to reset the timer the second she saw Roy Dobson roll up.

Tempted as she was to give him decaf, Darby decided that inviting any further karmic consequences might not be in her best interest at this precise moment.

"My sincere apologies, Roy," she said, pressing her hand to breasts he typically ogled. If you don't mind waiting for another ten, I'd be happy to brew a fresh pot just for you." She smiled so hard, her canines poked into her lower lip. "Or maybe I could interest you in a hot pour over?"

Your face.

Judging by his sigh alone, you'd have guessed that she'd just asked him whether he preferred to move Fort Warden Beach grain by grain, or empty the Puget Sound a thimbleful at a time.

"I guess I'll just take what you've already got." His gaze narrowed behind thick glasses. "But don't microwave it or I'll know."

He shoved the thermal cup he always brought from home through the window. Darby had the distinct feeling the tempestuous secondhand store owner did this not out of any conscience-driven need to lessen his carbon footprint, but for the fifty-cent discount she offered to anyone who brought their own cup.

"Wouldn't dream of it." If her forced smile got any wider, the tendons holding her jaw on were liable to pop like rubber bands.

Three customers away.

Darby stepped just out of eyeline and covertly glanced at *him* beyond the brassy beast of the espresso machine that had devoured an entire third of her initial business loan.

He hadn't looked at her once.

Something in the distance had his attention.

And not in a good way.

Arms folded against the solid wall of his chest, his angular jaw flexed beneath the tawny carpet of stubble she could still feel on her lips. Just as she could feel the press of his angular hips against her inner thighs. That rough palm clutching the sensitive skin of her throat as his thick fingers slid her panties to the side beneath her skirt, scalding her...*thumb*?

"Fuck," Darby hissed, sloshing more hot liquid on herself as she jerked her hand away from the steam wand. "Motherfucking fuckbiscuits! Sonova bitch that hurts."

Darby turned tiny sink tap onto cold and shoved her hand in the stream to calm her offended nerves. The relief was instant, but wouldn't last as she knew.

Steam burns were the literal worst.

Spotting the lavender essential oil one of her passing patrons had gifted to her, Darby liberally anointed the stinging digit and carefully rubbed in the unguent salve.

"Excuse me." Roy pecked on the aluminum siding of the service window. "Excuse me, but you *were* planning on refilling my cup, correct? Because I couldn't help but notice that you spilled a significant amount of coffee on*yeeep!*"

Darby's head whipped around hard enough for several vertebrae to crunch, her eyes going wide as duck eggs as she saw the reason Roy had broken off so abruptly.

Him.

He stood before the service window with a handful of Roy's button-up shirt gripped in one white-knuckled fist, the other cocked back like a wrecking ball.

"Can't you see she burned her hand you pointless, demanding fuck?" His bicep mounded beneath his sleeve as he hauled Roy's face closer to his.

Roy's mouth opened. Closed. Opened again. "I—but—tits," he stammered nonsensically.

"That's what I thought." He raked Roy with withering look. "Now you're going to back the fuck off and let her take care of it before I put my fist through the back of your flat skull."

Roy nodded and was released with enough force to send him stumbling backward. He sat down hard on one of the picnic table benches she'd painted a soothing seafoam teal in optimistic days unsullied by the scene before her.

Still tight with rage, her one-night stand's face swung in Darby's direction. Their eyes met, and recognition surged into his features like the tide. The eyelids lowering. The jaw unclenching. The mouth softening.

He knew.

He remembered her.

Darby stood at the window, her pulse pounding in her ears and her lips parted on a breath that refused to fill her lungs.

In what was perhaps the most shocking turn of events so far, Deep Dicking released his fists and calmly stepped back into line.

Or what was left of it.

Two of the other patrons had mysteriously vanished, apparently disinterested in being pummeled by the coffee bouncer should they ask for an extra shot.

The third seemed completely unfazed.

"Knew Sherriff Townsend had that in him somewhere," she said, wiping lipstick only a shade darker than Darby's fuchsia hair from her top teeth.

Darby's heart skipped a beat.

Sherriff Townsend?

No.

No way.

No way in *hell* that the man who'd had her leaving dental impressions in a plywood headboard clocked into a county job.

Darby's face prickled with the awareness of his gaze.

"Morning, Myrtle," she said, refocusing on the task before her. "What'll it be?"

The older woman squinted at the menu through the thick black frames of her bifocals, the white wisps of her spiky hair glowing like lightbulb filaments in the sunlight. "Can I get a double D Dirty Screw. Oh! And can I add a cream pie to that?"

"One Oreo Frappuccino with a double shot and extra whip coming right up," Darby said, grateful to have something for her hands to do.

"You can hardly blame poor Ethan after that business between Roy and his mother," Myrtle said conversationally.

"I'm sorry," Darby said, scooping cookie rubble into a compostable plastic cup. "Who?"

"Ethan Townsend. The guy who just made Roy's coin purse crawl into his colon."

Sherriff Ethan Townsend.

This was not the name of a man who gave you rugburn.

"Course, he may not be the Sherriff much longer," Myrtle said in a conspiratorial tone. Rumor has it, he's not the favorite to win."

Though she'd only rolled into town a couple months ago, Darby had quickly learned that gossip was a cornerstone of Townsend Harbor's civic structure. "Well, if he doesn't get elected, I can always hire him to do security."

Darby glanced up from her hand blender in time to see—Ethan? Sherriff Townsend? Whatever you called a man whose cock you could sculpt by memory, but to whom you hadn't been properly introduced—make Roy jump just by scratching his jaw stubble.

"If you're looking for help, I'd fill out an application. I know how to work a crowd." Myrtle raised onto the toes of her sassy red mules to peer through the window. "I used to be a dancer you know."

"Is that so?" Darby asked distractedly.

"Oh, yes," Myrtle warbled fondly. "In Paris. It was a long time ago, but I still have some of my costumes. They might need a sequin or two replaced, but they still fit. I haven't gained an ounce since my wedding day," she pronounced proudly.

On the contrary, she looked like she'd yielded a good deal of adipose tissue and muscle mass to the thieving ass-wrinkle of time.

"Of course, I only danced at the Moulin Rouge *before* I met my Frank, even though I almost never had relations with my customers. The French are such passionate men," Myrtle said on a wistful sigh.

Darby was so stunned by this new information that she

glanced up and involuntarily caught the Sherriff's eye over Myrtle's bony shoulder.

He no longer looked angry, he looked like he wanted to retract his head and legs into his ribcage and roll down the road like a sea anemone.

Darby put both Myrtle and Roy's coffees on the counter and took a step back. "I'm not looking for help at the moment, but I'll certainly let you know if that changes."

"Please do," Myrtle said, wrapping knobby knuckles around her cup. "The fertilizer business is in the shitter. No pun intended."

Roy kept his eyes averted as he shuffled up to collect his and scuttled away just as quickly.

"Wishing you all the breast!" she called after them.

And they were alone.

The individual air molecules seemed to thicken and darken despite the rising sun. She was no longer in her cozy little camper, but on a barstool one down from his. Her forearms on the sticky counter. The air hazy with neon-tinted smoke.

They hadn't spoken a single word to each other.

She'd sat down next to him. Ordered one of what he was having.

That granite jaw angled toward his hunched shoulder just enough to caress her with a languid peripheral glance.

He put his hand on her bare thigh. Brushed the crease at the back of her knee with the rough edge of his thumb.

Her drink came.

He'd pulled out his billfold, put down a twenty and picked up both his and hers.

She followed him out of the bar, up a set of stairs, to the door of a room he hadn't bothered locking.

Then he'd ruined her for the next five hours.

The time between then and now dissolved away. Her body came alive under the memory of his touch, her limbs going liquid.

Darby unwound the t-shirt from her head and tossed it to the side. Under a power not entirely her own, she lifted her nightshirt off as well, standing before him in her standard uniform of a cleavage-bearing bikini top that elevated her hardened nipples nearly to her neck.

No point in keeping up a façade now.

His footsteps sounded as loud as gunshots as he approached in slow strides, his eyes flicking to her breasts before finding her face.

"Welcome to Brewbies," she said. "What can I get started for you?"

His jaw flexed, then loosened as he lifted sky-blue eyes to hers. "I'm not here for coffee."

Heat flooded through her, pooling somewhere below the counter but above her ankles. Had he been driving by when, mirage-like, her glowing neon likeness summoned him for a second round. "What are you here for?"

The man who'd made her come so hard she blacked out reached into his back pocket and came back with a white envelope that he set on the counter before her.

"To shut you down."

About the Author

Cynthia St. Aubin wrote her first play at age eight and made her brothers perform it for the admission price of gum wrappers. A steal, considering she provided the wrappers in advance. Though her early work debuted to mixed reviews, she never quite gave up on the writing thing, even while earning a mostly useless master's degree in art history and taking her turn as a cube monkey in the corporate warren.

Because the voices in her head kept talking to her, and they discourage drinking at work, she kept writing instead. When she's not standing in front of the fridge eating cheese, she's hard at work figuring out which mythological, art historical, or paranormal friends to play with next. She lives in Texas with the love of her life and two fluffy cats, Muppet and Gizmo.

I **love stalkers! You can find me here!**
Visit me: http://www.cynthiastaubin.com/
Email me: cynthiastaubin@gmail.com
Join my Minions: https://www.facebook.com/groups/Cynthiastaubins/

Subliminally message me: *You were thinking of cheese just now, right?*

And here:

Also by Cynthia St. Aubin

Tails from the Alpha Art Gallery

Love Bites

Love Sucks

Love Lies

Love Binds

The Kane Heirs

Corner Office Confessions

Secret Lives After Hours

Bad Boys with Benefits

The Jane Avery Mysteries

Private Lies

Lying Low

Case Files of Dr. Matilda Schmidt, Paranormal Psychologist

Unlovable

Unlucky

Unhoppy

Unbearable

Unassailable

Undeadly

Unexpecting

From Hell to Breakfast

About the Author

Kerrigan Byrne is the USA Today Bestselling and award winning author of several novels in both the romance and mystery genre.

She lives on the Olympic Peninsula in Washington with her husband, two Rottweiler mix rescues, and one very clingy torbie. When she's not writing and researching, you'll find her on the beach, kayaking, or on land eating, drinking, shopping, and attending live comedy, ballet, or too many movies.

Kerrigan loves to hear from her readers! To contact her or learn more about her books, please visit her site or find her on most social media platforms: www.kerriganbyrne.com

Also by Kerrigan Byrne

A Goode Girls Romance

Seducing a Stranger

Courting Trouble

Dancing With Danger

Tempting Fate

Crying Wolfe

Making Merry

The Business of Blood Series

The Business of Blood

A Treacherous Trade

Victorian Rebels

The Highwayman

The Hunter

The Highlander

The Duke

The Scot Beds His Wife

The Duke With the Dragon Tattoo

The Earl on the Train

The MacLauchlan Berserkers

Highland Secret

Highland Shadow

Highland Stranger

To Seduce a Highlander

The MacKay Banshees

Highland Darkness

Highland Devil

Highland Destiny

To Desire a Highlander

The de Moray Druids

Highland Warlord

Highland Witch

Highland Warrior

To Wed a Highlander

Contemporary Suspense

A Righteous Kill

Also by Kerrigan

How to Love a Duke in Ten Days

All Scot And Bothered

CPSIA information can be obtained
at www.ICGtesting.com
Printed in the USA
BVHW031645220323
660956BV00012B/660

9 781648 393921